IN THE FOREST OF HARM

BANTAM BOOKS

NEW YORK   TORONTO   LONDON   SYDNEY   AUCKLAND

IN THE
FOREST
OF
HARM

SALLIE BISSELL

IN THE FOREST OF HARM
A Bantam Book / January 2001

Book design by Laurie Jewell
Map by Jackie Aher

Library of Congress Cataloging-in-Publication Data

Bissell, Sallie.
In the forest of harm / Sallie Bissell.
p. cm.
ISBN 0-553-80128-7
I. Title.

PS3552.I772916 I6 2001
813'.54—dc21   00-048621

Published simultaneously in the United States and Canada

Bantam Books are published by Bantam Books, a division of Random
House, Inc. Its trademark, consisting of the words "Bantam Books" and
the portrayal of a rooster, is Registered in U.S. Patent and Trademark
Office and in other countries. Marca Registrada. Bantam Books, 1540
Broadway, New York, New York 10036.

PRINTED IN THE UNITED STATES OF AMERICA

BVG   10 9 8 7 6 5 4 3 2 1

This book is dedicated to
Elizabeth and Carter Stringfellow

MY THANKS TO:

The Nashville Writers Alliance: Ronna Blaser, Kae Cheatham, Phyllis Gobbel, Martha Hickman, Nancy Hite, Amy Lynch, Madeena Nolan, Michael Sims, Steve Womack and Jim Young; Dr. Tracy Barrett of Vanderbilt University.

The Flatiron Writers of Asheville, North Carolina: Cathy Agrella, Alan Anderson, Perien Gray, Toby Heaton, and Heather Newton.

My agents, Robbie Anna Hare, whose belief in and hard work for this project were key to its success; and Ron Goldfarb, whose advice and counsel were invaluable.

My editor, Kate Miciak, whose wise suggestions made this a much stronger book.

Finally, to the best friends and first readers any writer could hope for—Genève Bacon, Cynthia Perkins, and Alana White.

Lyrics quoted on page 22
are from "All the Pretty Little Horses,"
a traditional American folk song.

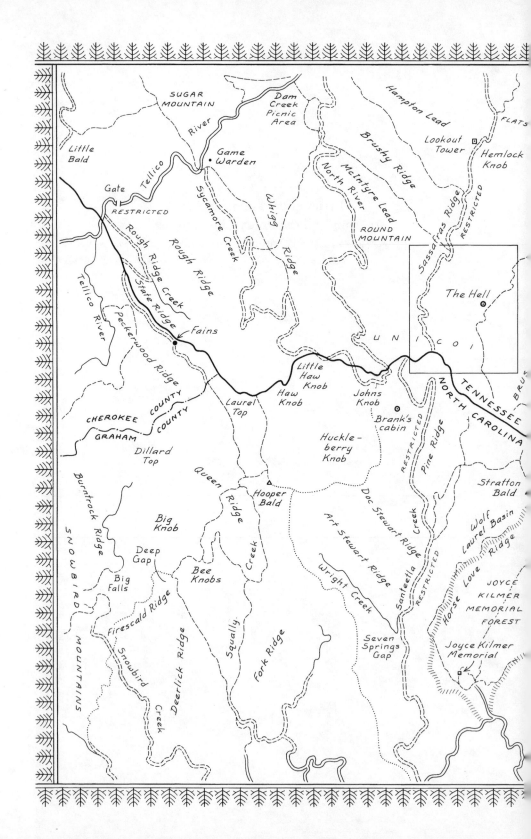

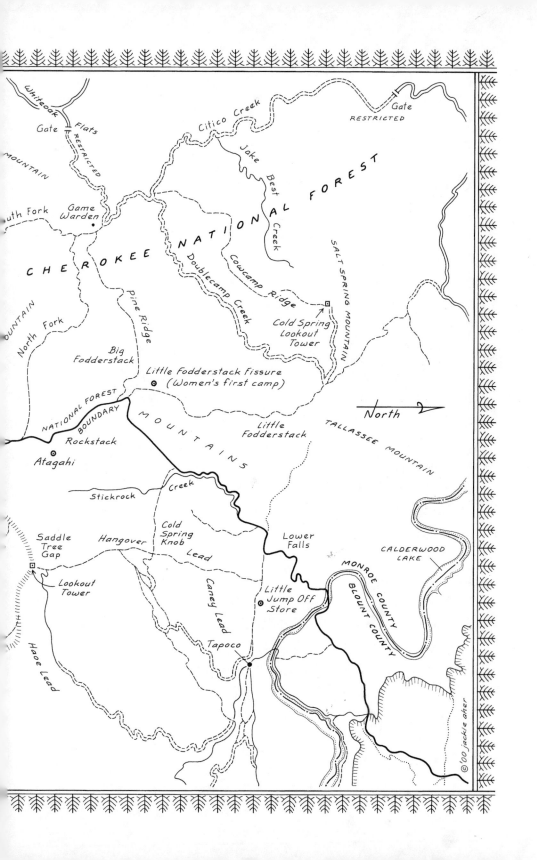

PROLOGUE

Mom? I'm home." Mary Crow tugged open the back door of the store, releasing the rich scent of curing hams and dried apples into the warm April afternoon. Inside, she could hear the ancient bait cooler wheezing over her mother's favorite oldies station, currently playing a scratchy version of "Hey Jude."

"Mom?" Mary repeated. "It's me."

She pushed her glossy dark hair back from her forehead, waiting for her mother's familiar "In here," but only her own voice echoed through the store.

With a shake of her head, Mary began to weave her way through aisles piled high with everything from laundry detergent to dusty, old-fashioned slop jars. Though her mother had worked here for ten years, the Little Jump Off store had been dispensing mountain merchandise since the days of cracker barrels and pickle jars.

1

"Mama?" Mary called louder as the bait cooler gave a grinding shudder. "I'm back. Sorry I'm late. I'll help you close up."

Again, there was no response. Mary felt a sudden odd coolness, as if someone had jerked a sweater from her shoulders. She frowned. Something was strange here. Something was not right.

"Mother?" Her call now rang edgy in the too-still air. She heard footsteps thudding from the store's front porch. Not her mother's light tread, but heavy steps, with a curious rhythm.

Quickly, she turned toward the checkout counter. She rounded the new spring seed display, then stopped, stunned, as if someone had slapped her hard across the face. At the counter the old wooden cash register gaped open like an empty mouth; change splattered on the counter, five- and ten-dollar bills littered the floor. For an instant Mary could only stand and stare, her stomach twisting into a sick, hard knot.

"Mom?" she called. "Where are you?"

She rushed to the front of the store, then gasped. Cans of baked beans rolled around the floor among boxes of oatmeal and burst bags of flour. Two ruptured six-packs of Coke spewed over the mess.

"Mom? Are you here?" Mary looked down the hardware aisle. Nothing. She checked behind the counter. Again nothing. She ran around to the corner of the store where her mother kept her loom; her heart turned to dust.

There, on the floor, beside a bag of wool scraps, lay Martha Crow. Her blue gingham skirt had been pushed up around her thighs; the front of her blouse was ripped away. Her face was the color of a fresh bruise and a line of large red blotches crawled up her throat.

Mary blinked as everything started to tumble—her mother, the store, her whole world. Her mind snatched at ideas as a dog might snap at flies. She should go to her mother, she should call the sheriff, she should run out on the porch and scream for help. But her legs felt like rubber, and at that moment she couldn't even remember where they kept their old black telephone. All she could do was stand there, staring mutely at her mother as the Beatles droned on and those heavy footsteps lumbered away.

"Mama!" she screamed, her voice gone tinny with terror.

"Mama?" Mary ran over and knelt beside her mother, pleading, praying. *Please let her open her eyes. Please let her smile.* "Are you all right?"

Martha Crow did not answer.

With the tips of her fingers, Mary touched her mother's shoulder. Her body was warm, still soft with life, but her chest remained motionless. As Mary gently shook her, a trickle of saliva threaded down from the left corner of her mother's mouth. Her hands—the hands that just this morning caressed Mary's cheek before she went to school, were bleeding. Every knuckle was scraped and one fingernail had been torn away, as if Martha Crow had fought someone very hard.

"Mama?" Mary shook her again, harder, and pulled the ragged blouse back across her chest. Though her mother's gold wedding band still encircled her finger, the Saint Andrew's medal, the one item of jewelry Mary had never seen Martha without, was gone. With a sob Mary touched the pale spot just above her breasts where the little medallion had always rested; the flesh there had already begun to cool.

She knew then exactly what had happened. Not the how, and not the why, but Mary Crow knew with certainty that the last person to leave this store had gone, taking her mother's life.

"Oh, Mama," she whispered. "Please don't leave me. . . ." With that plea Mary leaned over and buried her face in her mother's dying warmth, ignoring the footsteps fading from the porch, ignoring the Beatles crooning from the radio, ignoring everything except the thunderous breaking of her own heart.

ONE

I ndian bitch!" Calhoun Whitman, Jr., uttered his first words in court as he lunged
over the defense table. "Motherfucking
squaw!"

Mary Crow did not flinch as Whitman rushed
toward her. Jurors scrambled backwards in the
jury box while Whitman's defense counsel leapt
from his chair and threw himself at his client.
Though Whitman was a slender young man, he
had quick reflexes and astonishing strength. Even
with the beefy attorney clinging to both his legs,
Calhoun Whitman, Jr., writhed like a rattlesnake
toward the prosecutor's table.

The two bailiffs who normally dozed on
either side of the bench jolted forward. With a
flurry of grunts, curses and the final sick thud of
a skull striking the floor, the three men pinned
the just-convicted murderer at the foot of the
witness stand. An instant later both bailiffs had
their service revolvers pressed against the base of
Whitman's brain.

"Oh, my God!" Mrs. Calhoun Whitman, Sr., shrieked over the babble. "They're going to shoot him!"

"Order!" Judge Margaret McLean slammed her gavel on the desk. The sharp rap was swallowed in the din that enveloped the courtroom. "I will have *order* in this court!" She banged the gavel as if she were hammering nails. "Officers, put that man in cuffs and irons!"

"Oh, nooo . . ." Mrs. Whitman sobbed as one bailiff cuffed her son's hands behind his back while the other kept both his foot and pistol wedged against Cal's neck. Mary Crow sat motionless as the bailiffs snapped the leg irons around Cal's ankles and wrestled him to his feet. When everyone in the courtroom had retaken their seats and her heart had stopped its own rhumba in her chest, Mary stood up, as was customary, for Judge McLean to address the accused.

"John Calhoun Whitman, Jr., a jury of your peers has found you guilty of one count of sexual battery and one count of murder in the first degree upon the person of Sandra Dianne Manning. You will be sentenced by this court on Friday, November third, in accordance with the criminal code of the State of Georgia. Until that time, you are remanded to the custody of the State." Judge McLean scowled down at the strikingly handsome young man who now stood gasping before her in his torn Armani suit. "Take him away."

The two bailiffs grabbed Cal Whitman by his manacled arms and hustled him toward the door, his leg irons rattling like a cascade of dropped change. When they passed in front of the prosecutor's table, Cal locked his knees and elbowed both officers.

"Stupid whore!" he raged at Mary, his blond hair falling into his face. "Cherokee lesbo cunt! You're gonna pay for this!" Then he threw back his head and spit. Everyone gasped. A milky wad of saliva curved through the air, then plopped on Wynona, the small gray soapstone figure of an Indian goddess that Mary kept on her table at every trial. As his spit dripped from the little statue, Cal's pretty mouth stretched in a triumphant, mocking grin.

"Out of those spike heels, you're just a skinny piece of brown cooze!"

Mary felt her face grow hot. She despised men like Whitman, men who played rough with women and then expected their money or their power to put things right. She pressed her hands flat on the desk and leaned toward him, knowing the warm scent of her perfume would linger in his memory as an ever-present reminder of the day she hung him.

"Have a good time in jail, Cal," she murmured, not bothering to hide the pleasure in her voice. "I hear a few of the larger inmates are looking forward to being with you."

"I'll get you for this!" Cal screamed at her as the bailiffs dragged him out of the courtroom. "I swear to God I will!" The door slammed behind him, but his threats echoed crazily down the hall, fading only when they locked him in a padded, soundproofed cell.

"Ladies and gentlemen of the jury, thank you for your service. This court stands adjourned." With a brisk nod at the jurors and a sharp glare at Whitman's attorney, Judge McLean withdrew to the calm blue interior of her office. Then the true bedlam began.

Mary looked at the sputum-drenched Wynona and shook her head. At last this case, this crime of passion which some wag in her office had termed "the muff snuff," was over. Atlanta had been shocked when the younger son of one of its wealthiest real-estate developers had been charged with raping and then killing a Gap sales-girl, but when the papers had implied that political forces had put pressure on the DA's office to charge Calhoun Whitman, Jr., with the crime, the whole city had gone nuts. All Mary knew was that the case landed on her desk. Although the late Sandra Manning had shown a proclivity for multiple sex partners, the evidence had pointed over-whelmingly to Whitman. Her boss and the mayor and even the gov-ernor had wanted this political bombshell out of the papers, so Mary had gone to trial with the evidence she had. For the past two weeks she had prosecuted. Today the jury had convicted.

Kate Summerfield, the chief crime reporter for the *Journal-Clarion*, was the first to corner Mary.

"Hey, Mary, doesn't this make six convictions for six indictments?"

Mary fought the urge to grin and raise one fist in triumph. It would be better if the press did not find out how good it felt to nail scum like Whitman. It was a rush better than coffee, better than sky-diving, maybe even better than a talented man lingering between your legs. She glanced down at her papers and answered Kate's ques-tion with a modest nod. "Handsome Cal makes six."

Kate gave a low whistle. "That's amazing for one so young. Say, is it true that the old Cherokees chopped off one hand if someone killed a man, but two hands if someone killed a woman?" She scribbled in a long, skinny notebook that looked more suited for grocery lists than front-page headlines.

Mary laughed. "Who on earth told you that?"

"Read it somewhere. Is this old Cherokee tradition why you never bargain when the victim's a woman?"

"To tell you the truth, I've never thought about it one way or the other." Mary smiled, but did not elaborate. Actually, Kate had gotten it right. The old Cherokees were hand-lobbers and she didn't bargain when the victim was female, but Mary didn't want anybody attributing that to her over breakfast tomorrow morning.

"Is this the first time you've convicted someone from a prominent Atlanta family?"

It's the first time I've convicted someone whose aunt plays bridge with my grandmother, Mary thought, but again she smiled. "Kate, I go after whoever Jim assigns me."

Kate was about to ask another question when Mary felt a light touch on her arm. She turned. Her boss, Jim Falkner, stood there. He gave her a brisk hug, enveloping her in a cloud of oxford cloth and Old Spice aftershave. "Nice job, kiddo. You okay?"

"I'm fine." Mary held on to his comforting solidity for a moment. "Just glad it's over."

Jim scanned the courtroom in the unobtrusive manner of an ex-detective. "Let's get out of here," he said softly, his wary gaze lingering on Cal Whitman's older brother, Mitchell, as Mitchell draped a consoling arm across his weeping mother's shoulders. "We've gotten three more phone calls this morning."

"Same old same old?" Mary, as an assistant DA, had grown accustomed to a certain number of threats per case. Usually the callers commented upon her gender (cunt, bitch, whore) or her ethnicity (Cherokee cunt, half-breed bitch, Injun whore). The press, though, had used a small forest of newsprint on the Whitman case and the threats had risen proportionately.

"Not exactly." Jim's gaze flitted from person to person like a mosquito searching for a place to light. "Now they've used the B-word."

Though every entrance to the Deckard County Courthouse was equipped with a weapon detector and security for this trial had been doubled, Mary could tell by the way Jim kept ruffling his thick gray mustache that he was concerned. The B-word for Atlanta cops was *bomb*: ever since the Olympics, the police treated calls that threatened them as warnings from God.

"Hey, Falkner, let me borrow your handkerchief," she said.

Jim frowned as he dug in his back pocket. "You coming down with a cold?"

"I need to clean off Wynona." Mary nodded toward the little soapstone figurine. "Cal spit on her."

"Ugh." Jim pulled out a white linen handkerchief. "Just keep it. Or better yet, throw it away. Handsome Cal may have rabies for all we know."

Jim turned to confer with one of the cops on security while Mary dried Wynona. As she dropped his handkerchief into the wastebasket and slipped Wynona into her pocket, she could tell from the hum behind her that the press was interviewing the distraught Whitmans. Maybe she could slip through the crowd unnoticed.

She snapped her briefcase shut, then turned and began to weave her way to the door. News crews surrounded the Whitman family like hungry dogs waiting for scraps of meat. Calhoun Whitman, Sr., stood murmuring to his attorney, while his wife, Cornelia, huddled beside him, dabbing at her nose with a crumpled tissue. As Mary entered the center aisle of the courtroom, her eyes locked with those of Mitchell Whitman. Cal's older brother was giving his own interview to a reporter from Channel 9, but all the while he glowered straight at her. Mary had cross-examined him hard when the defense had called him as a witness, and she could tell by his furious eyes that he had not forgotten it.

"Of course we'll appeal," he declared as the reporter shoved a microphone in his face. "My brother was framed. This case was politically motivated."

"So who set Cal up?" two different voices demanded as the news cameras whirred.

Lord, Mary thought. What a zoo. She turned away from Mitchell Whitman and wriggled through a cluster of reporters talking on cell phones. Then she saw two familiar figures sitting in the back row of the courtroom.

Mary smiled. Tall, blonde Alexandra McCrimmon had been her best friend since their freshman year at college and had followed Mary, for lack of more compelling career plans, into law school afterwards. There they'd met Joan Marchetti, a diminutive Italian who'd lacked the stature to sing opera and fled south to study law. The three women had met when they'd wound up as the only females in their section of Constitutional Law. Mary had felt an instant kinship with Joan as a fellow outsider, while Alex was fascinated by Joan's sweet voice and scrappy attitude. Joan, who had never met either a cowgirl from Texas or an Indian from North Carolina, was thrilled to find two Southerners who didn't recoil from her Brooklyn accent or misunderstand her penchant for wearing black.

They formed a tight bond, and over the next two years, their grit, humor, and determination carried them through the tough Emory curriculum. Afterwards, while Mary had single-mindedly pursued criminal law, Alex and Joan had wound up as corporate attorneys, specializing in mergers and acquisitions. Both worked for the same sprawling law firm in one of Atlanta's newest high-rises. "It's dog-eat-dog," Alex liked to say. "But they pay us extraordinarily well to scoop the poop."

"Hi, girls." Mary plopped her briefcase down in the empty chair beside Joan. "How come you're here? Dull day in corporate takeovers?"

"We wanted to watch you nail handsome Cal." Alex eyed Mary's trademark black suit. "And since you're wearing Deathwrap without a blouse, we knew you meant business."

"So how'd I do?"

Joan winked. "You'd have made my Uncle Nick proud."

"Is this Uncle Nick of the killer lasagna?"

"No. This is Uncle Nick of the cement overshoes."

"Oh." Mary laughed, always enjoying the comic way Joan referred to her Italian relatives. "*That* Uncle Nick."

"I was a little worried about you for a minute, there, Mary," Alex teased, slipping back into the west Texas accent she'd tried for years to lose. "For a second I thought pretty Cal was gonna spit you to death."

Mary wrinkled her nose. "Pretty gross, huh?"

"And he's so good-looking." Joan sighed. "He probably owns his own tux *and* likes to dance." She shook her head. "What a waste!"

Jim Falkner joined them. He grinned at Mary, his mustache turning up on the ends. "Are you still bugging out for the weekend?"

Mary had asked, as final arguments began in the Whitman case, if she could take a long weekend off. "I need to go back home," she'd told Jim cryptically. "I've got some unfinished business to attend to." Jim had agreed, gladly. Mary had earned a rest. She was the finest young prosecutor he'd ever seen.

"I am," Mary told him now. "Alex and Joan are going with me."

"Camping." Joan rolled her eyes. "Can you believe it? A nice New York City girl like me?"

Jim smiled at the three women. "Just don't let Mary get eaten by any bears. We've still got a few thousand psychos to put away."

"And I bet you're saving them all for me." She laughed as she picked up her briefcase, but a chill skittered down her spine. For the first time in twelve years, Mary Crow was going home.

TWO

"What can I get for you, hon?"

Lou Delgado smiled up at the waitress, who stood with both her left breast and order pad poised above his right ear. "The usual, Marge. How's it going?"

"They come, they eat, sometimes I get a decent tip out of the deal." Marge cracked a wad of gum.

"You aren't referring to me, are you?"

Chuckling, Marge gave him a wink, then retreated to the counter. Lou settled back in the booth, appreciating the rhythmic jiggle of her bottom against the snug blue polyester of her uniform. All in all, the Copper Pot Diner was not a bad place to meet clients. The corner booth stayed empty in the late-night hours, the fluorescent lights allowed him a full view of the front door, and the waitresses knew how to keep their mouths shut if any cops came nosing around. Not a bad place at all, considering.

He drummed his fingers on the table and checked his watch. His next client should come walking through the door any minute. A young man, Lou thought, remembering the call from Perry that afternoon. Perry was an attorney who always sent Delgado his dirtiest jobs. Usually he was up-front about what needed to be done, but today the old shyster had been tight-lipped, saying only the new client was "someone you might recognize." Lou enjoyed coyness about as much as a root canal, but he had agreed to meet the guy. What the hell, he decided. He could use the money. Private dicking in Dixie was not the most lucrative of professions.

Headlights flashed across the front window as Marge placed a mug of coffee and a piece of pecan pie on the table. Delgado forked up his first bite as the door of a black Porsche opened. As a figure emerged from the car, Lou relished the warm, sticky sweetness that filled his mouth, then turned his dark eyes intently to the door.

A man wearing khaki trousers and a pale blue button-down shirt entered. The newcomer stood well over six feet, with broad shoulders and a thick neck. Ex-high school quarterback, Delgado guessed. Too tall for a wrestler. Not the right color to play hoops. His dark blond hair was combed back from his forehead, and he wore his shirt-sleeves rolled up to reveal the taut muscles of his forearms. Pumps iron, too, Lou decided. The young man scanned the diner like a lunchroom bully looking for his next victim, then nodded at Lou and strode toward the booth.

"Mr. Delgado?" The young man extended his hand.

"Right." Lou tried not to wince as powerful fingers mashed his fleshy paw.

"Mr. Perry sent me."

"Have a seat." Lou nodded at the other side of the table.

The young man slid into the booth and pulled a pack of Camels from his pocket. He flicked one out of the pack, touched what looked like a solid gold lighter to one end, and dropped both lighter and cigarettes back in his pocket, every movement precise as a close-order drill. He inhaled as if pulling the nicotine all the way down to his toes. Marge bustled back over, order pad in hand.

"You need a menu, sugar?"

He barely glanced at her. "Bring me a glass of water. With lots of ice."

Lou studied the young man as Marge went back to the counter. He looked familiar, like one of those actors in a late-night infomercial. The Porsche in the parking lot and the Rolex strapped to his wrist spelled money, but he was too young to have accumulated that kind of wealth on his own. Daddy's got dough, Lou decided. Junior's in some kind of trouble and Daddy's going to grease the slide.

"Okay." Lou started with his dependably disarming smile. "Tell me why a guy like you needs a guy like me."

"I need to find out someone's habits." He blew a plume of smoke toward Lou.

Delgado grinned. "You got a girl who's running around on you?"

"I wouldn't need a private detective to take care of that, Mr. Delgado," the young man replied curtly, pulling a newspaper clipping from his pocket. "I want to find out about this woman, here." He shoved the article across the table.

Lou looked down at the paper. The girl leaving the Deckard County Courthouse looked attractive, in a crisp, I-mean-business way. Long legs, nice tits, but all subdued behind an expensive black suit and a leather briefcase. He recognized her before the kid's fingers left the page. Mary Crow. Lou knew people who cursed this woman on a daily basis.

"So what did the famous Ms. Crow do to you? Not get all your speeding tickets dismissed?" Lou kept his voice light as Marge set a tall glass of water down on the table, ice tinkling.

"She just convicted my brother of murder."

Lou's face brightened. Suddenly it all fell into place. He *had* seen this guy on television. Not commercials, but the news. Every station in Atlanta had shown him sweating like a pig on the witness stand at his brother's trial. He didn't have the movie-star good looks of his killer brother, but the hair, the eyes—and the arrogance—were the same.

"You're that Whitman kid's brother," said Lou.

The young man nodded. "I'm Mitchell Whitman. Son of old Cal the real-estate king and brother of handsome Cal the killer."

"Sorry." Lou shrugged. "It seemed like a pretty airtight case."

"They set it up to look that way. My father has made a lot of money in his life, and a commensurate number of enemies. The only way they could get to him was through my brother."

"And the prisons are filled with innocent men." Delgado sighed. How many times had he heard that? "Just tell me how I figure into this."

Whitman drained half the glass of ice water, then set it down. "Like I said, I want to know as much about Mary Crow as you can tell me. Where she goes, what she does, who she does it with."

Lou choked out a little laugh. "Look, kid, I'll tell you right now I don't mess with officers of the court. And I sure as hell wouldn't mess with Mary Crow. I saw her going after you on TV. She squeezed your balls pretty hard."

"Nobody's asking you to mess with anybody." Whitman ignored Delgado's testicle remark. "I'm only interested in information."

Lou frowned down at the newspaper article. "So what terrible things do you figure she does on the side? Pose for porn? Fuck the mayor?"

"I don't know, Mr. Delgado. That's what I would be paying you to find out." Whitman bypassed the ashtray on the table and flipped his cigarette on the floor, grinding it out on the linoleum with the heel of his hand-sewn boot.

Lou gave up on his pecan pie. For some reason this Mitchell Whitman made him feel like he was sitting next to someone flicking matches at a half-empty gas can. Better to just get this over with, he thought, and be gone. "Okay. So I tail Ms. Crow. Then what?"

"Then report back to me. I'm sure this isn't anything you haven't done before."

Lou looked at Whitman for a long moment. Something told him there was a lot more to this, but something else told him it was better not to ask what. Suddenly an idea occurred to him.

"Okay," he said confidently, trying to regain control of the conversation. "You put five grand down on the table right now and you'll have me for twenty-four hours. Then I'm out of it, totally." Lou grinned. Rich people were the cheapest skates of all. A price tag like this would kill the deal cold.

Instead, Mitchell Whitman reached for his wallet and pulled out a blank check. Without blinking, he uncapped a fountain pen from his pocket and scrawled in: five thousand dollars.

Lou looked at the check as Whitman slid it across the table. It was already signed by Bill Perry and drawn on the Perry & Hendrix account. Thanks to Daddy's money, no trouble would ever come back to lie in this kid's crib.

"To be so young, you know the ropes pretty good," Delgado said.

"I'm a graduate student in applied computer science at Georgia Tech, Mr. Delgado. In six weeks I'm going to be installing a computer-operated hydroelectric dam on a small, very beautiful little island off the coast of Chile. I've spent the past three months helping my family wade through this pile-of-shit persecution. I would do most anything to leave the country without having to worry about my brother and the overzealous Mary Crow."

For the first time Mitchell Whitman smiled. Involuntarily, Lou stiffened. Whitman had a cold kind of mirth Lou had seen only once before, on an old man in Chicago who'd claimed to be the Führer's personal skinner-of-Jews. *Jesus*, he thought. *Who is this kid?*

"So have we got a deal?"

"Meet me here, eight o'clock Saturday morning. You'll get a twenty-four-hour slice of Ms. Crow's life. But I'm warning you, if she makes me, or any of my people, then I'm outta there and you and Perry are out five grand."

"Not a problem," Whitman said as he slid out from the booth and stood up. Delgado saw that his thighs were thick as small trees, and that he looked over the diner as if assessing how much firepower he would need to turn the whole place into a pile of greasy, smoking rubble.

"Saturday morning, kid. Then we're history."

Delgado watched as Whitman walked out into the night, the neon lights of the diner making the back of his neck glow a sick shade of green. He hopped into his car, the Porsche's lights came on, and Mitchell Whitman roared off, tires squealing against tarmac.

"Jesus." Delgado shook his head. "If that kid's engineering the future, then we're all fucked."

THREE

ood grief, Alex. We're spending
two nights in the Nantahala National Forest, not scaling K-2."

Mary stood in the parking lot of
her condo, skeptically eyeing the contents of
Alex's red BMW. The bright October sun
sparkled off the open trunk, revealing a bulging
teal backpack crunched in between a folded tent,
a giant cooler of food, and a gas stove that
looked like an early Russian space satellite.

Alex pushed the tent to one side. "Charlie
had all this stuff and insisted we take it. I couldn't
turn him down. He even packed us a lunch."

Mary set her backpack down on the bumper.
"Charlie had all this fancy gear?" Charlie Carter,
a lanky, gregarious veterinarian who had hiked
most of the Appalachian Trail in a pair of worn-
out Keds, was Alex's boyfriend. They'd met the
morning she'd brought her dog Daisy in to be
spayed, and by the time Daisy's stitches had
healed, Charlie and Alex were officially a cou-

ple. Since Alex had always tried to rehabilitate every hurt and abandoned animal she saw, Mary thought Charlie a perfect choice for her
friend. She'd never seen Alex happier with a man.

Alex rearranged the stove. "He bought this stuff to do Bryce
Canyon with his old girlfriend, but she got the cramps and couldn't go."

"Hadn't she heard of Midol?"

Alex squinted one eye. "I think they had some other issues." The
ends of her blonde hair brushed against the collar of an orange safety
jacket she was wearing over her favorite red plaid shirt. "Anyway, he
even bought us three of these jackets, just so we wouldn't get shot by
deer hunters."

"Greater love hath no man than to buy his honey a safety vest."
Mary didn't have the heart to tell Alex that they would be hiking far
too high in the mountains to even see a deer, much less a deer hunter.
"What's Charlie going to do while you're gone?"

"He's giving a paper next week at a veterinarian convention in
Toronto." Alex laughed. "'New Advances in Flea Control.' Charlie's a
major player in fleas."

Mary smiled, concealing a small pang of loneliness as they shoved
her backpack in the trunk. It had been a long time since she'd had a
man willing to buy her a safety vest and pack her a nice lunch. Most
of her lovers spooked quickly—unnerved by the grisly evidence files
stacked on her dining room table or saddened by the small shrine of
family photographs on her bedroom dresser. Rob Williams, the last
man she'd been serious about, had voiced it perfectly when he kissed
her between her breasts and murmured, "Sorry, babe. That broken
heart just doesn't have enough room in it for me."

Alex peeled off her Day-Glo vest and tossed it in on top of the
camp stove, then she saw the small metal toolbox Mary held in her
hand. "Hey, isn't that your old paint box from college?"

Mary nodded. "I thought I might do some sketching."

She balanced the box on the fender of Alex's car and snapped
open the lid. Inside was a neat array of pencils, a palette knife, a couple of tubes of aging oil paint and a small sketch pad. Also nestled
amid the art supplies were two tattered ticket stubs to *Dances with
Wolves* and a photograph of four college girls grinning from a bright
red London phone booth.

"Look!" Alex pointed at the photo. "That's us and the Willis twins! I haven't seen them in years . . . this paint box goes back a long way."

"*We* go back a long way, Alex," Mary reminded her, closing the box and shoving it between the tent and the sleeping bag. "I've lost count of all the crazy trips we've taken together."

"Which reminds me." Alex frowned. "You want to tell me why we're going camping in North Carolina? We haven't camped since college."

"Why shouldn't we go camping? It's a wonderful way to spend a vacation." Unconsciously, Mary fingered Wynona, tucked deep in the pocket of her jeans.

"Mary, I know you. I know what you like to do on your vacations. Your idea of fun is art galleries and bookstores and having hot coffee rolled in on a cart from room service. In all the years I've known you, never once have I heard you yearn to go sketch the piney woods of North Carolina." Alex slammed the trunk and turned to face her. "So. What's up?"

Mary looked at her oldest friend standing tall—shading her china-blue eyes against the sun, fully utilizing the lighthouse beam of a gaze she'd perfected in law school. She sighed, knowing that she was standing before the one person who could read her like an eye chart. Finally, she took a deep breath and said, "I want to go back to Little Jump Off."

"What?" Alex looked as if she'd just been doused with a bucket of cold water. "That store where your mother was killed?"

Mary nodded. "I need to see it again."

For a moment Alex stood speechless, all the joy drained from her pretty face. "But why?" she finally asked. "All that happened so long ago."

Mary shrugged. "I just need to do it, okay? It's like until I come to terms with all that, I'll stay stuck *here*."

Alex studied the strong, confident woman who stood before her and remembered the Mary Crow she'd met twelve years ago, when an elegant older lady in a linen suit had literally pushed a trembling, denim-clad teenager with a battered white suitcase into her college dorm room. "Why, hello, dear," the old lady had said in that soft Atlanta drawl that bespoke money and power and roots that stretched back to when Oglethorpe founded the colony. "I'm Eugenia Benne-field, and this is my granddaughter, Mary Crow. You two are going to be roommates!"

Oh, no we're not, Alex had thought. At the time she had been unable to imagine rooming for ten minutes with this quaking Mary Crow. Today she couldn't imagine living her life without her. Since that moment they'd met in their dorm room, Mary's quiet, unassum-ing *groundedness* had become an emotional safe harbor that she sailed into on a regular basis.

"Did you tell your grandmother you were going up there?" she demanded, lifting an eyebrow.

Mary shook her head. "I didn't want to get Eugenia riled up—she reads too many mysteries as it is. Anyway, Alex, I just want to look around. After we go to Little Jump Off, I'll totally devote myself to having fun."

"Promise?"

"Scout's honor." Mary raised her right hand.

"Well, okay." Alex sighed, only too aware of how stubborn Mary could be. "I've never been able to stop you from doing anything else you were determined to do."

"Thanks." Mary smiled.

"Can I ask just one more question?"

"What?"

"You're not planning on reopening any old murder cases, are you? Joan's edgy enough about this trip. She wanted to take us to New York to see *Tosca*."

Mary laughed. "My only plan is to forget all about Cal Whitman and enjoy the woods."

They drove to another of the thousand condos that ringed Atlanta, where Joan Marchetti sat perched on the bumper of her car, cutting the price tags off a new, black all-terrain fleece-lined anorak. An equally new black backpack lay on the ground, resting beside her barely broken-in black boots, while a new black camp watch marked the time from her left wrist. Joan's only garment over two weeks old was a battered black Yankees cap that shielded her eyes from the sun.

"Wow!" Alex hooted as she pulled the BMW up beside her. "New York goes Primitive." She got out of the car and sniffed the air extravagantly. "But you still smell like the perfume counter at Saks."

"Thank God." Joan brushed cigarette ash off her black jeans. "I could've bought three new pairs of shoes for the money I spent on this camping gear."

"You look terrific, Joan, but you're supposed to wear old ratty clothes when you camp," Mary told her. "Not go out and buy new ones."

"Oh, yeah?" Joan wrinkled her nose at Alex's tattered flannel shirt. "Well, I guess my wardrobe doesn't extend to ratty."

"That baseball cap looks pretty ratty," said Alex, turning and unlocking the trunk of the car.

"It may look ratty, but it's my lucky cap." Joan had stuffed her dark curly hair under the cap, exposing a slender neck the color of fresh cream. "My dad sent it to me the first time the Yankees beat the Braves in the World Series."

"Sounds like you're ready to camp to me." Mary hoisted up Joan's new backpack and put it in the trunk.

"But I wasn't ready to spend so much money." Groaning, Joan climbed in the backseat and waggled the anorak's price tag. "This better be a great weekend, you guys."

"When have our road trips ever not been great, Joan?" Alex laughed as she lowered the top of the convertible. "You're too much of a homebody. If it wasn't for Mary and me, you would just hole up in this condo every weekend, reading briefs and baking lasagna."

"I need to read my briefs. And I like baking lasagna. I especially like having Hugh Chandler over to eat it!" Joan protested ferociously, but she knew that Alex was right. Even though she'd lived in Atlanta for nearly nine years, she still felt intimidated by the hot, sprawling city with its honey-drip accents and countless Peachtree streets. Were it not for these two women, she probably would spend most of her time cocooned with Verdi and Puccini in the icy cool of her apartment.

"You can have Hugh Chandler over next weekend, Joan," promised Mary. "This weekend is Mother Nature's gift to girl attorneys who labor in the trenches of the law!"

"All right, already." Joan rolled her eyes. "Let's go!"

. . .

Alex pulled out of the parking lot and drove north. The morning begged for escape. The hot muggy fist of summer had loosened its grip on Atlanta, leaving behind a dry warmth that would linger until the first cool damp of fall inched its way down from Canada. With the CD player blaring, the three women sped along a chalk-colored interstate until it became U.S. 19, the ancient two-lane that connects the red clay hills of upper Georgia to the mountains of North Carolina.

The women drove on, Alex and Joan singing along to a Lucinda Williams CD. Mary smiled, listening as Joan's voice soared while Alex croaked along, struggling to stay in the right key. As their ears began to pop from the altitude, they crested a steep hill at the little town of Dahlonega, and the Grange-calendar landscape abruptly vanished. The clipped-green farms and sloe-eyed cows suddenly gave way to hazy blue mountains that rose before them, beckoning and forbidding at the same time.

"Are those our mountains?" asked Joan from the backseat.

"That's the beginning of them," Mary replied. "The Old Men, we call them."

"Gosh, I thought they'd be rocky and topped with snow," Joan said. "They look hazy. Soft, somehow."

Oh, but they're not, thought Mary. The same tiny chill she'd felt in the courtroom rippled through her as she scanned the deceptive-looking peaks. *Soft is the last thing the Old Men are.*

As the road traversed one of the few patches of flat ground, Alex spotted a lopsided billboard that commanded one corner of a small cow pasture.

"Hey, Joan." She glanced in the rearview mirror. "Y'all have anything like that in Brooklyn?"

The billboard asked, in flaming red letters, *Where Will You Spend Eternity? Heaven or Hell???* Wavy lines had been drawn around hell to indicate heat and an appropriate Bible verse was lettered underneath in smaller, more sedate script.

Joan frowned as the weathered sign flew by. "Jeez, I thought Sister Mary Xavier was nuts. Who on earth would put up a billboard about the afterlife?"

"Oh, the same folks who drink strychnine and kiss rattlesnakes," Alex teased. "Didn't Mary warn you? They eat Catholics for dinner up here. Roast 'em on spits in their backyards."

Joan started to object, but Mary turned around and gave her a wink. "Don't worry, Joan. The worst thing people eat up here is possum. And that's only when they can catch one."

"Oh, yeah? For a minute you had me worried. You know it's not too late to catch a flight to La Guardia. If we turned around now, we could be at the airport by three. We could eat calamari at my dad's restaurant tonight and see *Tosca* tomorrow."

"You're such a wuss, Joan," said Alex. "You know you've always wanted a walking tour of Hillbilly Heaven. Think of what you can tell the folks back home."

"Right." Joan fumbled in her purse and pulled out another cigarette. "I spent a thousand dollars to go sleep outdoors with my two crazy friends." She lit the cigarette and hunched forward. "Hey, Mary, show me again where we're going. I called my mother this morning and I couldn't even remember the name of the place."

Mary pulled a map from her purse and pointed to a tiny dot on the North Carolina–Tennessee border. "There. Santoah."

Joan frowned. "No kidding? I told my mom it was Nanook or Nirvana or something. She's already started lighting candles to the Blessed Virgin."

"It's in the Nantahala National Forest." Mary pointed to a pale green blob. "This shaded area here."

"But that must be a million acres." Joan traced the sprawling green outline with her finger. "It goes on over into, uh, Tennessee."

"Right. It's the Cherokee National Forest there," explained Mary. "But it's the same big stretch of trees."

"And this is where you grew up?"

Mary nodded. "We lived in Atlanta until my dad was killed in Vietnam, then my mom came back home." She tried to picture her father, but she had been only four when he died. She remembered the tautness of his cheek against hers, a laundry-starch smell, his voice singing her a lullaby in the dark, *Blacks and bays, dapples and grays, all the pretty little horses . . .*

Still looking at the map, Joan took a long drag on her cigarette. "You come back here a lot?"

"Not since my mother died." Mary's words fell flat on the sunny air. She closed her eyes and concentrated fiercely on the pungent smell of Joan's menthol-laced smoke. When she opened them, Joan was scowling.

"I don't think I've ever known what your mother died of, Mary."

For a long moment no one spoke; then Mary replied, choosing her words with care. "My mother didn't die of anything, Joan. My mother was raped and murdered."

"Oh, jeez." Joan shrank back in the seat. "How awful. I don't know what to say. I didn't realize it was anything like that—"

"That's okay. It's old news." Mary kept her eyes straight ahead.

"Hey, Mary. Tell us again where we're going." Reliably, Alex booted the conversation back up onto happier ground.

Mary cleared her throat. "A spring called Atagahi. Not many people know about it. My mom took me there a lot as a child. We used to soak in it like a hot tub. The Cherokees think it's visible only to those who need it. If you wash in Atagahi's waters, your wounds will be healed."

"Cool," said Alex. "You can jump right in and forget about the State of Georgia versus Calhoun Whitman, Jr."

"I can hardly wait," Mary replied, the hate-filled faces of Cal Whitman and his brother Mitchell flashing before her.

They sped on through the cooler, pine-scented air. The foothills grew steeper, and overall-clad farmers whittled beside Chevy pickups laden with mountain apples and sourwood honey for sale. Twice they had to stop to let Joan's queasy stomach calm down. Then Mary pointed down a gravel lane that sloped off the paved highway. "Turn left, Alex. There's a place I need to visit down there."

Alex turned the Beemer down the lane, gravel popping under the wheels of the car. The road skirted the base of a mountain, then crossed a shallow creek and broke into a meadow bright with golden-rod. On the far side of the field stood a small clapboard church. *Horton's Chapel U.M.C.,* read a hand-lettered sign by the front door.

"Gosh!" Alex gazed at the bright white church sparkling against the golden meadow and dark green pines. "This looks right out of Norman Rockwell."

"Park over there," Mary directed. "Near the cemetery."

Alex circled the church, pulling the BMW under a sprawling oak tree with a tire swing dangling from its lowest limb. Mary pointed at a split-rail fence halfway up the hill. It enclosed a number of white tombstones that erupted like jagged teeth from the thick grass. "My mom's buried up there. I'd like to have a look at her grave."

Alex glanced at her friend, trying to divine the expression in Mary's smoky hazel eyes. "Should we come, too? Or would you rather be alone?"

"No. Please come." Mary smiled. "I'd like you both to see it."

They got out of the car and walked up the hill, Joan and Alex following Mary through a cemetery that could have been in any churchyard in America, except for the names on the tombstones. Where most places you'd find Joneses or Smiths or Johnsons, here lay Owles and Saunooks and Walkingsticks and Crows. The three young women threaded their way through the graves. At a simple granite slab, Mary stopped.

Martha Joy Crow, the inscription read. *1948–1988*.

Joan's eyes filled with tears. "Gosh, Mary. Your mom was only forty."

Mary looked down at the gravestone. Alex had heard this story a thousand times. Joan had never heard it. Mary swallowed hard and began to speak.

"My mother died in the late afternoon on April eleventh. She was working in Norma Owle's store. Someone came in and did the Big Three—robbery, rape and murder." Mary rattled off her official version of her mother's death. She'd learned long ago that if she said it fast, it tasted not quite so bitter coming out of her mouth. "Not an uncommon crime for most of America. But a very uncommon crime for here."

"Did they ever catch her killer?" Joan spoke in a whisper.

"No. They scoured these mountains for weeks, but they never caught anybody. Finally they decided it was just some drifter who needed money for drugs. Nobody could ever explain why he needed to rape and kill my mother, too." Mary's eyes flashed. "Most of the money had spilled out of the cash register and was left behind on the floor. The only thing I saw missing was her Saint Andrew's medal."

Joan frowned. "Don't you mean Saint Christopher?"

"No. Saint Andrew. It was my father's. His grandfather had given it to him, and he'd worn it the whole time he was in Vietnam. They sent it back with his body. A knight, fighting a dragon. My mother put it on just before his funeral. She never took it off."

"Jeez, that's terrible." Impulsively, Joan wrapped her arms around Mary. "I'm so sorry. I can't imagine living through a hell like that."

Mary hugged Joan back. "It was awful," she agreed quietly. "But it's history, now." Over Joan's shoulder she smiled at Alex, remembering all the nights they'd lain awake in the dorm, Mary going over each detail of the murder scene and the hunt for her mother's killer a thousand times, Alex listening with unlimited patience and a diminishing pile of PayDay candy bars. Mary knew that without Alex, she wouldn't have survived the first week at Emory, much less the ensuing twelve years.

She squeezed Joan, then relaxed her embrace. "Alex pulled me through the worst of it."

From the pocket of her jeans she withdrew a plastic bag filled with six smooth, speckled stones. "The old Cherokees honored their ancestors with things of the earth," she explained. "I picked these stones from the little creek that runs behind my apartment in Atlanta."

Mary knelt down and kissed each small stone. Their grainy coolness against her lips brought that long-ago spring day rushing back— Reverend Hunt reading from his Bible, the redbud tree sending tiny magenta stars up against the darkening sky, the mourners huddling in raincoats around the dank hole in the ground that would embrace her mother for eternity. She'd felt like a murderer herself then. If she had just gone straight home that afternoon, this wouldn't have happened. She would have been there. She would have stopped whoever had done this. *Don't go, Mama,* she'd cried silently as they'd lowered the simple coffin into the earth. *Please don't leave me.*

Mary made a small pile of the stones just beneath her mother's marker. "*Sudali,* Mama," she whispered. "Six. Six stones for six convictions." For Hance Jordan, who poisoned his young wife to collect her insurance; for Wayne Creech, who fatally stabbed his girlfriend for not wearing a bra; for four more beyond them. One more, and she could place the seventh stone on her mother's grave. Seven. The number her people regarded as magical and redemptive as any plunge in a Baptist pool. One more stone, and Mary Crow would be at peace.

She stared at the little pile of six stones for a moment, then she rose and looked at her friends.

"Okay," she told them. "I'm done."

"Are you sure?" Alex asked. "We can stay longer if you want—Joan and I can wait for you in the car."

"No." Mary smiled as a shadow passed from her eyes. "I'm done. Let's go eat an early lunch, ladies. We've got a lot of mountains to climb before dark."

FOUR

SOMEWHERE IN THE NANTAHALA FOREST,

OCTOBER 2000

D*eath has a stink to it. It's blood and kum and the sea and the sour scent of a man humiliated, pleading for his life. It's sticky on your hands, and if you cram your fingers in your mouth and suck them like chicken bones, all that sweet death-marrow goes straight to your brain and makes you feel like God.*

Henry Brank laughed as he pulled the knife from the rabbit's neck. "This is a real piece of luck, Buster," he said to the snake that lay coiled inside the bag he'd carried over his shoulder all morning. "I thought for sure we'd only have cornbread tonight."

The snake made no response. Brank tied the rabbit's back legs together with a piece of raw-hide and slung it, along with the sack and his shotgun, over his left shoulder. He wiped the blood from his knife, stuck it in his boot and continued climbing up the slippery, pine-straw-covered switchback that would eventually take him to the top of Cowcamp Ridge. He'd walked east since dawn, and the once-warm sun had disappeared into a thick gray cloud bank that seemed to float up from the mountains themselves.

"We'll check the weather at the top of this ridge, Buster," Brank huffed, his legs burning from the near-vertical climb.

They crested the ridge just as the wind began to whip raw and sting his face. Out of breath, Henry dropped his gear next to a rotting log and looked out over the acres of forest spread below. Only the dark tops of pine trees poked up from the thick white stew of fog.

"Shit. Whited out." He turned northward and sniffed the wind. The sharp-iron smell of cold tingled his nostrils. Winter was coming, and soon. In a couple of weeks these gold mountains would turn a sullen brown, then pale blue snow would dust them like sugar. Right now, though, opaque clouds bloated with water swirled down from the sky, obscuring everything from trees to entire mountaintops.

He shifted the sack to his other shoulder. "We gotta find us a place fast, Buster. We don't want to get lost in the Hell."

Since midmorning Brank had skirted Godfrey's Hell, a huge tangle of laurel named for a long-ago bear hunter who'd once followed his dogs into the monstrous coil and had never been seen again. When Brank heard that story, all he could picture was a frantic man forever careening through a viney maze with a pack of frothy-mouthed dogs, and he'd given the Hell an extra-large dollop of respect ever since.

He squinted at the ground. A finger of a trail beckoned through the fog—nothing more than a dark track through the mist. He followed it carefully, keeping the ridge on his left, the Hell on his right. If he could just find a cave, or even an overhang to hole up and build a fire in, then he and Buster could wait out the weather.

He trudged on. He despised picking his way down a mountain like this, with clammy vapors icing your bones and putting blinders on your eyes. When he'd first come into the woods he thought whiteouts fun, like walking through giant swirls of cotton candy. But he'd been younger then, and losing yourself in a cloud was not a problem when lost was what you badly needed to be.

Suddenly he stopped. A noise, off to the right, coming up from the Hell. He sank to his knees and shouldered his shotgun. Maybe it was Trudy. He'd tracked her all the way from Nova Scotia, catching sight of her at dusk, slinking like a tawny scarf through the trees, at night screaming like some caterwauling demon. He'd been able to follow her by the remnants of what she ate—gnawed-out Holstein calves in Pennsylvania; mangled little shoats in Kentucky. These days she fancied fawns and feral pigs. Every place he'd tracked her though, she'd been too canny for the special trap he'd designed, and he'd never been able to draw close enough to get a shot off. *Shit*, Henry thought in disgust, aiming into the white nothingness. *You've wandered up and down these mountains for thirty years and you still can't beat Daddy's little girl.*

He listened, peering into the mist, but he heard nothing more. "Musta been a troll," he muttered, rising to his feet. Immediately his father's voice boomed through his head. *Der Kobold will come and pluck out your eyes, he said. Then he laughed that jouncing, beer barrel laugh. Hohohoho. Poor little sissy Heinrich. All these years and still scared of goblins.*

Brank shook the mocking voice from his head. His father was dead now, surely. His mother, too. All the Branks of western Pennsylvania were gone. All except him and Trudy.

He picked his way down the ridge, testing each step, careful not to veer off the trail and plunge headlong into the Hell. At a small gap the fog thinned, and he spotted a shallow limestone niche that a spring had eroded from the mountainside. He wouldn't be able to stand upright inside, but he could at least crouch away from the cold wind.

"Here we go, Buster." He flung his sack into the damp crack. "I'll build us a fire and we'll roast Thumper here for lunch instead of dinner."

It took him a while to find enough dry tinder beneath the damp leaves, but soon he had a small pine blaze built on the edge of the rock.

With four quick strokes of his knife he beheaded and eviscerated the rabbit. He pulled the skin off, then cut a green hickory branch from beside the spring and suspended the body over the now hot fire. Small droplets of oil began to bead up on the rabbit's flesh. Brank grinned. Rabbit had always been his favorite.

He stretched out his legs and pulled Buster out of his sack. The mud-colored snake was a yard long, the pattern on its back similar to that of a rattler. It twisted angrily in Brank's hand, annoyed at being plucked from its warm bed and thrust into the cool air. "Just get off your high horse, Buster," Brank warned the writhing reptile. "You've been sleeping on a hundred and twenty-seven primo coon skins all day. Not many snakes can say that."

The fire sent up wisps of thin gray smoke that carried the aroma of roasting meat. Brank put Buster back down on top of the sack and absently began to pluck the beggar lice that clung to his pants. Tomorrow, if the whiteout lifted, he would reach the Little Jump Off Post Office. There, people would ship his pelts to Michigan and sell him coffee and magazines. A shiver of anticipation ran through him.

The rabbit's juices began to drip down into the flames. The smell made Henry's stomach wrench with hunger. He smiled. Rabbit had been the first thing he'd learned to kill in the woods.

He was sixteen when he fled down here from Pennsylvania. He'd hung around the edges of small mountain towns, hungry for the sound of talk, finding thin comfort in the neon-lit windows of road-side bars. Even though he had his shotgun, the woods still terrified him and he lived on the sodden french fries and half-chewed steak bones that he dug out of restaurant trash bins. But what he had left behind at home had scared him even more and at night he always retreated into the woods where no one could find him. He would curl up beneath some tree, where every slithery sound the forest made sent a bolt of stark terror straight through him. Most nights he stayed awake, trembling, praying that God would arrange some kind of dispensation that would allow him back into civilization. Then, one morning while he shivered under a log on the north side of Big Stone Gap, a man appeared out of a locust grove. He wore a battered felt hat pulled down over his blind right eye and carried a shotgun with silver scrolling on the stock.

"Hidy, boy," he said, smiling an odd smile. "You look to be in a fair amount of discomfort."

That was how they met. Fate Lyons was a Vietnam vet from West Virginia who, in exchange for certain favors, taught Henry Brank tracking and trapping and the million other things he needed to know to survive these mountains. Though Fate's unrestrained appetite for boys eventually led to their parting, Brank still thought of him often, and with gratitude. He doubted he could have survived long without Fate Lyons's tutelage.

He wiggled the rabbit's haunch. It moved freely away from the body, golden-brown and glistening. He pulled the whole carcass from the spit and bit into the shoulder, putting a small chunk of the inside meat in front of Buster. The tiny forked tongue sniffed with interest.

"That's good stuff, Buster," Brank said, biting off a chunk of the meat. "Rabbit à la Fate."

He ate until he'd sucked the bones dry, then he threw the delicate skeleton into the fire and looked out into the thick wet cotton that surrounded him. There was no point in going further today—in two hours he'd lose what little light he had. If he continued down the ridge, he might find himself plunging headlong into the Hell like poor Godfrey and his hounds. It would put him behind schedule, but he'd do better to wait out the fog here.

With a deep sigh he took off his belt and unbuttoned his damp shirt. Icy wisps of mist chilled his flesh. He spread his shirt out close to the fire to dry, then turned, bare-chested, to his sack, from which he pulled a bottle filled with clear liquid. He uncapped it and took a long drink. As always, the first swallow scorched his throat and teared his eyes, but in a minute an easier, more pleasant heat radiated through him, turning him jocular and expansive.

"Damn, that's good," he whispered. He removed his boots and socks, and stood up, unzipping his pants and laying them beside the shirt. His body bore the marks of years of a hardscrabble mountain existence. Though he was half a foot taller than when he'd first come here, no fat covered his bones. Pale white skin stretched over a sinewy skeleton; the veins in his hands formed a bas-relief over the taut muscles of his arms. Scars from bites and scratches decorated him like tattoos. Five of his teeth had rotted away and a mis-set bear trap in Maine had nearly snapped off his leg. That day he thought he might die, in fact, prayed he would die, but he didn't. He'd bound his mangled shin and crawled off to chew up some pills he'd stolen from a hiker. After a month of fever dreams punctuated by a torturous thirst, he could walk again, though never as straight or as fast as before.

He crouched by the fire nude, his penis shriveling in the crisp air. He held his arms out to the thick white murk, as if to implore the weather to cease. In the firelight his pale body looked like a long sycamore branch come suddenly alive, and his beseeching motions linked him to an older time, when all men sat around fires and invoked the gods for good fortune.

When the whiskey had turned his frozen-up muscles warm and limber, he pulled another knife from his sack. He placed this one at the end of one log, then slowly, with inward-gazing eyes, he spread his fingers and felt inch by inch the skin of his skull, then the skin that lay beneath his dark, matted beard. "Good!" he grunted when he reached the point of his chin. "Nobody home."

He did the same thing to his neck, then his shoulders, then his chest. He stopped suddenly, half an inch below his left nipple. "Ha!" he muttered, parting the thick hair that grew there. "Here's one little bastard trying to suck my tit!" Pressing his long thumbnails together, he wedged underneath the spot on his skin and plucked out a tick the size of a dime. He held the creature up to the air, then he licked it with his tongue and placed it on the now-warm blade of his knife. The tick did not move.

Carefully he resumed his procedure, going down both legs, searching between his toes, then ending with the coarser hair that curled around his genitals. He leaned back and sighed with pleasure, as his fingers searched that damp, familiar territory. He had begun to think that maybe today there would be just the one when his right hand felt a bump between his penis and scrotum.

"Damn!" he said with delight. "It's always the sweet meat!" He took a deep breath, then jerked the tick out. He sat up and peered at his crotch. A single drop of blood had spattered against his thigh.

He stared at the squirming bug between his fingers. "You're gonna go dancing with your buddy," he announced, placing it next to the other tick on his knife. "It's not nice to suck people's blood."

He curled around the fire and placed the knife over a lapping tongue of flame. The ticks were oblivious to it. They would be at first. Then the blade would heat up and they would begin to crawl faster and faster, searching for a way off the red-hot blade, only to find that their only way off was into the fire itself. Brank chuckled as he settled down to watch the show. He loved tick dances. He held them most every night.

When the ticks finally plunged into the fire with a sizzle and a sputter he put Buster back in the sack and wrapped up in an old wool blanket. He wondered if he wasn't getting too old for all this damp cold. His leg ached every night and there was a stiffness in his shoulders that no longer went away. Maybe now was the time to head south. He'd read that living was easy in Florida if you could get past Disney World. 'Course there were alligators and coral snakes down there, but it was warm, and the Everglades were, to his knowledge, without cold and frost and the specter of his sister. He sighed. If he could just kill Trudy once and for all, heading south would be exactly what he would do.

He pulled his shotgun close beside him, curled himself around the fire and stared out into the cottony haze. Not being able to see anything made him edgy—his nose and ears had never been as good as Fate's. And who knew what madness Trudy or the trolls might do if they snuck up on him unawares? He hugged his rifle close and sighed. Maybe they couldn't see him, either. Anyway, there was nothing he could do about it now.

"Don't borrow trouble," Henry Brank chided himself as he settled down to rest. To hike these pelts to Little Jump Off without getting lost in the Hell or eaten by Trudy would be trouble enough of its own.

FIVE

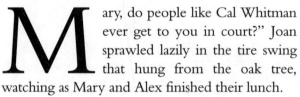

Mary, do people like Cal Whitman ever get to you in court?" Joan sprawled lazily in the tire swing that hung from the oak tree, watching as Mary and Alex finished their lunch.

"Oh, please don't get her started on that," Alex mumbled through a mouthful of one of Charlie Carter's special turkey-and-jalapeno sandwiches. "She's not convinced she's hung the right man."

"Really?" Joan sat up straight in the swing. That Mary might doubt a conviction surprised her.

Mary sipped a diet Coke, a faraway look coming into her eyes. "Not totally."

"How come? I thought you had that guy nailed from the get-go."

"His dick was hanging out of his pants when the cops got there," Mary replied. "Don't you think a man would at least zip his fly before he broke a girl's neck?"

Alex snorted. "Not if he'd raped her, and they were both stoned. It seems weird, but not impossible."

"Yeah." Joan spun around once in the tire swing. "Didn't the defense counsel say Cal had no memory of what happened that night?"

Mary nodded. "That's supposedly why he never took the stand."

"Well, then just take the dumb conviction and run." Alex finished her last bite of sandwich. "You stew about these things too much, Mary."

"I know." Mary frowned at the rust-colored mountains that encircled the little church and its placid graveyard. "Something about that case just doesn't feel right, though."

Joan lit a cigarette and shivered. "I envy your courage. I don't see how you can deal with that stuff every day."

"Our little Mary is tough." Alex leaned over and tapped Mary on the head. "See how hard that noggin is?"

"No, really," Joan persisted. "Don't you ever think about quitting the DA's office and doing what Alex and I do? We see a lot of corporate bastardy, but jeez, nobody winds up with their neck broken."

Mary looked toward her mother's grave. "I can't, Joan," she answered softly. "At least, not yet."

They packed up their trash and got back in the BMW. The white clapboard church and yellow meadow disappeared as they recrossed the creek and joined the main road. This time Alex drove more slowly, passing under a glowing bronze canopy of beech trees that rose as tall and magnificent as any cathedral.

The road twisted farther into the mountains. On the right a shallow river spewed white over iron-gray boulders while thick green rhododendrons tangled along its banks. To the left, the mountains thrust upwards with dark pines standing rank and file, thick as soldiers. High above the trees the sun shone gold; down here the mountains filtered the light to shadow, with only dapples of yellow coins dancing through the leaves.

"You know, up close these mountains don't look soft at all," Joan said as she peered at the woods that crowded against both sides of the road. "In fact, all these trees look kind of creepy."

"You're just not used to them yet." Alex grinned over her shoulder. "This time tomorrow, you'll be calling them all by name."

At a wide, gravel-lined clearing they passed a long cinder-block building that had begun life as a motel, then evolved, as a weathered sign indicated, into the "Demon's Den—A Private Club for Motor- cyclists of Distinction." Currently it was nothing but an empty, rust- streaked shell save for one lone figure who stood beside a wooden placard that read, *Have Your Picture Taken With A Real Life Cherokee.* The figure was a slender man, with the same dark hair and high Cherokee cheekbones as Mary, but he wore the full eagle-feathered headdress of a Sioux war chief. Mary watched his face stretch in a sur- prised smile as the BMW flashed by, his right hand raised in greeting.

Joan craned her neck. "Who was that guy? And why is he waving at you?"

"Gosh, I think that's Billy Swimmer!" Mary laughed as she waved out the window. It was amazing how little things changed around here. "I went to high school with him."

They twisted through a series of turns, then, on the right, between the road and the river, stood a long ramble of a building constructed of chinked logs. Half of it was two-storied, with small grimy windows overlooking the road. The rest of it just meandered along the creek bank, as if the owners had added on to the structure whenever time and money allowed. At the far end, the parking lot widened enough to accommodate a single gas pump and a rusty trash Dumpster. Mary's pulse ratcheted up as if she'd run a mile.

"This is where we need to stop, Alex," Mary said. She felt Alex's questioning glance, but kept her eyes straight ahead.

"Hey, do they sell cigarettes in there?" Joan asked as Alex nosed the BMW into the parking lot.

"Joan, do you realize how often we have to stop for you to get cigarettes?" Alex said. "I thought people who sang opera weren't sup- posed to smoke."

"Why do you think I quit?" Joan's voice quivered extravagantly. "One awful night I realized I had to choose between Verdi and Vir- ginia Slims. Nicotine won, hands down. The evil tobacco empire had me hooked. I was drummed off the stage, a hopeless addict."

"I thought they said you were too small," Alex countered.

"Well, that, too," admitted Joan.

Laughing, Alex shook her head. "That's what I love about you, Joan. Your unerring instinct for melodrama."

"Hey, you sing opera, you get melodramatic." Joan shrugged. "What can I say?"

Alex parked the car just beneath the Little Jump Off, North Carolina, Postal Service sign and turned off the engine. "Look at all that wood," she said, gazing at a line of slender upright hickory logs that stretched the length of the porch.

"Somebody must make bows here now." Mary's voice was a whisper; her legs had turned to stone.

Alex and Joan got out of the car, but Mary could not move. *Be calm*, she told herself, willing her racing heart to slow. *You wanted to come here.*

As Joan went ahead into the store, Alex paused and looked back. "Mary—are you sure you really want to go in there?"

"No," Mary answered softly as she stared at the wood-lined porch. "But I've got to try."

Alex shook her head, her face clouded with concern.

Mary got out of the car and followed Alex up the broad wooden steps. A cowbell jingled as Alex opened the door. Mary stopped for a moment, then she stepped inside. The familiar sweet smell of burned applewood permeated the ancient chinked walls. Where once an old stuffed boar head commanded the stone fireplace, several recurve bows now hung like delicate sculptures from the ceiling. The *Farmer's Almanac* calendar on the wall read 2000 instead of 1988. Otherwise, little had changed. Mary kept her eyes away from the far corner. *You don't have to look*, she reminded herself. *At least not yet.*

Across the store a dark-haired man was reading a newspaper behind the cluttered counter. He looked up. Mary caught her breath. Not twenty feet away sat Jonathan Walkingstick, her oldest friend and first lover. His dark eyes flashed once as he recognized her; then his face swiftly settled back into the noncommittal gaze that demonstrated courtesy for a Cherokee male.

"Jonathan." Her usually confident voice peeped out of her throat like a frightened sparrow.

"Mary." He said her name just as he used to—as if it were some charm that held a special magic just for him. Even now she could feel the caress of his voice all the way across the room.

A blush swept up her neck. "I had no idea you'd be here. I heard you were in the Army. England or somewhere."

"I was." Jonathan smiled and shrugged. "But I didn't make a career out of it."

"So when did you come back here? Has Norma Owle retired?"

"I've been back here since ninety-four. Norma died that fall."

"Oh." For a moment Mary didn't know what to say. Her mother was dead, but it seemed to her that everybody else up here should just go on living as they had been, timeless as the reruns of a TV sitcom.

"Well, it's good to see you again. Let me introduce you to some friends of mine." She babbled inanely, as if after twelve years she'd driven all the way up here just so she could introduce him to Alex and Joan. "We're going camping this weekend."

She walked toward him. He wore his hair longer than she remembered—tied in a ponytail with a leather thong. The slender muscularity of his youth had thickened into the powerful shoulders of a man in his prime. A postal-service badge hung crooked on his old Army jacket, which covered a faded denim work shirt. A half-finished *New York Times* crossword puzzle lay next to his cup of coffee, and the bone handle of the knife he called Ribtickler still protruded from his belt, just beneath his left arm. No paunch sagged around his waist and his mouth still tilted upwards in a wide, sensuous curve. Mary glanced quickly at his left hand. His fingers were bare. And he still looked at her as if he'd found some secret part of her only he could see.

She touched Alex's arm, willing her voice to courtroom strength. "Alex and Joan, I'd like to introduce an old friend of mine, Jonathan Walkingstick."

"Hi." Joan smiled at him, her dark eyes bright with curiosity. "Nice to meet you."

"Hello." Alex spoke softly as she extended her hand. *She knows exactly who he is,* Mary thought. *She remembers every word I ever said about him.*

"Good to meet you." Jonathan smiled his old lopsided smile; the blood seemed to sizzle through Mary's brain. "Where are you ladies headed today?"

"Someplace called Atagahi," Alex replied.

"That's a pretty good walk." He shot a curious glance at Joan's shiny new boots and stiff jacket. "You guys camp a lot?"

Mary shook her head. "We're taking it easy. I'm going to do some sketching, they're just going to relax. We should be home late Sunday."

"Going through the Ghosts?"

Mary smiled. "Maybe."

"Ghosts?" Joan looked at Mary. "What does he mean, *ghosts*?"

"It's nothing," said Mary. "Just a weird spot in the trail."

Jonathan asked, "Got tents and bags?"

Mary nodded again. "Alex's boyfriend loaned us some real high-tech stuff."

"Well, watch out for the weather. We've already had one snow, and it's only October."

For a moment, an awkward silence sprouted between them, then Joan spoke. "You got any Virginia Slims up here?"

"In the back left corner by the magazines." Jonathan pointed to the rear of the store.

"Any PayDay candy bars?" Alex was poking around the potato chip display.

"Middle aisle, over the outboard motor oil."

Alex and Joan went where he directed, leaving the two of them in silence.

Mary cleared her throat. "I thought I saw Billy Swimmer over at the Den. Has he started posing for the tourists?"

Jonathan nodded. "Ever since he lost his public job. Billy's doing everything he can, trying to raise enough money to get his fiddle out of hock. He's got a gig waiting with some bluegrass band."

Mary laughed. "Did he and Tammy Taylor ever get married?"

"Yeah. About three months after their son Michael was born."

"And you're the postman and bowyer?" Mary looked toward the back of the store where a number of bows hung unstrung against the wall. Longbows, recurves, double recurves—each one glowed in the shadowy light, elegant tributes to the skill in his powerful fingers. Mary could remember a time when those same fingers had smoothed the recurves of her own skin as expertly as they now shaped hickory and maple.

"Yeah. The bowyer, the fletcher, the candlestick maker. Three days a week I'm the postman, too." He looked into her face for a moment as if he wanted to say something else, then he laughed and retreated into politeness. "How about you? Happily married, I bet. With two kids and a Volvo."

Mary felt her blush deepen. "No, actually not. My work keeps me pretty busy. I'm an assistant DA in Atlanta."

"Lena Owle read you were famous down there. Said they called you Killer Crow or something."

Mary laughed. "Lena shouldn't believe everything she reads in the papers. So how about you? Two kids and a Volvo?"

He shook his head. "I was married for a while in Britain, but it didn't work out."

A Polaroid photograph taped to the cash register caught her eye. In it, Jonathan stood with his arm around a small, beautiful woman with luminous skin.

Mary pointed at the photo. "Isn't that . . ."

"Jodie Foster," he said proudly. "They filmed *Nell* up here. I was in the courtroom scene at the end."

"Hey, congratulations." Though she liked Jodie Foster, Mary had avoided that movie. Stereo and Technicolor brought the mountains too close for comfort.

"Just my five minutes of fame."

He laughed, then Joan's New York accent rang through the store. "Mary—come check this out."

Mary turned. Joan stood in front of a large cork bulletin board cluttered with the various chits of paper that marked peoples' passage up here—photos of hunters with trophy bears, notes advertising Plott hounds for sale, handwritten messages from one hiker to another. Mary walked over beside her.

Joan was looking at some photographs. They resembled Wanted posters, except the photos were not the mug shots of criminals, but people who had disappeared into the forest and never returned. They were pictures desperate relatives had ripped from family albums—one girl's high school graduation photo, another a gap-toothed little boy in an old Milwaukee Braves baseball cap grinning over a string of fish. Mary had seen the yellowed images so many times she felt like the missing people were old friends. Alice Andrews, nineteen, disappeared October 1, 1976, when she wandered away from a camp-out with friends. A year later Jimmy Reynolds, eight years old, let go of his father's hand on Butler's Bald for just a minute and was never seen again. Most people who got lost up here were found. Those two, though, had vanished. When she'd lived here they had haunted her, seeming to call to her through the trees every time she walked home alone.

Joan took off her sunglasses. "This is serious forest, isn't it?"

Mary shrugged. "Occasionally people don't make it out. Mostly, though, they do." She smiled at Joan. "We certainly will."

They walked back to the front of the store, where Alex had dumped six candy bars on the counter.

"You must not be into counting fat grams." Jonathan punched the keys on the ancient wooden cash register.

"Not today." Alex handed him a ten-dollar bill. "Me and my fat grams took separate vacations."

"Hey, life is short." He grinned, flicking open a brown paper bag. "And there's but a finite number of PayDays."

Joan reappeared with three packs of Virginia Slims and a bag of red licorice whips. She held up the latter. "I heard these were good to eat on the trail."

"Only if you like them in real life," said Mary.

"Oh." Joan fingered the candy, then put it back on the shelf. "Well, just give me the smokes then."

"You might try these instead." Jonathan grabbed a handful of Power Bars and shoved them in the sack with the cigarettes. "On the house."

He rang up the sale. "I understand you ladies are going primitive," he said as he gave Joan her change. "If you'd like one last shot at a flush toilet, you're welcome to use my facilities."

"Wow, that would be great," said Joan.

"Right over there." He pointed to a doorway beside an old ice-cream cooler that now chilled grubs and night crawlers.

Alex and Joan headed for the bathroom.

"Would you like to walk out on the porch?" Jonathan asked Mary when the door had closed behind them.

She looked at the sun, streaming in the windows. It would be like old times—Jonathan, close to her in the warm October light. She smiled, but shook her head. "Thanks, but I'd like to look around in here a minute."

"Sure." His smile faded, and she knew that he, too, was thinking of that long-ago afternoon. "I understand."

A sandy-haired man dressed in jeans entered the store, asking Jonathan about good spots to find trout. While they talked, Mary looked around. Little Jump Off was the same place it had been twelve years ago—still welcoming the mountain traveler with a little of everything and not much of anything. Although Jonathan now had a TV and a computer behind the counter, she knew if she stepped outside the back door, she would find an old well and a hog-killing trough and, further on, a cool, dark, hickory-scented shack where last fall's bear hams hung curing for Christmas. Further beyond that was the spot where she had said good-bye to him that awful afternoon. Involuntarily, she closed her eyes. Some things never change, however much you wish them to.

Slowly she walked over to the far corner where her mother's loom had once stood. It was here Martha wove the rugs and tapestries that tourists bought as souvenirs. Although the wide pine planks had been trod upon by a thousand different feet, the funny little discoloration in the wood was still there. Barely discernible to someone not looking for it, if you tilted your head at just the right angle you could see it. Mary knelt and covered it with her hand. It was here, at this point in the universe, that Martha Crow's heart had stopped and Mary Crow's heart had been broken forever.

She stared at the spot until she heard Joan and Alex coming out of the bathroom. Then she stood up quickly and turned away.

She used the bathroom herself, enjoying, one final time, the amenities of toilet paper and running water. Then she joined Joan and Alex, who were admiring Jonathan's snapshot of Jodie Foster.

"Ready, scouts?" she asked them.

"I am." Alex grabbed her bag of candy bars.

"I've got my smokes," added Joan.

"You ladies have a safe hike." Jonathan grinned, and raised one hand to Mary. "See you later," he called softly. "Be careful."

"'Bye." She followed her friends to the door. Pausing, she turned back toward the counter. "Say, Jonathan, who's the sheriff up here these days?"

"Stump Logan," he answered. "Same old fart as when your mother . . ." He stopped abruptly, horrified at the words he'd almost said. "He's fishing on Grapevine Creek," he amended quickly.

"Thanks," she replied. "Maybe I'll get in touch with him sometime." She smiled at him. "It was nice seeing you."

"Come back soon," he invited, his voice buoyant with hope. "No need to be a stranger."

She waved, then hurried to the car, almost bumping into the sandy-haired fisherman, who was ambling back to his car with a new fly for his rod.

"Yo, Mary, who was that hunk behind the counter?" Joan demanded from the backseat as Alex started the engine. "I'm sensing a little *historia* here, know what I mean?"

Mary stared at the store until Alex pulled out of the parking lot. "You sensed right, counselor," she finally replied. "*Historia* is the one thing Little Jump Off is lousy with."

SIX

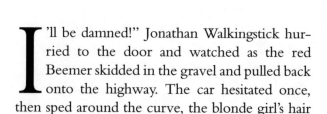

I'll be damned!" Jonathan Walkingstick hurried to the door and watched as the red Beemer skidded in the gravel and pulled back onto the highway. The car hesitated once, then sped around the curve, the blonde girl's hair blowing like flax in the wind.

Suddenly he felt as if he'd been kicked hard, and in the stomach. After twelve years, Mary Crow had just waltzed back into his life, and had looked damn good. Stylish in the way of city women, but different, too. Strong. Confident. Jonathan sighed and rubbed at an invisible spot on the windowpane. Mary must be doing okay.

He'd sneaked off to see her once in Atlanta, although he'd never told a soul. He'd accompanied his girlfriend, Lena Owle, to a teachers' convention, and while Lena attended her meetings he'd ridden the subway out to the Deckard County courthouse. He spotted Mary the instant he walked in the door. Black suit, spike heels, skirt just touching the interesting part of a woman's thigh. Her breasts pushed against the deep V of her suit lapels, and he'd felt himself growing hard just looking at her. She'd hurried into a courtroom, and he'd snuck in behind her and hastily taken a seat in the back row. For the rest of the day, or at least until he had to meet Lena, he'd watched Mary work the jury as cannily as a collie herding sheep. He had to leave before the case was decided, but he knew the accused was well on his way upriver. Afterwards he'd felt bad about the whole thing. He'd taken Lena out to an expensive Thai restaurant to make up for it. Later, when they'd made love, he took extra care to make her feel good, but he'd had to keep his eyes open. Every time they closed, all he could see was Mary.

"I saved you a seat," he said aloud now to the empty store, using their old line from high school. Back then he'd believed that he and Mary would go on forever, saving each other seats until the hearse arrived to take one or both of them to the grave.

"Too bad you took a different bus," he muttered as he walked back to the counter. He closed his eyes and breathed deeply, trying to hold the scent of her in his memory as long as he could. When he opened his eyes he scowled at the folded-up newspaper and tried to refocus on his puzzle. He needed a seven-letter word for "member of a nudist sect." He had just begun to write in "adahist" when the cowbell rang again.

"Hey, Jonathan!" Billy Swimmer, the skinny man who'd been shilling for photographs at the Demon's Den, stood in the doorway, his Sioux headdress tucked under his arm. "How goes it at Little Jerk Off?"

"Fine, Billy," Jonathan replied, scarcely looking up from his puzzle. He figured Billy must have spotted Mary and her friends as they drove past the Den. Like most inhabitants of small towns, Billy Swimmer could smell gossip in the air much like a mule could sense a coming storm. Now he was up here to sniff out whatever juicy tidbits Mary might have left behind. Jonathan concentrated on his crossword as Billy strolled over and hopped up on the counter.

"You haven't heard of anybody needin' help doing anything, have you? Nobody wants to have their picture taken and I still need a couple of hundred bucks to get my fiddle out of hock."

Jonathan looked up reluctantly from the paper. "Zell Crisp was in here saying you owe him a couple of hundred bucks, too."

"Well, yeah," admitted Billy with a helpless, snaggle-toothed smile. Jonathan shook his head. "Sorry. If I hear of anything I'll let you know."

"Say, wasn't that Mary Crow I saw drivin' up here in that red BMW?" Billy now revealed his true subject of interest, plucking a speck of dirt off one of the white pinfeathers at the base of the headdress.

"Yep."

"Is she coming back?" he asked just above a whisper, forgetting his feathers and staring at Jonathan with intense dark eyes.

Jonathan shook his head and peered at 14-Down. A six-letter word for "offspring of two gametes." "Nope. She's just going camping with some friends. They're going to Atagahi."

"Oh." Billy stopped short, disappointed. His brows pulled together in a frown. "Are you sure?"

"That's what she said. They loaded up on cigarettes and candy bars and took a whiz in the john. That sounds like women going camping to me."

"Well, hell, Jonathan. I don't see why she'd come up here just for that."

"This is her home, Billy. Why shouldn't she come here?"

"To go camping? They got plenty of campsites down in Georgia."

Jonathan looked up from his puzzle. "Leave it alone, Billy," he warned, his voice soft.

"I'm sorry. It's just a shame, everything that happened with you and her . . ." Billy's words trailed off awkwardly.

"Yeah." Jonathan began to print z-y-g-o-t-e upwards from *adahist*. "It is." He repressed a sigh. Everything Billy said was true, but what could he do about it? Mary was a hotshot DA in Atlanta. He ran the Little Jump Off General Store.

The cowbell jingled again. Jonathan glanced up, hoping that Mary had forgotten something, but a man he'd never seen before filled the doorway. The stranger wore hunting boots and carried both a shotgun and a battered canvas bag over his shoulder. His shirt and pants were standard Army camouflage, but with the name tag faded and the unit IDs torn off the sleeves. The sour odor of rancid fat and unwashed flesh wafted into the store. Billy gave a loud sniff and stashed his headdress safely behind the counter.

"Howdy, friend." The word *brain-fried* flashed across Jonathan's mind. "Can I help you?"

The man flared his nostrils like a dog smelling unfamiliar territory.

He turned in a slow circle, checking out the store, then he looked at Jonathan.

"I want to send a package." His voice creaked like a rusty hinge.

"We can do that."

"I got something that needs to go to Michigan."

Jonathan frowned. He couldn't remember ever having sent any-thing to Michigan. He searched under the counter for his postage chart. "You got it wrapped up?"

"No. I'll need to buy some kind of box off you."

Jonathan tossed his crossword puzzle beneath the cash register. "Let's see what you've got, then."

The man strode over to the counter. Jonathan tried to look at him without staring. His eyes were strange. Deep-set and light yellow, they glittered wolf-like beneath dark brooding brows. His nose was a thin wedge, and his skin had the texture of worn bark. His fingernails were long and dirty. He could have been as young as thirty-five or as old as sixty. He shot an angry glare at Billy, who hastily scooted off the counter, then he plopped his bag on the floor and plunged one arm in elbow-deep. With a sly grin, he fished out something that looked like an old rope and dropped it on the counter.

"Holy shit!" Billy leaped backwards, nearly knocking over the potato chip display. "That's a rattler!"

The snake, which had been asleep, uncoiled swiftly on the counter and flared its neck like a cobra. Jonathan stared at it, unmov-ing.

The man chuckled at Billy. "Don't piss your britches, Geronimo. It's just a little old hognose." He picked the snake up and cuddled it under his chin. "He guards my pelts when I travel. Most folks mistake him for a rattler, just like you." He curled his upper lip at Billy, then cut his eyes toward Jonathan. "And most folks don't stick their hands in my sack but once."

Still laughing, the man stuffed the snake inside his shirt and reached into his sack again. Billy eased forward in spite of himself, curious to see what the man was going to withdraw next. This time he fumbled around for a moment, then pulled out five luxurious rac-coon pelts.

Like many bowmen, Jonathan regarded trappers and their little bottles of musk with disdain, but he did appreciate a job well done. These were big, thick pelts, expertly dressed. "You're looking at a little money there, buddy."

"So I am," the man growled. "You got something to ship a hundred and twenty-seven of these to Michigan in?"

Jonathan stuck his pencil behind his ear. "I'll see what I've got."

He walked back to the storage room. A case of disposable diapers had arrived last week, and the boxy carton they'd come in might be big enough for a load of raccoon pelts. The deliveryman had kicked the carton over beside a barrel of tenpenny nails, and there it still lay, cardboard flaps open and ready for more cargo.

He carried the box out to the front and dropped it on the floor. "This is the biggest thing I've got."

The man stretched the largest pelt out flat and stroked the fur. The tip of the fluffy ringed tail just missed brushing the side of the box.

"I reckon this'll do." The man laid another pelt down, then a third. The box was wide enough for the skins to be layered perfectly in groups of three. Billy watched as the man fitted each thick, silver-tipped fur into the carton.

In ten minutes he'd packed them tight. Jonathan reinforced the sides and top of the carton with strapping tape. His postal scale only went up to ten pounds, so he lifted the carton and guessed its weight. "I put that at about thirty pounds," he said, bouncing the case up and down. He handed the box to Billy. "What do you think?"

Billy jiggled the box and nodded his head. "Sounds about right. Don't forget to charge extra for snakes, though."

Ignoring Billy's remark, Jonathan hefted the box on the counter. "Okay, buddy. Who are you sending these to?"

The man took out a worn piece of notebook paper from a leather pouch around his neck and handed it to Jonathan. "Send it there. C.O.D."

Jonathan copied down the Michigan mailing address. "You got a return address?"

"Just put Henry Brank. General Delivery, whatever this place is called. They'll send my money here."

"Okay." Jonathan filled out a label and slapped it on the carton. "You want insurance?"

"I'll take my chances without."

"It'll go out Monday." Jonathan looked up at Henry Brank, hoping this man's business was done. "Anything else I can do for you?"

"You got any shells?"

Jonathan nodded.

"Gimme three boxes of triple-aught."

Jonathan retrieved the ammunition and shoved it across the counter. He thought about warning this man that he was two months early on the gun season and that the wardens in both Tennessee and North Carolina would fine his ass proper if he came out of the woods with an illegal bear, but he remained silent. A big-time trapper like him ought to know the law. If this yahoo got stuck with a thousand-dollar fine for a poached bear, then so be it.

The man's gaze fell on the Polaroid of Jonathan and Jodie Foster. He grinned, exposing long teeth. "That your wife?"

"No." Though Jodie Foster had exchanged less than ten words with him, Jonathan suddenly wanted to stand in front of the photo and shield her from the man's inquisitive eyes. "She's an actress who made a movie over at Fontana."

"Jonathan here was in that movie," Billy piped up proudly. "Jodie asked him herself."

Jonathan remembered the lights, the tangle of cables that stretched over the ground, the crews of Hollywood people who'd all looked vaguely stunned, as if they'd been dropped on Mars instead of a rural county in western North Carolina. Though the real filming work had been tedious, the pay was good and Jodie Foster had been nice even to nobodies like him. It had been the cushiest job he'd ever had, and he wished some other big star would come along and make another movie.

The man dug a crumpled bill out of the leather pouch. "I'll give you five dollars for it."

Billy cackled. "He'd sooner sell his own grandmother."

The man looked at Billy as if he were some yapping dog to be silenced with a kick. "That may well be, Geronimo, but I'm not interested in his grandmother."

Jonathan shook his head, noticing a louse that had crawled out from the stranger's thick black beard. He tried to place the accent. This Henry Brank spoke mountain speech, but not with the twang of southern Appalachia. "Sorry. It's not for sale."

The yellow eyes flashed for an instant, then settled on the knife protruding from Jonathan's belt.

"That a Bowie?"

Jonathan nodded.

"You any good with it?"

Of all the things Indians were supposed to be good at, archery and knife throwing were the only two Jonathan Walkingstick had mastered. He'd never learned the Cherokee syllabary or the rules for stickball, but he could, without fail, make bows that sang true and plant the business end of Ribtickler anywhere he wanted.

"I've skinned a few squirrels." Unabashed, Jonathan looked the man full in the face.

"They're good knives." The eerie saffron gaze slid away as quickly as it had come. "Better than Barlows." Brank stacked his shells in a pile. "I need a few more things."

He shuffled up and down the aisles of the store, pondering the vitamin display, reading the cereal boxes, finally wandering over to the bulletin board.

He studied the wall closely, first looking at all the photos of hunters grinning over their dead quarry, then reading all the notes posted for Appalachian Trail hikers who were currently somewhere between Springer Mountain, Georgia, and Mount Kahtadin, Maine. His mouth twitched in an up-and-down motion as he scrutinized each one.

"You trap them coons somewhere near the AT?" Billy hopped back up on the counter and fished a piece of grape bubblegum from Jonathan's penny candy jar.

"Nope." The man smiled at the photo of Alice Andrews, who'd vanished two decades ago.

"Well, if you've got a picture of yourself and that snake, you ought to put it up there. You might win some kind of weird pet award."

The man wiped his nose with the back of his hand. "I kinda figured you were the weird pet around here, Geronimo."

Jonathan retrieved his crossword puzzle from under the register.

Billy folded his arms and chewed his bubble gum, watching as the stranger roamed the narrow aisles of the grocery. Eventually he made his way back to the counter with cornmeal and coffee, plus a giant economy size of Theragran-M's, a large box of chocolate Moon Pies and three magazines—*Newsweek, Esquire* and *Field & Stream.*

No sugar, Jonathan noted as he rang up the man's purchases. Not a blockader. Addled maybe, but not from drinking his own whiskey. "That comes to forty-nine dollars and forty-one cents."

"Don't forget your snake chow." Billy teased him like an insolent parrot.

The man ignored him as he withdrew a greasy wad of bills from the bag around his neck. He thumbed through it slowly, then peeled off two twenties and a ten. "Keep the change," he said. "I don't touch silver."

Jonathan slid the bills in the drawer and reached under the counter for a paper sack.

"I'll take 'em in here." The man opened the canvas bag he'd brought his pelts in and stuffed his supplies inside. Then he shouldered it and shuffled toward the door.

He paused once before he left and looked back at Jonathan. "I'll be back for my money in a week or two. Make sure you keep it safe." His mouth curled downwards in one quick, malevolent smirk, then he was gone.

Billy watched as the man closed the door behind him, then turned to Jonathan. "Man, did you get a good whiff of him? And see them piss-colored eyes?"

Jonathan frowned. "Yeah, I saw his eyes. I also saw an idiot in an Indian suit who sat there trying to goad that guy into a fight. Shit, Billy. He could've knocked the rest of your teeth out of your head. Don't you know better than to mess with a man who uses a snake for a personal security system?"

Billy plunged his hands into the pockets of his buckskin pants. "Hell, I wasn't scared of him. And I certainly wasn't afraid of his stupid snake. He's an escapee from some big-time Booger Dance if you ask me." Billy stuck out his chest and blew a pale purple bubble. He glanced at the front of the cash register, then his jaw dropped. He sucked the bubble back in his mouth and looked at Jonathan, his eyes wide. "Uh-oh," he said. "Lookee here."

Jonathan walked around the counter and looked where Billy pointed. The picture of Jodie Foster was gone.

"Son of a bitch!" Jonathan ran to the door, his fingers instinctively reaching for his knife. He rushed out to the porch, ready to yell first, then throw Ribtickler, but the stranger had vanished.

"What the hell?" Jonathan craned his head in every direction, but all he saw was an empty road twisting through a silent green forest. He turned to Billy. "Where'd he go?"

Billy scowled into the woods. "Don't know. Looks to me like he's solid gone, though."

Jonathan hurried down the length of the storefront, Billy scrambling after him. They went all the way to the gas pump, scanning the trees for a glimpse of camouflage or a swinging canvas sack, but not a twig moved. Everything looked as if it had been engraved in stone. Jonathan kicked angrily at an empty oil can. "That sunuvabitch has disappeared."

Billy looked around and scratched his head. "How the hell do you figure he managed to steal that picture? I watched that sucker the whole time he was in the store."

Jonathan shrugged; it was amazing how easily the man had stolen his picture and how quickly he'd disappeared. "Beats the shit out of me." Again he tried to place this stranger; he knew all of the Cherokee mountain men and most of the white ones, too. This man had appeared from nowhere and then vanished back into nowhere again.

"I'll tell you one thing, Billy," Jonathan said as he tested his knife's edge with his thumb. "Mr. Brank and I are gonna have a little chat when he comes back to pick up that check. If he doesn't return my picture he just might find his pelts have gotten lost in the mail."

"You let me know when you take that feller on, Jonathan," said Billy. "I want to get me some money down beforehand." He scratched his head. "Wonder why he was so taken with that bulletin board?"

Jonathan shoved his knife back under his belt and looked at a crow that landed on the porch roof. Everything seemed to be flying past him that day—first Mary, then his silly little picture of Jodie Foster, now this odd stranger. "Everybody reads that bulletin board, Billy. It's like a great big scorecard that tells who's alive, who's dead, and who's about to be eaten by the crows."

SEVEN

H a, you smart-assed Cherokee bastard. Wouldn't sell the picture of your girlfriend, would you?"

Brank wagged the photo of Jodie Foster through a clutch of bright yellow witch hazel. He'd slipped into the forest just in time to see the fun, chuckling as the Indian rushed out, knife in hand, storming up and down his storefront, followed by his little Tonto sidekick. Brank shook with laughter as the tall one hurried down to the gas pump waving that long Bowie, all set to carve him up like a pumpkin and not finding a single thing to take a swipe at. He relaxed into the witch hazel as both Indians finally gave up and trudged back, defeated, into the store.

Brank smiled. This mail drop had turned out to be a lot of fun. Buster had made the short one shit his pants, he'd made off with the Cherokee's snapshot, plus he'd gotten a good long gander at that bulletin board.

"That kid in the baseball cap." He shook his head in wonder. "And the girl with the class ring." He hadn't thought about them in years, but there they were, both of them, grinning like they'd won some kind of prize. He chuckled as he patted the snake that lay curled next to his belly. "Guess those two are gone for good, eh, Buster?"

He remained under the bush clutching the photograph for a moment, then he studied the image the camera had captured. The young Indian stood tall, dressed in a coat and tie, his arm resting on the slender woman's shoulders as if she were made of glass. She had assumed a serene pose that made her long white neck look as graceful as a swan's. Her cobalt eyes slanted upwards, and there was a spareness about her smile that implied intelligence more than the thick red lips of sex.

"She'd be something to fuck," Brank whispered, reaching down and softly squeezing his balls. He blew a piece of fuzz off the photograph, then buttoned it carefully inside his shirt pocket. He would take it out later, when he had the time to devote to more serious fun.

He pushed the witch hazel away from his face and crept out from under the thick green leaves. He'd have to settle the issue of the photograph with that Indian when he came back to get his money, but he would think of something. Maybe he could lure him into the forest with it and make him reveal where all that Cherokee gold was hidden. Brank chuckled. That would be wonderful, but it would never happen. Cherokees might be stupid and lazy, but they weren't fools.

He squinted through the lacy trees, checking the angle of the sun. Maybe he'd travel west for a little while and see if he could pick up Trudy's trail. It would be nice to relax down in Florida without her scaring him shitless every time the sun set. He glanced once, thoughtfully, at the store, then he shouldered his sack and walked out of the shadows. The Little Jump Off folks could rest easy. Today he was hunting his sister.

With his load lightened by thirty pounds, he slipped through the forest like a shadow, barely ruffling the leaves as he passed. The smell of damp earth rose from the ground as he traversed the crenelated ridges that led away from Little Jump Off. He searched for the chewed-up groundhog or mangled fox that would indicate Trudy's presence, but he saw only an occasional squirrel and several bright mountain grosbeaks that darted like fierce blue arrows through the golden trees.

By midafternoon hunger began to crimp the edges of his stomach. In an upland meadow he found a small clearing that had once held some farmer's cabin, and he flopped down in the cool shadows beneath an ancient charred rock chimney.

It felt good to be still, to stretch out his legs for a while. He scratched his back against the chimney rocks and looked at the trees that surrounded him. Though the sun shone bright and the breeze blew warm, the woods seemed quieter than usual, as if his presence had stilled the birds and hushed the sleepy hum of the crickets.

He untied his sack and pulled out his Moon Pies. He hadn't had chocolate in months. He freed one of the flat cookies from its cellophane wrapper and bit into it. A pleasant dark sweetness flooded his mouth, reminding him of a Christmas cake his mother had made. His mother. He wondered about her sometimes. What had she done that afternoon when his father had run back to their kitchen, Trudy in his arms, Henry nowhere to be found? She had always seemed to love him a little. Cried, he decided. She'd cried for both her children, then gone ahead and put up pickles and kraut and done all the things she'd always done while his father had waged his private war against him.

He took another bite of Moon Pie. Suddenly two rangy shadows darkened the sky. He looked up. A pair of large black birds swooped low over his head, their wingspans casting long shadows on the ground. They glided over the clearing once, then turned sharply to land in the top of a rotted-out elm. Brank stopped eating and smiled.

"*Cathartes aura,*" he proudly recalled one of the Latin names Fate Lyons had taught him. Turkey buzzards. Ugly as sin. Most people despised them, but he found them to be presagers of great events. He'd often followed kettles of them to locate the dead and dying, and he regarded the birds as just another battalion in the vast army of Death.

"Hello, boys." Brank gave a polite nod to the pair. "Something around here about to die?"

They cocked their dull red heads to one side and stared at him beady-eyed. Wings still spread, they perched in the tree as if waiting for some internal signal to swoop over and sink their talons into his flesh.

Brank frowned as he chewed the sticky chocolate. It did seem a little odd. Buzzards did not usually fly in pairs or roost so close to upright, healthy human beings.

"Join me in some lunch?" He broke off two tiny pieces of the cookie and tossed them beneath the tree. The birds remained motionless, their eyes glowering straight at him.

"Picky little bastards, aren't you?" Brank stuffed more Moon Pie in his mouth and chewed vigorously. Tossing them two crumbs had already been extravagant; he was not going to further waste his Moon Pie on such ungrateful creatures.

Their gaze stayed on his face. His cheeks grew warm and he began to feel slightly uneasy, as if the birds knew something he didn't. He patted the barrel of his gun.

"Don't forget who's got the gun here, pals," he muttered through his food.

The larger buzzard folded its wings but continued to stare, its scrutiny sharp as the point of a knife.

Brank was about to throw one of the loose chimney rocks at them when something else caught his attention. A new sound suddenly whispered through the woods. A step. Then a pause. Then the faintest rustle in the grass.

"Ahhhh." He continued his conversation with the buzzards as he shifted his hearing to the woods. "I get it. You boys are hanging around because you figure you'll soon be getting some meat to eat."

He kept his eyes on the birds, but dropped his food back in his sack and eased the gun onto his lap. He shoved a new shell in each chamber, then turned by inches to the right and peered into the surrounding forest. Tree trunks stood festooned with gold leaves while black grapevines dangled down like serpentine. Nothing unusual for a mild autumn day. Nothing out of the ordinary at all.

Then he heard it again. From deep within the trees, the long, slow rumble of a bottle being rolled down a hall. The hair rose on the back of his neck. He'd heard that sound before. Trudy was here.

Brank's heart began to race as he squinted into the underbrush, trying to catch a glimpse of her huge amber eyes. "Here, Trudy, old girl," he crooned softly as he curled a finger around both triggers of his gun.

Again he heard the low, menacing rumble. He drew his legs up and balanced the gun on his left knee, waiting for her to make a move. Was she brave enough to attack him in the daylight, he wondered as his heart tripped and his hands grew slippery on the gun. He didn't think so. Trudy, like the trolls, preferred to prey on him at night, when his eyes couldn't pierce the darkness and his imagination made up the difference.

Brank tried to keep the gun steady on his knee. It occurred to him that just as he had followed other buzzards in times past, this particular pair must follow Trudy, waiting for her scraps. With a sick lurch of his gut he realized that for the first time in his life, he himself was, at this moment, the short end of the food chain.

"If you're thinking I'm gonna be lunch, you're mistaken, old sis," he whispered to the fiend hidden in the forest.

He held his breath and concentrated on the trees. Gold and russet, the leaves shimmered in front of him, rustling like a woman's gown. He sat rigid, waiting. The minutes dripped by. Sweat began to run into his eyes. He could hear the rapid thud of his own heart. His hands clutched the gun so tightly they began to shake. He'd just begun to think that maybe he'd imagined the whole thing when the weeds beneath a yellow buckeye gave a single swift shudder and a roar enveloped him like a freight train. All at once Trudy stood in front of him, not ten feet away.

Huge hungry eyes now more green than amber pinned him where he sat. She was far bigger than he remembered. She crouched with her tail twitching, gauging the distance to him just as a house cat might measure a leap to a kitchen table. Shiny black lips curled away from long yellow fangs. Brank began to tremble. When he'd last shot Trudy, she hadn't looked nearly so scary as this.

EEEOOOOOOOWWWWW!

Her scream filled the universe, ricocheted through his head. He had half a second to get his shots off before those fangs sank into his throat. Mad, mad, she was so mad—he had killed her so many years before. Now he was going to kill her again. With shaking hands he aimed at her broad breast. He drew a bead on where he guessed her heart would be, then sucked in his breath and pulled both triggers.

The gun bucked as it never had before. The double recoil knocked him against the chimney. Brank's head snapped back into the sunbaked rocks, sending grit and dirt stinging into his face and eyes. For a moment he couldn't see, then when he'd wiped away the dirt, he opened his eyes. Trudy should be stretched out and bleeding like a sieve, her pink tongue protruding from those nasty black lips, but the ground was empty. The clearing was as vacant as it had been when he'd arrived.

"What the hell?" He jumped up and walked to the spot where Trudy had been. Surely he had wounded her. Surely there would be a path of blood leading to wherever she'd fled. He'd fired two loads of triple-aught buckshot from point-blank range. But there was nothing. A slight indentation in the long grass was the only sign that Trudy had ever been there at all.

Brank's gun sagged downward as he stared at the ground. All these years of tracking. All those nights that awful unearthly cry had pierced the darkness and pulled him from the edge of sleep, twisting his stomach and turning his bowels to brown soup. Always, he'd gotten up and hurried out with his gun, only to come back empty-handed. Today she'd practically presented herself as a gift and still he couldn't kill her. He felt sour inside, as if something within him were spoiling. He looked over at the tree. The buzzards stared back at him, their wings seeming to droop with disappointment.

"What the hell are you looking at?" he cried, rage boiling up inside him. "Miss your damn meal ticket?"

The buzzards did not move.

"Here." Brank shoved another shell in the gun and raised it to his shoulder. "See if you like this." He aimed at the smaller vulture and fired. The elm branch shattered as the bird exploded in a mist of blood and feathers. The other bird leaped into the air, spreading its broad wings and lifting over the trees before Brank had time to shoot again.

"Stupid sons of bitches," he screamed, stamping back over to the chimney and gathering up his sack. "Stupid motherfucking sons of bitches!"

He picked up his gear and strode off into the woods. Trudy would be ahead of him now, slipping through the trees, watching and waiting for the next time he let his guard down. He would just have to try twice as hard, Brank told himself as his legs began to shake and sweat rolled down his face to cling like raindrops to the end of his beard.

"I'll get you before I leave here," he vowed to Trudy as he pushed through a laurel thicket. "By God, I will."

EIGHT

Mary stared out the window as Alex drove to the trailhead. So that's what Little Jump Off looks like now, she thought as the woods sped by the car in a dark blur. The same fireplace, the same bait cooler, the same knotty-pine floor where your mother died. Only now your ex-lover is the proprietor, *and you want him just as badly as you ever did.* The words swept through her brain like wind through parched grass. As much as she longed to sit still and sort it all out, she would have to do that later. She'd promised Alex that she would devote herself to having fun after Little Jump Off, and she never welshed on her deals with Alex.

"There's our turn." She pulled herself out of Jonathan's grasp and pointed at a battered sign that read War Woman Road.

Alex turned left onto a gravel path that led to a small unpaved overlook, where she braked beside a tangle of wild honeysuckle. Thirty feet to the right, a tiny footpath seemed to plummet off the edge of the world.

The three women got out of the car and walked to a crumbling stone wall that skirted the overlook. Alex hopped up on the wall, putting her hands on her hips as she surveyed the expanse below.

"Holy shit!" she exclaimed. Her cry floated out over the mountains like a bottle launched upon an ocean.

For miles, a sea of trees undulated away from them. Still green at the lowest elevations, it swelled to red and gold and brown until distance tinted it mauve, then lilac. Finally it disappeared, miles away, into a hazy blue nothingness. As they watched two faraway hawks glide on a high thermal, the only sound they heard was the breath that rose from the forest itself. Cool and unwavering, it carried the fecund smells of growth and decay and made the fine hairs on their arms stand erect.

"Jeez," Joan murmured, standing beside Alex. "And I thought Central Park was something." She fumbled for the disposable camera she'd stashed in her purse. "I gotta get a picture of this."

Mary watched as Joan snapped away. She knew from experience that her pictures would come out disappointing—the colors would be flat, the scope less majestic. Photography was frustrating that way. Only the images etched in your memory remained crisp, with colors undiluted.

"Can you imagine how the pioneers must have felt the first time they saw all this?" Alex spread her arms, as if all the acres below were a wild empire that belonged only to her.

Mary smiled. Alex's imagination had always been able to soar at the slightest provocation, thrusting her back into history or forward into some crazy future. Though it made for interesting conversations, sometimes when she stood next to Alex she felt as dull as a stump.

"If we got lost could we follow those electrical wires out?" Alex pointed at a phalanx of power lines that stretched over the trees like strands of some giant spider's web.

Mary squinted at the TVA cables linking the Cheoah and Calderwood dams. "I suppose, if we could climb a high enough tree to get a fix on one. It's probably a day's hike from pole to pole, though."

Joan stared at the vastness before her and frowned. "Mary, are you sure you can find one little Cherokee hot spring in the middle of all those trees?"

"If this were New York could you get us to Coney Island?"

"Absolutely."

"Okay," said Mary. "Then just think of this as my Manhattan."

"Great, but when you take the subway to Coney Island, all you've got to deal with is muggers and street gangs and your basic New York loonies. Here you've got a jillion acres of God-knows-what hiding in the trees." Joan pushed her Yankees cap back on her head. "I don't know if I'm up to this, guys. I smoke, remember? I don't know a fox from a ferret and I don't jog every day like you two."

"I haven't jogged in six months," Alex told her. "Anyway, I'll take care of you. You'll be back at the office Tuesday raving about the fun you had."

Joan scowled. "If I pass out, will you give me CPR?"

"In a heartbeat." Alex's laughter was rich and genuine. "I swear you'll have a good time up here."

"Well, okay," Joan sighed. "But just remember I'm supposed to have dinner with Hugh Chandler next Saturday. I don't want to have a broken leg or poison ivy or anything."

"All you'll have is thrilling tales of hiking through Appalachia," Mary assured her. "Hugh will think he's eating with Superwoman."

Joan shot Mary a dubious glance, but she followed her two friends to the car and watched Alex unlock the trunk.

"Good grief!" Alex cried, hoisting Joan's backpack out onto the ground. "What in the world did you pack? Free weights?"

"No." A flush of embarrassment pinkened Joan's cheeks. "Just my things. Clothes. Makeup. Wine. Something to read."

Alex shook her head. "It feels like most of our law library. Unbuckle that pack and pull out everything that's not absolutely vital to your survival."

Grumbling, Joan knelt and unbuckled her pack. Moments later she'd fished out three pairs of jeans, two wool sweaters, five cans of soup, a Coleman lantern, two bottles of Chianti, two extra pairs of shoes, and a hardback biography of Beverly Sills.

Alex looked at Joan's supplies and started to laugh. "I've seen less junk crammed on a moving van. You'll have to ditch about half that stuff."

"Half my stuff?" cried Joan. "What about half *your* stuff? Your trunk doesn't exactly look empty, Alex."

"You guys sound exactly like you did three years ago when you had to share that office," Mary reminded them. "Why don't we all ditch half our stuff? Then we can fit everything into two big packs, and one of us can always be traveling without any extra weight."

"Well, I will if she will," agreed Joan grudgingly. "But are you sure you wouldn't like some wine tonight?" She held up one raffia-covered Chianti bottle.

Mary shook her head as she discarded a bulky sweater from her own pack. "Not enough to carry it uphill all day. Anyway, I brought some brandy in a plastic flask."

They each pared their supplies in half, then Alex helped Joan repack her gear. As Mary attached the tent to one pack frame and the stove to the other, Joan held up a tiny cell phone.

"Shouldn't we take this? In case of an emergency?"

Alex smiled. "We won't need it. Charlie already put one in my pack."

"Can I make a call on it?"

"Of course you can."

"Cool," said Joan. "I'm going to call my mother as soon as we get there and say, Hey, Ma, I'm in the middle of Nantootlah!"

"Nantahala," Mary corrected.

"Okay, okay, whatever."

When they got everything repacked, Alex locked the Beemer and shoved the keys deep in her pocket. She shouldered the heaviest pack while Mary carried the other, giving Joan the first easy shift. For a moment the three friends grinned at each other like children who'd managed to play some incredible piece of hooky; then Mary led the way down into the leafy green sea.

To Mary's great relief, the Little Jump Off Trail had escaped the notice of both the current timber barons and the latest crop of

Cherokee teenagers. The ancient oaks that towered above it had not been clear-cut and planed into coffee tables, and no discarded condoms or flattened beer cans littered the path. The trail cut through the mountains as rough and rutted as it had been when she'd first walked it with her mother. Back then she hadn't wanted anything to do with the forest. She hated it here, with these strange people who ate something called bean bread and used words she didn't understand. She missed her father and french fries and wondered why they couldn't go back and stay with the Andersons at Fort Bragg. The Andersons had offered. But her mother said no. *"Sometimes we have to be brave, baby,"* she had whispered, holding her tight. *"As much as we want to stay put, sometimes we just have to go forward."* Then her mother had smiled, and helped Mary put on her jacket. *"Go get your crayons. I'll take you to a magic place and we can draw some pretty pictures."*

"Hey, Mary! What do you think happened to those missing people on that bulletin board?"

Joan's question came out between little gasps of breath. The trail from the highway had bottomed out in a stretch of wild ginger, and they were at the foot of a trail that twisted steeply through tall sweetgum trees, ascending one of the minor Unicoi Mountains. Beads of sweat decorated Joan's and Alex's foreheads and Mary could tell by the trudging way both walked that they were already beginning to feel the hike in their legs.

"I don't know." She stopped, removed her pack, and sat underneath a tree to allow her friends to catch their breath. Alex pulled off her pack and flopped down beneath another tree while Joan rummaged in her pocket for a cigarette.

"Got lost, probably. It's easy to do." Mary opened her paint box and dug out her sketch pad and a small piece of charcoal. "I mean, look at how thick these woods are. If I walked ten feet off this trail you probably wouldn't be able to see me."

"That's why I'm not letting you out of my sight." Joan sprawled beside Alex, her cigarette bobbing in her mouth as she talked. "Consider us joined at the hip until we get back to Atlanta."

Mary looked down at her sketch pad. The image of two people joined at the hip brought Jonathan Walkingstick back to mind. A wife in England. She tried to picture the woman's hands, her mouth. What had she cooked for Jonathan? How had she made love to him? *Stop it,* she scolded herself as she felt a catch in her throat. *Don't think about that now.* "Sit still, Alex," she commanded as she grasped the charcoal and started to sketch.

"Not a problem." Alex lay collapsed against the tree. "Work as long as you want. Draw a masterpiece."

With a sudden yelp Joan leapt up as if she'd sat on a pin. "Is that poison ivy?" She pointed to a scraggly green vine curling up the tree trunk.

"Has it got three leaves?"

"No." Joan squinted at the plant. "Five."

"Don't worry about it. It's probably Virginia creeper."

"You wouldn't kid me, would you?" Joan frowned as Alex snickered.

"Honest Injun," Mary reassured her. "That one particular part of the forest will not harm you in any way."

Joan folded her arms across her chest and looked nervously around the woods. "You know, I don't think I've ever seen as many trees in my life. It's spooky—almost like they're alive."

Mary laughed. "They are alive, Joan. They're breathing in carbon dioxide right this very second."

"That's not exactly what I meant," Joan whispered as she peered into the shadows.

Altering her pose for a moment, Alex pried up a spiky brown sweet-gum nut. "Hey, Mary, did your mother teach you woodlore and herbal medicine and stuff?"

"Some," Mary answered, bent over her drawing. "Things like what plants are poisonous and how to splint a sprained ankle." She shrugged. "At the time I thought the whole Native American thing was pretty hokey. Now I wish I'd asked her more."

Joan inhaled greedily as a yellow maple leaf spiraled gracefully to the ground. "My great-aunt in Sicily used to brew up some pretty weird cures. I wonder, though, if all that herbal medicine stuff isn't just wishful thinking."

Mary looked up from her drawing. "Beats me. My mom and I just took aspirin."

. . .

They switched packs and climbed higher. The trees grew more intense in color—red sourwoods mingled with gold poplars and crimson black gums, all standing stark and vibrant against a brilliant sapphire sky. They stopped often at streams, where Joan would sit and smoke, Alex would dangle her bare feet in the icy water, and Mary would lie back in soft, mossy beds of galax, the old smells and sounds of the Little Jump Off store fresh in her head. After they climbed one of the higher ridges, the trail split in two directions. Mary stopped and shrugged off her pack.

"Okay, scouts, we've got a decision to make here." She pointed to the right, where the trail escalated into a high, unending stand of bright orange maples that glowed like lit matches.

"That way is the official Little Jump Off Trail, which goes over Chestnut Knob. It's high, it's hard, but seventy years ago it was blazed by the Babcock Lumber Company."

Joan was scratching at a mosquito bite. "What do you mean *blazed*?"

"They cut a path through the woods and carved marks on the trees along the way."

"Okay," puffed Joan, beads of sweat now dotting her upper lip. "One hard, but marked trail. What's behind Door Number Two?"

Mary turned left, toward a much fainter footpath that tunneled between two rows of dark, low-limbed spruce pines. "That will lead us to where we want to camp through more level ground. There's just one thing you need to know about it."

"What?" Alex's face was flushed with exertion.

"It goes through the Ghosts."

"The Ghosts?" Joan's voice rose. "That thing Jonathan was talking about?"

Mary nodded. "I'm not sure how to explain the Ghosts. When we were kids we thought it was where the old dead Cherokees hung out. Now I'm guessing it's some kind of underground spring that's eroded the top of a mountain. It's weird. I've never seen anything like it anywhere else."

"So is it, like, *haunted*?"

"No, but it's seriously foggy. The only danger is getting separated from each other." Mary looked at her friends. "If we take the Babcock trail, we'll have go slow. If we go through the Ghosts, we'll have to be careful."

Joan looked at Alex. "Isn't this just *sooo* Mary? Take this way to get lost, or that way to have a coronary. We should never have let her go into criminal law, Alex."

Still winded, Alex just grinned and wiped her forehead with the back of her hand. "Since my lungs are on fire and my legs feel like limp spaghetti, I vote for anything that's *not* uphill."

"But we don't want to get lost," Joan added. "Especially in fog."

"Let's make a caravan," suggested Mary. "I'll lead. All you two will have to do is follow me."

"Are you sure it'll be safe?" Joan sounded skeptical.

Mary nodded. "I've crossed that way before."

They rested another moment, watching as a flock of lively black chickadees chattered through the trees, then they reshouldered their packs and trudged on. When they entered the tunnel created by the overhanging trees, the cool air turned cold, instantly chilling the sweat on their skin. Though it felt like winter and smelled of Christmas, beyond the first rank of trees the woods seemed strangely aware, as if unseen eyes were watching them.

"When do these Ghosts start?" Joan asked in a whisper.

"Just about now," replied Mary, peering toward the end of the tunnel. Already she could see it—or rather see the lack of anything resembling forest. Thick white mist curled up from the ground, punctured only by the occasional spiky thrust of a tree. Jonathan always hated this place, she remembered. *"It's just like someone pulled a plug, and all the colors drained out of the world."* She'd forgotten how much he'd loved color.

At the end of the spruce pine tunnel, the trail vanished into a white soup. The three women stopped and stared into a foggy void.

"This reminds me of last summer, when we went to San Francisco and that fog just rolled in from nowhere." Joan's voice took on an edgy cheeriness. "Remember? One minute you guys were looking in that antique shop in Chinatown, and the next minute all I could see was white goop."

"Yeah." Alex snorted. "And then that gorgeous writer from Australia appeared and we didn't see *you* for three days!"

"Peter," Joan recalled with a coy smile. "What can I say? He was crazy about old Italian chests."

Mary laughed. "Here." She turned to Joan and held out her backpack. "You and your old Italian chest hang on to this strap. That way you'll stay attached to me. Alex, you grab the strap on Joan's knapsack, and you'll be attached to her. We'll caravan that way. If anybody loses their hold, yell and I'll stop."

"We cowboys call this a pack train in Texas," Alex grumbled as she grabbed Joan's knapsack.

"Well, we Indians call it a caravan in North Carolina. Although I guess by now we've crossed over into Tennessee." Mary noticed Joan's pale face. "Don't worry. I know this looks spooky, but it's really not that bad."

"Are you sure you know the way?"

For an instant Mary wondered if she was being foolish—overconfidence was what killed most people here. But she'd trekked through the Ghosts a thousand times with Jonathan, and the woods were slowly beginning to seem like home again. She could do this. Anyway, the Ghosts weren't what frightened her out here. "Just pretend we're on that subway to Coney Island," she told Joan, smiling.

With Alex and Joan tethered behind her, she took a deep breath and stepped into the thick vapor that curled catlike around her shins. The ground was spongy beneath her boots. Moss furred the tree trunks and the only sound that reached her ears was the muted footsteps of her friends. As she watched thin fingers of mist caressing the dark trees, Mary wondered if perhaps she'd been wrong to decide this was an underground spring. Maybe she and Jonathan had been right the first time, when they'd chalked it up to ghosts.

"This is really creepy," Alex muttered.

"I can't see past my nose. Anything could be watching us from the trees." Joan's voice rang high and thin.

"Don't think about it," Mary replied. "Keep your eyes closed if it makes you feel better."

"No, I'm okay." Joan gave a jittery laugh. "This must have been a hell of a place for a Halloween party, though."

They walked on, pushing resolutely through the gauzy white silence. Mary realized she hadn't heard Alex in a while. "Hey, Alexandra, are you okay?"

"Just enjoying the view." Alex's muffled voice came out of nowhere. "Which is either a solid cloud bank or Joan's butt."

"You got a problem with my butt?"

"No, but if you break wind, I'm a dead woman." Though they all laughed, Mary could hear the tension in Alex's joke. For someone who'd grown up under the broad blue skies of Texas, traipsing through this soupy white miasma must be disconcerting.

"How much longer is this trail?" Alex called.

"Maybe half a mile."

"Well, at least it's mostly flat."

They walked on in silence, as if wishing to pass unnoticed by whatever the mist might conceal. Whispers echoed like thunder here, quiet words resounded as shouts. Alex started to whistle, but her bouncy little tune sounded vaguely desperate in the still air, and she finally gave it up, trudging along accompanied only by the soft *squish* of her own footsteps on moss and rotting leaves.

Then, as abruptly as it had begun, the Ghosts ended. The trail emptied into a wide clearing, where two woodpeckers busily drilled for bugs in a copse of sun-speckled pawpaws.

"Boy," Joan said as the warm sun began to dry the sweat from the back of her neck. "I'm glad that's over."

They rested, tasting the sharp, piney smell of the breeze, then hiked on, still going up. By the time they crested the one minor Unicoi mountain they'd begun climbing in the early afternoon, the sun was falling westward into the trees. At a tall hickory Mary found the trail that veered up to a place she hoped would be as she remembered—a broad but shallow cave that went about ten feet into the side of Big Fodderstack Mountain. Deep enough to accommodate a tent, the cave would give them shelter on three sides and a terrific view of the mountains below. Unless a bear had beaten them to it, it would be a perfect place to camp for the night.

She tightened the pack on her shoulders, then led Joan and Alex up the final hundred feet of trail. At its end, she found it just as she had known it years before, a wide triangular hole gouged in the mountainside.

"Okay." She smiled at the others. "Here's our room for the night."

"We're actually going to camp in there?" Joan peered dubiously into the cave.

"We are if nothing got here before us." Mary dug her flashlight out of her pack and beamed it into the semidarkness. She saw only stones and rubble, but to make sure she found a long pine branch and systematically poked along the back of the small fissure. Nothing pawed at her stick or rushed snarling out to attack.

"Nobody here but us chicks," she reported, standing up straight and patting the cool, rough roof of the little cave with the palm of her hand.

"Won't it be cold?" Joan eyed the dusty rocks.

"With all the gear Charlie sent us, we could weather a blizzard on Mount McKinley."

Alex sniffed. "You can laugh now, but you'll thank me in the morning, when you wake up all warm and toasty, with coffee brewing on my special stove."

They quickly set up their camp. Every piece of Alex's equipment proved to be a marvel of space-age engineering. In twenty minutes the blue and white tent was up and functional, with three sleeping bags lying side by side on an insulated tarp. Just outside the cave Alex assembled the stove on which she swore she could both boil freeze-dried lasagna and bake brownies. While she cursed one reluctant leg of the stove, Mary went back down the trail to gather twigs for a traditional fire.

"Are you going to start it with flint like they do in the movies?" Joan followed like a puppy as Mary carried an armful of small dead limbs to the far edge of the cave.

"Not hardly." Mary dusted off a circle on the ground and piled tiny pieces of dried leaves and twigs in the middle of it. She took a piece of chemical fire starter from her backpack, lit it, then shoved it beneath the tinder. Instantly, a small hot blaze swelled up. She added pine kindling, then the twigs she'd found—and the campfire began to crackle. "See? Cherokee woman's fire burn all night. Alex's stove's just good for dessert."

Joan looked at her with awe. "I've always known you were cool, Mary Crow. But I had no idea you were *this* cool."

Her fire built, Mary moved to the edge of the cliff and dangled her legs over the vastness below. It felt good to be still. Already her thighs ached and her shoulders were sore. Tomorrow, she knew, they would each wake up with leaden feet and cracking knees, but they could spend the day soaking their aches away in the steamy waters of Atagahi. For a moment she watched as Joan filled a pan with bottled water and Alex stirred her brownie mix, then she turned back to the mountains.

The Old Men have been kind today, she decided, remembering their names as her mother had taught her—*Dakwai, Ahaluna, Disgagistiyi*. They'd allowed her to guide her two best friends through the forest without harm. *Thank you*, she said silently, as a sudden gust of wind stroked her cheek. For once, you have made me feel welcome.

NINE

"Okay, Buster, just one more mile to go." Brank shifted the sack on his shoulder. For the last hour he'd toiled up through an unending growth of slippery green thorn bushes, and even the almost empty canvas bag he carried lay heavy across the top of his left shoulder.

"Maybe we'll have us a party when we get to Simpson's Bald," he wheezed like a splayed-out accordion. "Or maybe we'll just sit down and try to recover from the getting there."

He pushed his way through a stand of goldenseal that cluttered the trail. It was odd to see a flatland weed growing up so high, but these mountains always did do strange things. Birds that belonged in Maine roosted in Tennessee; trees that covered the cliffs of Nova Scotia sprouted up in Georgia. His immediate destination, Simpson's Bald, was strangest of all—the bare top of a mountain that reputedly got its name from a Union spy who'd been hanged from the lone oak tree that grew there. The soil was a sick shade of gray beneath the limb-span of that old tree, and the mountain people teased their children with tales of witches and boogeymen who held horrific ceremonies in the wide circle of blighted earth.

Brank, however, found Simpson's Bald restful. He was accustomed to the single, ineffectual ghost that haunted the place, and no one else ever bothered him there. The mountaintop afforded a 360-degree view of the surrounding terrain, and the huge roots of the old hanging tree coiled so thick and deep that a man could lie down between them and wait out a blizzard without getting wet. It was solitary, it was safe, and it was also the one place he knew he could get a clear shot at his sister.

"Scheisse!" he cursed as he stubbed his toe on a rock hidden in the goldenseal. Lately he'd found himself cursing in German, the language of his childhood. Though he had not heard a word of it in thirty years, for the past several weeks it had floated on the top of his consciousness like a bobber on a fishing line.

"*Scheisse* meant shit," he explained to Buster as he recovered his footing. "*Esel* meant stupid. *Wiesel* meant me."

He trudged higher. The goldenseal gave way to a scraggly stand of white pines, which shrank into an even thinner scrub of rhododendrons. He decided that green things must run out of juice this high: all the effort devoted to growth at lower elevations up here went to pure survival. He scrambled over a final patch of lichen-covered rock, then he was there.

In the dying daylight the mountaintop glowed a pale green. The single oak tree thrust up from the earth like a bone-yellow hand begging something from heaven. Brank guessed most people would find this tree unsettling, but he admired its stubborn defiance, and the odd, hardscrabble shelter it offered.

"Fate Lyons would have hooted at all these silly hillbillies, Buster," he chuckled to the snake. "This old bald's just a place where witches land their brooms."

He walked across the mountaintop and threw his sack down beneath the gnarled tree. His shoulders and legs burned from the final mile of the trail, and the cold wind that whipped around the mountain made his eyelids feel like sandpaper. With spare, practiced motions he quickly unfolded his blanket and laid it in a deep trench between two of the thickest roots. Punching his near-empty sack up like a pillow, he nestled down inside the trench. The hard earth felt good against his back, and for a while he just lay there, relishing the sensation of not moving. He would build a fire, but later. Right now he just wanted to be still.

When the almost-full moon rose he got to his feet and snapped off some of the lower limbs of the tree. Dead to the point of being powder, they broke off with a groan rather than a crack, and a few minutes later they lay in a pile, orange flames licking their undersides. Brank huddled close to the small aura of light and warmth the old branches produced and stared into the fire. Though he'd missed his best shot at Trudy, the day hadn't been a total loss. He'd mailed his pelts off and had some fun stealing that Cherokee's photograph. He patted the pocket of his shirt and smiled. Tonight he had his own personal little movie star, right in there, waiting just for him.

When the fire had burned down to a ruddy glow, he dug into his sack again, pulling out his Moon Pies, his whiskey, and his vitamins. "Ten thousand units of vitamin A," he read aloud, squinting at the label in the firelight. "Two thousand units of Vitamin C. Every antioxidant known to man." Chuckling, he opened the bottle, tossed three tablets in his mouth and washed them down with a swig of whiskey. "Whoa!" He shook his head at the potent combination. "Guess I'm antioxidized now."

He leaned back against the tree and ate two Moon Pies, looking at the brightly colored advertisements in his *Esquire* magazine. Fate would be proud of the way he was taking care of himself, and keeping his mind up-to-date. By the time he finished eating and reading, the fire seemed to be the sole orange spot in the middle of a steely-blue universe. He put the magazine away and drank several more swallows of whiskey, eager for its warmth to reach the stiff muscles of his buttocks and thighs. Good whiskey's like a slow fuck, he thought, then he remembered his photo. He unbuttoned his pocket and looked at Jodie Foster's silvery face.

"*Schön,*" he murmured, tracing the outline of her neck with his finger. "And tonight you're all mine."

He turned and balanced the photograph against the knuckle of a tree root. He'd just begun to unzip his pants when he heard a creaking, high above his head. He thought he knew what it was, but it never paid to be too cocky on Simpson's Bald. Grabbing his gun, he slipped the picture back in his pocket, then sat by the fire and waited.

It didn't take long. In a moment it came to him as always, floating down from the tree, its blue uniform in tatters. A noose dangled from its neck, and it rolled its green head from side to side, blinking bottomless scarlet eye sockets directly at him.

"Hello, bro." Brank nodded. "Still haven't gotten rid of that necktie, have you?"

The apparition gazed at him pitifully, then clawed at his neck, as if he might tug his head off in his efforts to remove the noose.

Brank scowled, suddenly irritated at the spectral interruption. That stupid ghost pulled the same dumb trick every time he came up here. It had grown as predictable as a train.

"Don't you know the war's over? You won. The Union is saved. Go back to hell and celebrate."

The ghost looked surprised for a moment, as if it wanted to speak, then suddenly the red eye sockets opened wide and the specter grew, stretching to the top of the tree, then swelling high above it. Brank watched, gooseflesh rising on his arms. The crazy thing had never done anything like this before. It had always been nosy, but manageable. When it began to tower fifty feet above him, Brank pulled back the hammer of one barrel and fired.

The shotgun's deep boom split the night. The ghost screamed— an agonized wail that turned Brank cold inside, then, in an instant, it shrank into a shiny red ball of vapor a foot away from Brank's head. It glittered there for a moment, pulsing with crimson light like a mad heartbeat, then imploded into a pin-spot of icy blue, and vanished.

"Jesus!" Brank whispered, blinking at the mist where the ghost had loomed above him moments before. "It's been practicing something new." His heart pounding, his fingers still wrapped around his gun, he waited. Minutes passed, but nothing more happened. He lowered the gun into his lap, and the mountaintop's sad, sighing emptiness returned.

When his breathing became normal he started to reach in his pocket again for the picture, but changed his mind. The ghost would probably only come back to distract him, and he'd have the movie star for another two weeks. Instead he took another slug of whiskey and rolled up in his blanket, hoping for a slow easy slide into unconsciousness. He took a deep breath and closed his eyes, allowing the night sounds that kept most men awake to lull him to sleep. His muscles relaxed, warm and heavy. Dark colors danced on the inside of his eyes. He'd almost drifted away when suddenly he sat up, wide awake, staring into the darkness.

He heard something—a sound that did not belong, a noise that fit nowhere. It was not Trudy's low growl, nor the silly natterings of the ghost. This was something else entirely.

His pulse quickened as he listened to the dark. Had it been a dream? He could hear nothing now but the hiss of the wind over the mountaintop. He continued to listen, straining to catch whatever it was. There. He heard it again.

Quick as a shadow he was on his feet, shotgun in hand. He hurried over to the west edge of the bald and peered out over the mountains beyond. The night pressed close against his face. He squinted into the thick darkness, once more hearing nothing for so long he wondered if this might not be some new bit of nonsense the ghost had dreamed up. Then, the noise came again. If he cocked his head when the breeze blew from the northwest he could hear it, crisp as a snapped twig. It was the sound of women. Laughing.

He pulled at his left ear. This was not possible. Women would not be out here in this wilderness, miles from any civilization, thousands of feet above the nearest settlement. It must be some freakish television signal, bouncing around the sky. He gazed out into the blackness and willed his eyes to open to everything.

At first he saw just a million dark, sleeping trees and the night animals that scurried among them. Then, slightly to the left of his center of vision, he saw it. A tiny dot of flickering light suspended between forest and sky. All at once he knew what it was. Women were camping in the fissure of Big Fodderstack Mountain.

His heart drummed in his chest. *Women.* Catching Trudy was one thing; catching women was quite another.

He gulped, and opened his eyes to the wavering light. Soon they appeared, swirling before him, shimmering like Loreleis. Their flesh was pale, their eyes reflected the orange of the fire, and their lips were moist and red. They threw back their heads and their breasts bounced with the laughter that bubbled up their throats. He could see the blood flowing in their veins, the quivering hearts that pumped the blood, and further down the viscera—the food in their stomachs, the sludge in their guts, the eggs in their ovaries waiting to ripen.

Saliva flooded his mouth as if he'd just licked a lemon. He lowered his gun as another tinkle of laughter reached him, and stared at the flickering light. Women were a different sport from sisters. Far less exciting to track, but infinitely more gratifying when caught. He chuckled as he turned away and headed back toward his bedroll beneath the tree. What a gift! Fate must still be looking out for him!

Grinning, he looked up into the nighttime sky. In just a few hours morning would bring sunlight and the women and maybe even Trudy again. He'd better get to sleep fast. Who knew what kind of prey he might run into tomorrow?

TEN

D o you guys remember the day we met?" Joan studied Mary and Alex across the fire. The flames gave her face the look of an eerie pumpkin.

"I do." Mary sat on the lip of the fissure, the moon rising huge and yellow behind her shoulder. "Dr. Walker's section of Constitutional Law. Mondays at nine."

"You sat beside that blond guy from Indiana who wore a coat and tie." Alex grinned. "You always borrowed his notes. Mary and I used to wonder if you had anything going with him."

"No," said Joan. "He was gay." She shot Alex a dark look. "But I always wondered if *you* were sleeping with Mark Holcomb."

"Mark Holcomb?" Alex crinkled her nose. "Dopey Mark Holcomb? I'd rather go to bed with a personal appliance."

"You'd probably have more fun," Mary chuckled.

"Which brings me to you, Mary Crow,"

Joan said, scooting closer to the flames. "I want to ask you a question."

"Okay," replied Mary. "What?"

Joan hunched her knees up close to her chest. "Tell me about you and Jonathan Walkingstick."

Alex cleared her throat loudly, as if to signal Joan to *shut up*, but Joan ignored her and kept her eyes on Mary.

Mary swirled her brandy under her nose, allowing the sweet, potent aroma to fill her head. "Not much to tell, really. Rings, proms, the whole high-school sweetheart thing." She glanced at Alex, who was looking at her with a hesitant smile.

"Oh, come on," Joan nudged. "My *amore* genes are picking up vibes. There's a lot more to you two than just high-school sweethearts."

"Joan!" This time Alex glared at Joan across the fire, but again Joan ignored her.

Mary watched a charred pine log collapse into the embers, throwing up a shower of fiery sparks. Up to now she'd trusted only Alex with this story, but Joan had long been a close friend, too. Maybe it was time to let her in on the secret as well.

"Jonathan was my first friend here. In grade school the other girls considered me odd—light skin, no father, a mother who'd married a rich white boy, then come back a widow and tried to weave tapestries for a living. They called me Crazy Crow. Old Crow. Scarecrow.

"Jonathan, though, didn't care how much the other kids teased me. He lived up the mountain. The two of us and Billy Swimmer played together every day. Our yard was a thousand acres of forest. We blazed trails and swung on grapevines and pretended we were Robin Hood and Tarzan."

"You didn't play cowboys and Indians?" Joan's voice rose in surprise.

Mary shook her head as she took a sip of brandy. "Nobody was ever willing to be the cowboy. Anyway, when we got to high school, Jonathan and I began to date. We were just as happy as a couple as we had been as friends. We never went out with anybody else."

He looked at her differently that day on the school bus. New eyes—

hungry, questioning eyes probed her as if she were some fresh creature invented just for him that very morning. Her palms grew damp. In a way he scared her. In another way, she didn't want to ever leave his side. "Save my seat," he'd whispered as he got up to go borrow someone's science book. She'd never forgotten the way those words rang in her head.

"So what happened?" Joan hunched forward eagerly. "Why did you guys break up?"

Mary held the cup of brandy against her cheek and closed her eyes. *Here comes the hard part,* she thought.

"Jonathan and I were together on the afternoon my mother was killed." She stared at a gray rind of ash along one sooty log. "It was the first time we'd made love—the first time I'd made love with anybody."

It's Thursday night, and they'd dawdled their way home from band practice, unwilling to leave the heady spring evening for the rigors of geometry homework. They sit on an old moss-covered log, laughing about Mr. Mooney, the band director. Jonathan removes his shirt. His chest is sculpted and hairless, and reminds Mary of the torso of Hermes in her World History book. Though she knows she shouldn't, she reaches over and touches him. His skin is tight and warm; she can feel the rapid drubbing of his heart. Suddenly his hand is under her blouse, and electricity jolts through her and then they are behind the log, discovering each other in that sweet April air. They do not speak. He is warm and heavy and smells clean, like new grass. The first time she flinches at the small sting of pain. The second time she figures out to rise and meet him and together they ride away on a velvet horse of their own invention.

"I got back to the store about a minute after my mother was murdered," Mary said. *You heard footsteps and you couldn't even go to the window to see who was walking away.* Her old coward mantra started ringing in her head. The years had not dimmed its power to condemn. Suddenly she felt herself shrinking, the strong muscles in her body withering as she sat there.

"Oh, my God!" Joan's eyes were dark pools in the firelight. "How awful!"

"I used to think that if I'd just come straight to the store that afternoon, nothing would have happened." Mary fought to keep her voice even. "Sometimes I still think that might be true."

Joan reached over and squeezed her leg. "Don't—you think like that, you'll drive yourself crazy."

Mary looked back into the fire and thought of the stones at the base of her mother's grave, and of the six men she'd hungrily convicted of murder. "Sometimes I wonder if I'm not crazy already."

"Don't go there, Mary," Alex said. "You're no crazier than the rest of us."

"Is this the first time you've seen Jonathan since your mom's death?" Joan's question floated above the fire like a wisp of ash.

"Oh, I saw him at her funeral. He was as horrified as everybody else. He and Billy ditched school for a week to search for her killer." Mary leaned over and rearranged a half-charred log. "I saw him alone only once more, then my grandmother came and took me to Atlanta." She looked up. "And what could I have said to him, anyway? 'Hey, Cherokee-boy, if we hadn't been fucking, my mom might still be alive?'"

Suddenly a single thunderous boom shattered the air above them. Then that sound was replaced by a high, piercing scream that wavered somewhere between human and not.

"Jeez!" Joan leapt to her feet, her collapsible cup tumbling to the ground, spilling brandy onto the rocks. "What the hell was *that?*"

Mary stood, too, and stared into the blackness. The first sound she recognized—the simple deep report of a shotgun. The second noise she couldn't place. No animal she'd ever heard up here made a cry like that.

"Oh, it's probably just some juiced-up hunters trying to scare each other." She tried to make her voice light.

"What would anybody be hunting in the dark?" The flames deepened the hollows underneath Joan's cheekbones.

"Bears, maybe. Somebody could be poaching red wolves. They've reintroduced wolves to the forest and a lot of people don't like it."

"Isn't it illegal to hunt at night?" Alex looked up at her.

"Not necessarily." Mary shrugged. "And anyway, who's up here to write them a ticket?"

"Gosh, they won't hear us and think we're red wolves, will they?" Joan rubbed her arms as if she were cold.

"No. Wolves are smart, but they don't drink brandy around camp-fires at night." When Joan did not laugh, Mary answered more seriously. "They're probably miles away. The sound travels funny up here."

"Everything travels funny up here, if you ask me." Joan fished in her pocket for her cigarettes.

They huddled around the fire, that old fighter-of-night that the Cherokees regarded as a living spirit who both kept their secrets and revealed their dreams. When the low, shimmying flames had warmed them again, Joan spoke.

"Mary, I'm sorry for making you dredge up all that old stuff about your mom. It seems like every rock you turn over in this forest, something nasty crawls out."

Mary gazed into the fire and thought of the Old Men. "That's just quid pro quo for the mountains. If they give you something, they always expect something in return."

They poured another round of brandy, then Alex started folding herself into a yoga position called the Crow.

Mary laughed as Alex's long arms and lanky legs stuck out like pipe-straws, but even as she laughed, she kept one ear tuned to the forest. That scream had unnerved her more than she was willing to admit. If something strange was roaming around out there she wanted to know about it before her friends did. She peered past Alex into the darkness beyond, waiting for whatever it was to shriek again, but everything remained silent; their own voices were the only noises in the glittering black stillness of the autumn night.

They talked on, the familiar chatter of her friends comforting her. Alex carped on about how there were only three people in Atlanta who could give you a decent haircut; Joan's accent took on a decidedly Brooklyn edge as she complained that the shoe sales at Saks almost never included size five. When the embers had burned down into mere pinpoints of orange, Mary was calm again—the gunshot and the strange, inhuman cry had receded into just another odd memory of a forest night.

She got to her feet. "I'm hitting the tick, ladies."

"You're what?" Joan exclaimed, horrified.

"Going to bed." Mary laughed as she pulled her sweatshirt over her head. "That's mountain speak. I don't know about you guys, but I'm whipped."

"Me, too," said Joan. "My legs feel like concrete."

"Just wait till tomorrow," Alex warned. "They'll feel like concrete *underwater*."

Inside, the cave was dark and smelled of dry dust. Zipping themselves into their tent, Alex stripped down to her long johns and jumped into Charlie Carter's arctic sleeping bag while Joan took off her boots and curled up in her new bag. Mary climbed into her old flannel bedroll between them.

"Anybody need to pee?" Alex asked, her hand on the lantern's switch.

"Not bad enough to leave this tent," answered Joan. "It's too long and cold a walk in the dark."

"I'm okay, Alex," Mary replied.

Alex started to switch off the light, then she grinned and made a face above the lantern. "Anybody want to tell ghost stories? I know some good ones."

"No, Alex. You ask that every time we sleep in the same room. Nobody wants to hear any ghost stories. Spending the night in this cave with you is scary enough." Joan tugged her sleeping bag over her head. "I'll see you guys in the morning."

"Good night, Alex," Mary said, laughing at the crestfallen look on Alex's face.

"Good night," Alex sniffed, turning off the lantern. "And sweet dreams to all who *deserve* them."

Darkness enveloped them like a glove; then in a little while Mary felt a soft tug on her sleeping bag.

"Mary?" a voice whispered. "Are you awake?"

"Yes." Mary smiled knowingly in the dark. Joan always saved her most troublesome questions for last.

"Do you really think those hunters are miles away?"

"Absolutely." Mary snuggled into her sleeping bag, breathing in its woodsy, cedar-chip smell. "If they're locals, they know not to try this trail at night. If they're not locals, then they couldn't find this trail even if they wanted to. Don't worry. We're safe."

"I hope so," Joan replied through a yawn. "Goodnight, then. *Buona notte.*"

"Goodnight." Mary turned on her side and closed her eyes. At first she saw nothing, then Cal Whitman's face and her mother's slain body floated before her. Footsteps echoed, walking away. She shuddered. Too bad Joan hadn't let Alex tell her ghost story. A mythical monster would be preferable to the real ones that roamed through her dreams.

ELEVEN

Lou Delgado had just taken his second bite of warm pecan pie when a shadow fell across the sunny table. Coffee sloshed over the rim of his cup as someone jostled his booth. He looked up. Mitchell Whitman slid into the seat across from him.

Whitman tapped the Rolex on his wrist. "It's eight o'clock, Saturday morning, Mr. Delgado."

Lou forced down his pie, its sweetness suddenly a sticky, sodden lump in his mouth. "I got what you wanted."

Whitman folded his hands and waited, as if expecting to be dealt a lucky hand of poker. "And?"

Lou picked up a manila envelope from the seat beside him and plopped it down on the table. "These just came from the darkroom."

Whitman opened the envelope. Inside was a photographic contact sheet—36 tiny black-and-white pictures all on one piece of paper. Turning the sheet sideways, he looked at the images. Three women loading camping gear into the trunk of a BMW, the car traveling down a gravel road, the three again coming out of some hayseed general store. The final picture showed the Beemer parked in some forest.

He looked at Lou. "So Mary Crow's gone camping?"

"Sure has. Somewhere between East Bumblefuck, North Carolina, and Nowhere, Tennessee. It's written on the back of the sheet."

Whitman turned the page. "Little Jump Off Trail?"

"Hillbilly country." Lou winked at Paula, the morning waitress, as she freshened his coffee. "Where the feds managed to piss off the locals so bad they lost that Rudolph guy."

Whitman's eyes darted up at Delgado. "Who?"

"Eric Rudolph. The guy who *allegedly* blew up that abortion clinic in Birmingham. He got his ass up in those mountains and the cops haven't seen him since." Delgado chuckled.

Whitman shrugged, disinterested, as he began to reexamine each picture. When he looked up again, his lips drew back in that awful smile. "Mr. Delgado, you've just opened a whole new realm of possibilities for me."

"Oh yeah?" Lou sat back in the booth and stirred his coffee. "Possibilities for what?"

"Like I told you before. Mary Crow knows too much. I intend to see that she has nothing more to do with the prosecution of this case."

"Look, kid, there's something you don't understand. The DA's office is like a real deep baseball team. Mary Crow gets benched, another lawyer'll step up to the plate. Stopping Mary Crow ain't gonna stop this case. Your brother's already been convicted."

"You don't understand. We're the Whitmans, for God's sake . . ."

"Wouldn't matter if you were the Jesus H. Christs. You whack somebody, they'll come after you."

Mitchell clenched his teeth. "Then let's just say it's personal. Something between Mary Crow and me needs to be resolved."

Delgado frowned, feeling as if he were about to set something very bad into motion. "And how are you gonna resolve this personal thing?"

Whitman spread the fingers of his right hand and studied his palm. "Haven't decided yet."

"You wouldn't be thinking of going up in those woods, would you?"

"What if I am?"

"Because my guy says it's pretty rough where they went."

Whitman's fingers curled into a fist. "I led tactical ROTC squads every semester in undergraduate school. And my Dad and I have hunted all over the country. Alaska. Maine. The Canadian Rockies. I don't think the Smoky Mountains would present too much of a challenge."

"I think you're wrong."

Whitman frowned. "Why?"

Delgado leaned forward. "Because even if you were the General Patton of your ROTC unit and bagged every moose in Maine, you still got no business hunting lawyers in the jungle. Trust me, kid. You do that, and you're in way over your head. This Mary Crow's like a bad dog with a big bone. You don't want to piss her off."

For the first time Whitman threw back his head and laughed, revealing a mouthful of square white teeth. "You actually think I should be *afraid* of her?"

"She roughed you up pretty good on the witness stand, didn't she? Everybody in town was laughing about it."

Whitman's smile faded as his eyes abruptly took on a sheen like black ice.

Delgado shook his head. "Kid, you got an old man who can throw enough money at the system to get your brother off on appeal. So this chick DA made you look like a yo-yo on TV. People will have a little chuckle about it, then the next chump will come along. Go get laid. Go build your dam in South America. It'll work out better for everybody in the long run."

Whitman grinned at Lou as if he had him in the crosshairs of a gun sight, then he slid the contact sheet back in the envelope and closed the clasp.

"Thanks, Mr. Delgado." He clapped Lou hard on the back as he rose from the table. "You've no idea how helpful you've been."

Mitch Whitman pulled his car out of the Copper Pot parking lot and turned south on I-75, heading toward Georgia Tech. *Mary Crow roughed you up on the witness stand*, Delgado's voice rang in his ears. *Everybody in town was laughing about it.* He put the thought out of his mind as he sped around a wobbling truck carrying chickens to market.

Camping, he thought, glancing over at the pictures on the seat beside him. *The fucking bitch hangs us all out to dry and then goes on a nature walk.* He'd assumed she would do what most career girls did on Atlanta weekends—shop at Phipps, dinner in Virginia Highlands, then drinks in Buckhead. He figured Delgado would bring him a list of restaurants and nightclubs along with the name of some lover, and he could have had her taken care of at some place where she felt at home.

But camping. This was far better than he'd ever expected. He laughed out loud as he exited off the highway and pointed his Porsche toward Mincy's Sporting Goods. For the first time since his little brother had graduated from diapers, things were looking up. With just a little careful planning, he would be able to enjoy a woodsy autumn weekend and make sure Mary Crow would never squeeze anybody's balls again.

Three hours later Mitch Whitman stood in his old bedroom in his father's house. Though he'd kept his apartment near Tech, he'd moved most of his stuff back home after Cal had been arrested. His mother had been too much of a basket case then, and his father had asked him to come home and "keep her company."

"Her damn friends won't call her anymore," he'd told Mitch. "You can take her mind off things."

Mitch thought that the Jack Daniels his mother sipped from noon through Oprah Winfrey kept her mind off most things, but he did what his father had asked. Few people, he'd noticed, ever denied a direct request from Calhoun Whitman, Sr.

Now he stood, dressed in jeans and a yellow Georgia Tech T-shirt, surveying the array of equipment spread out on his bed. Beside his sleeping bag and camp stove was an unusual selection of high-tech gear. Night-vision goggles, a handheld VHF radio, and a GPS positioner lay next to a Colt Light 30.06 with a long-range scope. A 9mm Beretta pistol gleamed dully next to the rifle, amid three different kinds of survival knives and a dozen boxes of ammunition. Mitch smiled. He had enough firepower on this bed to bring down any animal in the southeast United States.

Prepare for everything. Mitch remembered his father's admonition before every hunting trip they'd taken together. *And expect the worst.* Mitch wished he'd remembered that at Sandra Manning's house that night, but there was nothing to be done about that now.

"Did you know Sandra Manning before she was killed, Mr. Whitman?" Thanks to his brother's asshole attorney calling him as a character witness, that question had kicked off the worst hour of his life. Mary Crow had leaned right up against the stand when she'd cross-examined him—stood so close that he could see the tiny vein throbbing on one side of her long throat. Her heart beat calmly, delicately, while his hammered in his chest like a drum.

"No." That lie was his first mistake.

"Really?" Mary Crow prissed over to her table, the kick pleat in her slim black skirt revealing shapely legs. "Then why on earth would Sandra's phone records indicate that she called your apartment every day for the past six months?" Mary Crow held up a thick stack of papers.

His mouth froze; became unable to form words. How could he have forgotten about the fucking phone records? Mary Crow walked back to the stand.

"Who do you think Sandra Manning called there, Mr. Whitman? Your roommates?" Mary Crow checked her records. *"And why would Sandra talk to them for fifteen, twenty, thirty minutes at a time?"*

"Well, maybe I did know her," he admitted, his face heating up. The reporters in the back of the courtroom perked up. They were looking at him, whispering and scribbling on their notepads as he squirmed.

"Bitch," he repeated now, aiming the rifle at his reflection in the bedroom mirror. "Before I'm done, you'll wish you'd finished me off in court."

With a hot anger rising in his gut, he put the rifle back on the bed and sat down at the desk that had served as his worktable since he was fourteen, when he got his first computer. On top of the plans for the dam in Veracruz de Calbuco were three pictures of Mary Crow. One showed her tonguing a blonde woman; in another she straddled a black man. The third was a nude shot of Mary alone, her legs spread wide, sprawled in a leather chair. Mitch looked at the pictures and smiled. Of course none of them were really Mary Crow—all were just her head pasted on porn shots he'd downloaded from the Net. Earlier that morning, though, with just a few clicks of his mouse, he had hacked into some French guy's screen name and E-mailed the shot of Mary with the Negro to everybody in the Georgia legal system. He chuckled. His little electronic masterpiece would cause Mary some embarrassment. Too bad she wasn't going to survive the weekend long enough to suffer through it.

He thumbed through the papers on his desk until he found a pink sheet with all of Mary Crow's numbers on it—Social Security, driver's license, address, telephone, credit cards. Yesterday afternoon he had maxed out her Visa and tanked her credit. This morning he had humiliated her with a dirty picture. Tomorrow he would take care of Mary Crow forever, and the cover was perfect. When she didn't show up for work on Monday, people would figure that having her affair with the black buck exposed had frightened her off. After her credit card scandal broke they would assume the heartbroken and disgraced Mary Crow had just flapped her wings and flown off into oblivion. Nothing else had ever worked out so well in his whole life.

He slipped the photos and credit card numbers in a folder and filed it in the bottom drawer of his desk. From the same drawer he pulled out another folder labeled "Alternates" and flipped it open. Paper-clipped together in four small stacks were four separate identities—driver's licenses, credit cards, draft cards, one even with a card from Blockbuster for a video store membership.

"Okay." Mitch riffled through the cards. "Who do I want to be today?" He looked at them all, then chose Mitchell Keane, a registered Republican and card-carrying Rotarian from Athens, Georgia. Digging his wallet from his back pocket, he slipped Mitchell Keane's IDs behind his own, then he locked the other papers back in the drawer.

With expert ease he stowed his gear in a large backpack and grabbed his rifle. Along with a camouflage suit, he had food and supplies for a week. If he couldn't get this job done in that amount of time, then he might just fly down to Chile early and not bother coming back home.

Downstairs his father's voice thundered from the library, demanding an answer to some legal question. Mitch stashed his pack in the dark closet at the end of the hall and walked to the double library doors. He cracked one open. Some idiot lawyer was catching hell. He hoped it was the same incompetent fucker who'd put him on the stand. His father stood at his massive desk, a phone glued to his ear, his finger stabbing at some paragraph in a thick legal tome. Whoever it was, Mitch was glad *he* wasn't on the other end of that call.

"I tell you she shouldn't even be in the Georgia legal system," Cal Whitman roared. "She's a goddamn Cherokee. According to the treaty my own damn ancestor wrote, she's an illegal alien. She ought to be out in Oklahoma, frying bread for tourists."

Mitch stepped forward as his father listened on the phone. "Hey, Dad. I just wanted to tell you that I'm flying up to D.C. for the week-end—"

His father put the receiver to his chest, ignoring the voice still buzzing from the phone. "Your brother just got convicted of murder and you're going to Washington?"

Mitch felt his stomach shrivel, as it always did when he talked to his father, but he ignored it and planted his legs wide apart.

"I'm meeting some guys from the dam project there," he replied. "I'll be back next week."

Big Cal regarded his strapping firstborn a moment, then he lifted his hand in farewell. "Be back here Wednesday. And tell your mother where you're going."

"Yes, sir," Mitch said as he backed out the door. "Maybe I'll bring you a present, Dad. Something that will help you sleep better at night."

Cal, Sr., didn't reply.

Mitch turned and walked back through the hall to the den. His mother and Lucille, their maid, sat together shelling pecans and watching some man weeping on the Jenny Jones show. Daytime television had become their diversion-of-choice. Since Cal's arrest they had probably watched enough talk shows and shelled enough pecans to send a pie to every drug-abusing, wife-beating bisexual transvestite in America.

"Mom, I'm going to D.C. for a couple of days."

"Fine, dear."

"I've got a meeting about the dam."

"Fine, dear."

"I'll be back soon."

He did not wait to hear the third "Fine, dear." Instead, he turned and walked toward the closet in the hall, wondering what her response would have been if he'd announced his true intentions.

"Mom," he would have said. "I'm going to kill Mary Crow."

"Fine, dear. Have fun."

TWELVE

C ome look out the window," the voice commands. "You can't do anything for your mother now. Come look out the window!"

Mary looks up from her mother's body. She cannot move. Her feet feel nailed to the floor.

"The window," the voice insists again, then Mary hears something else. A dull thudding that grows louder. Footsteps. Slow. Methodical. Moving closer. This time coming for her.

"Mary! Wake up!"

Mary opened her eyes. Brilliant light surrounded her. Someone was kneeling in front of her, talking.

"Mary?" Alex's voice hummed above her as her face and blonde hair came into focus. She was frowning, her blue eyes squinting as if she were peering into a microscope. "Are you okay?"

Mary sat up, breathing hard. "Someone was stalking me."

Alex threw one arm around her shoulders. "You were dreaming, honey. Nobody's here but Joan and me."

Mary closed her eyes, the earthy-sage smell of Alex's flannel shirt stilling her panic. "Alex, I heard the footsteps again," she said, her mouth dry as a cracker. "I haven't heard them since college . . ."

Alex squeezed her shoulders, then started to rub her back in slow circles. Outside the tent, birds chirped and buttery morning sunlight streamed through the open flap.

"You know, Mary, maybe the mountains aren't where we need to be right now. Why don't we pack up and hike out? We can throw our stuff in the car and drive back to Atlanta. We'll have a nice dinner there tonight and just table the rest of this trip."

"No." Mary couldn't stop trembling. "This is what we planned. We're almost there, and I want you guys to see Atagahi."

Sighing, Alex sat back on her heels. "Honey, you can't come up here and visit your mother's murder scene and pretend it's some picnic in the country. Stuff like that takes a toll. Let's go home and come back another time. I'll come with you again."

"No, Alex. We're already here and Atagahi really is special. One cup of coffee and I'll be fine. I promise." Mary peered through the tent flaps. "Where's Joan?"

Alex snorted. "In the middle of her morning *toilette*. Sunscreen. Moisturizer. The whole nine yards." Alex rolled her eyes. "She's as bad as my mother." She scooted backwards out of the tent, summoned by a thread of steam that whistled from a small kettle of water heating on top of her stove. With a wide grin she waggled a packet of instant coffee. "Since you're determined to stay up here, would you like some nice fresh coffee from the stove you made such fun of yesterday?"

"Please." Mary rubbed her eyes, trying to erase all vestiges of her nightmare. Maybe this was mountain payback. You nose around some, the Old Men lob over a tiny little psychotic flashback in return. Just like a psychic tennis match.

She crawled out of the tent as Alex poured the coffee. Overnight a blanket of mist had arisen from the forest floor, and Alex looked as if she were about to tumble into a cloud bank. Mary sat cross-legged by the fire and took the cup she offered. It was not her usual freshly brewed French Roast, but it was a marginal jolt of caffeine that would bump her into the day. She had just taken her first sip when Joan materialized through the fog, makeup kit and canteen in hand.

She sang some vaguely familiar aria as she walked, her light soprano trilling through the damp air.

"Morning, Joan." Mary smiled, suddenly grateful for Joan's taupe eyelids and the scent of perfume that preceded her. The fact that one of them had risen and was singing opera helped to rivet her to the here and now, away from the manic tangle of her dreams. "Your first night in the forest must have been okay."

Joan stopped singing and rotated her shoulders. "Are you kidding? My feet feel like petrified wood. My thighs are on fire. I have an awful pain in my right shoulder and I just popped three Excedrin for a sinus headache. And if that isn't enough, Alex snored all night."

"I did not!" Alex snapped. "I never snore."

"Well, then it must have been some bear that slept outside our tent," Joan retorted. "Or maybe it was that ghost you were dying to tell us about."

Relishing Joan and Alex's wrangling, Mary stretched her legs out in front of her. In the crisp morning air, her nightmare seemed far away and silly, nothing that a grown woman should be afraid of.

"Hey, Mary," Alex asked, "when can we hike on to the spring?"

"Soon as the mist burns off." Mary looked out across the huge cauldron of thick white mist that roiled just beyond the lip of the fissure. Only the tops of the mountains pierced through the swirling clouds. The view reminded her again of San Francisco, only here the mountains were the whales, dark forms breeching in a wispy white sea.

Joan flopped down between them. "Is all this fog why they call these the Smoky Mountains?"

"*Shaconage,*" Mary said without thinking.

"Excuse me?"

"That's Cherokee. It means 'land of blue smoke.' Although actually," Mary continued as she warmed her fingers around her coffee cup, "we're in the Unicoi mountains, which comes from the Cherokee word *Unaka.*"

"Which means?"

"White mountains."

Joan laughed. "You're a regular thesaurus, Mary."

"Don't get excited. Ten more words and we'll be at the end of my Cherokee vocabulary."

Alex fixed them oatmeal with raisins for breakfast, then they waited for the fog to lift. By the time they struck their tent and repacked their gear, rust-colored mountains began to reappear as the thick white mist drained away. Overhead the sky turned from white to dazzling blue, and the breeze carried the aroma of apples and damp earth. It promised to be one of the singularly gorgeous fall days for which the Appalachian Mountains were famed. Mary grinned at her friends, suddenly exhilarated. "Are we ready for the final assault on Atagahi?"

"I'm ready for any kind of hot tub," replied Joan. "Electric, solar, or thermonuclear. These old bones need to soak in some nice warm water."

Alex laughed. "Joan, you're only thirty."

"That's in Atlanta years. Up here I feel three hundred."

They doused the fire, buckled on their backpacks and followed Mary as she began to pick her way down from the cave.

Each step down the steep path sent currents of pain up their shins. The packs they'd worn so lightly the day before rubbed against sore muscles and stretched tendons, and the air itself seemed against them—buzzing with small, nearly invisible gnats that hovered around their eyes and stung their faces.

"How much farther?" huffed Joan when they stopped to rest at Blacksnake Creek.

"Not much," Mary replied, her own breath coming in short gasps. "It's a stiff climb, but it won't last more than half an hour."

"That's what you said two hours ago," Alex growled, shifting the backpack on her shoulders and wiping the sweat from her forehead. "There's not going to be much left of me after these damn bugs get through."

They pushed on, climbing a steep path that blazed with red sumac. The forest slanted away to their right, trees stretching up from a waist-high carpet of electric-green ferns. Soft pine needles brushed delicate fingers against their cheeks, and at a rushing mountain stream, Alex pointed to a cluster of thick black berries that dangled from the pink stem of a poke plant. "That looks like one of those sci-fi films where the earth's been nuked and the plants are fifty feet high and the people are the size of ants."

"Don't talk so much, Alex," Joan said grumpily, her face the color of a stop sign. "It takes too much effort to listen."

They climbed higher, the rush of the creek growing fainter and fainter until they heard it no more and finally saw it only as a silent flash of distant silver far below them.

"How much farther now?" Joan panted, slurping from her canteen as they plodded along.

"Over this ridge," Mary promised. "Then we're there."

They walked on, no longer stopping at creeks or listening to birds, just doggedly planting one foot ahead of the other, determined to make their destination. They crested the mountain, then Mary led them around the jutting roots of a massive overturned maple.

"There." She grinned triumphantly and pointed below them. "Atagahi."

A hundred yards away, ringed by huge boulders, a clear green pool glistened iridescent as a hummingbird in the sunlight. The calm waters glittered like an extravagant emerald on the finger of a czar.

Alex gasped. "Good grief! That looks more like Acapulco than Appalachia."

"It even smells different." Joan sniffed the air. "More like flowers instead of forest. And there aren't any of those awful bugs!"

But Mary couldn't speak. Atagahi was even more beautiful than she remembered. She could almost hear her mother's laughter tinkling up over the water as they'd lain floating on their backs, watching white clouds sail across a blue sky.

Hurrying now, the three women picked their way among the rocks to the spring, ditching their backpacks under a drooping willow tree, their aches and complaints forgotten in the excitement of reaching their destination. At the lowest rim of rock they knelt and dipped their hands into the water.

"Hey, it is warm." Joan looked up at Mary in surprise. "You weren't kidding."

"How deep is it?" Alex was peering into the fluorescent green depths.

"I've never known anyone who's touched the bottom." Mary sat down and began to unlace her boots. "But in a minute I'm going to try."

She undressed. Her clothes made a small pile on the rock. She stood naked in the warm sun for a moment, then she poised on the edge of the pool and dived, her skin flashing pale bronze as she arced over the water. Seconds later she surfaced ten feet away, her black hair slicked back and shining.

"This is incredible!" she cried exultantly. She arched her back and exhaled, floating, letting her weary arms and legs relax in the warm green water.

"Did you touch the bottom?" Alex called, fumbling with the buttons on her shirt.

"Nope. I saved that just for you."

"Are you sure nobody will see us naked?" Joan, who felt uncomfortable in the dressing rooms of Bloomingdale's, peered around anxiously.

"Only that gun-toting red wolf we heard last night," Alex replied. "And of course the ghost who slept outside our tent."

"Oh shut up, Alex!"

Mary closed her eyes and smiled as her friends' voices danced in the air. They could swim or not, as they pleased. She would be content to float here for the rest of her life. In a few moments, though, she heard a western *Yee-hiii!* and felt a splash. Alex swam beside her; a moment later Joan did, too.

Her mother's body is sleek as an otter's. Martha smiles in the sun and dives headfirst into the spring as if she might find diamonds hidden in the deep green water. Her head breaks the surface and she calls to Mary. "Come on in, baby. Don't be afraid. I won't let anything hurt you!" Mary strips down to her bathing suit and leaps into the water with far less grace than her mother. Down, down she goes, bubbles nibbling at her toes like tiny fish. She looks back up above her and sees the sun shining gold through the water and she gives one strong kick and surfaces in the honeyed air.

They swam for an hour, diving, splashing, laughing, letting the warm water soothe away the rigors of the trail. Joan sang little bits of

Rigoletto; Alex tried to yodel. It was only when their fingertips shriveled like prunes that they decided to climb out and relax in the sun.

"Mary, I've got to give you credit. I was doubtful at first, but this was worth every sweat-soaked step," Alex declared, positioning herself spread-eagle on a sunny boulder.

"I agree." Joan dug through her clothes on the rock and stepped into her underpants. "It's just too bad you have to walk so far to get here."

Alex looked over at her and frowned. "Why are you getting dressed? I'm not moving an inch until the sun goes down."

"Misericordia girls don't sit around naked in the woods," answered Joan primly. "Sister Mary Xavier would have a *stroke*."

"I'm getting dressed, too," Mary told them. "I want to go back up the trail and sketch that old maple tree."

"You mean I'm the only one who's going to rest *au naturel* on this rock?"

"Looks like it," said Mary.

"Suit yourselves, then," Alex sighed with contentment. "I'm going to stay buck naked in the woods for as long as I possibly can. Tuesday will come soon enough, and then ugh! It's back to suits and heels and panty hose."

Joan frowned as Mary pulled on her jeans and quickly laced her hiking boots. "You won't be gone long, will you?"

"No. The tree's just up there, behind those boulders. My mother and I used to sketch underneath it." She pointed at the high ridge behind them. "I'm going to make a couple of drawings. It shouldn't take me more than half an hour."

Alex lay flat on her back, one knee bent, one arm under her head. Her hair shone gold and the sun made her skin glow like the petals of a lily. She squinted up at Mary. "Hey, Killer, throw me a PayDay before you leave, will you?"

"And my smokes?" Joan added.

Mary dug the candy and cigarettes out of Alex's backpack. She tossed the candy to Alex, the cigarettes to Joan.

"Thanks." Alex grinned. "We'll be right here stoking up on nicotine and sugar. Holler if you need us."

"Right." Mary looked at her friends and smiled. They looked like goddesses fresh from a hunt, lying with their faces raised to the sun. *Thank you*, she said silently to the Old Men as she glanced at their distant peaks and began to climb up to the tree. *Once again, you have been kind.*

THIRTEEN

Mitch Whitman grinned like a college boy as he stepped up to the Delta Air ticket counter. "Hi," he said, cracking a wad of chewing gum. "I'm Mitchell Whitman. Flight 646 to Washington. My ticket should be on your screen."

A skinny black woman with long purple fingernails checked her computer. "You purchased this morning on-line, billed to your American Express card?"

"That's correct." Mitch Whitman continued to grin.

"I need to see a picture ID."

Mitch dug out his driver's license from his wallet and handed it to the girl. She glanced briefly at his face, then pecked some more numbers into her computer.

"Any seating preferences?"

"An aisle seat near the front, if you've got one. I like to stretch my legs."

"Are you checking any luggage?"

"No. This fits overhead." Grinning, Mitch held up an unforgettably gold Georgia Tech gym bag as if it were a bowling trophy. The girl giggled.

"And did anyone other than you pack your bag?"

"Nope. I haven't left it unattended either, and nobody has asked me to carry any packages for them."

"I guess you know the drill." The girl smiled at Mitch, her dark eyes coy.

"I've been on a plane a couple of times before."

"Well, then, Mr. Whitman, you have a nice flight." She handed Mitch a boarding pass. "Concourse A, gate seven. Departs at 3:05."

"Thank you." Mitchell gave her one final smile. "You've been terrific. I might write a letter to your boss."

The girl giggled again. Mitch winked, then he picked up his gym bag and headed toward the gate. It was only when he was out of her sight that he stashed the boarding pass in his back pocket and headed toward the down escalator. After losing himself in a crowd of chattering Arabs, he made his way over to the line of rental car companies.

"Hi," he said to another young black woman who stood at the Avis counter. "I need to rent a car for the weekend."

"Driver's license and insurance card," the woman said perfunctorily, slipping her lipstick in a drawer.

Smiling, Mitch dug in his wallet again and pulled out a whole stack of identification. "Driver's license is on top. Whatever else you might need is there, too."

The woman stared at the license for a moment, then began to fill out a form. "Mitchell Keane," she read as she keyed his name into her computer. "Athens, Georgia."

An hour later, his identities and alibis firmly established, Mitch Whitman tucked his black Porsche in a dark corner of the long-term parking lot, and sped toward the mountains in a new white Taurus, his gear and rifle stashed in the trunk.

He roared, as much as the rented Ford could roar, north along Highway 441. Though filmy clouds wisped through the blue sky, the air held a sullen heaviness that reminded him more of August than October. He rolled down the window and drove faster, letting the wind ripple through his hair. His heart was beating fast. He'd killed elk and moose and one old black bear, but this would be different. This would be his first assassination.

"Too bad I can't put it on my resume," he said aloud, his thoughts suddenly turning to all his friends from Tech, who were getting ready to go to Veracruz and lay the groundwork for his dam. Though they'd all watched Mary Crow demolish him in court, nobody had said a word about it. No doubt they were all laughing at him behind his back. That idea made him sick with fury. After he got through with Mary Crow, everyone would know he was nobody to fuck with.

"All this because of my stupid shithead brother," Mitch said as he punched the Taurus up to ninety. Cal had been a fuck-up since the day he was born. At nine he'd superglued a fellow Cub Scout's protuberant ears to his head. When he was fourteen he'd been thrown off the school tennis team for screaming obscenities at a line judge. By the time he was sixteen he had been arrested twice for selling drugs. His father had bailed him out of juvie while his mother consulted a battery of adolescent psychiatrists. Drugs were prescribed, more involvement in sports was encouraged; one idiot shrink suggested that Cal start boxing at a gym. That, of course, was the one thing he responded to. By the time Cal followed Mitch into Georgia Tech, he had several new drug addictions, a fearsome right cross, and a temper that could turn on a dime. Who knew how much money his father had doled out, bribed with, and ultimately pissed away in attorney's fees to keep Cal out of jail. Mitch sighed. He'd done his share of helping Cal, too, but now he was sick of it. The time had come to close the great sucking hole that his brother's life had become.

"A fuck-up you were born, Cal. And a fuck-up you will die," he promised as he punched on the radio. "After I get Mary Crow, I'm coming after you."

By midafternoon, he crossed into Ramon County. "Thaddeus Whitman country," Mitch mused aloud. All his life he'd listened to his father expound about their ancestor, the great Thaddeus Whitman. About how way back in the eighteen hundreds Thaddeus had ridden up here from Charleston on a mule, then found fat gold nuggets in a stream on Cherokee land. Ultimately he'd headed a contingent of white Georgians who rode to Washington and convinced Andrew Jackson that it would be advantageous to fledgling America if the peaceful Cherokees were relocated as far away from that gold as possible. For years Thaddeus's old musket had hung above the fireplace in his father's library. Now he, Mitch, had a musket of his own, all set to relocate yet another Cherokee. Mitch smiled. There must be some kind of karma in that.

He drove on, cruising through a string of ramshackle towns that clung to the highway along with the kudzu-draped trees and fencerows. As the sharp smell of curing tobacco stung his nose, he pictured Thaddeus riding in on his mule. What had this country looked like when the old codger had discovered his fortune? Not nearly as pathetic as this, he decided as he pulled into a single-pump gas station that sold Cokes and lottery tickets from a grimy office decorated with a hundred battered hubcaps. Mitch dropped a twenty-dollar bill in front of a toothless old man who dozed at the desk. Not as pathetic as this at all.

He topped off his tank and pulled back on the highway. The mountains lay before him like giants slumbering under blankets of orange trees. As the cooler air chilled the skin on the back of his neck, he was suddenly back in that courtroom, Mary Crow hard at him.

"Are you close to your brother, Mr. Whitman?" she'd asked, a faint rosy blush now rising from the cleavage between the lapels of her black suit. She wore no blouse. Hell, she might not even be wearing a bra.

He felt everyone looking at him. He knew he'd sweated through his shirt; he could feel the cold, soggy stains beneath the sleeves of his suit. Mary Crow had hammered at him for almost an hour, yet her clothes were still dry, her eyes just as bright as before. Christ, did she never need to pee or eat or get a drink of water?

"I suppose." His voice came out in a croak.

"Would you lend him a tie if he needed one?"

What the hell kind of trick question was this? Loaning Cal a tie was not important. "Yes," *he replied.*

"A clean shirt?"

"Yes."

"So you're in the custom of sharing your things with your brother?" She smiled at him, her eyes innocent as a dove's.

He gulped, despising the way this woman made him squirm. "I suppose I am."

"So since we've already established that you knew Sandra Manning, and had gone out with Sandra on more than one occasion, may we then assume that you might even share Sandra Manning with your brother?"

"Objection!" the defense attorney shouted as a rumble of suspicion rolled like soft thunder through the courtroom.

Mitch blinked and tried to relax his grip on the steering wheel of the car. His knuckles had grown white and the ends of his fingers were tingling. He took a deep breath and flexed his hands. He had to stop revisiting that awful hour. Right now he didn't need to relive his discomfort in the courtroom with Mary Crow. Right now he needed to consider his options when he came upon Mary Crow in the forest, face-to-face.

He shrugged his shoulders hard, trying to soften the muscles in his neck. The best thing to do would be to put a bullet in her brain when she was away from the two others, then slip back into the trees. But what if that opportunity did not present itself? Most women wouldn't even go to the bathroom by themselves. In a forest they'd probably stick together like glue. If he sniped them with his rifle, they'd scatter like chickens. That would not do. He would have to think of something else.

As he tried to tap the feeling back in his fingers on the steering wheel, it came to him. Just wait, he realized. Wait until they're asleep. Most likely they'll all be in the same tent. You won't even need the rifle. Just slip out of the trees, then pop, pop, pop with the Beretta and Mary Crow won't be coming after anybody anymore. By the time they find her body, you'll be working on your tan in Veracruz.

He sped on, until he came to a gas station where bright handmade quilts flapped behind a sign that read FISHING & CAMPING SUPPLIES. There, he made a hard turn and pulled in.

He locked the Taurus and walked inside. Behind the counter a fat blonde girl sucked on a pale blue drink as she watched wrestling on a minuscule TV. There was a prettiness about her, despite her weight and heavy makeup, that reminded him of Sandra Manning. A sudden sadness struck him. I'm dirty now, too, he realized. And I've got Cal to thank for that.

All the things people ran out of—motor oil, toilet paper, baby food—lined several shelves beside the beer cooler. At first he didn't see what he wanted; then, between dashboard fuses and light bulbs, he found it. Duct tape—giant gray rolls of the stuff you could temporarily mend most anything with.

Quickly, he grabbed three rolls of the tape, then found two packages of clothesline. Not the nylon shit that slipped, but the cotton kind that got tighter when it got wet. On his way to the cash register he added a carton of Camels and a pack of spearmint gum. Might as well get everything while I'm here, he decided. There won't be any stores in Injun country.

He placed his items on the counter. With a heavy sigh the girl pulled her attention from the wrestlers that flailed away on the tiny TV screen and looked at Mitch's purchases.

"You got a clothesline needs fixin'?" she asked with a nervous laugh, black eyes glittering like marbles beneath green shadowed lids.

"Maybe." He pushed his sunglasses higher on his nose.

She rang up his bill. "Thirty-five seventy-two with the cigarettes."

He dug out a fifty from his pocket. She counted out the change in his hand, pudgy fingers brushing against his palm.

"Have a good one," she chirped as she closed the cash drawer. "Don't go tyin' nobody up."

For an instant he couldn't breathe. Was he that transparent? Could this yokel read the inside of his head like a road map? If she could tell what he was planning, then she could turn him in to the cops. Suddenly he was keenly aware of the Beretta nestled beneath his left arm. Should he put a bullet in her head before she lifted the phone?

He looked at her face. The ends of her mouth quivered upward, as if she were hoping he would find her amusing. Again, he thought of Sandra.

"Yeah, right," he laughed, realizing that it was just her lame version of a joke. "See ya."

He hurried outside to the Ford. When he unlocked the door he looked back toward the store. The girl's blank stare had returned to the TV screen, her frosty blue concoction once again plugged into her mouth. No interest in what he was doing at all.

"Lucky for you, fat girl," Mitch mumbled as he turned the key in the ignition. "Being brain-dead just saved your pathetic little life."

FOURTEEN

By the time the morning fog lifted, Henry Brank had put several miles between himself and the ghost of Simpson's Bald. He'd awakened before dawn with his heart like a feather, and now he strode along in the bright sunshine with his vitamin-filled sack swaying behind him, singing in anticipation of the day to come.

"Sluts and tramps, chicks and dykes." He made up the words as he walked along. *"In the woods they're all alike."*

He wondered, as he moved through the trees, what sort of women you would find way up here. College girls camping with their sorority sisters? Or harder, jackbooted women who wore leather and enjoyed fucking their own kind? He'd found both sorts before. Coeds usually flirted with him at first, hoping that would change their fate. The dykes started out swinging, brash as young men, but their best punches consisted mostly of poorly aimed kicks at his groin.

Had their little karate instructors not warned them about how easy it was to catch an upturned ankle and twist it into agony? He chuckled as a blue-tailed skink slithered like liquid sapphire off the top of a warm rock. It made no difference to him what kind of women they were. All made good sport for a while, but they all wound up the same.

The thought of them, though, made him move faster through the forest. His breath began to come hard as he traversed the spine of the mountain range he'd climbed just two days before. The trail twisted around boulders that seemed to thrust up from the bowels of the mountains themselves. Though hiking this fast through the warm, thick air strained his back and bad leg, he kept pushing onward, like a shark drawn to the scent of blood.

He stopped only when he reached the ancient black gum tree that marked the trail to the Big Fodderstack fissure. Dropping his sack, he flattened himself against the brown scaly bark, breathing deeply and listening. No voices floated down from the little cave; no pans clattered in preparation of a midday meal. He nodded. He'd pegged it right: the women had broken camp and gone on to wherever they were headed. Probably he could strut up there brash as John Wayne. Nonetheless, he slid his knife from his boot as he eased out from behind the tree. Better to be careful around women.

He crept up the trail silently, his ears keen for any sound another person might make. Although the rocky footpath revealed few clues, he found one fresh track left in a patch of mud. He measured the depth with his finger and smiled. Some not-very-heavy person had recently walked up here in a pair of brand-new boots.

The breeze carried no particular smell of close humanity, so he crawled up to a huckleberry bush that grew where the trail widened into the ledge. He crouched behind its leaves, listening. Nothing. Cautiously he stood and crept onto the ledge itself. It was as he'd expected—an empty granite shelf sticking out from a vacant cave like a pouty lower lip. The only clue that the area had recently been a camp was the small dark circle of a neatly constructed fire. He squatted down and touched it with his palm. The dirt still felt warm.

He sheathed his knife and flopped down inside the cave, rubbing his cheek hard against a crack along one wall that smelled of cigarettes and perfume. Here their odors hung in the air. Deodorant, toothpaste, brandy, coffee. It was even better than he had hoped: in all that reeking bouquet of smells nothing bore the slightest scent of a man. He closed his eyes and imagined the women still here, underneath him, wrapping their legs around him while he thrust himself inside them. How good that would feel. Hot and soft as bread fresh from the oven.

He returned to his pack and fished out a Moon Pie, stuffing it in his mouth while he scanned the woods for their trail. He found it easily. Like most hikers, they had made no attempt to cover their tracks, and their trail of matted-down grass stretched out before him as plainly as if it had been lined off by the highway department. Brank chuckled as he licked the chocolate crumbs from his fingers. There would not be much sport to this, but there would be an awful lot of fun.

"I'll have them in an hour," he predicted to no one in particular as he reshouldered his sack and set off down the matted grass trail.

The women, though, had not taken some Audubon Society bird stroll. They'd gone up one side of a mountain so steep he thought his lungs would burst before he reached the top. Halfway up, with his shirt wet and clinging to his skin, he sat on a shady log and paused to rest. They're going somewhere special, he decided. Nobody would hike up this high just to watch the leaves change. On a whim he untied his sack and dug out his vitamins. He opened the jar and shook out half a dozen. "I might need some extra C," he muttered, remembering one of Fate's old caveats about protecting himself against disease. "You never know what sort of germs you might run into."

He dropped the vitamins back in his sack and saw Buster, coiled tightly against the remaining Moon Pies. With one hand he unbuttoned his shirt as he lifted the snake from the sack with the other.

"How're you doing, old Buddy?" He looked into the snake's beady black eyes.

The snake darted his tongue toward him. It didn't appear hungry or in pain. Brank cuddled it under his chin.

"We're gonna have some fun here in a little while," he promised as the creature slithered around his arm, seeking warmth. "You help me out, I'll give you something real good to eat."

The snake coiled tighter in response.

"Atta boy." Brank unwrapped the reptile and tucked it inside his shirt. "Just sit still for a little while longer."

The snake felt cool against his damp belly. He retied his sack and climbed on.

When he finally crested the mountain he stopped in a shoulder-high thicket of red elderberries. He settled himself to listen and looked out at the hundred lesser mountains that rolled away from him. At first the breeze brought nothing but the echo of a flicker drilling a tree. Then, all at once, on a puff of wind from the west, he heard the same voices he'd heard the night before.

They floated up so clearly you could almost hear what they were saying. Words, then laughter, then something that sounded like someone singing. Suddenly he knew exactly where they were—Slickrock Springs, a hidden-away place the Indians considered holy. An easy walk from here. He grinned as he pushed out from between the dense branches. Slickrock Springs meant bad medicine for a white man, but today the Great Spirit would just have to make an exception.

Brank waded into a tangle of wild fox grapes, zigzagging silently through the thick foliage. In twenty minutes he'd reached the edge of the spring. Out of breath, he looked up.

Slickrock had always reminded him of a small volcano—a broad mound of giant sandstone boulders rising fifty feet to cradle the hot spring that gurgled in the center of them. He could still hear the women's voices, fainter though, as if they hovered on the air above his head. An outcropping of rock jutted forth a third of the way from the top. If he could climb up there, he could see what awaited him without being detected.

He hid his sack and rifle under a hawthorne bush, then began to climb. By wedging his toes and fingers into the cracks between the boulders he could pull himself up like a lizard scaling a wall. But the sandstone offered little purchase; once, his foot slipped out of a crack, banging him noisily against the rocks. Panicked, he pressed himself against the boulder, praying the women hadn't heard. He held his breath through a long bubble of silence, then their conversation resumed. With sweat now streaming from his forehead, he climbed on. Just below the outcropping he balanced on his toes, stretching full length and reaching up until his fingers curled around the edge of the ledge. Then he hoisted himself up. Every muscle in his back and shoulders screamed, but with one final effort he thrust with his feet and managed to fling himself belly-down on the ledge, gasping, sweat stinging his eyes.

When his heart had slowed to a gallop, he turned around and straightened up. If he stretched as tall as he could, he would be able to peer over the rocks and see what was going on. Higher and higher he rose, until finally everything came into view.

"Sweet fucking shit," he whispered, as the world suddenly turned gold around him. "It's Trudy. And one of her sidekicks."

Two women lay on the boulders beside the pool. One had dark hair and wore a sweatshirt and underpants. Trudy, however—the one that took his breath away—lay naked. She had a mane of blonde hair that looked like a puddle of sunlight. Her arms cradled her head and lifted her breasts towards him. The rosy points of her nipples rose to the mountain air. Her belly was flat and ended in the small mound of her crotch, the inner workings of which were hidden by a thatch of darker blonde hair. She had the longest legs he'd ever seen. She was eating a candy bar while her friend smoked a cigarette. One would laugh, and the other would join in. The sound jingled on the air like a wind chime. He watched them until he could stand it no longer. With his penis stiff as steel he crouched down on the ledge and relieved himself in three quick strokes. A tornado ripped through him as he splattered against the rocks.

"Ahhhh, Gott," he groaned, his heart rattling inside his chest.

He crouched, trembling, on the ledge until the fire inside him cooled to an ember. He needed to find out for certain if they were alone. Carefully, he stretched up again. The women lay there happy, content. No guns or fishing tackle had been left beside them by boyfriends who might have gone off to explore. Except for a pile of cast-off clothes and two bright backpacks under a tree, his sister and her little pal could have been dropped down from heaven purely for his own enjoyment. He watched as she rearranged herself on the boulder, then he squatted back down on the ledge.

He looked up into the sky. A wide V of Canada geese flapped

southward across a field of blue while the sun fell like warm honey on his forehead. A crazed, delirious hum spun in his brain as he began unlacing his boots.

"At last," he whispered, offering his thanks to whatever gods had delivered unto him that day his rightful and most long-awaited prey. "Trudy, old girl, in a few minutes you're finally gonna belong to me."

FIFTEEN

J oan felt the shadow first. A small interstice
of darkness fell across the bright sunlight
that bathed her face. A cloud, she thought.
But the chill did not move. Reluctantly
she opened her eyes to see what was obstructing
the light that had just a moment ago warmed her
so deliciously. A colossus stood above her. Its
face blocked the sun, and she could see nothing
but a black shape haloed with a corona of blinding light.

"Mary?" she asked tentatively, an instant
before she looked down and saw that the figure
stood barefooted. Dark hair covered the tops of
the feet; the nails were thick as claws. A snippet
of bright green grass clung to one dirty toe. Joan
opened her mouth to speak, but the foot moved.
Fast, as if stomping a cockroach, it slammed
down on her throat, crushing her vocal cords.
When she next opened her mouth it was only to
suck in air, to hang on to the slender thread that
tethered her to this life.

"You make one sound and I'll sic my little friend on you." A man's coarse whisper rasped flat on the air. He held up a long, twisting snake. Joan stared at it, unable to take her eyes, off its darting, flicking tongue.

"Did you say something?" Alex's voice rose in a question, somewhere to her right.

Joan struggled beneath the foot to reply, to warn Alex, but faster than any thug she'd ever seen on the subway the man knelt and pressed the edge of a hunting knife flat against her throat. The blade felt like ice beneath her jaw and her pulse throbbed hot against it.

"One word and this rock'll look like a hog-killing."

"What?" Joan heard the surprise in Alex's voice. She squirmed to see her raising up on one elbow; then Alex, too, registered what was happening. "What the fuck . . ." she began.

The man turned suddenly and dangled the snake over Alex. Her blue eyes grew huge and wide and she began to gulp air as if she'd just come up from the bottom of the spring.

He sheathed his knife and arranged the snake in a heavy coil on Joan's chest. The creature rose up like a cobra, its eyes glittering like shiny black seeds. Panic surged inside her. "Don't you move, now," the man said. "I'd hate for you to get bit."

The man pulled some thin rope and a red bandana from inside his shirt and forced the bandana between Alex's jaws. He knotted it at the back of her head, then rolled her, unresisting, on her side, pulling her arms and legs tight behind her and binding them with the rope.

"Be still!" the man ordered as Alex stared speechless and terrified, her back arching like an inverted hobbyhorse.

He tied her arms and legs, then patted her hip as if he'd just won a contest in a rodeo. Licking the tip of one index finger, he reached for Alex's nipple.

"No!" Joan screamed before she realized what she'd done. The man jumped and turned back to her. His eyes blazed and she saw the index finger that had been bound for Alex's breast stop and curl into a fist. It rose, then roared down out of the sky like lightning and collided with the bridge of her nose. Bones snapped as her face melted in a furnace of pain.

"You don't tell me no," the man said. "You may be Trudy's partner, but don't you ever tell me no."

The man looked down at her. His face darkened with a deeper rage, then he smiled slightly, as if some good idea had just occurred to him. He forced Joan's mouth open. His hands smelled like rotten meat and the cloth he stretched between her jaws tasted like kerosene. He pulled her head forward by her hair and tied the cloth tight against the base of her skull. Her tongue seemed to double, to triple in size. There was not enough room for it and the rag in her mouth. She tried to suck in more air, but she couldn't. *This is how you will die*, she realized. *You will not be stabbed. You will not be bitten by the snake. You will die simply trying to breathe in air.*

The man put the snake around his neck and raised Joan's arms high above head. He pulled up her sweatshirt. The air felt cold on her bare breasts, the sandstone boulder rough against her back. She saw nothing beyond the black underside of her sweatshirt. She tried to keep breathing as she felt hands jerking her underpants down the length of her legs.

Hail, Mary, full of grace, she began to repeat inside her head, picturing the pretty pink rosary beads that she'd left, where, in her jewelry box? In the bathroom drawer with her birth control pills? She couldn't miss taking any of her pills; she had a date with Hugh Chandler in just a few days.

The hands pried her legs apart, then squeezed her sex as someone might coax juice from an orange. It burned from the outrage while her legs jerked as if she'd just grabbed an electrical wire.

Blessed art thou among women . . .

The hands traveled up her belly to her breasts, pinching her nipples with sharp fingernails. She gasped with pain, but then the fingernails disappeared, replaced by a hot wet mouth that sucked her right breast until it went numb. She squirmed to get away, to fold herself into the rock, but the hands grabbed her hips and jerked her forward. They grabbed her thighs and pushed her legs so wide apart she feared they would snap off like twigs. *I am not wet*, she thought, *this will not work*, and she tried to twist back into the woods or the rocks or even into the dark green depths of Atagahi itself. But she could not move.

A weight pinned her legs flat as something began to batter an entrance to her vagina.

Blessed is the fruit of thy womb, Jesus. He rammed into her harder; she couldn't remember any more of the rosary she'd known since she was four. She thought of Times Square and the Christmas windows on Fifth Avenue and her Aunt Carla the ex-Rockette. Her legs would not break off like this. Aunt Carla could put on her tap shoes and turn this man's balls to hamburger and the smile would never leave her face. *Un vero angelo,* her mother laughs when she talks about Aunt Carla. Joan thought of her mother and her mother's kitchen, where the sun slants across the red linoleum floor and the walls are redolent of garlic and lemons and the yeasty smell of dough rising. Renata Tebaldi, her mother's favorite soprano, sings from the stereo. *Giovanna,* her mother calls her by her Italian name. She wished with all her soul that she were back in that bright, warm, infinitely safe kitchen. If she could ever get back there she would never leave again.

He pummeled into her until finally, like a poorly stitched seam, her tissue tore and gave way. The stranger was within.

Time stopped then. Joan felt the beginning of each stroke, its path and its thumping end. She endured each without thought as to when this might cease, knowing only that when the choking in her head met the fire that was ripping up through her vagina, she would die. Surely God would grant her that mercy. Finally, just as she decided to quit breathing, she felt something spew up into her, and it was over. He quivered inside her for an instant, then shrank away. The hands left her hips; a coolness enveloped her.

Then she left, as fully as he did. She flew to a faraway place where her grandmother squabbled with Mrs. Cannanero about the best place to buy tomatoes, where nuns smelling of lavender repeated their prayers like pigeons cooing, and where, on an afternoon just like this one, you could get a hot dog and an egg cream and feel like the world belonged to you.

SIXTEEN

Mitch Whitman sighed at the aging Dodge pickup trundling ahead of him. Though its right taillight had blinked for the past twenty minutes, the truck had ignored an obvious turn and chugged on into the mountains ahead of him, one worn back tire wobbling.

Behind the truck, Mitch held his temper in check, trying to ignore the oily fumes that spewed from the bouncing tailpipe. Several times he'd been tempted to pull around and pass the vehicle with his middle finger raised, but something held him back. Two Confederate flag decals decorated the Dodge's battered bumper, and a lethal-looking pump shotgun lay racked across the back window. The brawny left arm of the driver periodically emerged to heave empty Budweiser cans out the window, and every half-mile or so the passenger's cowboy-hatted head would peer back to see if Mitch still followed them. Between the two men Mitch could see the smaller outline of a blonde woman who wore a black leather jacket with the collar turned up.

Wonder if they're brothers, he thought. *Wonder if that girl belongs to the driver or the passenger?*

He scowled as another beer can sailed toward a pine tree. Probably neither, he decided. Probably all three are from the same litter. Isn't that what they do up here?

Just as he started to pull off the road to let the beer drinkers get farther ahead, they abruptly turned down a narrow gravel path that slid off the edge of a cliff. *Wonder what they're going to do*, he thought, watching as the old Dodge became just two red taillights bouncing down the mountain. *Fuck, probably, then fight.* Mitch felt a sick ripple in his gut. *What would it be like to put it to your sister?*

He turned his gaze away from the bouncing taillights and sped up the road, for once grateful that Cal was the only sibling he had to contend with. His burst of speed was short-lived, though. The road twisted like a strand of curling spaghetti, and the Ford's automatic transmission hesitated, unable to decide between second and third gears. As he gained altitude the wind that whistled through the trees grew so cold he had to raise the window and turn the car's heater on. He couldn't imagine what it would be like to haul up these mountains on foot.

"Maybe old Thaddeus actually earned some of that gold," he said, grimacing at the thought of dragging a mule up into this flinty, dark wilderness.

For an hour he crept along a crumbling asphalt road that twisted through the peaks. According to his map, the Little Jump Off Trail should be up here, but he saw no hiking trails leading off the highway, nor any signs pointing to anyplace called Little Jump Off. Frustration heating his insides, he parked on one side of a wide curve and unfolded the Geological Survey map he'd bought in Atlanta. Pale green swirls like huge fingerprints indicated mountains and altitudes on the paper; darker lines followed the contours of the land. Red-and-white candy stripes illustrated medium-duty roads, broken black lines were jeep trails, and faint dotted lines represented footpaths. According to the map, Little Jump Off lay in the far right corner of the page, a dotted line springing from the single candy stripe that twisted through the sprawling Unicoi range. He checked his compass and his GPS positioner. By all indications, Little Jump Off should be exactly where he now stood.

"Well, fuck," he said aloud. "Does the U.S. Government not even know where this shit hole is?"

He scowled at the map, wondering if maybe Lou Delgado had been right. Stopping Mary Crow would not stop any ongoing investigation of him. Still, she might well be the only one who could piece it all together. The only one who had the *passion* to piece it all together. He'd felt it, on the witness stand.

"Mr. Whitman, now that we've established that you not only knew the deceased, and that you would have, if need be, included your brother in some of your moments together, how would you now describe your relationship with Sandra Manning?"

"I'm not sure I understand your question." Though he was exhausted, he was still determined to play his own version of coy. He was not going down easy for this Mary Crow. He saw his brother sitting beside his attorney, smirking at him. Cal was actually enjoying this! And he was up here sweating, trying to save both their asses.

"I mean, would you describe your relationship with Sandra Manning as platonic? Romantic? Intimate?"

Suddenly, his brain locked up. He knew every eye in the courtroom was staring straight at him, but all he could do was look at Mary Crow, his mouth moving in some vapid semblance of speech.

Then she pivoted, like a cat pouncing on a bird. "Were you not intimate with Sandra Manning, sir?" she demanded. Her voice flicked like the end of a whip.

"I'm . . . I'm not sure what you mean." It seemed to him he squeaked like a mouse.

"Intimate means sexual, Mr. Whitman," she said, in his face, hard. "Sexual means that the two of you engaged in sexual intercourse. I'm assuming you know what sexual intercourse means, Mr. Whitman. If you don't, I'll be quite happy to pause to let you consult your little brother!" She smiled at him then, her eyes the color of stone as everyone in the courtroom howled. His friends, the reporters, even Stacy Lamb, a girl from school he'd gotten to know. Cal was roaring, even his ashen-faced attorney was smiling as the judge pounded her gavel.

"You fucking bitch." Sitting in the car, he suddenly wanted to tear her picture into shreds. "When I find you, I'm gonna make you pay."

Yeah, right, he thought. *But first you've got to find her.*

He studied the map once more, then decided to start all over again, back at that fat girl's convenience store. He must have taken a wrong turn somewhere. He restarted the Taurus and for what seemed like hours he twisted through the mountains. Sometimes the scenery looked vaguely familiar, sometimes the contorted, acid rain–scalded trees made him wonder if he wasn't on another planet. He squeezed his eyes shut as a headache began to throb at the base of his skull. Just as the sun began to set he rounded a curve, skirting a peeling white concrete building that had once been a motel. In its weedy parking lot sat a lone figure dressed in buckskins and a full feathered headdress. Beside him stood a small, hand-lettered sign that read *Have Your Picture Taken With a Real Life Cherokee.* A rangy brown hound dog sat at the Indian's feet, his long pink tongue flopping from one side of his mouth.

Mitch pulled in. Maybe this Real Life Cherokee could tell him where the Little Jump Off Trail was.

"Hidy!" The Indian seemed to awaken as the shiny white Ford pulled beside him. He hopped up and walked over to the door, the dog ambling close behind.

The war bonnet topped a small, thin man with several teeth missing from his lower jaw. He grinned at Mitch. "Want your picture taken with a real Cherokee Indian?"

Mitch tried not to laugh. Though the Indian's sharp features were a dusky cinnamon, his manner was obsequious, his accent more Gomer Pyle than Sitting Bull.

Mitch was about to shake his head when suddenly an idea came to him—unbidden, yet full-blown and beautiful. A gold nugget dropped from the ancestral lap of Thaddeus Whitman. It might entail another murder, but after three, who would be counting?

He pushed his sunglasses higher on his nose and gazed sternly at the Indian. "Are you familiar with this area?" he asked, assuming his father's best command voice.

"I reckon I am," the Real Life Cherokee said. "Lived here all my life."

Mitch turned off his engine. "Do you know a trail called Little Jump Off?"

"Why, sure. It's over near the Tennessee line. You're way lost if you're looking for that."

Mitch dug in his wallet and flashed Mitchell Keane's Georgia student ID in front of the Indian's eager eyes. "My name's Keane. I'm with the Deckard County Sheriff's Department. I have urgent business with an attorney of ours who's supposedly vacationing on the Little Jump Off Trail."

The Indian gave a big grin. "You mean Mary Crow?"

For a moment Mitch didn't know what to say. He hadn't expected this feathered fool to actually know Mary Crow. "Possibly," he replied carefully. "Can you identify her?"

"About this tall." The Indian held up one hand at eye level. "Too skinny for my taste. Pretty, though. And smart as a whip."

"You know her?"

"Sure. Grew up with her, till her grandma stole her away to Atlanta."

"Look, I'm not familiar with this territory. If you can guide me to Mary Crow, there's a thousand dollars in it for you." Mitch pulled five hundred-dollar bills out of his wallet and held them between two fingers. "Half now and half when I reach her."

The Indian's eyes widened. He looked as if he'd never seen that much money in his life. He swallowed hard. "Let me go get Jonathan Walkingstick," he said. "He's the real tracker. Mary and her friends went up to Atagahi. Me and Jonathan can lead you up there in no time."

"The more trackers, the less pay," Mitch said decisively. "You bring in your buddy, your cut goes down by half."

The Indian took off his headdress, revealing badly cut dark hair sweat-plastered to the angular bones of his skull. He shrugged, disappointed. "Well, okay. I can get you where they're going. How about we leave at daybreak tomorrow?"

"How about we leave now," Mitch insisted. "Like I said, my business is urgent."

"We won't have but a few hours before dark."

"The pay goes down tomorrow." Mitch held firm.

"You can't go like that." The Indian eyed Mitch's thin yellow T-shirt and blue jeans. "It's cold up there."

"My gear's in the trunk," Mitch explained. "I can be ready in five minutes."

"I'll need to go home, then. Change my clothes and get a pack."

Mitch unbuckled his seat belt. "By the time you get back here, I'll be ready to go."

"Okay. Give me half an hour."

Mitch watched as the Indian tucked his headdress under his arm and hurried over to an ancient Toyota pickup. The dog trotted after him, leaping into the truck bed. Mitch scratched his head, amazed at how easily the Indian believed him. No wonder old Thaddeus had been able to move these nitwits to Oklahoma. "Hey, what's your name?" he called, half expecting the guy to say Crazy Horse.

"Billy Swimmer," the Indian replied as he tugged open the door of his truck and chugged off to get his supplies.

SEVENTEEN

Mary squinted at the thick maple limb as she made the final shadings on her sketch. When she was eight this tree had stretched up to heaven. She and her mother had often sat on its bench-sized roots—Mary drawing, her mother painting, both happy to sit under its sun-dappled shade. Sometimes her mother would hum an old tune, her eyes growing wistful. Mary guessed she was missing Jack Bennefield then, the handsome young husband and father they'd both known for far too short a time. Or maybe she was wishing that the spring would heal her wounds and deliver somebody new for her to love. But if her mother had hoped Atagahi might produce another love for her, she had died disappointed.

Now, Mary could almost see her sitting there, the sun casting blue highlights on her glossy black hair. She frowned. Her mother would now be over fifty. What would she have looked like? Chubby and diabetic like so many

Cherokees? Or would she be merely an older version of the pretty, slender woman with the infectious laugh? Death left a small recompense for your pain, Mary supposed. It took the ones you loved, but left them unblemished in your memory. She smudged in one last shadow on the page with the tip of her little finger and closed her paint box.

She climbed off the maple roots, listening for the voices of her friends. The soft Atagahi breezes usually carried words like the fluff of a dandelion, but only a raspy chorus of jar flies greeted her as she picked her way through the coarse sedge that grew among the boulders surrounding this side of Atagahi. Alex and Joan were probably fast asleep by now, she decided. They'd hiked hard as bear hunters these last two days, and they were just three tenderfeet Atlanta attorneys.

Rock by rock she began to climb. The sandstone felt like warm pumice on the palms of her hands, and she scaled the old boulders as she had as a child—leaping from rock to rock, nimble as a goat. With a final jump she reached the top and stood straight, smiling, hungry to see the whole vista of Atagahi spread out below her. Suddenly her smile froze. Though the bright green water still lapped lush and inviting, two women no longer sunned themselves on its rocks. The place was empty. No one was there at all.

Mary blinked. The warm wind ruffled her hair. *A joke*, she told herself, ignoring the sudden stillness of the place. *This has Alex's fingerprints all over it. They've decided to hide and see what I do.*

"Very funny, Alex and Joan!" she called. "You guys are real comediennes."

No one stood up from behind the boulders. No muffled giggles rose from the rocks.

"Okay, you guys," she called louder, now irritated. Mostly she loved Alex's goofy sense of humor, but she was not finding this prank amusing. "It worked. I was scared for a full two seconds."

Again, her words fell on hushed air.

Mary stared at the blank tableau, uncomprehending, then a tremor of fear rippled through her. *Something has gone wrong*, she realized as her heart began to beat like a snare drum. *Something has gone very wrong.*

"Joan? Alex?" she called, scraping her shins on the boulders as she raced carelessly down the rocks, desperate to hear one of Alex's goofy wisecracks.

No one answered. Her paint box slipped from her fingers, clattering down the steep incline in front of her. She passed the boulders as if in a dream—each stood like a mute sentinel, yielding none of Atagahi's ancient secrets.

"Joan! Alex!"

Only the rising wind sighed in reply. Frantically, she began to retrace their steps. They had dived in the water here, floated to there, climbed out here, sunned on the rocks there. *There.* Mary focused on one smooth rock. Could that long splotch on the far side of the boulder be blood?

She raced over, then her heart froze. A body lay sprawled on the rocky ground, the face covered with a black sweatshirt.

It was Joan. The legs were short, a small gold cross glittered between her breasts. Mud streaked across her upper thighs. Bloody teeth marks ringed one nipple. *Raped.* The word echoed through Mary's head. *Just like Mama.*

"No!" she cried. The rocks echoed her protest back at her, mocking her outrage.

She knelt and yanked the sweatshirt away from Joan's face. A blood-soaked cloth stretched her mouth in the rictus of a smile; her pretty white skin was blue. The delicate, sculpted shape that had once been her nose had been smashed into a grotesque red mangle. Mary put her hand against her cheek. It was cold. Joan was dead.

"No," Mary cried. "Not again!"

She wrestled the rag from Joan's mouth. What was it that you're supposed to do to people who can't breathe? Cover their noses and breathe into them? What if there's no nose left? Shit, she'd only seen this done on television. She reached inside Joan's mouth and pressed her tongue down with her thumb. With a huge gulp of air, she covered her friend's lips with her own and blew.

The sharp taste of blood filled Mary's mouth. She sat back and stared at Joan's face. Nothing. Joan remained motionless; her skin waxen. Breathing as if inflating a reluctant balloon, Mary tried a second time. Again, nothing.

"Come on," she demanded. Once more she filled her lungs until she felt light-headed, then she exhaled hard, willing every last molecule of her own oxygen down into Joan's body. There was no response.

"Joan!" She grabbed her bare shoulders and shook her, hard. "Breathe, dammit!"

For what seemed like an eternity Joan lay motionless, then suddenly her chest jerked as if she had the hiccups. Her belly began to rise and slowly the purplish cast seeped from her lips. Her eyes flickered once, and she woke up coughing, like someone pulled drowning from the sea.

"Oh, please keep breathing." Mary scooped her up in her arms and held her close. "Please . . ."

She clasped her for a long time, desperately trying to infuse her with her own warmth and strength. Slowly, the pale cheeks grew pink. Mary loosened her embrace and looked down at her. Joan's eyes were open but focusing a thousand lifetimes beyond Mary's shoulder. Her breath smelled of bile and blood.

"Joan?" Mary smoothed strands of sweaty hair away from the battered forehead. Joan stared straight ahead, seemingly unaware of her. "Joan, it's Mary. Can you hear me?" She did not respond. Mary turned and looked at the rock where Alex had lain. It bore neither the scuffed marks of a struggle nor the bloody detritus of a rape. Neutral, it revealed nothing. Alex might have been there ten minutes ago; Alex might have been a mirage they'd both imagined. She turned back to Joan, and said in as calm a voice as she could muster, "Joan, do you know where Alex is?"

Joan blinked. She tried to speak, but only a hoarse grunt issued from her throat.

Mary looked into Joan's eyes, willing her to establish some kind of connection. Though she wanted to scream and shake the words out of her, she took another deep breath and kept her voice low. "Joan, you've got to tell me what happened to Alex."

Joan swallowed, wincing in pain. "A man . . . came," she finally said in a reedy, old-woman voice. "Barefooted. He tied her arms together. Then he put a snake on me and pulled down my pants." Her words emerged as if English had suddenly become her second language.

Mary frowned. This sounded absurd. A barefooted man with a snake? She held Joan tight. She would squeeze the answers out of her if she had to. "But what happened to Alex?"

Joan shook her head, her body jerking as if she were having some kind of fit. "He tied her up. He put a snake on me. After that . . . Oh, Mary, I don't know!"

Joan's voice disintegrated into a high wail. Mary rocked her, repeating her name, trying to soothe her as a mother soothes a baby. A man had found the two of them. He'd raped Joan. But what had he done to Alex? A rage began to race through her veins. This could not be happening. Not again.

"Joan, I've got to find Alex."

"No!" Weeping, Joan grabbed Mary's neck and clung to her like a terrified child. "Don't leave me. Don't! He hurt me!"

"I've got to, Joan. Alex may be tied up and hurt, too." Mary unwrapped Joan's arms from her neck and got to her feet. "Sit right here. I'm going to look around the spring. You can watch me the whole time."

Joan grasped at Mary and kept keening, but Mary circled the spring, running like a frantic animal, looking for a boot or some blood or even a candy wrapper, but the water gave no clue and the rocks remained blank as untracked sand.

Please, she beseeched the Old Men as she searched. *Don't let me find her like Mama. I can bear anything except that.*

With Joan's cries reverberating in her brain, she worked her way to the tops of the boulders, finding nothing. She looked over the rocky walls that lifted Atagahi on two sides, dreading to see Alex sprawled there, her spine snapped against the boulders, but the cliffs were as empty of clues as the spring. As Joan's whimpers faded, Mary pushed through the spiky weeds that encircled the north and east sides of Atagahi. At the willow where they'd left their supplies, she found only the paint box she'd dropped when she fled down from the tree, and Joan's underpants, crumpled in the dirt.

Her breath was coming in hard gasps that scalded her throat. She had to stop. To think. She looked over at Joan. She'd stopped crying, but sat on the ground befuddled, like a newly hatched bird fallen from its nest, her face slick with tears and blood. Mary lifted one hand in a

wave, then stooped beneath the willow. She would get Joan a cigarette. That would make her feel better. Hell, maybe she would even
smoke one herself. She hurried to the tree, then her stomach
clenched. The spot where their packs should have been was empty.
Their clothes, their food, all their supplies had vanished. She gasped.
A cold night was coming and she and Joan were stuck in the middle
of a forest with only one complete set of clothes and a madman out
there, waiting to strike again.

EIGHTEEN

Mary peered into the shadow beyond the willow tree. At first the dark green pines and yellowing grass seemed no more revelatory than any other stretch of forest, but then something caught her eye. If she tilted her head at a certain angle, she could see a small line of trampled weeds heading west, up into the mountains. Instantly her pulse began to thrum like a timpani. She knew what had happened. The barefoot man had taken a prize, and that prize had been Alex.

"Not that," she pleaded out loud, her voice sounding like something trapped inside a jar. "Please don't let it be that."

She stood there, almost woozy, beseeching the Old Men for some other, more acceptable scenario. But nothing happened. As always, the mountains remained aloof, unaffected by her anguish. When their chilling breezes brought her nothing but the sad moaning of a million trees, she turned away from the willow and walked back down to Joan.

Joan sat small and trembling, her sweatshirt tugged down tight over her knees. Her gaze focused inward, as if she were struggling to make sense of some private horror movie that played on the back of her eyes. Mary sat down beside her.

"How are you doing?" She put her arm around Joan's shoulders.

"I'm cold." Joan's teeth chattered. "Where's Alex?"

"I don't know."

"What do you mean you don't know?" Joan's mouth curled down in surprise. "You're supposed to know these things, Mary. You always know these things."

"I don't know where Alex is, Joan. There's a trail leading west from the willow tree." Mary shook her head. "I think the barefoot man took her with him."

Joan made a choking noise that could have been either a laugh or a cry.

"He took our supplies, too." Mary noticed Joan's delicate little toes poking out from under her shapeless sweatshirt. "All we've got is what we're wearing."

"You've got lots of clothes," Joan tittered with a brittle hilarity. "And paints." She sniggered. "And my underpants!"

"That's right." Mary nudged the dirty white panties that lay beside the metal box at her feet. "We've got all that, plus one hell of a drawing of a maple tree."

Joan kept laughing, like Mary had just told her the best joke in the world.

Mary put her head down on her arms. At that moment she hated Joan. Hated her accent, hated her whining. Hated the mole on her thigh and her sophisticated perfume-and-tobacco smell. It was all she could do not to slap her and run into the mountains, screaming for Alex like a lunatic.

Stop it, she ordered herself, digging her nails into her palms. *Don't think like this now. Just concentrate on how to survive. Because if you don't, we'll all die.*

She turned her face up to the afternoon sun, a hot orange ball sliding down a blue sky. They might have two more hours of warmth, then it would be dark. And what would darkness bring? Frost? Bears? The barefoot man returning for some late-night fun and games?

Mary looked over at Joan. Her manic laughter had stopped and she sat picking at the dried smear of blood on her leg. A thin rope of snot dangled from her nose. Joan was crying without making a sound.

Mary rubbed her eyes, then said gently, "Why don't we go wash off? The warm water will make us both feel better."

Joan sat motionless as if she'd grown deaf. Mary repeated her question, then she finally stood up and pulled Joan to her feet. Wrapping one arm firmly around her waist, she led her toward the spring. Joan's legs moved stiff and bowed. When they reached Atagahi, she locked her knees like a balky brat and refused to go any further.

"Come on, Joan, just a few more steps. It'll make you feel better." Mary coaxed her toward the water.

"No!" Joan stared at her as if she'd never seen her before, as if they hadn't been close friends for the past eight years. "You can't make me go in there!"

"But it's just water." Mary knelt down and splashed water on her own face. "It feels good."

"Stop!" Joan shook her head in horror. "You don't know what he might have put in there!"

Joan's quivery words caught Mary so by surprise that she stopped splashing and let the water drip from her chin. She stared at Joan, then she realized what had happened. Joan was standing there, yet she wasn't. The real Joan had flown away, to someplace where the spring and the barefoot man and even Mary were not allowed admittance. The thing that stood before Mary was just a small, frightened husk of Joan. *You've got to take care of her,* Mary told herself, wiping the water from her eyes. *And hope the real person returns.*

"Maybe you're right, Joan," she answered quietly. "Maybe washing isn't such a great idea. Why don't you put your underpants back on, though? That way you'll stay warmer."

Joan stood frozen, still gazing at the water. Her face was badly bruised, one eye swollen shut. Blood leaked from her nose. Mary grabbed her panties and held them out in front of her. Obediently, Joan stepped into them, but Mary had to pull them up over her hips.

"Put these on, too," Mary said, shucking off her own jeans and holding them out. "You need them more than I do."

"What's this thing?" Joan fished Wynona out of the pocket while Mary snapped the jeans around her waist.

"Just the little statue my mother made me." Mary held out her hand. Joan had seen Wynona what—fifty, a hundred times? "Nothing for you to worry about."

"What are we going to do now?" Joan wobbled on her feet, as Mary stashed Wynona in the pocket of her sweatshirt.

"We need to find a safe place to curl up for the night." She bent and cuffed up the pant legs for Joan, a full five inches shorter than Mary. "It'll get cold when the sun goes down."

Joan said nothing.

Mary looked around the spring. If the barefoot man came back here, they would be trapped. It would be better to hide back in the forest, but it would also be considerably colder and much easier to lose their way. Mary frowned, then she spotted the top of the old maple tree, its yellow leaves fluttering over the highest Atagahi boulder.

"Let's go back up to the maple. The ground's soft up there, and the tree's big enough to protect us from the wind. It'll be easier to hear if anyone sneaks up."

Joan's unswollen eye rolled like that of a horse about to bolt. "Who do you think is going to sneak up on us?"

"Just some animal." Mary gifted Joan with a lie as she reached down and grabbed her paint box. "If a skunk decides to pay a call, I'd really like to have some warning." She smiled.

This quieted Joan and she followed Mary meekly back up to the maple tree, making no further protests. Already the air beneath the tree was blowing far crisper than Atagahi's caressing breeze. Mary knew that if Joan became hypothermic she would die, and at this time of year they would be lucky if the overnight temperature stayed above forty degrees. She shook her head. Joan had survived a rape and a horrific beating. Now Mary had to figure out how to keep her from succumbing to a simple nighttime chill. She unlatched her paint box and emptied it on the ground. Oil paint and drawing pencils tumbled into the grass along with her little sketch pad. That and the palette knife were all the tools they had to survive.

"Joan, do you feel strong enough to sit on this root and keep watch?"

"Watch for what?" Joan's eyes darted around as if panthers might be slinking through the trees.

"Skunks. Coons. Possums. Just sit there and let me know if any four-legged beast comes by."

"Okay." Gingerly, Joan lowered herself to the ground and peered intently into the forest.

"I'm going to scoop out a trench with this paint box," Mary explained. "We'll line it with pine needles to make it soft. Then we'll pack ourselves with leaves, lie down and spread more leaves over us like a blanket. That way we'll stay warm tonight."

Mary began to scrape furiously at the ground with the metal edge of her paint box. With dead eyes, Joan watched the woods.

Later, as the cool evening air rattled through the dying leaves, they sat beside a small trench lined with pine needles. Mary lifted her sweat-soaked hair off the back of her neck; her shoulders burned with fatigue. A job that would have taken twenty minutes with a shovel had taken her and her paint box two hours.

"This looks like a grave." Joan's voice twanged through her grotesquely swollen nose.

"I know," Mary replied, breathing in the trench's damp earth and pine aroma. "But it'll keep us out of the wind."

They watched a vermilion sun sink behind a crowd of inky trees, then Joan touched her nose and whimpered and started to cry again. Mary handed her two soft willow fronds she'd stripped from the tree near the spring. "Chew these," she told Joan. "They'll make you feel better."

"Is this what the Cherokees used?" Joan sucked the willow like a lollipop.

Mary nodded. "My mother said people used willow before they had aspirin."

Suddenly, Joan pulled the leaves from her mouth and began to sing. Though the tune was pretty and the notes came out in perfect pitch, they sounded ragged, like a bell with a damaged clapper.

"That's Puccini," she announced proudly when she'd finished, tears smearing the blood on her face. "What do you think?"

"Sounds great, Joan." Mary smiled. "Beautiful."

"Liar." Joan's upper lip curled in a vicious sneer. "It sounded like shit and you know it."

She sucked the willow fronds for a while, then yawned. "I want to go to sleep," she whined.

"Okay." Mary stood up and walked over to the pile of yellow maple leaves she'd managed to gather. "Then let's get ready for bed."

Joan followed Mary to the leaves, now docile as a lamb.

"I'm going to stuff these inside your shirt," Mary told her gently. "They'll help keep you warm."

She filled the back of Joan's sweatshirt with leaves, then she did the same to the front and the sleeves. Finally she pulled the hood up and tied it tight under Joan's chin. "There." She smiled. "You're insulated."

Mary gathered up the rest of the leaves and knelt beside the trench. "Which side do you want?" she teased.

Joan shrugged. Stiffly, she lowered herself into the trench and curled up tightly. Mary got in beside her and piled the remaining leaves and pine needles over them. She fitted her hips and legs close against Joan's back and wrapped her arms around her, in an embrace of survival. Not exactly a thermal blanket, she thought, but it would have to do. She only hoped it would be enough.

The leaves crackled as Joan twisted to face Mary. "You're not going to sleep, are you?" she asked fearfully, the quiver returning to her voice.

"No. I'm going to stay awake and make sure you stay warm," Mary promised.

"All night?"

"All night."

"You don't think the barefoot man will come back, do you?"

"No. I think he's gone far away." *And taken Alex with him.* She tightened her arms around Joan.

That seemed to satisfy Joan. She turned away and spoke no more. Mary could feel the tension slowly uncoil from her small body as her arms and legs relaxed into an exhausted slumber. "Sleep well, Joan," Mary breathed. *"Buona notte."*

For a long time she lay with her eyes open in the darkness, her friend cradled in her arms, keeping watch as the moon floated across a field of stars. Questions about Alex pricked her like stings, accompanied by a chorus of guilt. *How could you let this happen again?*

"I didn't mean to," she said. But then, she had never meant to do anything. She had never meant to make love to Jonathan that afternoon. She had never meant not to defend her mother. She had never meant to go off sketching when her two best friends needed her most. Yet somehow, she had failed them all.

She squeezed her eyes shut and pressed herself closer to Joan, the hard lump of Wynona digging into her stomach.

"Make me strong as Eagle," she whispered, repeating the old bird prayer her mother had taught her. "Swift as Hawk, and clever as Crow. And let me wake up tomorrow." She added her own final line, "with some idea about what in the hell to do."

NINETEEN

I wonder if I ought not to go back and stick that girl, just to be sure."

The man's voice rumbled above Alex's head like thunder. She grimaced as one of his boots pressed hard against the back of her neck, mashing her right cheek into a prickly carpet of pine needles. She lay belly-down on the ground, the tight red bandana stretching the corners of her mouth back in a stilted smile while her heart pounded in her chest like a triphammer.

"If I kill her for sure I'll rest easier," the man mused, sticking a pinch of tobacco inside his lower lip. "But going all the way back to Slickrock will put me an hour behind the light." He unbuttoned his shirt and withdrew the snake, holding the creature in his lap and pensively stroking the underside of its blunt head. "Sometimes, Buster, it's hard to figure out the best thing to do."

Alex looked away from the private moment

that had arisen between man and serpent. The dead pine needles beneath her smelled like turpentine and stung her cheek. Even though she was gagged, with her arms bound behind her, she wondered if now was not the time to throw a kicking, screaming, cactus-in-your-ass fit. Something like that might make this monster forget all about returning to the spring. Conversely, a fit might also make him mad enough to bustle back down the mountain just for spite.

"On the other hand, it would be a waste of time to go back down there. She's probably already a goner." His heavy boot pressed against Alex's neck. He hacked up something from his throat; a dark brown wad of goo splattered on the earth an inch from her nose.

"What about it, Trudy? Can your little buddy vaporize herself as good as you can?"

Alex felt him scowling down at her, waiting for her reply. Her jaws worked vainly to spit out words, but his foot shoved her face brutally against the ground.

The man laughed. "Well, of course she can't. You're the champ at that. What does she change into when you do the cougar? A skunk, probably. She'd got black pelts at both ends and all that white skin in between."

She used to sing opera, Alex protested silently as the man chuckled at his own joke. His laugh reminded her of a donkey, braying and snorting at the same time.

"Hell, she's been fucked good and kicked off a boulder and all she's got to wear is her little shirt and panties. Most women die pretty quick from silly shit like that." He laughed again. "As a special favor to you, Trudy, I won't go back. I'll leave her just like you used to leave those poor little half-eaten calves in Virginia. The cold always got them by morning. I expect it'll do the same to her."

Sensing the finality of his last remark, Alex closed her eyes. She had decided to do anything to keep him here. Thrash on the ground, pull him bodily through the trees, or hurl herself straight at him, tied up as she was. If she could just keep him away from that spring, then maybe Mary and Joan might make it out alive. She herself would likely be dead soon, but they still had a chance. She was almost certain she'd seen Joan move slightly before they left. Even if Joan was badly hurt, Mary could get her back to civilization.

Removing his foot from her neck, he buttoned the snake back inside his shirt, then grinned down at her. "Anyway, Trudy, you and I need to put some miles between us and Slickrock." He held up Mary's pack. "Gotta ditch this thing somewhere along the way."

Her small hope that whatever this was might end soon flickered and died. She was not going to be killed quickly, while she still had enough energy and courage to fight back. Her time would come later, after he'd worn her down physically and exhausted her resolve. *That's what it's going to be for me,* she realized as she fought back the scream that boiled up in her throat. *A damp, moldy death in some mountain cove courtesy of this maniac and his snake.*

He rose and jerked the long cord that tethered them together. Already it had cut a deep, raw welt around her waist. "Get up," he ordered, every trace of humor gone from his voice.

What would happen if she refused to move? She knew people always had a better chance if they acted quickly after an abduction. Maybe she should make her last stand right here, right now. She was almost as tall as he; it would be hard for him to hoist her over his shoulder and haul her through the mountains like a sack of meal.

"Get up, I said!" He gave the cord a vicious tug. It sliced into her bare skin like a hot knife. Still she did not move.

"Trudy!" he bellowed.

Out of the corner of her eye she saw his left leg jerk back, then felt pain rip into her side. The breath whooshed out of her involuntarily as a wave of agony engulfed her chest.

He tugged the cord again. "I'm telling you to get up, unless you want to kiss a few more ribs good-bye."

She lifted one hand in surrender and squeezed her eyes shut, willing a rising tide of nausea to recede. When she could breathe again, she raised up on her arms and pulled her legs beneath her. Her whole right side throbbed in a wall of fire. Ribs, he'd said. She'd never before realized how much pain could radiate from the bones that encased one's heart and lungs. Biting back a whimper, she pulled herself upright. Her legs buckled, as if she'd drunk too much tequila. He laughed when she fell and prodded her with his foot.

"That little love tap was for yesterday afternoon, when you snookered me with those buzzards. But that's all I'm gonna do about that, Trudy. The important thing to remember from here on out is that even though you're older than me, I'm in charge. Not Papa. Not Mama. Me. Little Heinrich, and my rule is this: People who don't mind get hurt. *Gehorchen* the next time I tell you to get up!"

Gehorchen? Alex blinked, bewildered. What language was he speaking? *Gehorchen* sounded nothing like the Spanish she'd grown up with in Texas nor the French she'd muddled through in college. Another tug seared across her midriff and she struggled to her feet, wobbling dizzily.

Tugging Joan's Yankees cap low on his head, he picked up his sack, slung his gun over his shoulder, and pulled her deeper into the shadows.

She staggered along behind him, clasping her throbbing side, sickened as the mottled camouflage pattern on his back blended into the dappled forest. Everything had happened so fast. She had been lying on the rock when she heard Joan say "Mary?" then she'd opened her eyes to see his hungry yellow gaze, then the snake, then his fist turning Joan's nose to mush. When his hands began scurrying over Joan's body like crabs, she'd closed her eyes, thinking crazily that if she didn't see it, it might not be happening. But she couldn't close her ears to Joan's soft mews of pain or the dead slaps her buttocks made against the sandstone. They'd gone on forever, then after one final expulsive groan, she heard scrabbling in the rocks, a muffled thud, then silence.

She waited, then, for his hands to start crawling on her. Instead, the cord that bound her legs loosened. He'd jerked her head forward and dragged her to her feet by a fistful of her hair.

"Come on, Trudy!" He'd tugged her off the rock and over to the willow tree. To her shame she'd obeyed him, docile as a naughty child being led away for a spanking, too scared to do more than sneak a hasty glance at Joan.

"Which one of those pursey-books is yours?" He'd pointed his gun at the two packs. She'd nodded at the green one. He'd fitted it on her naked back and then retied her hands in back of her, forcing her breasts to thrust out and together.

"*Saftig,*" he'd chuckled, caressing her right nipple with one filthy fingernail. He jammed her socks and boots back on her feet, then pulled out a long leather cord from his sack. "This time I've finally got you," he laughed, tying one end tight around her waist, then looping the other end around himself.

He hoisted Mary's backpack over his shoulder, then pulled Alex into the woods as someone might lead a mule. She craned her neck, desperate for one last glimpse of Joan or Mary. She thought she saw something once through a small gap in the trees, but the view was as elusive as everything else in these mountains, and soon the spring disappeared into a lattice of golden leaves.

Now with every step she stumbled as she tried to keep up. Who was this man? Who were Mama and Papa? He spoke a language she didn't recognize; he called her Trudy. He seemed to think that they had some kind of history together. Could he be some crazed environmental storm trooper that her corporate papermill merger had somehow pushed over the edge? No. Enviro-nuts tied themselves to trees or sabotaged chain saws. They didn't stalk attorneys like prey. And even enviro-nuts didn't wear live snakes for undershirts. That kind of psycho stuff was Mary's terrain.

Mary. At the thought of Mary, her throat tightened. What on earth had happened to Mary? Was she still sketching a tree somewhere? Or had he found her first and killed her without a sound? The realization hit her like a kick in the gut. Mary was dead. He must have sneaked up on her as she sketched and stabbed or strangled her. Otherwise she would have warned them, somehow. Mary. Killer Crow. The kind, quiet, haunted girl she'd loved since they were both eighteen. The woman she played racquetball with every Sunday morning and met for lemongrass soup at Bo-Thai's, and spent whole Saturdays following from bookstore to bookstore. The last time they were at Borders she'd gotten impatient with Mary, called her a hopeless bookworm who would rather read about sex than actually have it. She blinked back tears. Now she would happily carry Mary Crow on her back to every bookstore in America, if she only had the chance.

Another thought occurred to her. Her captor certainly looked old enough. And powerful enough. And he was definitely at home in these woods. The odds were astronomical, but not impossible. Her heart flopped in her chest. Could this snake charmer be the same man who murdered Martha Crow?

She looked up into the crystal-blue sky, struggling to clear her mind of all emotion. She must not allow herself the luxury of fear or rage or sorrow. Her feelings would consume her if she let them. Right now she had other things to take care of.

She straightened her shoulders and marched a little more briskly behind him. Although every movement sent a shock wave of pain up her right side, she began to test the knot that bound her wrists together. It was a thin rawhide rope, tied securely. She couldn't budge it, and wiggling her hands only seemed to pull it tighter. No dice there, she thought. She turned her attention to the cord that tied her to him. This was the same kind of rope, only thicker. A complicated knot rested just above her navel; the other end was laced around the man's waist. There was no way she could untie it with her hands bound behind her, and the rope was too thick to break with her weight alone.

Damn, she said to herself, touching the greasy-tasting bandana with the tip of her tongue. *Asshole's thought of everything.* For an instant she panicked, certain she was going to throw up and gag on her own vomit. *Center yourself*, she thought, remembering the one thing she'd learned in a hundred yoga classes. *Center yourself. Ride on the breath.*

She tried as best she could. Though every breath burned like fire, she concentrated on the mottled-green man ahead of her and breathed, trying to float above her pain.

Okay, Sarah Alexandra McCrimmon. You might not be able to get out of this alive. But just once, before you die, you're going to make this bastard pay for Mary and Joan and maybe even Martha Crow. He's going to wish that on this particular Saturday he'd picked wildflowers instead of women.

TWENTY

Billy Swimmer leaned into the sharp curve of Bear Wallow Road, the bald back tires of his truck squealing. Homer, his Plott hound, braced himself against the side of the truck and turned his nose to the wind, his ears blowing back like little wings on either side of his head. Billy punched the pickup into third gear and climbed the rest of the way up the hill hunched forward over the steering wheel, as if that might propel the old truck faster. An impatient stranger with a thousand dollars was waiting for him, but who knew for how long? Billy figured he had about fifteen minutes to pack his gear and break the news of his adventure to Tam.

He turned up the steep, weedy driveway that led to their trailer and pulled the truck up by the front door. He hadn't had time enough to think of a way to make this go down sweeter, so he guessed he would just have to tell Tam the truth. He grabbed his feathered headdress from the passenger seat and raced to the front door, Homer following at his heels.

"Billy!" Tam looked up, surprised, as they came in the door. She sat cross-legged in the faded green La-Z-Boy that sprawled in front of the TV set. Pink rollers sprouted from her head and she dabbed gold eye shadow on her upper lids while a lady on the shopping channel cooed over a fake diamond bracelet. "How come you're home so soon?"

"Something happened." Billy placed the headdress in the middle of the card table they used as a dinette. Homer's toenails clicked on the linoleum as he headed for his water dish in the kitchen.

Tamara's blue eyes darkened with fear. "Zell Crisp didn't try to beat you up again over that money you owe him, did he?"

"No, nothing like that." Billy took a deep breath. This was not going to be easy. Tam had been planning this evening for months. He walked over and knelt down beside her chair.

"Tam, I need to tell you something, and it's God's own truth. A few minutes ago a man came by and offered me a thousand dollars to lead him to Mary Crow."

Tam snorted. "Yeah, right, Billy. And Dick Clark just dropped by here with balloons and a big ol' check from the magazine sweepstakes." She checked one eye in her makeup mirror.

"No, honey, it's true. I swear." Billy sat down on the floor and put a tentative hand on Tam's foot. "This man's from Mary's law office down in Georgia. They need her for some kind of emergency. Probably some criminal's escaped and she needs to help catch him."

"What's Mary Crow doing back up here? I thought she lived in Atlanta with that rich old grandmother of hers."

"She's gone camping with some of her friends." Billy shrugged. "I talked to Jonathan this afternoon."

"Then why don't you let Jonathan go after her? He's the hotshot tracker. And he'd like nothing better than a good excuse to go running after Mary Crow."

Billy stared at the floor, guilty. "The man said the more who track, the less the pay."

"So?" Tam began to dab moisturizer under her left eye.

"So this fella's in a real swivet—he needs to find Mary as soon as he can. I'm going to lead him up to Atagahi by myself." Billy coughed. "So I guess we won't be going out tonight."

Tamara turned her eyes away from her mirror and stared at him, stunned. "We *what?*"

Billy kept looking at the floor. "I don't reckon we can go out. Not tonight, anyway."

"Billy, this is our anniversary! We haven't been anywhere in months. My sister's coming all the way from Robbinsville to watch Michael."

"I know, Tam, but do you know how far a thousand bucks would go? I could get my fiddle out of hock and pay off Zell. Then I could stop wearing those stupid feathers and make some real money playing music. We might could even take Michael to Dollywood."

Tamara glared at him, unsmiling. "Billy, if this is just some scheme so you can get more money to waste gambling with Zell Crisp, I'll kill you—"

"No. I swear. This guy just drove up in this brand-new Taurus while I was out by the picture stand. He's big and strong, but he talks just like a lawyer. He's waiting for me right now." Billy inched his hand up Tam's leg.

She started to blink away tears. "Couldn't you just *tell* him how to get to Atagahi? We could use old grocery sacks and some of Michael's crayons and draw him a map."

Billy shook his head. "I don't think he'd pay me a thousand dollars for a map on a grocery sack."

"Oh, Billy." Tam wiped at her eyes with the back of her hand. The gold shadow smeared. "Do you have to?"

"I'm sorry, honey," Billy pleaded. "I'll make it up to you, I swear. When he gives me my thousand dollars we'll spend the first hundred of it on us. Just ourselves."

"Promise?" Tam's voice sounded like the mew of a kitten.

"Cross my heart." Billy made an X over his chest.

"Promise you won't go betting any more money on the football games with Zell Crisp again? Ever?"

"Never again," Billy swore. "This time I learned my lesson." He got up from the floor and kissed her. At first she held her mouth hard against him, then slowly her lips softened, forgiving him once again.

"Well," he said finally, hating to pull away from her. "I guess I'd better go pack."

Tam frowned. "You pack quiet, Billy. Michael's got the earache again and I just got him down for his nap."

Billy tiptoed into the bedroom. Two-year-old Michael lay in the middle of the bed, a small hump covered by a red wool blanket. Billy leaned over and looked at him. The child slept curled on his stomach with his mouth open, his nose encrusted in green snot.

Billy remembered the last time they'd taken him to the clinic, sitting in a smelly waiting room crowded with other Indians. The old woman next to them had blistered her fingers on a hot skillet; the man on the other side had pneumonia. They'd waited for hours, Michael crying, pulling at his ears, then finally lying limp with fever in Tam's arms.

"This child has chronic otitis media," Billy remembered the young doctor had told them when their turn finally came. "If you'd put tubes in his ears, you'd solve all his problems," the doctor had said, his voice scolding. Billy and Tam could only look at each other, their faces hot with rage and shame. They could barely afford Michael's antibiotics. There was no way they could pay to have tubes put inside his ears. Before any more light-eyed doctors in crisp white coats could offer any more advice, they put the boy's jacket back on him and hurried out of the clinic. The memory still brought a bitter taste to Billy's mouth. Didn't that doctor think he would buy Michael tubes for his ears, if he could?

"Maybe now, Big Guy." Billy leaned over and kissed the little boy's thick black hair. "This tracking job is gonna turn things around, I know it." Michael smiled once in his sleep, then stuck his thumb in his mouth and snored on.

Billy unbuttoned his buckskin Indian suit and hung it in the closet, next to Tam's old prom dress. Maybe, he thought, this job really would be some kind of turning point. The Freight Hoppers were holding a place for him, if he could ever get his fiddle back. Everybody loved their music, and they made shit pots of money. He fingered the fringe on the Indian suit and sighed. Maybe, if things went just a little right this time, he would never have to dress up in these stupid feathers again.

He pulled on a pair of old jeans and the hooded Tennessee sweatshirt Tam had given him three Christmases ago, then he carefully tugged his bedroll from beneath the bed, trying not to jiggle the mattress and disturb his son. After lacing up his field boots, he grabbed his harmonica from the dresser and reemerged to face Tam once more.

"Look, Tam, since you've already got your sister lined up, why don't you and Lena Owle go on out tonight?" He walked over to the feathers and pulled two five-dollar bills from inside the headband. "Here's what I made today. Take it down to Robbinsville and play some bingo. Maybe you can win the coverall."

Tamara sniffed loudly. "You know I never have any luck when you're not there."

Billy knelt down beside the La-Z-Boy and smiled. "I bet you will tonight, though. I've been feeling lucky ever since that man drove up."

"When will you be back?"

"Day after tomorrow, I reckon. Atagahi's a day and a half away."

"And you'll really have a thousand dollars?"

Billy nodded. "That's what the man said." He leaned over and kissed her. Her breath smelled like peppermint, and the sweetness of her tongue flooded his mouth.

"I'll miss you, honey," he whispered.

"Me, too."

"Gotta get going now, though." He stood up. "Before that fella finds somebody else to take him. We got anything I can take to eat?"

"There's the cornbread and chicken from Thursday night. I thought we'd go to the store tomorrow."

"That's okay," Billy said. "It'll be enough." He went into the kitchen, where he wrapped some stale cornbread and a chicken leg in an old dishtowel and stuck it down the front of his shirt. Then he picked up his bedroll and walked toward the door.

"Aren't you taking Homer with you?" Tamara asked. The dog sat by the front door, his eyes imploring Billy.

"I hadn't thought to."

"Oh, take him with you, Billy." Tamara climbed out of the La-Z-Boy and put her arms around his neck. "Look at the way he's looking at you. He'll just keep me and Michael up all night, whining."

"Oh, okay." Billy smiled. "Come on, Homer."

The dog's tail thumped against the front door at the sound of his name. Billy kissed Tam one final time. "See you later. Go out and have some fun with Lena tonight."

"You just come home with that thousand dollars, Billy Swimmer," Tam said, smiling as Billy gathered Homer and his bedroll. "You find Mary Crow and come on home. And don't you spend a dime of that money before you walk back in this house."

"Not a chance, darlin'," Billy said, winking at her. "Not a chance in the world."

TWENTY-ONE

Brank dragged Alex higher into the woods. He hauled her up the mountain without speaking, stealing little glances at her over his shoulder, his eyes glittering beneath the Yankees cap. After a time he seemed to relax about her escaping; from then on he would turn and ogle her breasts with a slack-jawed gape, as if he'd never seen a human female before. At first his leering humiliated her, then it made her mad. By late afternoon she wished she could sharpen her nipples and poke out his eyes with them.

After twisting through a dense growth of buckeyes and sugar maples, they turned onto something that had once been a kind of road. Waist-high weeds and scrub cedar trees choked most of it now, but a faint flat bed was still discernible. She figured it was probably pointless, but she began walking slew-footed, dragging her feet through the long grass, trying to mark a trail. Her brothers would be proud, she thought, picturing the three of them as she surreptitiously bent the thorny stalk of a thistle. Alexandra bought the farm, but she left a hell of a good trail buying it.

But then a current of excitement sizzled through her. How could she be so stupid? She had a weapon! She had something the Snake Man knew nothing about! Right this moment she was carrying the tiny cell phone that Charlie had slipped in the bottom of her pack. If she could somehow hold on to it until this maniac fell asleep, she'd be able to call for help. *All right,* she told herself as she continued to bend thistles with her feet. *Just thirty seconds alone with that phone and this little kidnapping will be over.*

When the western horizon turned fuchsia, they stopped on a ridge where a narrow river boiled thirty feet below them. The man dropped his sack and gun, but he did not loosen the leather cord that bound them together. He moved closer to Alex and grinned. "Now we'll see what you've got in your little bag."

He turned her by her shoulders and opened her pack. *Not the phone,* she pleaded silently, wincing as his hands nudged the straps against her blistered back. *Please don't let him dig deep enough to find the phone. . . .*

"Hey!"

She froze.

He pulled out a fistful of candy bars and several packets of freeze-dried food. "We've got candy, lasagna, chicken titty-something. Gosh, Trudy, you were gonna eat like a queen up here."

I sure was, Alex thought, holding her breath as he rummaged deeper in the pack. *Regular five-star dining alfresco.*

"Here's some little underpanties and some little makeup things and—lookee here! What's this?" His hand plunged deeper into the pack. She closed her eyes.

"Uh-oh," he said in a singsongy voice. "Look what I found!"

She opened her eyes. The small red cell phone waggled before them.

With a great sagging in her chest, she watched as he unfolded the phone.

"Sorry," he giggled, holding the thing to his ear, and miming a conversation. "Trudy's not here. I don't know where she went, but she won't be back for a long, long time."

Stop. She wanted to beg him. *Just let me make one call. Let me tell my Mom good-bye.* But he took the phone away from his ear, cocked his arm back like a baseball pitcher, and threw it toward the river. It riffled through leaves, then she heard nothing but her own breathing, as if she were the last person left alive on earth.

He untied her hands, yanked off her backpack and loosened the cord from her waist. He pulled the sour bandana from between her lips, then he began to speak. "Now, Trude," he said, his beard tickling her cheek, his breath hot in her ear. "Even though you can't talk on your pretty phone, you can still scream as loud as you want. There isn't anything to hear you up here but chipmunks and meadow mice. *Verstehen?*" He tied her ankles together with rope. Of course she understood that. She could scream, but no one would hear. She could run, but only in hobbled strides that would carry her nowhere.

Alex slumped on the ground as the man pawed through the rest of her supplies. After finding Mary's fire starter, he dragged a pine log and some twigs together and soon a bright orange blaze crackled into the chilly blue air. Though the log popped with resin and sent fiery sparks exploding up like tiny rockets, Alex scooted as close to it as she dared, seeking to warm away the damp cold that had seeped into her bones. He looked up as he tinkered with the backpacker's stove and saw her shivering.

"Here," he said, plucking her denim jacket from her pack. He tossed it toward her. "That should warm you up."

She nestled into it gratefully, drawing her legs close to her chest and tucking her chin beneath the collar. The jacket smelled of the cedar closet under her mother's stairs, and without warning she was back in Texas, in the old house on the edge of a cottonwood grove where the earth lay white and flat as a biscuit. The sounds of her family in a spring twilight came to her clearly: her mother clattering pots on the stove while Jacinta the cockatiel shrieked a commentary of the news on TV. The screen door banged and her father clomped into the kitchen, his barn boots covered with dust. Outside, the dry desert wind that whispered all the way from Mexico rattled the windows, carrying with it the sound of her brothers' backyard football game.

"Go long, Jack!" David yelled. "Go *long* and cut right!" Alex smiled. It all seemed distant as a fairy tale. Tears dampened her eyelashes as she pulled the coat close against the dankness. Though she had lived most of her adult life trying to scrub away the yellow dust of Texas, she would give everything right this minute if she could go back and breathe that dry air and tell them all how much she loved them.

"You get spaghetti tonight, Trudy." The man thrust a pouch of hot food at her, then sat down. "I get lasagna. Eat it before it eats you."

They ate to the sound of the fire crackling and popping. The man shoveled the sticky pasta into his mouth. Alex ate slowly with her fingers, forcing down little bites.

After they finished, the man sipped what she assumed was moonshine, offering the jar to her with a wink and a tipsy display of his yellow incisors. She shook her head and said:

"I want some water." Her voice squeaked like a rusty hinge.

"Why, Trudy!" The man's eyebrows shot up in surprise. "You can talk. Here I was thinking the cat permanently got your tongue." He pulled the water bottle off her pack and handed it to her. She uncapped it and drank. The water cooled her parched throat and made her feel suddenly sharper, as if she'd awakened from a deep sleep. Maybe now would be a good time for a little voir dire, she decided. Find out the truth, so you'll know what you're up against. She lowered the water bottle from her lips and cleared her throat.

"Who exactly are you?" She flinched at the bluntness of her question, but she couldn't call her words back.

"Who am I?" The man grinned. "You know who I am. We left Pennsylvania on the same day. And you've dogged my trail for the past thirty years. 'Course mostly you've had four legs and big teeth instead of those big tits."

Schizophrenic, Alex thought. *Truly nuts.* Still, she had to keep going. "Refresh my memory, then," she told him, forcing a smile. "Changing from one species to another takes a toll. A lot of brain cells die in the process."

"I bet they do," he chortled. "Surprised you have any left at all."

Alex took another sip of water. "You say we lived in Pennsylvania?" she asked tentatively.

The man nodded. "Papa was Herr Fleischman's butcher."

"Are we German?"

"Papa had been a POW. He spent most of the war raising hogs in Alabama."

"I can't remember our last name."

"Brank," the man replied. "Papa was Rudy, Mama was Anna. You were Gertrude but we called you Trudy. Remember what you called me?"

"What?"

"*Esel. Dumpfbacke.* Queer. You thought all those names were a scream. You know what I thought?"

"No."

Brank gave a low chuckle. "I'm gonna show you what I thought," he promised, with a leer. "Later."

She was about to ask him about Martha Crow when abruptly he leapt to his feet. "Time for something else now."

He tossed the water bottle over by the pile of clothes and jerked the jacket from her shoulders. Slowly, his eyes riveted to hers, he began to remove his clothes. First his boots and socks, then his pants, then he pulled the snake from his shirt.

It's not poisonous. The realization stung her as he flung the reptile back into his sack. *He conned Joan and me. He snookered us with some harmless thing you'd find in a garden.*

Finally he stood before her naked, with his knife in his right hand.

Her heart raced like a hummingbird's. It was her turn now. He was going to get even with her for everything this Trudy had ever done to him.

He pushed her backwards on the grass and pulled her feet-first over to the fire. Then he balanced the knife on a stone, suspending the blade over the hot embers. The skin above his beard glowed like some ancient bronze mask.

"Now," he said softly. "Raise your arms over your head. And don't try any of your tricks, Trudy. I can slit your throat a lot faster than you can grow fangs and a tail."

She stared at him, mesmerized and unable to move.

"I said get 'em up!" He jerked her arms above her head. The blisters on her bare back burned like a hundred tiny flames.

"There," he muttered, when he'd positioned her to his satisfaction. "That's better." He straddled her and sat down, resting his whole weight on her stomach. His scrotum felt like a sack of clammy dough against her belly, and his greasy, curdled smell made her gag.

He smiled. "You probably pick up a lot of these things, living in the trees and all." He put his thumbs together and spread his hands like a fan. Then he placed his fingertips at her hairline and slowly combed through her scalp, stopping once at the crown of her head, then traveling down to the nape of her neck. Alex squeezed her eyes shut and bit back a scream.

"None there!" he announced. He ran his fingers over her face, then down her neck and over each clavicle, ruffling the pale stubble in her armpits. He continued down both arms, then returned via her shoulders. When he reached her breasts he scooted down so he straddled her hips.

She opened her eyes and watched him fondling her flesh. He stared, grinning, at her breasts, caught up in some interior fantasy of his own design. "Good old Trudy," he whispered. "I've wanted to do this for so long."

He rolled off her and worked his way down her legs to her feet, then back up the inside of her thighs. She felt his breath on her pudenda, then his fingers explored her pubic hair. She clenched her jaw, waiting for him to jab his penis inside her, but that did not happen. Instead, he left her and spread out on the other side of the fire and repeated the entire process on himself. At last he sat up, disappointed.

"No tick dances tonight," he said wistfully.

Alex lowered her arms then. Whatever he had just done, he had apparently finished. She kept one eye on him as she sat up and pulled her jacket back on. Curling herself into a tight ball, she watched as Brank stared into the fires; then the dancing, hypnotic flames pulled her in, too.

She remembered the night before—how irritated she'd been when Joan had pressed Mary about Jonathan, then how happy when Mary had told them both the whole story. How many lifetimes ago had that been? If she closed her eyes she could hear the happy, brandy-tinged laughter of their campfire, yesterday, when they were whole and safe and unaware that this Brank creature even existed.

Suddenly she almost laughed out loud. Before they went to sleep she'd wanted to tell them *ghost stories*, for God's sake.

Brank stood up and stumbled over to her. "You need anything?"

She shook her head.

"Then I'll just tuck you in for the night." Grinning, he tied her ankles tighter together and bound her hands in front of her. "See what a good brother I am?" He threw her jacket on top of her.

"Tomorrow we'll talk more." He raised one eyebrow at her and chuckled. "I hate for anybody to think there was a serious case of sibling rivalry between us."

Alex watched as he moved to the other side of the fire and folded himself into his bedroll. "Sweet Jesus," she said softly. "I am in so much trouble."

TWENTY-TWO

Mary's eyes flew open. She lay flat on her back in the trench, shivering in only her sweatshirt and underpants. All night she'd struggled to stay awake and listen for the snapping of a twig or the rustling of leaves, but exhaustion finally relegated her to a jittery no-man's-land between sleep and reality, where she was buffeted between a dark nothingness and the feeling that fat, black spiders were crawling up her legs.

Now she lay fully awake, but she was unable to bring herself to look at Joan. She was terrified that she'd failed again, and the living, breathing woman she'd tried to keep warm last night would now be a corpse—a dead thing whose soul had been sucked away by the deep forest cold. *And what will you do then, Mary Crow?* the Old Men seemed to murmur.

Taking a deep breath, she extended her left hand. Her fingers crackled through their leaf-blanket, then she felt Joan's shoulder. Her skin still felt warm. Gently, Mary touched her arm. Almost imperceptibly, a muscle twitched.

Thank God. However damaged Joan might be, at least she's still alive.

She got up quietly and stretched her cramped arms and legs, then started to make her way back down to the spring. She had to make sure the trail she'd glimpsed yesterday hadn't been some wishful hallucination. When she reached Atagahi, she hobbled over to the willow tree and peered into the woods. In the morning light, the tamped-down grass still beckoned like a ribbon, leading up the mountain. Her heart flopped in her chest. Alex's trail. Mary knew it as surely as if someone had lettered a sign with an arrow pointing straight ahead.

Troubled, she walked back to the spring and sat down beside the water. She needed to think. That Joan needed to get back to civilization was clear. Doctors and rape counselors could surely salvage the rest of her life. But what about Alex? If Mary took Joan back to Little Jump Off now, it would be at least eighteen hours before any kind of official search could be launched for her, and Mary already knew how most official searches ended. A sudden, cold realization blew through her. If she took the time to take care of Joan, she would never see Alex again.

"I can't let that happen," she said aloud. Alex had never deserted her. Never. She couldn't just walk Joan back to Little Jump Off and leave Alex stranded here alone.

And yet, if Joan was still in the terrible state she'd been in last night, how could she do otherwise? What could you do with someone who could barely pull up her own underpants?

She gazed up at the mountains. Now the color of dusty plums, they seemed to be mocking her. *Little Mary Crow has really gotten herself in a fix this time.* Here she sat in the middle of a half million acre forest with one friend gone in body, the other gone in mind. Could she possibly save both? *Little Mary Crow,* the Old Men seemed to sneer, *would more likely save neither.*

She watched as the sun glittered over the top of the highest Atagahi boulder. It would be hard, perhaps impossible, but she had brought Joan and Alex to this place. It was up to her to bring them home. "Both," she vowed, glaring at the Old Men as she rose to her feet. "I'm going to save them *both.*"

She drank some water, then climbed back up to the maple. Joan slept on, her position unchanged. She breathed with her mouth open, blood crusted on both nostrils. Her right eye was swollen shut, the left one caked with mucus. Mary touched Wynona in her pocket for luck, then crawled close to whisper her name.

"Joan?"

"Stop!" Joan's legs twisted in the trench, as if trying to squirm away from something.

"Joan . . ." Mary whispered again.

"Stop!" Joan wailed. She began to slap at Mary, flailing her face and shoulders.

"Joan." Mary grabbed her hands. "Wake up. You're having a dream."

Joan jerked her hands away, then turned toward Mary and tried to open her eyes. "I can't see!" she cried, sitting up, feeling her face. "My eyes! He's done something to my eyes!"

"It's okay," Mary soothed. "Hold still." She pulled the waistband of her sweatshirt up, spit on it, and gently wiped Joan's good eye. Slowly, the lids parted and revealed a slit of pupil.

"What's wrong with my eyes?" Joan's cry tore at Mary's heart.

"Nothing." Mary stroked her cheek. "Your right eye is swollen because your nose is probably broken. Your left eye had crusted with some mucus."

"Are you sure?"

"Yes. Your eyes will be fine."

Joan crawled away from her and huddled in a tight knot at the edge of the trench, trembling. "These leaves itch. I'm cold."

Mary leaned over and pulled off a leaf that dangled from Joan's matted hair. "Let's go down to the spring," she suggested. "We can wash. That'll make us warmer. You'll feel better then."

Joan made no further protests as she rose from the trench. Mary helped her shake more leaves from under her sweatshirt, then, with Joan clutching her arm like a frail old woman, the two picked their way down through the boulders.

At Atagahi, tendrils of steam curled into the chilly morning air. Mary heard the familiar trill of a warbler, and farther off, the cawing of a crow.

"I'm going to wash off now," she told Joan as she pulled off her sweatshirt. "You might want to do it, too."

Mary knelt and rinsed her chest and neck, watching to see what Joan would do. Her friend did not move.

"Here." Mary stood up and reached for Joan's sweatshirt. "Let me help you."

"I can do it myself," Joan snapped. She pulled off her sweatshirt and dropped to her knees, splashing water clumsily over her neck and arms. Mary noticed that red streaks now radiated from the bites on her bruised breasts. The barefoot man had marked her.

"They say Atagahi will heal you if you get your wounds in battle," Mary said as Joan rinsed underneath her arms.

Joan's laugh sounded like splintering glass. "I hate to break it to you, Mary, but I think they lied."

Joan began to feel her face with her fingers, tentatively exploring the newly arranged contours of her nose. Once pert, it had become a bulging topography of angry red tissue, topping the purple bruise that stained most of her throat and jaw. She looked at Mary.

"How bad am I?"

"It probably feels worse than it looks," Mary lied, feeling like some absurdly optimistic nurse in a field hospital.

Joan's bloodshot eye glittered. "Mary, tell me the truth."

"It looks bad." This time Mary answered honestly, but she still did not tell Joan that it looked far worse than bad; that it really looked like some cleanup hitter for her beloved Yankees had mistaken her face for a fastball. "But it's fixable."

"Yeah, right." Joan's chin began to tremble. "Maybe with enough plastic surgery, I might someday approach human again."

Joan pulled her sweatshirt back on. Mary watched her, searching for some better words of comfort to offer. Everything she came up with sounded so inadequate. *All my words are weapons*, she realized. *They condemn. They convict. Comfort is not an active part of my vocabulary.*

"I'm hungry," Joan announced, staring into the spring.

"Drink some water." Mary pulled on her sweatshirt. "It'll fill you up."

Joan eyed the pool. "Is that safe to drink?"

"It'll probably give us diarrhea."

"Terrific."

As Joan began to slurp handfuls of water, Mary studied the boulder where Alex had lain. It stood there as unrevealing today as it had yesterday. Atagahi had divulged all the clues it was going to reveal, but the trail was something else. With a quickening of her pulse, she turned and looked again at the trampled grass that beckoned into the forest. All at once she knew what she must do.

Bracing herself, she turned. "Joan, I need to tell you something."

"What?"

"I'm going after Alex." She blurted the words out quickly, as if she were confessing something shameful.

The spring water dribbled from Joan's hand as she turned to look at Mary. "What did you say?"

"I'm going after Alex. There's a trail. I can follow it. I'll build you a little nest under that boulder over there. You'll be safe here until I come back."

Joan squinted her good eye. "That's not funny, Mary. The man who took Alex is a monster. He'll smash your face to pulp, then he'll kill you."

"I'm not kidding," Mary told her steadily. "And I'll take a rock or a stick or something to use as a weapon."

"Hey, that should really shake him up," giggled Joan. "Mary Crow and her big, bad rock."

Mary blushed. Her words did sound ludicrous. Women with rocks didn't subdue men armed with knives. "It doesn't matter about the weapon. I'll be careful."

"You'll be *careful*?" Joan's brows lifted. "I'm so glad, Mary. I'd hate for anything to happen to you."

Mary blinked at Joan's sarcasm. Yesterday she'd been a trembling, dazed victim whom she'd warmed in her arms. Overnight she'd grown a hostile edge that she swung like a scythe. Mary felt like she was talking to a stranger.

Joan broke the painful silence between them. "Can I ask just one question before you leave?"

"Sure."

"What about me? That man hurt me. I haven't eaten since yesterday and I've shivered all night in a leaf-lined grave not fit for a rat. Any chance of my seeing some kind of doctor?"

"I'll take you to one when I get back."

"But I need to go now!" Joan cried, a deep red flush crawling up her throat. "I need food. I need clothes. I need to wake up in a bed that's in a room with a door that has a lock on it." She buried her hands in her thick, snarled hair. "I want to go home!" she wailed.

"If I take you back," Mary said, "We'll never see Alex again."

Joan raised her head and blinked, incredulous. "Mary, Alex was kidnapped by a madman. You don't seem to understand . . ."

"No—"

"Mary, she's already dead! She was probably dead yesterday, before the sun went down—"

"Shut up!" Mary raised her hand as if to ward off a blow. If those words touched her, they might come true. "It doesn't matter, Joan. I'm still going after her."

"And what am I supposed to do while you're gone?"

"Rest here. In three days they'll miss you at your office, and Jonathan knows where we went. Somebody will show up looking for us. And I'll be back." She looked into Joan's savaged face. "I wouldn't suggest this if I didn't think it would work."

"Of course you would," Joan sneered. "Don't you think I know that Alex is the only thing you care about?"

"That's not true, Joan."

"Yes, it is. Everybody talks about it."

"It's not like that, Joan . . ."

"You two are worse than an old married couple." Joan's mouth puckered into a vicious line. "You're disgusting."

"I'm sorry you feel that way." Her face burning, Mary bent down and began to tighten the laces on her boots.

"So you're just going to tie your damn shoes and go?" Joan's taunt crackled with anger.

Mary concentrated on her boots. "I'm sorry you're hurt. I'm sorry you're upset. But right now, you need to stay here. And I need to find Alex."

"No!" shrieked Joan, her fists clenching. "I won't stay! Look what happened the last time you left me alone! If it wasn't for you, none of this would have happened!"

The trees, the mountains, the universe itself seemed to reverberate with the words Joan had uttered. Had they been a lie, or even an exaggeration, Mary could have shaken them off. But she knew too well the truth of them, and the weight of that truth felt like shackles clamped around her heart.

"That's a pretty heavy load, Joan," she finally managed to utter.

"Oh, yeah?" Joan ran her fingertips along her mauled nose. "Well, why don't you try wearing my new face for a while? See what kind of load *that* is."

Mary sucked in her breath. "Okay." She glared at Joan, trying to squelch a sudden fury of her own. "Here's the deal. I'm going after Alex. You can either stay here and be safe, or you can come with me. It'll be uphill the whole time, through country far rougher than this. You'll be colder and hungrier, and you might just come face-to-face with that scary old barefoot man again, but if you'd rather do that, fine."

"I would rather lie in hell with my back broken than stay here another second," Joan snarled.

"Terrific," snapped Mary. "Then let's go."

TWENTY-THREE

They started from the willow tree, Joan wearing her own sweatshirt and Mary's jeans, Mary clad only in her sweatshirt, underpants and hiking boots. Before they left they both scribbled notes in charcoal on an Atagahi boulder. Mary explained what had happened and where they were going; Joan wrote an odd, disjointed letter half in Italian, saying good-bye to her parents in Brooklyn, her brother in Chicago, her sister in Washington, D.C.

"Here." Mary opened her paint box as they started to follow the trail. She handed Joan a small silver tube. "I've got a job for you."

"This looks like toothpaste." Frowning, Joan uncapped the tube and squeezed out a dot of bright yellow pigment.

"It's oil paint," Mary answered. "Cadmium yellow light. I want you to put a dot on the trees as we pass."

"Hunh?" Joan wrinkled her nose as if the paint smelled bad.

"Dot the trees with this paint as we go." Mary held the open end of the tube against the bark of a pine tree. "That way, if we get lost, we can at least find our way back here."

"But I didn't think you ever got lost, Mary," said Joan, her hostile side swiftly returning. "I thought you knew these woods just like I know Manhattan."

"Not all of them, I don't." Mary fought another flash of irritation with Joan. "Look, if you don't want to do this, just say so."

"No." Joan grabbed the paint. "I'll do it. God forbid I not help save your precious Alex."

With Mary leading, they turned away from the spring and began to follow the narrow trail that twisted deep into the mountains. They trudged single file, Joan hobbling close behind Mary, complaining and berating her, until they came to a dirt path that snaked through a stand of cedars. Far beneath them to the right, Atagahi glittered through the trees. Mary stopped for a moment, as if she were bidding farewell to an old friend, then she turned and gazed into the forest. She was certain that Alex was still alive up there, somewhere. But who or what else was up there with her?

"Walk quietly," she cautioned Joan as they started to climb. "You never know how close they might be. And be careful not to step on anything sharp."

"If he catches us, he'll hurt me again," warned Joan. "He'll hurt you, too."

Mary closed her eyes. "I know," she said wearily.

The sweat began to trickle between their breasts as they started their ascent through a series of switchbacks. Though Mary walked through the woods barely whisking the grass, Joan crashed along behind her, limping off the trail to dab paint on the trees, her breath wheezy as someone on a respirator. Every bird-chirp and twig-break made her jump, and sometimes, for no apparent reason, she would cry aloud.

"What was he like, Joan?" Mary asked softly, finally sitting down on a fallen walnut tree. Maybe if Joan caught her breath she would walk with less commotion.

"Who?"

"The man who hurt you."

Joan slumped down beside her, gulping air through her mouth. "Tall. Filthy black hair and beard. Old Army uniform. Awful fingernails." She shuddered. "He smelled like veal gone bad."

Mary frowned. "What do you mean, old Army uniform?"

"Those green-spotted suits they wear in the jungle."

"Did he wear anything besides that?"

She gave a thin rasp of a laugh. "Just his pet rattlesnake."

"That's not possible." Mary wiped the sweat from her brow. "Nobody keeps a rattler for a pet."

"He did. The thing had diamond shapes on its back. And it swelled up like a cobra."

Clever, Mary thought. Barefoot had commandeered Joan and Alex with a hognosed snake, a benign creature whose chief defense was its resemblance to the poisonous timber rattler. "Did he say anything?"

"He said *That's about enough from you*. Then he smashed my nose."

"Did he say anything to Alex?"

Joan laughed as if Mary had told her a joke. "Sorry, Mary. I didn't eavesdrop. I was too busy trying to stay alive."

A pine-scented breeze chilled their faces while the hot sun drilled into their scalps. As they hiked higher, the air grew bright and humid, and droplets of sweat clung like dewdrops to the ends of their hair. Though Joan dotted the trees with paint as Mary had asked, she still careened through the woods, sometimes sullen with anger, other times giddy, singing Italian songs.

We're thundering through here like a troop of scouts, Mary thought. *I hope the barefoot man isn't nearby.*

"It really burns when I pee," Joan complained when they'd stopped to rest beside a stream. "That man hurt me a lot down there."

"Maybe we'll find a creek deep enough for you to sit in for a few minutes," Mary told her. Wonder what the Cherokee remedy for savaged vaginas was? Something her mother had surely never dreamed she would have need of knowing.

Slowly they made their way up-country. Mary led by her instincts when the trail became hard to read; Joan laughed every time she dabbed the trees with paint. At midafternoon Mary spotted a cluster of oyster mushrooms growing out of a fallen limb.

"Oh, look!" she cried, tearing the fungi off the bark. "Slicks!"

"Ugh." Joan sniffed the delicate pink underside of the mushroom Mary handed her. "What did you call these?"

"Slicks," replied Mary, her mouth full. "Oyster mushrooms. They're delicious."

"Aren't they poisonous?"

Mary shook her head. "It's the only mushroom I can absolutely guarantee. Try some. They won't hurt you."

Joan took a tiny nibble. "*Funghi trifolati*," she announced, starting to laugh again.

When they'd eaten all the mushrooms they could find, Joan tapped Mary on the shoulder. "Do you think we're on the right trail?"

"It's the only fresh one up here," Mary replied, remembering a game she and Jonathan had made up. Search and Destroy, they'd called it. One of them would run through the woods for thirty minutes, then stop and hide. Then the other would start tracking. Jonathan was always much better at the game, but eventually Mary had become adept at reading the almost invisible signs that betrayed where a person had passed.

Joan chuckled. "You know what I can't figure out?"

"What?"

"Why he didn't kill me."

Mary glanced at Joan's brutalized face. "Maybe he thought he already had," she answered softly.

They pressed on, wading through a creek where yellow beech leaves floated brilliant against a dark mirror of water. Mary pointed to a spot higher up on the tree where long strips of bark had been ripped away. "Bears have been here. That's how they sharpen their claws."

"Terrific," shot back Joan. "Now we can worry about bears, along with everything else."

"They shouldn't be a problem," Mary explained. "They're holing up to hibernate now."

Once when they crested a rise Joan grabbed Mary's arm.

"Did you hear that?" she demanded, her eyes wide and terrified.

"What?"

"Alex!" Joan cried. "Her cowboy yell. The barefoot man's coming! Hide!" Turning, she thrust herself into the cover of the trees.

Mary did not move. Had Alex escaped? Was she headed back to Atagahi as fast as she could, the barefoot man behind her? She listened carefully for what seemed like hours as Joan crouched fearfully behind a log, but she heard nothing that sounded anything like Alex's famous yee-hiii. Finally she realized that Joan had been tricked by the mountains—the faraway shrill of some hawk or even some tall sycamore branches, scraping together in the wind.

"Come on out, Joan. Alex isn't here."

"She is, too, Mary," Joan insisted fiercely. "I heard her cowboy yell. I'd know it anywhere."

"If you say so," Mary agreed, realizing that Joan had zoomed through three different personalities in the past three minutes. "But she's gone now. We'll have to keep following her trail."

They hiked on in silence, Mary studying the grass, wondering which Joan was going to pop out next. At length they came to a narrow, overgrown track that cut across the contours of the land. Mary reached down and pried up a small dark rock embedded in the grass.

She remembered a long-ago afternoon when she and her mother had carved a pumpkin for Halloween. Her mother had sold one of her tapestries and splurged at K-Mart on a store-bought costume for Mary. Impossibly proud and resplendent as Wonder Woman, Mary had watched as her mother's sharp knife coaxed eyes and a grinning mouth from the blank orange face of their pumpkin.

"There's a place you must never go," her mother warned, her luminous *eyes serious. "It's called Wolfpen, and it's where men came long ago and cut down all the trees."*

"Is it haunted?" she'd asked, hoping for another of her mother's crazy *Cherokee ghost stories.*

"No. Just dangerous. Rotten floors, rusty nails, broken glass. You could get hurt. The place was falling down when my grandfather was a boy. A man named Babcock built it."

Mary looked at Joan, who now stood trembling beside her.

"See this?" Mary held up the black rock.

Joan nodded.

"It's coal. There's supposed to be an old logging camp up here," Mary explained quietly. "This is probably the railroad bed that led to it."

"Does anybody live there?" Joan's voice rose with hope.

"No. They logged out this part of the forest after the First World War."

"Too bad," Joan said glumly, but Mary didn't hear her. She'd just noticed a tall purple-headed thistle on the verge of the path. The stalk was bent. Someone who wanted to conceal their trail would never leave such an obvious marker. But somebody who wanted to be found would. She let the piece of coal fall from her hand. If the trail they had followed since morning really was Alex's, then they were still on it. Barefoot had made no effort to cover their tracks. *Figures,* Mary thought. *He feels safe. He doesn't know about me and he thinks Joan is dead. Who else would be up here tracking him?*

"We're going to follow this road from along the bank on the other side," she told Joan. "That way we'll be going in the same direction, but still stay hidden."

They darted across the exposed roadbed and scrambled up the bank, plodding on.

As the afternoon shadows grew long, a feeling of dread began to churn in Mary's stomach. She felt as if every tree or bush or fallen log might reveal something she didn't want to see—Alex raped, Alex strangled or Alex dead, gutted like a field-dressed deer. But the forest held no such surprises. All she and Joan saw were trees and leaves and an occasional bird. The only sign of Alex lay twenty yards to their right, where the thin trail of trampled grass continued to bisect the old narrow-gauge railroad bed.

"Shouldn't we stop soon?" asked Joan, her face wan in the shadows, her swollen nose angry and purple. "Won't we need to find a safe place to stay before dark?"

Mary looked up at the fading sun, then nodded. "You're right. Look for a fallen tree, or one with big roots. We can dig a trench like we did last night." She ignored Joan's complaints.

They walked on, scouring the forest, when suddenly Mary's gut shriveled. She dropped to the ground, pulling Joan down behind her.

"Is it the barefoot man?" Joan cried. "Do you see him?"

"No! Hush!" Mary pointed. "It's Alex's shirt!"

In a small clearing in the old road below them, a red plaid shirt lay rumpled beneath a blackberry bush. Alex had worn a similar one yesterday, laughing about how garish it had looked against her orange safety vest.

Joan frowned through the shadows. "Are you kidding?"

"No. You stay here and be quiet. I'm going to go have a look."

"Wait! It might be a trap!" Joan grabbed Mary's sweatshirt. "What if this is just a way to get us someplace where he can hurt us some more?"

"I don't know," Mary replied bluntly. "You stay here and watch. If anything happens, run like hell back to Atagahi."

"And then what?" Joan snarled. "Call 911?"

"You insisted on coming with me, Joan."

"Just go and see if it's Alex's shirt." Tears leaked from Joan's eyes as she shrank back timidly into the weeds.

Mary crept down to the road. Shafts of hazy sunlight slanted through the silent forest. Nothing seemed to have followed them, and nothing seemed to await them ahead. From where she crouched she could see no lifeless body pulled behind a rock, no shadowy figure in camouflage waiting to pounce upon her. She took three deep breaths, then sprinted across the roadbed, dropping to her knees beside the shirt. The soft flannel still bore the faint aroma of sage; the faded label read "Abercrombie & Fitch, Size 10." Alex's size from Alex's favorite store. Mary pressed the shirt against her face, inhaling Alex's smell, her aliveness. For once she'd guessed right. They had found Alex's trail. This was her shirt, and maybe, just maybe, Alex might still be alive. *Thank you*, Mary whispered to the Old Men as she held the shirt aloft and motioned for Joan to join her.

TWENTY-FOUR

The screech owl perched on the lower limb of the oak tree, as two men and a dog came crashing through the dark woods. It eyed the trio, its saffron-yellow pupils dilating into enormous black orbs, then it spread its wings and soared a foot above their heads, whistling a quivery *skreeeee* as it passed. This thundering trio had frightened the tiny vole the owl was about to pounce on; now the bird would have to fly on to quieter hunting grounds. *Skreeeee*, it trilled, again voicing its disgust.

"Shit!" Mitch Whitman ducked. "That damn thing's flying low."

"They do that in the fall," explained Billy. "Close to where all those ground squirrels are digging up acorns."

"Makes sense, I suppose." Mitch peered up into the night sky as he pulled his jacket closer around his neck. "Gotta go where the game is."

The men and the dog trudged on. They

SALLIE BISSELL

hiked for a time in silence, then Billy spoke. "You about ready to stop
for the night?"

"As long as we've gotten a good start on the trail for tomorrow,"
Mitch replied.

"We're about a third of the way there," Billy told him. "I know a
place we can camp, just a little ways away."

They'd made better time than Billy had expected. This Mitch
Keane was in good shape. He followed along up one mountain and
down another without complaint, breathing heavy only as they clambered to the tops of the highest ridges. When he took his sunglasses
off, Billy had expected to see the usual jittery look of people who
weren't used to the deep woods, but Mitch didn't appear nervous at
all. He just took it all in, his gaze cold as a winter pond.

The hike, though, seemed to have spoiled him for conversation.
He'd barely grunted when Billy had tried to tell him about Michael's
ears and his own fiddle problems, and when he started talking about
taking Tam to Gatlinburg, he'd yawned right in his face. Billy had
taken no offense, though. Mitch was probably pondering on Mary
Crow, and didn't want to hear about his little pissant problems.

When they came to a deep waterfall that plunged thirty feet into a
narrow creek, Billy stopped.

"Mind your step," he warned as he led Mitch down the weedy
creek bank, then along the slippery rocks that lay like huge flat turtles
at the base of the falls. "We'll get a little wet here, but it won't be too
bad," he called over the roar of the falling water.

He jumped from rock to rock, Homer splashing haunch-deep in
the creek behind him, then they leaped behind the curtain of water,
landing on a wide rock ledge. Billy stood waiting for Mitch to follow,
but the sound of footsteps did not reach his ears. "Come on, Mitch,"
Billy called. "Just do what I did."

A moment later Mitch appeared, squinting into the darkness
between the rock wall and the falling water.

Billy grinned. "Come on in. It's a nice place for a fire."

Mitch hesitated, then stepped inside the hidden cavern.

"See?" Billy's voice echoed as if coming from the bottom of a
well. "It's downright cozy back here."

Mitch glanced around the dark, wet walls. "I'll be damned. I once camped in a spot like this in Mexico."

"What were you hunting down there?"

"Poontang, mostly." Mitch laughed. "Latina girls are nice."

A little while later, as he was nursing some dry pine twigs into a fire, Mitch unpacked the slickest equipment Billy had ever seen. He set up a propane stove that lit on the first try and then unrolled an all-weather aluminum sleeping bag that looked like something you'd roast an ear of corn in. Billy felt almost shamed by his own threadbare bedroll and the soggy chicken and cornbread he'd brought for him and Homer, but Mitch had seemed happy to share the fancy freeze-dried stew he'd cooked on his stove. Homer had turned his nose up at it, but Billy thought it tasted as good as anything he'd ever eaten at Shoney's. After they'd washed their plates in the waterfall, they sat across from each other by the fire.

"Ol' Homer's confused," Billy said as the dog paced back and forth, panting. "He thinks we're going coon hunting."

Mitch studied the rangy hound. "Is coon what you hunt up here?"

"That and boar. Wild turkey and whitetail, if you go down to the flats." Billy pulled his harmonica out of his pocket. "Maybe if I play some music he'll calm down." He played a scale, then launched into several verses of "Old Joe Clark." Homer finally lay down with his head on his paws as notes bounced off the dank walls like chips of bright sound. After Billy had run through "Pretty Polly" and "Columbus Stockade," Mitch held up one hand.

"Enough. The dog's calm now."

Billy frowned. "Don't you like harmonica music? It cheers most people up."

"I'm topped off with cheer as is." Mitch stretched his long legs out by the fire.

"This thing's kept me company ever since I was a kid." Billy stole a glance at Mitch's black Colt rifle. This fella might be a lawyer in Atlanta, but he carried hunting gear Billy had seen only in Jonathan's magazines. "I guess I'm used to it."

"I wouldn't want Mary Crow to hear it."

"Oh?" Billy cocked his head. "We're not trying to sneak up on her, are we?"

"Nah." Mitch's face cracked into a grin. "I'd just hate to wake her up if she's asleep or something."

"Well, unless she's got ears like a bat she isn't gonna hear us. Atagahi's still about six hours away."

"I see." Mitch poked at one fiery log with a stick, then he looked at Billy. "So you're a Real Life Cherokee?"

"Yep."

"And you grew up with Mary Crow?"

"Went all the way through school with her. She's one brainy gal. It was a shame about her mama and everything."

Mitch cocked his head. "Her mama?"

"Yeah. The way she got murdered at the store. They never could catch who did it."

Mitch gave an odd smile, as if he'd just learned a secret that gave him pleasure. "Never did, huh?"

"Nope." Billy peered into the falling water. "They finally decided some drifter must have killed her, but you never know. It might have been a maniac who could still be out there right now, just a-waitin' for another throat to slit."

Another moment of silence passed; Billy said nothing as Mitch stared into the crackling flames.

"I don't reckon he's out there, though, what with all these Hell Benders around."

"What's a Hell Bender?" Mitch looked up.

Billy nodded toward the water. "That old river dog over there, a-givin' you the evil eye."

Mitch turned. A long, squat four-legged shape stood just inside the falls, looking straight at them. Tiny pig eyes glowed with pinpoints of firelight as the creature grinned the soulless smile of a lizard.

Mitch laughed. "That thing looks like something you'd flush down a john."

The Hell Bender eyed the two men for a bit, then waddled along the ledge, its tail slapping wetly on the moist rock.

"Take it out of here, Homer!" Billy commanded.

"No, wait!" Mitch reached behind him and grabbed his rifle.

"Hold on!" Billy cried. "He's not worth—"

But before he could finish his sentence, the cave erupted in a roar that made Billy squeeze his eyes shut and cringe down into his clothes, his ears ringing as if he were sitting on the inside of a bell. When he opened his eyes, the spot where the Hell Bender had been was just a smear of bright red blood. Mitch's bullet had disintegrated the thing. Billy clapped both hands over his throbbing ears, while Homer ran around the cave like a dog gone berserk.

"Good God, Mitch!" Billy cried. "Don't you know better than to fire a gun inside a cave? That old lizard didn't mean you no harm!"

Mitch's mouth moved, but Billy couldn't hear what he said. Mitch leaned his rifle back against the cave and both men sat for a long time staring at the fire, waiting for the ringing in their ears to subside. When Billy could finally hear Homer's whimpering, he put the harmonica to his lips again. The mournful notes of "Wayfaring Stranger," his Daddy's favorite song, began to float through the damp air. This time Mitch made no complaint about the music.

When he came to the end of the tune, Billy slipped the harmonica back in his pocket.

"Sorry about the lizard," Mitch said gruffly. "I haven't fired that rifle since I hunted elk in Montana with my dad. I guess I wanted to see if she still shot straight."

"I'd say she does all right," grumbled Billy. He sighed. He was surprised that Mitch would do such a stupid thing, but he'd known other people who'd gotten trigger-happy in the woods with much worse results. He guessed there was no point to getting all huffy about having your head rung like a church bell.

"So how come you're fetching Mary Crow back to Atlanta?" he asked, changing the subject.

Mitch's mouth drew tight. "There's a problem with one of her convictions."

"Oh? Did somebody escape from prison?"

"Not exactly."

"I bet y'all have some right fierce criminals down there," surmised Billy with a wink.

"Some are." Mitch's voice took on an edge. "Most are just fuck-ups."

"You hunt a lot on your off-time?"

"I go with my dad."

"Sounds like y'all have tracked some pretty exotic stuff."

Mitch looked at the fire. "Elk in Montana. Moose in Maine. Once we even tried brown bear in Alaska, but we didn't get anything."

"I hear those brown bears are crazy. They'll even kill their own kind."

Mitch shrugged. "So would most of the human race."

"Oh, yeah?"

"Yeah." Mitch turned to Billy. "I once knew a man who set up his own brother after he killed his girlfriend."

"Really?" said Billy, his eyes wide. "What happened?"

Mitch laughed softly. "Nothing. The asshole brother got caught. He's rotting in jail right now."

"What about the other fellow?"

"He took some heat on the witness stand, but the DA couldn't put it all together. Guy's a free man now. Builds dams in South America. Goes hunting every chance he gets."

"So one's in the pokey and the other's free as a bird."

"Just about," Mitch agreed.

Billy shook his head. "That doesn't make for a right happy family, does it?"

"No." Mitch gave a careless shrug. "Guess it doesn't."

Billy stood up and walked to the edge of the falls. The moonlight shone through the falling water like a liquid silver curtain, and the soft, constant gurgle of the water soothed him like the tide of the ocean he'd never seen. A fine, cool mist dampened his face and the smell of iron laced the air. *This creek is probably full of sapphires*, he thought, watching as the moonlight danced on the water. *Rubies, too. If anybody had the time and the equipment to dig them out, they'd probably wind up a rich man.* He smiled, then wondered how Tam had done at bingo. Maybe she'd won the coverall. If she'd come home with fifty dollars in her pocket then she might not be so disappointed about him coming up here with Mitch. He touched the five hundred-dollar bills that lay curled deep in his front pocket. Mitch would give him the rest as soon as they found Mary. That would get him his fiddle back, and he would never tie up with Zell Crisp again.

He turned and walked back to the fire. Mitch had already tucked into his corn-roaster sleeping bag and pulled the flap over his head.

Billy unrolled the old flannel bag he'd used since he was a kid and wrapped it around him, curling up close to the flames. Bathed in the silver glow of the waterfall and the golden glow of the fire, he felt as if he were sleeping in some great hall that blazed with the colors of the stars. He closed his eyes, feeling content. Tomorrow they would find Mary. Tomorrow he would get the rest of his money. Tomorrow his life would begin to take on the richness of the colors that surrounded him.

TWENTY-FIVE

Alex lay with her eyes open. She curled not in her usual tight coil, but flat on her back, open like a flower, her boots laced tightly on her feet.

Brank lay beside her. Alex knew without looking that he was asleep; his snores droned steady as waves on a beach. For hours she'd feigned sleep, watching from under her captor's ragged tent as the nearly full moon glided across an indigo sky.

That night he'd left her legs untied when he pushed her under the tarp, and the prospect of flight had tantalized her ever since. He'd gone to bed woozy from his moonshine, and ever since she'd lain awake, trying to figure out what to do. Murder tempted her—the thought of easing the knife out of his belt and plunging it deep into his chest brought a smile to her lips. But she hadn't seen where he'd put the knife when he'd collapsed on his blanket, and if she woke him fumbling for it, she knew she'd be the one who would wind up with a blade through her heart.

That was when she'd decided on escape. Although running through the blackness of the forest with her hands bound would be dicey, anything was better than being Henry Brank's plaything, listening to his weird Germanic ramblings about mad Trudy and Papa and Pennsylvania. She took a deep breath. The moon had already passed its apogee. If she was going to escape, she needed to go now.

He lay on his back, his mouth open, snoring the easy sleep of a man unbedeviled by dreams. Cautiously, she pulled herself upright. A shock of pain flared down her rib cage, but she inhaled deeply through her mouth, tamping it down to the point that she could bear to move. The nylon sleeping bag beneath her seemed to rustle with every eye blink, betraying her movement. She glanced over again at Brank, certain she'd awakened him, but he snored on, apparently undisturbed.

She started to pull her long legs beneath her, then realized that struggling upright without the leverage of her hands would make far too much noise. She would have to roll over and push up from her stomach. Keeping her eyes on Brank's face, she rolled to her left. Hot fire instantly consumed her battered body, but she ignored it. Broken bones could not concern her now.

Every motion sounded like a cannon shot. Her sleeping bag rustled like a chorus of high-pitched violins. Her breath came in shallow, rapid gasps. *Any second now he will open his eyes and see me.* For an eternity she crouched motionless, holding her breath until her lungs burned, waiting to see what would happen. Her forehead grew damp with sweat. He snorted once in his sleep, making her dizzy with fear, but then turned his head away from her; his snores resumed.

So far, so good, she told herself. Cautiously, she rose to her knees. Then she brought her left knee forward, balanced her elbow on top of it, and lifted herself up. Her knees wobbled and nearly buckled, and she had to stoop to keep from hitting the top of the low tent, but at last she stood upright and untethered. She nearly wept with joy.

Standing seemed to make even more racket than turning over, but still Brank snored on. Now she had only to slip out of the tent. Then she would be free.

She held her breath and turned. Three more steps and she would be outside. It would be treacherous to find her way at night, but the moon still shone bright overhead and she'd taken extra care yesterday to try to memorize their trail. If she could run fast enough and long enough, she might be miles away before he even knew she was gone.

She took a step, then stopped. The nylon bag rustled, but still Brank did not move. The next step took her to the end of the bag. One more step and she would be free of the tent and into the forest. She pressed her arm against her right side and looked at Brank one final time. He slept on, still as death. Steeling herself against the pain, she ducked beneath the ragged flaps. The cold, dark air caressed her like a lover. She had done it. She was free.

She wasted no time. With rapid strides she slipped past their smoldering campfire, desperate to avoid any twigs that might crunch beneath her feet. Tall hemlocks thrust up into the night about twenty feet away. If she could reach them, she could slip into their shadows. . . .

She had to fight the urge to cut loose as she had done on her high-school track team. *Go slow*, she commanded herself. *Go quiet. Just get into the trees. Then you can run.* She took two more long steps. She longed to look over her shoulder, to make sure Brank wasn't coming after her. *Don't stop*, she told herself. *Just get to those trees.*

Three more quiet steps, then two, then the forgiving branches of the hemlocks reached out and enveloped her. Their pungent aroma reminded her of Christmas. Her heart pounded as if she'd sprinted a mile. Her breath came in gasps. *I've done it*, she thought, tears spilling from the corners of her eyes. *I have gotten away.*

She twisted to look back at the tent, still expecting to see Brank roaring out like a madman, waving his gun in the air. But nothing moved. She knew, though, that would all soon change. He would wake up and find her gone. She had to put as much distance between her and that moment as possible. For an instant, however, she crouched beneath the hemlocks, breathing in their sharp, clean scent, remembering the Christmas she'd gotten a shiny blue twelve-speed bike.

"Whatever happens after this," she said softly, gripping one branch tight in her hand, "at least I escaped once."

She stood up and turned toward what she hoped was east, where the trees cast thick smudges of shadow on the ground. She might not remember the trail exactly, but she knew she must go opposite from where Brank had been taking her. Impulsively, she turned back to the tent and poked up the third finger of her right hand. "Fucken-sie you," she said under her breath. "You and your dumb cat-woman sister." With that she turned and ran into the night.

At first she thought she'd stay beneath the trees, hidden from sight. The hemlocks, however, were thick; picking a path through them slowed her down and often led her far away from the old roadbed. At last she realized that if she was not to get hopelessly tangled in the forest, she would have to drop down to the trail. It would expose her to Brank, but it was the only way she knew to get back to the spring. She crept down to the roadbed and began to run.

It was harder than she'd thought. She tried the old, mile-chewing pace of her cross-country track-team years, but with her hands tied in front of her she couldn't find the right rhythm. If she approached anything near speed, she lost her balance. If she worked at keeping her balance, then her pace slowed to a crawl.

"Bastard," she cursed Brank aloud. "You just had to tie the hands, didn't you?"

Finally she settled into an awkward, shuffling lope. She felt ridiculous, fleeing from a monster at a whopping two miles an hour, but it was the best she could do. Her moments of darkness were ticking away.

She ignored the pain in her right side and pressed on until the soft gray moonlight turned colorless and a few birds began to chirp. Soon it would be dawn. Soon she would have to decide whether to hole up and hide or keep running. That he would be after her, she had no doubt.

A raccoon scampered into the woods ahead of her, startled by the two-legged creature bursting into its universe. She clambered over a fallen tree she remembered climbing over the day before and smiled. She was on the right track.

Just as the sky grew pink in the east, she stopped, breathing hard. Water gurgled from some boulders at the top of a small rise. She hadn't had a drop of water since the night before. Her throat felt like sandpaper: she knew if she was going to succeed, she must keep herself hydrated. She lifted her face to the icy spray of water. Her skin felt stung by a thousand frigid bees, but she didn't care. She had just begun to scoop some water into her mouth when something flickered in the corner of her vision. She turned, then gasped. A gray scarecrow hobbled towards her, elbows flapping like the stubby wings of an ostrich.

It was Brank. And even with his scrambling, hunched-over gait, he was covering ground fast.

"Shit," she cried. She sprang back onto the trail and ran. No time to worry about falling now. She clasped her hands tightly against her chest and tried to make her strides long and fast. *Get ahead of him*, she urged her tired body on. *Then hide.*

She threw herself along the trail, searching the dying shadows for any place that might give shelter. Thorns tore at her bare legs, her feet slipped on slick pine needles. She put her head down and concentrated. *Run.* He was probably at the top of the rise now. *Just make it to this curve, and he won't be able to see you.*

Her breath rattled in her throat. Her legs pumped like pistons. She risked a glimpse over her shoulder. The scarecrow had crested the rise. She blinked. He was lifting one arm.

"Hey, Trudy!" He had seen her. His gravelly voice rang out through the trees. "We were just about to have some fun!"

"No!" she cried. Every stride sent a new shock of pain through her ribs, but she willed her legs to move faster. She couldn't stop now. She couldn't give up. Maybe there was a rock or a dead branch she could grab and smash his head in. But she couldn't stop to find a weapon.

"Trudy!" His voice sounded closer. She turned. She saw his face. His mouth gaped open, but his eyes seemed to burn into her flesh, as if to brand her as his own.

She asked her legs for more, for the kick she'd always had in high school, but they did not respond. She was exhausted. "Please," she begged, trying to dig in with her toes. Brank was gaining ground. She could hear his footsteps slapping the ground behind her.

"Please," she whimpered one final time, just as her right foot snagged on the hidden branch of a tree. Desperately, she tried to recover her balance, and for a moment, she succeeded. She stayed upright, but then she hit the ground flat on her face, her breath escaping like air from a balloon. Instantly he fell on top of her, his sharp nails digging into the tender flesh of her shoulders.

For a while both of them just gasped, then his weight left her body and she felt a rope grip her left ankle. In another moment her right ankle was trussed up the same way.

"What's the matter with you?" He sobbed above her. "We were getting along so well."

He retied her ankles, but this time he left only about a foot of cord between them.

She rolled over on her back and looked up at him. "I can't walk like this."

"I guess you'll have to." Wheezing, he wiped his nose on his sleeve. "Papa always said you were a handful. Looks like he was right."

Alex shook her head, her eyes bright with fury. "Papa didn't know me!" she screamed. "Papa has no idea what I'm like!"

He tied her old rope around her waist. "Then maybe I'll just have to find out what you're like," he growled as he pulled the knot tight. "Maybe from now on I'll make it my business to do just that."

TWENTY-SIX

C ome on!" Brank jerked the rope. "Your little escapade may have cost us the day. A wind's blowing up that's gonna turn our faces to jelly."

She sat and stared at him. He scowled back, his thick brows drawing down over his eyes. "*Gehorchen*, Trude. You don't want to be a big old tall girl with a jelly face. You won't get any boyfriends that way."

She did not move until he pulled his right foot back. Then she remembered her ribs, and the penalty for not *gehorchening*. Without further protest she rose to her feet. She followed him back to the camp with tiny, crippled steps, stumbling like a comic character in a flickering silent movie.

The sun had climbed well above the mountaintops by the time they reached the tent. He tied her to a tree while he gathered his supplies, then he walked over and began to loosen the rope around her wrists.

"Take off that jacket," he ordered when he'd freed her hands. "We're going to do it a little different than we did yesterday."

Slowly, she removed her jacket and stood naked in the sunlight.

"Now you're gonna see what happens to girls who run away." Brank stuffed her jacket into his sack. He threaded her arms through her pack from the front, pressing her breasts hard against the aluminum frame as he tightened the straps. Though she winced as the straps bit into her skin, she pressed her lips together and refused to cry out.

When he'd secured the heavy pack to her chest, he took a length of rope and tightened it around her neck. He took a long piece of cane he'd found in the woods and whacked her across her hip.

"There," he chuckled. "Girls who run away get driven instead of led." He whacked her again, raising a welt on her backside. "Giddy-up. You balk like a mule, then you'll get treated like one. Walk on, Trudy."

With the rope tight around her neck and the pack now saddled to her chest, she started forward.

For hours she limped in front of him, her head bent against a stiff headwind that blew across the mountaintop. Though the pack was much more uncomfortable against her breasts, she didn't mind walking this way. She didn't have to look at or smell Henry Brank, and she could almost imagine, until the rope tightened around her neck, that she was out here all by herself.

The wind blew incessantly; as they walked around a wide tangle of bushes Mary had called laurel, it turned her face raw and stiffened her already swollen knees and ankles. She had known howling prairie wind in Texas, but that was playful as a spring breeze compared to this. Just when she feared she might scream from the endless whine in her ears, the laurel ended. They began a slow descent into a valley that spread below them like an undulating carpet.

Immediately the hike grew easier. The wind calmed to a breeze; the sun warmed rather than blistered. If timber had ever been harvested here, there was no trace of it; the mountains bulged with ripe autumn abundance.

Out of the wind Alex felt stronger. The tiny steps she had to take came easier and she'd figured out just the right distance to stay beyond the reach of the cane pole. It was impossible, though, to bend any weeds as they passed. Whatever trail she had managed to mark had ended on the other side of the laurel. Once she thought of Charlie and almost burst out laughing. Here she was, being driven like an ox through the Appalachian Mountains while he was in some cushy Canadian hotel, lecturing on fleas. He would phone her midweek, but he would not think it odd for her to be out. No, she thought, as her urge to laugh floated away like milkweed on the breeze. It would be Friday before Charlie started to worry. By then, she would be dead.

At midafternoon Brank pushed her into a weedy meadow. There, in the distance, she saw two log cabins connected by a covered sidewalk, just like a touristy ghost town she'd once visited in Arizona.

She stopped walking. She had assumed he was going to drive her through the woods yammering in German until he made up his mind to kill her. That they were headed for a specific place had never occurred to her. Now, apparently, they'd reached their destination. *Destination.* The syllables thudded, final as death.

"Is this where we're going?" The words spurted out of her mouth before she could stop them.

He walked up beside her and stared at her. That she spoke and had emotions always seemed to take him by surprise. "Yep."

"Why are we coming here?" She may as well find out as much as she could. There was no percentage in just musing about how you were going to be murdered.

He took off his Yankees cap and grinned. "We're gonna get to know each other a little better, Trudy. I've been thinking about this since you ran away. We're gonna rewrite the Brank family values."

He slapped her again with the cane. She stumbled along blindly, a wave of nausea rising from her belly. She was going to be reeducated into the ways of a madman. This was to be her destiny, just as this awful place was her destination. *Okay,* she decided, looking up at the sky, realizing that her options were dwindling fast. *Just let me think of a way to either kill him, or get him to kill me fast.*

The cabins had once been substantial, but spindly walnut seedlings now sprouted in the crumbling mortar of the chimneys, and jagged panes of shattered glass served as the only windows. A small creek boiled through the back of the property, while the mountains ringed it like sentries on the other three sides. It was a perfect place for someone who did not welcome unexpected guests.

"Home, sweet home," Brank announced as he pushed her through the thick mat of weeds that overran what had once been a yard. When they came to one of the cabin doors, he pushed it open first and pulled her in behind him.

A vaporous stench stung her eyes.

"Goddamn bats made this mess," he grumbled, squinting. "See? Over there." He pointed to the far wall. A wide splash of grayish droppings splattered down the timbers and into a heap on the floor. "I bet I've shot five hundred of 'em, but they keep coming back." He peered up into the shadowy eaves of the cabin. "They roost under the roof and crap in here." He laughed and poked her with his elbow. "I guess everything likes having a warm place to shit. This cabin used to be the bunkhouse for a logging camp," he explained, continuing his tour. "Now it's my storage room."

He walked over to the corner, where an old copper kettle sat. A long copper coil sprouted from its top. "This is Gertie." He patted the tub affectionately. "I named her for you, but I don't use her for making whiskey. Sugar and corn cost too damn much and dope's just too easy to grow."

Alex watched him and waited.

He grinned, then pointed at one of the toothed iron rings that hung from the cross-beam of the ceiling.

"You know what these are?"

She did not answer.

"Traps." He nudged one of the rings, setting it swinging like the pendulum of a clock. "This one's for bear, that one's for fox. This one here I made special for you, Trude. Watch."

He stepped out onto the porch, then returned with a log as thick as his arm. He positioned the wood in the middle of the Trudy trap, then jabbed upward. With a sharp crack, the jaws slammed shut, and the log clattered to the floor, sheared in half.

"That's what it was supposed to do to your leg." Brank chuckled.

Alex started to tremble. The reality that she would truly die here finally sank in. Before, in the woods, she'd banked on the slight chance of getting away. Here, in the cabin, she was cornered. Why hadn't she had the guts to try and stab him the night before? He probably would have killed her, but at least she wouldn't have to be tortured to death in this homespun hell.

He pulled her back outside and tugged her along the porch to the second cabin, opening the door with a flourish. "This is where I live," he announced with a wink.

The dry smell of old dust greeted them. Animal skulls grinned down from the walls, and a row of raccoon skins stood on little ironing boards in front of the fireplace at the far end of the cabin. A rumpled cot was set beneath one shattered window, a stack of ragged paperbacks and old magazines piled beside it. In one corner of the cabin stood a curious table heaped with items from a flea market. Three yellow plastic Frisbees lay next to a stringless guitar; baseball caps were piled on top of an old stereo; cheap jewelry and fishing lures spilled from a tackle box. An array of snake skins dangled from the rafters overhead like gypsy beads.

"Some of these things I brought with me," Brank explained. "Others are souvenirs from people I've run into over the years."

It suddenly made a kind of perverted sense to her. Henry Brank was a trophy hunter. Pelts from raccoons, Frisbees from children, tattered Stephen King paperbacks from mountain vacationers. He took what he found, and stole whatever he wanted. Was Martha Crow's Saint Andrew medal tangled in that tackle box, along with the fake pearls and beaded necklaces?

He pulled a battered cardboard box from beneath the cot. "Remember what Papa used to do to us when we were bad?" he asked, dropping the box on the squeaky cot.

She shook her head.

He laughed. "Of course you don't, Trude. You were never bad, were you?" He sat down on the cot, his eyes glittering beneath his brows. "When you were bad, you were always smart enough to blame it on me. I was the one who always got taken to the garage because of some shit you did."

Keep playing dumb, she thought, raising her shoulders in an apologetic shrug.

"Well, that's too bad, Trude. Looks like we're gonna have to reeducate you from the ground up."

She lowered her eyes. Whatever he might do, she was never going to give him the pleasure of seeing her cry.

"First, though," he announced, "let's have something to eat. We'll need all our strength for this."

He set the box aside and unhitched the backpack from her shoulders. While she relished the feeling of freedom, he pulled out the box of Moon Pies from his sack. He took two for himself, then offered her the last one.

She shook her head.

"You should try these, Trudy." He bit greedily into the pie, oblivious to her harsh gaze. "They taste like that old *Kuchen* Mama used to make. They'll give you enough energy to get through what we're going to do."

Suddenly her fear left, replaced by a fury that electrified every cell in her body. "Guess what, Henry," she hissed. "I don't give a shit about *Kuchen* or Mama or any of our fucked-up family values. If you want to know the truth, I think you're still the pathetic little toad you always were."

He stopped chewing and looked at her, his yellow eyes hard as glass. "Don't you talk to me like that."

"Oh?" She smiled, deliberately taunting him. "What are you going to do? Hit me with another stick? Or just dangle that stupid snake in my face?" She shook her head. "Worked once, asshole," she said. "Won't work again."

His face grew red. "You shut up!" he cried, spewing half-chewed Moon Pie all over himself.

Though she tried hard to contain them, Alex couldn't quash the ripples of her own laughter. This was insane. Her mountain monster spat Moon Pies when he was pissed. Quickly, she sat down and put her face between her knees, laughing uncontrollably.

When she stopped she heard a quietness, as if the earth were readying itself for some volcanic eruption. Her body instinctively tensed. Then she felt his hands wrap tight around her throat. With one motion he jerked her upright; the bones in her neck cracked.

"Are you laughing at me again?" he screamed, his face an inch away from hers. "*Are you?*"

She clasped her hands together and tried to spike him between his legs, but he saw the blow coming and twisted away an instant before it landed.

"Don't you do that!" he screeched. His left arm pulled back across his face, then her left cheek exploded in pain. "Don't you *ever* laugh at me! Why the fuck do you think I killed you before?"

"I don't know!" she cried. "Why don't you tell me?"

"Don't you remember the fall of sixty-eight? Old man Parsons' cornfield? We were hunting deer. I wanted to shoot one so bad, just to show Papa I could do it." His eyes bored into her, hot chips of saffron fire. "But you wouldn't give me time. You were such a show-off. You cut in front of me and killed my deer, then you called me names. *Wixer! Hosenscheisser!* You made me mad."

He pressed closer to her. "Got you back, though, didn't I? The first bullet got your knee; the second really mangled your throat. You were crying and bleeding like a stuck pig." He laughed at the memory. "You even wet your pants!"

Her cheek burning, she tried to make her features expressionless, but he pressed her jaws backwards with his thumbs, bending her face up cruelly to meet his. She could feel the pulse in her throat fluttering like a bird caught in a trap.

"Now maybe I'll make you wet your pants again."

He jerked her back onto the porch and around to the side of the house, where several nailed-together boards lay on the ground beneath the window. Clutching her tether, he lifted the boards up, uncovering a pit about two yards wide. He grinned and pulled her toward the hole. "Go ahead, Trudy. Call me a *wixer* now!"

Trembling, she peered down. The pit at her feet was deep, with black earthen walls. At its bottom a writhing knot of rattlesnakes coiled in on each other like the entrails of some beast. For an instant, she feared she'd faint.

"Mostly I sell these to Bible-thumpers who are too busy tattling to Jesus to do their own snake-catching," Brank informed her. "But I've also found that if I uncover this every night, *nobody ever* climbs in my window." He snickered.

"But the thing you need to be aware of"—Brank picked up another long piece of cane and jabbed down into the pit —"is that if I ever again hear the slightest tinkle of laughter coming from your mouth, I want you to know that this pit's about four feet taller than you are."

She stared at him, then she looked down into the shadowy pit. *End it now, Alexandra,* the voice in her head urged. *Just jump in and let them have at you.*

She took a step forward. *It'll hurt like hell, but it'll be over fast. He'll never be able to put his hands on you again.*

She was at the very edge of the pit when she felt the cord bite into her neck.

"Not yet, Trude," Brank warned. "Our fun's just about to start."

"You want to bet?" Alex asked, tensing against his rope as she gave him the darkest of smiles.

TWENTY-SEVEN

The big Huey helicopter rose like an oversized wasp from the flat coastal plain of South Carolina. It stirred up a maelstrom of dry orange dust, causing the small herd of Holstein cattle grazing in the field below to flee at a stiff gallop as the powerful rotor *whopped* low over their heads. The two-man crew chuckled at the panicked cows, then set a west–northwest course toward Tennessee.

The copilot, a rangy blond man originally from Indiana, shook his head as he checked the altimeter. "Can't believe we're crossing the Appalachian Mountains for fifty pounds of barbecue. Don't they make the stuff down here?"

The pilot slipped on his sunglasses. "Not to suit General Claiborne. He's a Tennessee boy. Folks from Tennessee figure they're the only people on the planet who can cook pig."

"Damn, it's just food. In one hole and out another."

"You ever had Angeline's Barbecue?"

"I've never even been to Tennessee."

"Well, then." The pilot looked over and chuckled as he pointed the chopper towards the western mountains. "You're in for a real experience."

In the Nantahala forest below, Harold Hobart scowled up at the sky. "What the hell is that?"

The sudden top-limb breeze and heavy *whump-whump* of a rotor had made the boar, which Harold had been tracking for the better part of three hours, turn. The pig seemed to grin at Harold for a heartbeat, then he pivoted and scampered off into an impenetrable thicket of fox grape and rhododendron. Harold knew at once that he'd lost him. The boar could shimmy through brush like that and not quiver a leaf. A whole day's hunting was over, and he hadn't even nocked an arrow.

"Beats me." Jonathan Walkingstick peered up into a small patch of brilliant sky between the thick trees. The throaty hum of the engine indicated a big machine—not the little skimmers the North Carolina dope patrols used, or even the larger birds from Tennessee. This sounded like one of the CH-47s he'd served on in the Gulf. He listened for others, thinking perhaps the 82nd was on maneuvers, but no more followed. Jonathan shook his head as the low thump dopplered away.

"Are y'all in some kind of flight path here?" Harold Hobart asked, his hair curling in angry red wisps beneath his hunting cap. Brent, Harold's sixteen-year-old son and heir apparent, looked pointedly at his watch and sighed.

Jonathan shook his head. "Most aircraft avoid this part of the Appalachians. The wind's shifty and the weather can change fast."

"Well, if it hadn't been for that damn 'copter I'd have had that boar," Harold carped on.

"Dad, can we go back now?" Brent swung his bow like a baseball bat and drilled an imaginary line drive into the forest. He shot a dark look at Jonathan. "This trail *sucks*."

"May as well." Harold wiped the sweat from his forehead. "We're done for the day." He turned and began marching back up the trail they'd just crept down. Brent plugged in a set of ear buds and, with a smirk at Jonathan, lumbered through the forest behind his father, his head bobbing to music only he could hear.

Jonathan was glad this job had been cut short. The Hobarts had called from Greenville, South Carolina, saying they wanted boar, but he realized twenty minutes out that as hunters and bowmen, father and son were not up to the challenge. Jonathan had flushed that particular boar on purpose. He'd chased the animal for the past three years himself, and he knew the little guy was fast enough to give the Hobarts a good chase, and smart enough not to get shot. Setting them up like that was probably not the most sporting thing to do, but what the hell. The Hobarts got to feel like real bow hunters, and the boar was no worse for the wear. Both parties would live to prey another day.

Lena Owle stood on the porch of Little Jump Off, a pink gingham apron tied around her waist. She smiled as Jonathan thumped the top of the Hobarts' gleaming black Cadillac with the flat of his hand and headed them back home.

"Good trip?" Lena called as the big car purred out of sight.

"Terrific," Jonathan replied. "Hobart can't shoot and his kid can't even pick his nose." He frowned up at Lena, who stood holding her big French butcher's knife. "Did you hear a chopper fly over about three hours ago?"

She shook her head. "Been too busy cooking. Sunday dinner, remember?"

Jonathan looked blank.

"Cassoulet, Jonathan. French country stew. We planned it last weekend." She folded her arms under her ample bosom. "I bought two bottles of wine and fresh raspberries for dessert."

"Oh, right." He nodded vigorously, trying to look enthusiastic. Lena was nice to come over and cook. Nicer still to linger and make love to him afterwards, but beyond that, she made him uncomfortable. She always wanted to stay, sometimes for days at a time, rearranging his books, straightening his closet, once even lining up his spices in alphabetical order. He liked her, but she needed things nailed down, defined. He thrived on the vagaries of life.

"You forgot, didn't you?" Triumph tinged her voice, as if she'd caught him in a lie.

He faked a smile. "No. Cassoulet. Lena. Sunday night. I'm sure I jotted it down in my day-planner."

"You're such a teaser." She laughed and bustled back into his kitchen.

He followed her into the store, wondering what forest emergency might have called in a chopper that big. A lost hiker? A heart attack victim at the bottom of a cliff? The image of Mary and her friends flashed across his mind. They were just going to Atagahi, but that was a stiff hike for three city women. Maybe he ought to check on them.

Don't be a jerk, he scolded himself as Lena clattered a pan upstairs. Mary's probably already back at her desk in Atlanta, nursing shinsplints and poison ivy. He walked over to the cooler and opened a Coke. Still . . . It was foolish, but maybe if Lena got involved in a TV show later he would walk to the trailhead, just to make sure that red BMW was gone.

Mitchell Whitman was lying on his back with his eyes closed as the helicopter approached. Though he lay on a high mountain bald in Appalachia, Mitch was really drifting in the aquamarine waters of Rio Blanco. A sultry breeze carried the smell of brine and shrimp up from the river's estuary and the laughter of the fisherwomen fell like soft petals around him. His mouth filled with the sweet taste of sugarcane, and he felt like someone new. Someone who would not have a simpering brother or a sot for a mother, or a father who roared like a dragon. To him they suddenly seemed like people you read about in the paper: damaged people you feel pity for, grateful they did not belong to you. Then the hum of the helicopter roared through his dream, and suddenly he was back on the sixth floor of the Deckard County Courthouse.

"Mr. Whitman," Mary Crow said in the now-hushed court. "In the last very long hour, we've gone to great lengths to establish that you knew Sandra

Manning, that you had a relationship with Sandra, that you might have even been willing to include your brother in your moments with Sandra. But you insist that you do not have any idea why your brother might have wanted to kill her." Mary Crow paced in front of the jury and scratched her head. "It's funny how you can know so much, and yet so little, isn't it?"

He sat there, hoping this might be the end. Mary Crow had pried up and exposed every nasty, humiliating little corner of his life, but so far she hadn't been able to come up with anything he could be indicted for. As juicy an entertainment as his testimony had provided, Cal was still the only Whitman sitting in the defendant's chair.

"I just have one more question." She turned and faced him, her eyes suddenly sharp as a hawk's. "Why did Sandra Manning call your apartment approximately three hours before the police found her dead?"

He took a deep breath. He could hear the sweat oozing from his forehead, feel his heart thudding like an executioner's drum. He turned his eyes on Mary Crow.

"I don't know," he lied in as sincere a voice as he could muster.

"I don't know, either." Billy Swimmer squinted up into the sun as the helicopter thumped above their heads. He and Homer sat opposite Mitch, eating cornbread and watching two male mockingbirds squabble over a tree limb heavy with arrowood berries.

"Huh?" said Mitch, rushing back so fast from the Deckard County courtroom that he felt he was riding a roller coaster.

"You said I don't know. I agreed with you. Lost hikers and dope growers are what they're after most of the time."

"Oh." Mitch blinked. "You mean the helicopter."

"Right." Billy gave Mitch a curious look as he fed Homer the last piece of cornbread. Then his expression grew alarmed. "Say, you don't reckon somebody else from your work might be looking for Mary, do you?"

Mitch's face paled. He stared up at the sky, his brows knotted in a frown. "I don't think so. If they planned to send out a helicopter, they didn't tell me."

"Well, I wouldn't worry about it none," Billy reassured him. "These trees are too thick for choppers to find most people. Anyway, they're going the opposite direction from Atagahi." He winked at Mitch. "You'll probably be the hero of the day, after all."

"I sure hope so," replied Mitch, rubbing the stubble that was beginning to grizzle his chin. "I'd hate to have come all the way up here after Mary and have someone beat me to her."

Mary Crow was squatting behind a bush when she heard the oncoming whump of the helicopter. The various waters she and Joan had consumed were carving new paths through both of them, requiring them to stop often and defecate behind whatever tree or bush was handy. Sometimes they had enough warning to scoop out a cat hole with sticks and the palette knife; other times their bowels would give way and it was all they could do to drop and squat, trembling in the grip of a microbic demon that froze their legs and seared their foreheads at the same time.

At first she thought the sound over her head was thunder, then she recognized the growl of an engine. Hastily, she pulled up her underpants and ran to a small break in the forest.

She shielded her eyes and searched the sky. Far away in the southeast, a gray dot flew toward her.

"Hey!" she yelled, even though she knew they couldn't hear her. "Over here!" The copter came closer. She jumped up and down, waving her arms, desperately looking around the clearing. There were no logs she could arrange in an X, and she had no means for a quick fire. Surely, there must be something. She ran back up to the spot where she'd been squatting. The little palette knife lay there, half-hidden in the tall grass. She grabbed it and wiped the blade on her shirt as she ran back to the clearing. If she could just get the angle of the sun right, maybe she could flash the blade and attract the helicopter's attention.

"Over here!" she yelled again. The chopper dipped closer, but still too far to the north. She raised the palette knife over her head and tried to catch the sun. She couldn't tell if the angle was correct, but the thing did seem to make some sort of glimmer if she held it just so and wiggled it gently.

"Over here!" she hollered, the helicopter whirring closer still. If she squinted she could read letters on its side—SCNG-107C. Frantically, she flashed the knife. The big helicopter seemed to hesitate, hovering like a massive dragonfly over a stream. She yelled again, louder, expecting to see the thing circle and land, but the helicopter began to churn away.

"Stop!" she screamed, throwing the palette knife to the ground and stripping off her sweatshirt. She waved it over her head like some crazed person with a semaphore flag.

"We're here! We're here!" She careened in a wide circle, making as much noise and movement as she could, but the helicopter flew on. The SCNG-107C on its side grew smaller, the roar of the engine faded. If it had been searching for them, then it had missed them by less than a hundred yards.

"We're here!" Mary called again, watching as the aircraft diminished into a tiny speck in the sky.

"We're here!" she called one final time, her voice dying as she stood sadly in the middle of the clearing, once again alone.

Joan huddled above the logging road, in the exact spot in which Mary had left her twenty minutes ago. Her eyes were closed and she was humming to herself, waving one hand as if she were conducting an orchestra. Her nose had darkened from red to deep purple, and her blistered feet were obscenely swollen. She jumped as Mary crashed through the bushes.

"Did you see Barefoot?" Already Joan was halfway to her feet, ready to run.

"No," Mary replied. "I saw a helicopter."

"A helicopter?" Joan's eye brightened. "Were they looking for us? Did you flag them down?"

"I tried." Mary sighed. "They didn't see me."

"Jeez, how could they not see you? Did you run around and yell?"

"I did my best."

"You don't have enough voice," complained Joan. "You can barely carry past the jury box. I bet I could have gotten them to land."

Mary glared at her. "Okay, Joan. Next time we hear a helicopter, you just go out and cut loose with a little *Madame Butterfly*. They'll land in a heartbeat." She picked up a stick and hurled it at a hickory tree. "Hell, they'll probably ask for your damn autograph."

Joan shrugged. "Don't blame me if I've got a voice and you don't."

For a moment, they glared at each other, then Joan turned her face away from Mary and looked up into the bright arc of sky. "What are we going to do now?" she asked softly.

Mary followed Joan's gaze. The sky was as blue and empty of helicopters as it had been a thousand years ago. Maybe it hadn't been real. Maybe she'd just seen a bird and imagined rotors whirring, imagined numbers on its flank. They'd had virtually no food and little sleep. Maybe she was even now imagining things—that Alex was still alive, that this trail would lead them to her. Maybe Joan had been right and Alex really had been murdered and dumped in some nameless, unfindable ravine. Maybe everything else was just wishful thinking. Her throat grew hot and aching. She was beginning not to know what to believe.

"We'll go on," she told Joan. "If another helicopter comes, we can worry about it then."

"Are we going to be walking over those cactus things again?"

"Probably."

Joan greedily eyed Mary's feet. "Then can I wear the boots for a while?"

Maybe another helicopter will come, Mary thought as she knelt down and unlaced her shoes. *Maybe Charlie and Jonathan will figure this out and send a whole fleet of helicopters. And Joan can sing the* Alleluia Chorus *from the mountaintops, just to help them land.*

TWENTY-EIGHT

fter the helicopter passed, the weather turned sour. For the rest of the afternoon, biting wind with icy chips of sleet whipped from the sky as Joan and Mary picked their way over slippery rocks high above a rushing mountain river. Though the tracking itself was laughably easy, they progressed at a pitiable pace, sliding backwards on the slick rocks each time they pushed themselves forward. Still, they shared their one pair of boots and struggled on. As long as Alex kept marking a trail, Mary was determined to follow it.

They had just thrashed through some weeds into a small clearing along the river when they heard a high, barely audible whistle coming from the clouds above their heads. They looked up just in time to see a reddish-brown streak plummet down from the sky. Before they could speak, before they could even breathe, a dark shadow swooped to the earth not ten feet ahead of them. Something scurried frantically among the wet leaves; then they heard one panicked shriek of anguish and surprise. Dark wings flapped twice, and the brown shadow rose again, this time lifting another creature high into the air. One more terrified scream reached their ears, then there was silence. It was over before they realized what had happened.

"Jeez!" Joan cried. "What was that?"

"A hawk, I think." Mary watched as the bird flew away, its awesome wings thrusting it upward.

"It killed something, didn't it?" Joan kept her eyes on Mary, away from the creature still squirming vainly in the hawk's talons.

Mary nodded, her palms suddenly clammy. "A squirrel. Or maybe a rabbit. They scream like that sometimes."

"Oh, jeez." Joan knelt down on the ground. She huddled beside Mary, trembling and rubbing her arms. "Are they now just dropping out of the sky?"

"Who, Joan?"

"The hunters," she sobbed. "The things that kill."

Mary knelt beside her and hugged her. She kept forgetting how little Joan knew about the woods. "It's part of nature," she tried to explain, her own voice shaky from the suddenness of the bird's attack. "Hawks are not herbivores. That's how they survive."

Joan took no apparent comfort in Mary's words. She remained crouched on the ground, not speaking, her body trembling as if she were freezing.

Mary stood up and sighed. In the past few hours, Joan had grown a little more like her old self. The hawk, though, had reduced her to a quivering, barely articulate heap. It seemed pointless to press on any further now. The rain and fog were growing thicker and the nonexistent sun was about to set. She scanned the woods around them. A rotting sycamore, its trunk three feet wide, lay on the ground twenty feet away. For once, they would have good shelter for the night.

"How about we call it a day?" she said to Joan. "You rest here and I'll go over and dig a trench beneath that tree."

Joan nodded her head.

Mary walked over to the sycamore and with one edge of her paint box started to hollow out a trench on the south side of the bark. She wished she could dig down deep and just pull the dirt back over them, but clay soil was a lousy insulator, and Joan refused to sleep in anything that looked like a grave.

As she scraped the slick mud into her paint box she uncovered a colony of squirming white grubs. With her belly on a long, slow boil from hunger, she picked out three of the plumpest ones and popped them in her mouth. She swallowed them without chewing, then waited to see if her stomach would bid them welcome or send them back up. Nothing happened. Her gut did not recoil but neither did the glowing coals of her hunger abate. She shrugged and resumed digging. Three grubs, she decided as she wiped her nose with the back of her hand, do not a feast make.

After a time Joan wobbled over. Her tears had made slender pale streaks through the grime on her face. Mary knew that she had been weeping for the little creature that had wound up as dinner for the hawk. Without thinking, she picked three more grubs from beneath the log and held them out to Joan.

"You gotta be kidding," Joan cried, horrified.

"It's protein," Mary said. "You need to eat something."

Joan backed up a step.

"Don't chew them. You won't taste them at all." Mary grabbed Joan's hand and dropped the squirming insects onto her palm. Joan stared at the fat pearlescent bodies, then she looked at Mary, her mouth curling in disgust. "Is this part of nature, too?"

Before Mary could answer, Joan flung the grubs back at her and ran toward the riverbank. At first Mary started to run after her, but then she stopped. She was tired. This was the way things happened in the woods. If Joan needed to recover from the shock of seeing a hawk grab a rabbit, then she would have to do so. Mary had a trench to dig, and not much time to do it. She bent down and scraped her paint box harder into the earth, working double-time against the fading light.

Suddenly, she stopped digging. She heard something—a cry of some sort, like a small animal in pain. Had the hawk returned? She stood and cocked her head toward the river. Above the muffled roar of the water, it came again. A sharp, plaintive ping of a cry.

"Joan?" She frowned, searching the woods for her friend. Where had she shuffled off to? A thick copse of pines and sycamores rose from the very edge of the gorge. Mary dropped her paint box and broke into a run.

Again, the cry came. This time louder. A desperate, pleading sound. Not a rabbit.

"Joan?" Mary reached the trees but saw nothing. She scrambled through scraggly rhododendron that sprouted between the rocks of the gorge. Then, without warning, the ground crumbled beneath her feet. She tumbled—leaves, rocks, twigs and branches falling with her, bumping down what felt like the sheer side of a shale cliff.

Protect your head, she thought as she rolled, but she was falling too fast. The earth passed by in a painful blur of rocks and bushes.

I'm going to drown, she decided. *I'm going to fall off this cliff and into the river. I'll never see Alex again.*

She began to scramble, then, with her arms and legs, trying to break her fall against the roots of trees, clutching at the slick rocks as she skidded past them. Flint sliced into her bare legs, and as she fell she felt something pierce the fleshy part of her shoulder. Finally she came to a stop. Her back felt wrenched in a thousand directions, and her head spun dizzily as the rock and the trees and the sky all swam around her.

At first she lay still, trying to figure out where she'd landed. Dirt and pieces of leaves filled her mouth, but she was afraid to move, afraid that the rock beneath her would crumble and the whole sickening plummet would start again. Finally she looked around and realized that she lay on a huge outcropping of solid limestone rather than the treacherous shale above.

She spit dirt out of her mouth and checked to see if anything was broken. Her bare legs bled from a hundred scratches, but her ankles flexed, and her scraped knees bent. She felt a hard lump against her belly. Wynona, still miraculously nestled in the pocket of her sweatshirt.

"I'm okay," she whispered. "Now, where's Joan?"

Another cry floated up from the river. Mary looked around, but saw only the high, rocky gorge, speckled with scrub cedars and rangy stands of laurel. Scrambling forward, she lay belly-down on top of the big rock. From there she could see the whole ravine. "Oh, my God," she breathed as she looked below her.

The shale had tricked Joan just as it had her. Like Mary, she'd stepped wrong and fallen: only Joan's tumble had been much farther and her landing spot far more perilous. Somehow she'd stopped just before she'd plunged into the river. Now her arms were wrapped desperately around the root of a tree that sprouted from a small, rocky ledge while the lower half of her body dangled in the air, twenty feet above the racing waters.

"Mary!" she begged, her face pinched and white with fear. "Help me!"

"Be calm," Mary replied, trying to make her voice steady. "I'm coming."

"Hurry," gasped Joan. "I can't feel my arms . . ."

Mary crawled off the boulder and eased herself down. Here the cliff face was mostly limestone—firm, but wet and slick from spray. Joan was wearing the boots, so Mary had to clutch the slippery boulders with her toes. Cautiously, she climbed down the cliff as Jonathan had taught her, keeping her hands and feet touching the rocks at all times.

"Are you hurt?" she called, sliding as her fingers failed to grip a slimy rock, then biting into the earth with her fingernails to stop her fall. The mist from the river rose like an icy wet cloud; droplets of stinging sleet blinded her.

"I don't think so," said Joan. "My arms, though. They're numb."

"I'm eight feet away. I'll be there in a flash." Mary tried to sound reassuring, but even as she spoke her right foot slipped and she had to fling herself forward to keep from falling. These rocks are so fucking slick, she thought, remembering how she and Jonathan used to think how stupid people were who fell to their deaths at waterfalls. Now she knew how easily it could happen.

She climbed on, like an elderly spider. One foot here, the other there. In the deep cut of the gorge, the cloudy daylight had faded to dusk. Ten minutes more and she would be climbing in the dark.

"Mary?" Joan's voice floated up, nearer, but closer to panic, too. It was hard to hear over the noise of the river boiling below. "Are you still coming?"

"Yes. Look just above your head."

"Oh!" Joan cried. "I can almost touch you!"

"Don't let go of the roots, Joan!" Mary commanded sharply. "Keep your arms folded tight around them!"

Joan's response was lost in the water's roar.

Moving now by miserly inches, Mary lowered herself to the ledge above Joan. The tree roots she clung to belonged to a young sycamore, an errant offspring of the taller ones that clustered on the gorge high above them. Mary sat down and wrapped her legs around the trunk of the small tree, then lowered the upper half of her body over the ledge. Joan clung just below her, hugging the slender roots while her legs dangled in the wet air.

"Thank God." Joan's lips were blue in her ashen face. "I was afraid you wouldn't hear me."

Quickly, Mary studied Joan's position, trying to figure out the best way to grab her. The sub-ledge was too narrow for her to climb down and push Joan up from behind. She would have to try something else.

"Joan," said Mary. "This is what we're going to do. I'm going to wrap my arms around you. Then when I start to pull you up, let go of the tree and grab on to me."

"Oh, Mary," Joan whimpered. "Are you sure? I weigh a lot."

"Don't worry," Mary replied with a confidence she did not feel. "I'm braced up here. I can hold you."

Mary wrapped her legs tighter around the tree, then leaned over the ledge and grasped Joan under her arms. She took a moment to position herself, then breathed deep and closed her eyes.

"Okay," she whispered, knowing that if this young sycamore could not support their combined weights they would both drown in frigid water, shattered by the sharp rocks below. "Let go, Joan. *Now!*"

As Mary pulled, Joan reluctantly loosened her grip on the roots. At first Mary feared she'd misjudged, and they both seemed to be sliding into the oblivion below. But she tensed the muscles in her legs and back and pulled with all her might. Joan edged up, slightly, toward her. Mary pulled harder. Finally Joan's legs pushed up from the fragile roots and up she came, fast, tumbling over on the ledge on top of Mary.

Gasping for breath, they lay without speaking. The cold, wet air that had before seemed like a shroud now felt good, cooling their sweat-soaked skin. Joan sat up and scrambled back from the ledge. Then she began to weep.

"I thought I was going to die just like that rabbit," she sobbed. "I thought I was going to drown."

"It's okay." Mary sat still, her breath coming hot and hard. "Once we climb out of this gorge, we'll be safe."

"But we can't climb out now!" Joan wailed. "It's almost night."

Mary looked up at the slate-gray sky. "If we hurry, we can make it out before dark. The climb up won't be so bad."

Joan gaped at her, unbelieving.

"You can go first," said Mary. "I'll tell you where to step, and I'll be right behind you in case you fall."

Joan did not move. Her tears and her body language betrayed the depth of her terror. She was so frightened, she could get them both killed, Mary knew.

"We have no shelter on this ledge, Joan," she explained. "If we don't climb up now, the cold will kill us before dawn."

"I can't do this any more, Mary," Joan sobbed, shrinking back against the rock face. "That man hurt me. He hurt me a lot!"

Suddenly a rage enveloped Mary. "Don't you think I know that?" she yelled, leaping forward at Joan. Longing to slap her stupid weak face, instead she grabbed her by her shoulders and pushed her hard against the rock. "Don't you think I know exactly how that man hurt you? He beat you, Joan. He raped you. He nearly killed you."

Joan shrank back further from the blaze in Mary's eyes.

"I know all that, Joan." Mary leaned in closer. "But I know something else. I know how strong you can be!"

"No." Joan shook her head. "I can't."

"Yes, you can," cried Mary. "Any little girl from Brooklyn who's fought her way into opera and then fought her way into Emory Law and is now fighting her way up the corporate career ladder in Atlanta is plenty tough enough to climb one lousy cliff." Mary tightened her grip on Joan's shoulders. "Joan, you can do it!"

"But I've never . . ."

"Doesn't matter!" Mary would not let Joan turn away. "I haven't done it, either. But we've got to try. We may wind up breaking our necks in that creek, but we've got to try!"

Joan peered at Mary through her tears. "You really think I can do it?"

"Absolutely."

Joan looked up at the rock face looming above her. Trembling more than ever, she looked back at Mary. Then, slowly, she got to her feet. "Okay," she said, her voice like a child's. "I'll give it a try."

Mary stood, too, and studied the mass of dark rocks that rose above them. The limestone down here was stable, but dangerously slippery. The shale above crumbled like puff pastry. Now, in the dark, she had to figure out which rock was which. All she could do was guess, and hope her luck held. She rubbed her fingertip against Wynona, deep in her pocket.

"Where do I step first?" asked Joan.

"Put your left foot here." Mary touched one flat plane on a rock. "Then put your right foot over there. Stay crouched down low, and use your arms as well as your legs."

"Okay." Joan put her foot where Mary directed. "Here goes nothing."

With Joan going first and Mary following, the two women began to climb. Wearing boots, Joan had better footing, but the soles would often slip on the wet rocks, sending blinding showers of dirt and pebbles down into Mary's face.

"Where now?" she called tentatively after Mary had directed her halfway up the rock face.

"Try that pinkish rock straight ahead."

"I don't think it's strong enough." Joan's voice wobbled. Mary knew she was on the edge of giving up again.

"Try it anyway," insisted Mary. "Everything else is shale."

Joan stepped forward. Keeping both hands and her other foot where they were, she shifted her weight timidly to the pink rock. Though a few pebbles tumbled off into the gorge below, the rest of the thing held firm.

"It's okay," Joan called down to Mary, and Mary realized she had been holding her breath for so long her lungs burned.

With the roar of the water diminishing below them, they climbed to the top of the gorge just as the last light died. In darkness they threw themselves down on the grass, trembling and exhausted, but grateful to be alive.

For a long while Joan wept quietly. Mary knew she should apologize for her harsh words, but she was too tired. She relaxed into the hard, damp earth as if it were a feather bed. From now until sunrise her legs would not have to push her up over sheer mountains or out of rocky gorges; she was free to relish the exquisite pleasure of being still. As raindrops began to patter through the leaves above them, she felt Joan raise up and turn toward her.

"You know you saved my life back there," she snuffled.

"Oh, you probably could have climbed out on your own," Mary said, although she knew without a doubt that Joan's lifespan had stretched no more than six inches beyond that narrow ledge.

"That's not true." Joan shook her head. "Look, I know I've been a real bitch lately. But I would have died today if you hadn't come after me. I just want you to know that I'll try to do better from here on out."

Mary gazed into the dark, listening to the rain fall on a million trees she could no longer see. "It's okay, Joan," she replied. "Considering all that's happened, I think you're doing just fine."

TWENTY-NINE

Jonathan locked the front door and flipped the OPEN sign to CLOSED. Dusk had deepened into darkness, and Little Jump Off had dispensed its last six-pack of the day. He turned off the store's overhead lights, then walked upstairs to the apartment. Lena Owle stood at his kitchen counter, having changed from her jeans and gingham apron into a tight black dress. She poured white wine into two slender glasses.

"Something smells good." Jonathan flopped down at the kitchen table, letting the heat from the small stove warm his backside. He stretched back in the chair and flexed his shoulders. Ever since the Harold Hobart helicopter fiasco, the day had soured like milk left in the sun. Nothing he'd undertaken had gone right, from re-fletching an arrow for Bill Landing to his mini-repair job on the wheezing ice-cream freezer. Now Lena stood here smiling, expecting him to be good company for dinner and even better company afterwards. He sighed. He should feel lucky, he supposed. So why didn't he?

"That's the cassoulet." Lena handed him a wineglass. "As soon as the bread is done we'll eat." She nodded at a thick stack of newsprint on the table. "I brought you a Sunday paper from town. You can get started on the crossword if you want."

"Thanks." Jonathan took a sip of wine and picked up the heavy Sunday edition of the *Atlanta Journal-Clarion*. He skimmed the front page, then turned to the op/ed section, where, according to the editorial writers, Atlanta should enact stricter handgun laws, Republicans should not think the state of Georgia is in their back pocket, and traffic snarls on 285 had better be addressed, and fast. Jonathan yawned, then a moment later snapped the paper to attention in front of him.

"Hey," he said. "Here's an article about Mary Crow. She's just sent up some rich guy named Whitman."

"Really." Lena clattered a pan in the sink.

"Yeah . . . It says that Atlanta's lucky to have such a dedicated young assistant DA . . . 'who comports herself with grace and passion in the courtroom. The recent Whitman case showed her to be a prosecutor of the first rank. It would be . . . ' " Jonathan turned the page, " 'hard to find another like her, said District Attorney James Falkner.' "

Lena sniffed the cassoulet and laughed. "Well, I hope it won't be too hard for Billy. He needs the thousand dollars."

Jonathan looked up over the paper. "Huh?"

"The thousand dollars that man's paying him to find Mary."

Jonathan frowned. "Fill me in here, Lena. We must not be on the same page."

Lena smoothed a wisp of dark hair back from her forehead. "I thought you knew. Yesterday a man from Mary's office drove up to Billy's picture stand and offered him a thousand dollars to take him to Mary Crow. Tam was thrilled. It was all she could talk about last night at bingo."

Jonathan refolded the paper, then asked, "Was this man a cop?"

"I don't know. Tam didn't know, either. She said Billy was packed up and gone in five minutes." Lena bent to check the French bread browning in the oven. "Just think, Jonathan. Billy might finally be able to get his fiddle back."

Jonathan sat back in the chair and stared into his wineglass. Lena made some joke about the stove, then slipped onto his lap and kissed him, her tongue teasing against his lips. He kissed her back, but just barely. He was thinking about Mary. Something was not right. If someone from Atlanta needed Mary Crow, they'd contact Stump Logan, the county sheriff, who would probably contact him. He'd worked with city cops before, even the Feds. Nobody in legitimate law enforcement would just drive up and hire Billy Swimmer in his Sioux war bonnet. He gave Lena a disengaging peck, then shifted backward in the chair. "Have we got a couple of minutes till dinner?"

"A couple." Lena raised a wary eyebrow. "Why?"

"I think I might walk over to the trailhead and see what's going on."

"Nothing's going on, Jonathan." Lena seemed to press down harder in his lap. "Somebody just needed to find Mary. Somebody hired Billy to help. What's the big deal?"

"It sounds odd. I'd like to check it out."

She stood up quickly and folded her arms. A flush of irritation pinkened the bridge of her nose. "Should I wait dinner?"

"No. I'll be back by the time the bread gets done."

Jonathan hurried downstairs before Lena could say anything more and wove through the darkened store to the front door. Outside, the cool air felt good against his skin, the breeze a crisp relief from the suddenly cloying aroma of simmering stew.

He hurried off the porch and strode west, where the Little Jump Off Trail began. Mary had taken up a lot of space in his head since she'd stopped by the store two days ago. Every time he passed the Coke cooler he thought of when they'd sat and washed salted peanuts down with two small-sized Cokes. Often he could hear her laughter echoing through his room, and for the past two nights he could almost feel the warm weight of her body on the bed, as if she lay beside him instead of his old pillow. *If only*, his thoughts would crank up like a chorus of manic cicadas. *If only you'd just walked her home that afternoon*. What then? He would never have had to see that terrible look in her eyes, nor would he have ever felt Stump Logan's official wrath pointed straight at him like the barrel of a shotgun.

I understand you and Mary Crow were together when the murder occurred.

Jonathan had nodded, his eyes downcast. "Have you got anybody who can testify to that?" Jonathan's mouth felt like the inside of an old cornhusk; he could only shake his head. Stump's eyes bored into him. "I don't suppose you'd like to tell me what you two were doing?" Jonathan looked straight at him then. There was not a man on earth, white or Cherokee, who could pull that answer from him. Stump stared back, then the very ends of his mouth twisted up in a sardonic smile. "Well, boy, that kind of puts you right at the top of the suspect list, don't it?"

"Let it go," he whispered, turning away from the twelve-year-old tape that played inside his head. "You can't change history."

He lengthened his stride, hurrying to the trailhead. No point in making Lena any madder than she already was. As he walked, the moon began to peek over Little Haw Mountain, illuminating the shallow, rushing river that tumbled along the left side of the road. Jonathan could hear the splash of trout as they leapt against the current, and along the bank one die-hard bullfrog bellowed a hopeful love song to a breeding season long past.

"Better get buried fast, buddy," Jonathan called to the frog. "Or your ass is gonna be ice cubes."

The road curled away from the river in a tight curve through the mountains, then the trailhead came into view. Jonathan pinged a rock against the grapeshot-peppered sign that read SCENIC OVERLOOK and turned from the highway up onto the narrow access road. His footsteps crunched in the gravel as he walked to the small, flat area that had been graded off to accommodate cars. He stopped and looked around. At one end of the tiny lot sat three cars, near a Park Service garbage can. The red Beemer Mary had driven up in glowed burgundy in the moonlight. Beside it stood the battered silhouette of Billy's rusted-out truck. Next to that sat a gleaming white shape Jonathan did not recognize. He walked toward it, his steps making not a sound.

The driver had backed in, revealing only a front license plate from a car rental agency. Jonathan approached the car carefully, then recognized the lines of a new Ford Taurus. He touched the hood with one finger. The finish felt like silk.

"Damn," breathed Jonathan. "I bet this car doesn't have a thousand miles on it."

The doors were locked, so he peered inside the driver's window. All he could see was a crumpled gas receipt and a manila envelope on the passenger seat. He cupped his hands around his eyes and pressed his face against the glass. Then his heart stopped. On one corner of the envelope, printed in bright red letters, was the name *Whitman*.

THIRTY

"Are you going to Atagahi before we even eat?" Lena clutched a long wooden spoon, the cassoulet bubbling merrily on the stove beside her. He nodded from the kitchen chair as he tightened the laces of his boots.

"Jonathan, we're just about to sit down to a four-course dinner with two different kinds of wine. You've already tromped around the woods most of the day." She scowled at him, then sought to soften her voice. "If you're that concerned about Mary, why don't you call Sheriff Logan?"

"Because Stump won't get his lazy ass in gear until daybreak," he replied. "If I leave now, I'll have half a day's head start."

"But you don't even know anything's wrong. Maybe she and her friends were having so much fun they decided to stay longer."

"Lena, she just nailed some rich bastard named Whitman for murder. Don't you think it's a bit coincidental that the guy who hires Billy to find her leaves an envelope with the name Whitman on the front seat of his rental car?"

"Not if he's from her office. It probably has something to do with the case she was working on."

"Nobody from the Deckard County DA's office would drive up here and hire Billy Swimmer out of the blue. It just doesn't work like that."

"It could, though." Lena turned the heat off under the cassoulet, her lower lip beginning to tremble.

He looked at her and felt a pang of guilt. "Hey, I'm sorry, but I've got to check this out. Just put the stew in the freezer. We can eat it next weekend."

"It's not stew, Jonathan. It's cassoulet and it won't be any good next weekend." She tossed the wooden spoon in the sink.

Jonathan reached for the phone on the wall and dialed a number. Busy. He hung up and dialed another number. A moment later, he slammed the phone down.

"I'm going to grab some gear," he told Lena, who wouldn't look at him. "Would you try Stump Logan again in a few minutes? Tell him what's going on, and tell him I'm on my way to Atagahi to make sure everything's okay."

"Isn't Atagahi a whole day away?" She grabbed his old pink dish sponge and began to scrub at the counter.

"Yes. But I figure if I leave now and hike fast, I can make it there by dawn."

The small muscle in her jaw twitched as she scoured the stained grout between the tile. For a moment neither one spoke, then Jonathan broke the silence.

"Lena, why are you acting like this?"

She turned to him, her brown eyes moist with tears. "Because I have spent most of three days and a week's salary on this meal that we both agreed last week would be a lovely thing to do." She flung the sponge in the sink beside the wooden spoon. "Of course that was before Mary Crow showed back up."

"Oh, for Pete's sake. Mary's an old friend. She might be in a lot of trouble."

"That's why we have a sheriff, Jonathan. And tribal police *and* the

Forest Service. You just pick up the phone and dial 911 and let them deal with it."

"Give me a break, Lena. Mary's not in the Quallah boundary. She's somewhere either in North Carolina or Tennessee. The tribal cops would be way out of their jurisdiction and the Forest Service guys can't find their asses with both hands." He stomped into the bedroom. In a few moments he returned, his old army pack on his back.

She was still standing in front of the sink, her face tight with disappointment, her eyes brimming with tears.

"Look," he said softly. "I'm sorry to ruin your supper, but I need to check this out. We'll eat the stew another time, okay?"

"Cassoulet," she whispered as he moved toward her. He held her lightly in his arms. When she felt his mouth brush against hers she wrapped her arms around the back of his neck and opened her lips. She tried to pull him deep inside, but his tongue danced with play instead of passion, and in a moment he pulled away.

"I'll see you when I get back," he told her, hurrying downstairs to the store. "Don't forget to call Stump, okay?"

She tried to ignore the brightness in his eyes and the high color of his cheeks as she watched him grab his shotgun from under the counter and disappear behind the cigarette display. She heard him walk to the candy aisle, then his footsteps crossed the room.

"Bye," he called. The door banged behind him and she stood alone in silence, save for a final gasp of steam that hissed from the now cooling cassoulet.

"Bye," she replied to the empty store. For a long moment she stared at the pot on the stove, counting the hours she'd spent preparing this meal. They were much like the hours she'd spent waiting for Jonathan to call her, or slip his hand in hers, or even kiss her first in greeting each time they met. Suddenly another door slammed inside her head, and she realized that here, at Little Jump Off, "cassoulet" would always be "stew" and Mary Crow would always be the real dish Jonathan Walkingstick hungered for.

"You bastard," she hissed as she lifted the lid of the pot and dumped a hundred dollars' worth of food and a three-hour trip to Asheville in the sink. A moist cloud of clove and garlic boiled up as she turned and pulled the bread from the oven. She ripped it in half and dropped it on the cassoulet, then fired the raspberries on top, one by one. When the mess looked repulsive enough she took the half-empty Pouilly-Fumé bottle and smashed it against the edge of the counter. Glass and wine exploded all over the tiny kitchen.

"You damn bastard!" she screamed, as hot tears rolled down her cheeks. Sobbing, she turned and looked at the telephone. She should, she supposed, try and call Sheriff Logan. Good old Lena would certainly do that. Good old Lena washed clothes and cleaned up kitchens and provided sex and Sunday papers. Surely she could make the small gesture of dialing the three digits that might save Mary Crow's life. After all, Jonathan had asked her to.

"To hell with that!" She jerked the receiver off the wall and threw it in the sink, where it sat like some bizarre garnish on top of the rest of the ruined meal. If Jonathan wanted to call Stump Logan that badly, then he could just damn well dial him himself. She had wasted too much time here already. She grabbed her coat and hurried downstairs to the front door. She had a life of her own, goddamn it. If she started right this instant, she might be able to find it before it became as lost as stupid Mary Crow.

Jonathan loped straight down the middle of the road. No cars approached from either direction, and his footsteps broke the moonlit stillness with a rapid, staccato cadence. In the glittering sky, Orion was rising in the east, out for an evening's stellar prey. Jonathan remembered another, long-ago hunt.

"We don't know who we're looking for," Stump Logan said to the men clustered around the map unfolded on the hood of his cruiser. "Other than a male who knows his way through the woods. I want you to divide into two-man teams and choose a section of the forest to search. If you see anything, radio me back here. Do not attempt a capture and don't try to be a hero. I don't need anybody else getting themselves killed." Jonathan and Billy had listened, then stepped forward. Logan had glared at them, but the teenagers had signed their names to the farthest, most difficult section. They didn't care about the danger, and they didn't give a shit about what Stump Logan wanted. They would bring back the head of Martha Crow's killer and lay it at Mary's feet; then they would eat the heart on a cracker. Hell, they were

young Cherokee bucks with the blood of the great warrior Tsali in their veins. It probably wouldn't take them the morning.

Five days later they returned with nothing. Not a trail or a sign, or a shadow of a clue. Stump Logan had only shrugged when they reported their utter failure, but Mary had watched eagerly as Jonathan climbed the steps to her house. How hard it had been to look into her face and tell her they hadn't found her mother's killer.

How long ago that had been, Jonathan realized as he turned his gaze away from the stars and shifted the pack on his shoulders. Billy had all his teeth, he had reliable knees and they both had legs that could run forever. Still, they came up short. Tonight, he thought, maybe it'll turn out different.

He glanced once at the pale silhouette of the Taurus as he crossed the trailhead parking lot; then, carrying a single small flashlight, he plunged into the forest.

Immediately he surprised two possums snuffling beneath the low branches of a pine tree. They looked up, their retinas flashing red, then ambled into the underbrush, naked pink tails curling behind them.

He watched them disappear, then he ran through a mental checklist about Mary. *What do you know about her,* he asked in the ancient tradition of the tracker. *That she's smart. That she's probably in fair physical shape. That she's very capable in the woods.*

What do you know about her pursuer? Nothing, other than he'd driven up in a rented Ford and paid Billy Swimmer a thousand bucks to lead him to Mary. Could he hike? Did he know how to track? Jonathan shook his head as he splashed across a shallow creek that glinted silver in the rising moon. It didn't matter what the guy knew. He had Billy Swimmer, and Billy knew the woods better than the strings of his fiddle.

For three hours he moved through the dark forest. Along a streambed, where the trail grew muddy, he knelt and beamed his flashlight on the ground. Footprints in varying sizes indented the mud, all going the same direction. The smallest set bore the crisp ridges of new boots. All the other prints were worn. Adds up, Jonathan thought. The dark-haired girl with the Brooklyn accent was new at camping. Mary and her taller friend had camped before.

He hiked on, hurrying through the hours, weaving through the moonlit trees like a shadow. At last he reached the point where the trail divided. He looked once toward the Ghosts and felt the hair rise on the back of his neck. Then he tightened his grip on his shotgun and turned right, where the trail rose like an escalator through a stand of trees.

He climbed until that odd hour of the night when the earth belonged to neither sun nor moon. As he approached the last mountain before Atagahi, he blinked. Lights. Thirty yards to his right. He saw lights. Someone was camping.

"Mary!" His impulsive cry broke the silence like a gunshot. There was no reply. *They're sleeping*, he decided, trembling with relief. *They took the harder trail home and staked lights around their campsite before they went to sleep.* He ran forward, crashing through the underbrush. "Mary! It's Jonathan!"

He splashed through a creek, cold water soaking his pants up to his knees. The lights were clustered just ahead, around both sides of the stream. He ran faster. "Mary!" he called again.

Suddenly he stopped. He realized what he was running toward. What he was seeing through the trees was not the flares of campers, but just a growth of fox fire. The luminescent fungi that people attributed to everything from fairies to spacemen.

"Fuck!" he cried, kicking at one incandescent chunk of decayed log. It tumbled rotten into the stream, still shining brightly as the water swept it away.

He took his pack off and sat down on a log. What an idiot he was! A big-time guide being fooled by fox fire. Next he'd be heading for the caves to consult with the *Nunnehi*. Keeping his shotgun close beside him, he stretched out on the ground and considered the facts he knew. The three women had come this way, yet he had seen no sign of them other than their footprints. If he didn't find them tomorrow at Atagahi, then he would retrace his steps and go through the Ghosts.

He put it out of his mind and closed his eyes. Cullasaja, the last mountain that guarded Atagahi, was too treacherous to climb in the dark. He might as well get an hour or two of rest and start again at first light. Leaning back against the log, he cradled his rifle in his arms. Suddenly he was years away; strong, and incredibly young.

"I heard your grandmother is coming for you," he said to her. They sat side by side on the back porch of the funeral home, he throwing Ribtickler in a nervous game of mumblety-peg.

"I don't want to stay here, Jonathan," she replied. She wore a white blouse and a blue gingham skirt that came to her ankles.

"It wasn't your fault, Mary. It wasn't our fault. There was nothing any-body could have done." He tossed words at her willy-nilly, hoping a few would come close to what he wanted to say.

"That's what they tell me."

"And they're right," he insisted, flicking the knife in the dirt.

"My grandmother wants me to do this, Jonathan. She wants to send me to college."

"But what about us?" He had not touched her since that afternoon. He longed to feel her skin against his, to twine his fingers through hers. "I love you."

She looked at him for what seemed like forever. Her eyes reminded him of the mottled creek stones that lay under clear water. "I love you, too," she replied. "But that doesn't change a thing."

An ovenbird woke him, its happy *teacher-teacher-teacher* call carrying through the woods. He sat up and looked around. For a moment he thought he'd heard Mary. Then he realized that it was a bird; that Mary was still just as gone as she had been when he drifted off to sleep. He forced himself to be optimistic. The day was new: he would surely find them lolling in the warm waters of the spring. And Billy was no fool; if this mystery man from Deckard County meant Mary any harm he would piece it together. Right now he was probably leading the man surreptitiously back toward Stump Logan's jail. Jonathan opened his pack and drank a warm Coke, then, shouldering his gear, he began to climb.

The trail snaked upward through hemlocks and cedars. The morning air was heavy with moisture and his breath came in white puffs, as if he were smoking a pipe. This would have been a hard climb for women unused to the woods, he thought, as a thorn branch snagged his pants leg. Higher and higher he pushed. By the time the dawn had turned the color of a pale egg, the armpits of his shirt were ringed with dark circles of sweat. Three more turns, fifty feet on the trail, the big maple tree, and he reached the rocks above Atagahi. Finally he was there. He looked down at the spring.

"Oh, God," he cried, his voice raw as an open wound.

THIRTY-ONE

He leapt down the boulders, his feet barely touching one rock before they thrust him onto the next, his gun banging against his shoulder blades. *Should've come down here loaded,* he thought as he slid and nearly fell on loose gravel. But there was no time now to shove any buckshot into his gun. He jumped over the last rocks and threw off his pack. The air from Atagahi rose warm and moist against his face; faraway he heard the warning *caaaawww* of a crow.

The body floated facedown in the green water. Hair clung like dark tar to the skull, the hands bobbed outstretched, as if beseeching someone beneath the water.

"No," Jonathan said under his breath.

He shrugged off his gun and knelt by the spring. Leaning out over the water, he could just touch the right ankle with his outstretched fingers. He grabbed the leg, then an arm, then he hoisted the body out of the spring. Maybe he wasn't too late . . .

Billy had not yet bloated or stiffened, but his skin looked like unmelted paraffin and felt like a well-chilled steak. Blood and water oozed from the dime-sized hole in the middle of his stomach.

Jonathan's brain went numb. All he could do was cradle Billy's head in his lap and stare into his face. Billy's mouth seemed to gape open more in surprise than terror, an expression Jonathan had seen often on his friend in high school, after they'd been caught smoking in the boys' bathroom.

Billy's hands bore no signs of struggle. The knuckles were unsplit and the fingers hung limp, frail as the bleached bones of a dead bird. They would coax no more music from horsehair and gut.

"Oh, Billy," Jonathan said thickly. There was a hard angular lump in the pocket of Billy's sweatshirt. Jonathan reached in and pulled out a small harmonica. It was waterlogged, but untouched by any bullet. Jonathan lifted it to his lips. He blew a cluster of sad, tinny notes into the air, then he buttoned the harmonica in his own breast pocket. He would give it to little Michael. The boy was too young to understand now, but someday they would sit on the porch at Little Jump Off and Jonathan would tell him about his father—that he had been a good man and a fiddler like no other.

"I'm so sorry," Jonathan moaned, wishing he could speak the words in Cherokee. He pressed his forehead against Billy's. He held him for a moment, then he examined the bullet hole more closely. The orange fabric of Billy's sweatshirt was charred around the edges, and a thin smear of blood trailed along the rocks for almost twenty feet. Whitman, the stranger who'd lured him up here with the promise of a thousand dollars, had shot him in the gut from point-blank range. Ever the Cherokee, Billy had spent his last moments trying to crawl to the healing waters of Atagahi.

The sharp taste of anger rose in Jonathan's throat. If Whitman had already killed Billy, then he might well have murdered Mary, too, and now be on his way back to civilization. But Jonathan had passed no one on the trail; he hadn't seen the slightest trace of anyone heading east. Could Whitman still be here, in the forest, waiting?

Quickly, he laid Billy on the ground and picked up his shotgun.

He loaded two shells and circled the pool, trying to stay inside the deep purple shadows cast by the rising sun. He peered into the small crevices between the boulders, his ears keen for the scratch of a pebble or the cock of a gun's hammer. When he found nothing but the same blank boulders that had stood there for the past ten thousand years, he climbed up into the bigger surrounding rocks, steeling himself to find more bodies, but hoping to find anything that might give him some kind of clue. Again, the rocks revealed nothing. He crouched beside a boulder. Could Mary and her friends have gotten lost in the Ghosts? Did the three women even make it this far? If that was the case, why did Whitman kill Billy here?

He turned that over in his mind as he searched the rest of the rocks. He'd just crept past one huge boulder that protruded upward from the others when he heard a whimper.

"Mary?" he called out, his voice lifting with hope.

He heard another, sharper cry. Under a small outcropping of sandstone, a familiar face peered up at him. Dark brown eyes, floppy ears alert for danger.

"Homer!"

The dog whimpered as he leapt into Jonathan's arms. Wagging his tail like a buggy whip, he plastered Jonathan's face with sloppy, ardent kisses. The weight of sixty twisting pounds of joyous hound pushed them both backwards into the dirt.

"Homer, what happened?" Though Homer wiggled with delight, Jonathan could feel his rangy muscles shivering. Whatever had transpired before Billy's death was still terrifying his dog.

A bloody gash creased the top of the animal's head, the result, Jonathan surmised, of a poorly aimed bullet. Other than that, Homer was okay, though there was an edginess about him that Jonathan had never seen before. He scratched Homer underneath his chin, then got to his feet and shouldered his gun.

"Come on, old boy. You can help me out here."

He searched the remainder of the clearing, Homer at his heels. No one else, dead or alive, was hiding anywhere at Atagahi that morning. More puzzled than ever, Jonathan climbed back down and sat beside Billy. Homer nudged Billy's hand once with his nose, then nestled close beside Jonathan and again started to shiver.

Jonathan stared at the hole in Billy's chest as he considered differ-ent scenarios. Had Whitman killed Billy, then killed the three women and left them somewhere else? Had he buried them? Why bury three victims and leave the last floating? And why not kill Homer, too? Surely a man who would gut-shoot another man would have no qualms about dispatching a dog. If—he had just begun to postulate a third possibility when he noticed two dark splotches on a boulder beyond the spot where Billy's bloody trail began. He jumped to his feet and ran to get a closer look.

Two chalk markings decorated the sandstone. The lines and loops looked like they could have once formed words, and it seemed to him a single line was scribbled at the bottom of each block. Just like two separate letters with two signatures. He traced the edges of them, as if that might tell him what happened here, then he touched one block itself. It was dry. He leaned over and licked it. The bitter taste of burned wood stung his tongue.

He frowned. There must be something else here, something he'd missed. He surveyed the spring again, this time softening his focus, allowing his gaze to absorb everything.

Halfway through a slow scan of the area, he saw it. A narrow, trampled trail through the grass that led past the willow and up into the mountains, weeds bent along both sides, wide enough for one person to walk. A dot of color caught his eye. A yellow fleck dotted the old willow.

He hurried over to the willow and touched the lemon-colored spot. It felt sticky; a bit of yellow came off on his finger. He sniffed it. Oil paint. Mary. She had come up here to paint, and she'd left this dot of yellow pigment five feet up the tree. Why? Because she had to go into woods she didn't know, and she was marking a trail to lead her back here.

"Okay, Homer," he murmured as he scanned the trees up the mountainside, searching for more dots of yellow paint. He saw none, but surely there must be more. Mary wouldn't have marked one tree and then quit. "We might have the start of a trail here. Now we've just got to find the rest of it."

He began to move quickly. Homer followed at his heels as he

pulled a tarp from his pack and spread it beneath the willow. Then he walked back to the spring and gathered Billy in his arms. His body felt lighter than he'd expected. Jonathan carried him to the tree, remembering all the sweet summer evenings Billy's fiddle had sung at weddings and wakes and barn dances, for free, just because he loved to see hard-knuckled farmers and their taciturn wives jumping like crickets to his music. As he thought of that, Billy's body grew leaden in his arms, and he felt as if he were carrying some dead part of himself as well.

Homer watched, ears pricked, as Jonathan laid the corpse squarely in the middle of the tarp, then turned it so Billy's head pointed west. He knelt there, trying to call up some Cherokee prayer that would send Billy off, but he couldn't remember any Cherokee words. Suddenly a dark, hot rage shot through him. Some rich white fucker in a rented Ford had killed his oldest friend, and he hadn't been able to do a thing about it.

He stuck two fingers of his right hand into the wound in Billy's stomach. He pulled them out, dark with clotted blood, then closed his eyes and smeared the blood across his cheeks and nose. A single stroke, left to right, as he once read the great Tsali had done; then he looked up at the sky. Though he knew it was crazy, at that moment he felt just like one of the old warriors—hot and strong and utterly without limits.

"I don't know if the old ones did it like this, Billy, but I swear to you that you shall have the heart of the one who killed you."

THIRTY-TWO

S hit!" Mitch Whitman spat as he threw himself up the steep trail. A dense fog had arisen suddenly from the ground, clutching at his legs with wispy fingers. In ten minutes the world had gone from a clear, dark green to a nebulous gray.

Pausing to wipe the sweat from his forehead, he peered through the swirling mist until his eyes stopped on the next yellow-dotted tree. He climbed up the trail till he reached the tall pine, then he collapsed beneath it, happy to sit and let his lungs refill with air. It was only when he closed his eyes that everything came rushing back.

He hadn't meant to kill the Real Life Cherokee. But before he could stop himself, he'd burst out laughing when he read Mary's note scrawled on the rocks. From then on, things had gone downhill fast.

"What's so funny?" The Indian had turned to him, his dark eyes flashing with suspicion. "Mary's note says she's in big trouble."

Mitch took a step back and tried to explain. "I'm laughing because Mary's so brave. It would be just like her to try and rescue her friend."

"But she and her friend got hurt." The Indian's eyes bored into him. "Can't you tell how scared they are?"

"The great Mary Crow wouldn't be scared of a little rapist," said Mitch. "She deals with scum like that all the time."

"Bullshit," the Indian replied. He reached down as if to re-tie his boot, then, quicker than Mitch would have dreamed possible, the Real Life Cherokee pulled a hunting knife and was pressing the sharp, cold point into the hollow of his throat.

"Turn around, Mr. Keane. I'm not sure what all you're about, but your guided tour of the Smoky Mountains has just ended."

Mitch froze as the damned hound began growling behind him, then, cautiously, he began to inch his hand toward the Beretta nestled under his arm.

"Move it, Keane," the Indian said softly. "Me and Homer got you covered."

"Fuck you, Tonto." Mitch pulled the Beretta out and shoved it into the Indian's gut, squeezing the trigger twice. Two muted pops sounded. For an instant, the Indian looked astonished, then his eyes focused inward and he crumpled to his knees. Mitch winced as the damned dog started licking the blood that gushed from his master's wound.

The Indian groaned. With his knife still clutched in his right hand, he began to crawl toward the spring.

"I don't think you're in any shape for a swim," Mitch taunted as the wounded man inched forward, leaving a slug-trail of shiny blood on the rocks. The dog yapped and ran circles around them. Mitch watched, amazed, wondering where the Indian intended to crawl with half his stomach blown away. He seemed determined to get to the spring, but just as he stretched out his hand toward the green water, the knife fell from his fingers and his legs lost their strength, merely twitching when they should have been pushing him forward.

"Tam?" said the Indian, his voice no more than a husky echo.

Mitch could not look away. Though he'd seen game dying in the field, this was the first time a man had bled out at his feet. Like a passerby who stops to gawk at some grisly accident on the highway, he could not pull his gaze away from the Indian's quivering legs or his strange, mumbled words that could have been either curses or prayers.

Then as always, whether it was a moose fallen on the ground or just some dumb deer, there was that tingle that started in Mitch's scrotum and made him weak with desire. He enjoyed the prickly warmth that spread through his loins, but it left as swiftly as it had come, rendering him angry and unfulfilled.

"Oh, come on," he said gruffly, acting on his own discomfort. "Let's put you out of your misery."

He stuffed the gun back in his holster and walked over to the Indian. Grasping him by the seat of his jeans and the collar of his Tennessee Vols sweatshirt, he picked him up and flung him into the spring. He floated facedown, blood seeping into the water like ink from an overturned bottle.

Under the pine tree, Mitch opened his eyes. "Actually, not such a bad way to go," he decided. "Certainly more heroic than poor old Sandy Manning."

What had the Indian's name been? Billy or Willy or something. Poor dumb fucker. He'd babbled on about his kid's ears and his hocked fiddle, truly believing that a thousand dollars was going to turn his life around. Mitch chuckled. A thousand bucks might punch up your weekend, but turn your life around? Shit. Anyway, it didn't matter now. For the Real Life Cherokee, getting his life turned around was no longer an option.

The damp, humid air had left a film of moisture on Mitch's clothes that looked like dew. Around him, all he could see were tree trunks, poking up black through the mist like ghostly pikes on some medieval battlefield. Of all the places he'd hunted, this sodden, foggy country was the strangest. All these trees, all these mountains, and he'd only seen one owl and some kind of lizard. Not a rabbit or a chipmunk or even a squirrel. It was as if they had sensed his coming and just ceded him the whole half-million acres. Maybe it was just as well, he thought, remembering that turd-looking thing he'd shot the night before. Animals were not what he was hunting today, anyway.

He hadn't done as well with Homer as he had with the Indian. At first he thought he might bring the dog with him, but when the Indian hit the water the hound started barking like crazy. Mitch had tried to call him, but the damned animal snapped at him every time he came within a few steps. That was the trouble with dogs. Kill their masters and they turned against you. Immediately and forever. Mitch had finally taken the Beretta out again and aimed at Homer's head. Blood spurted after he fired, but the old dog didn't fall. Instead, he bounded up into the rocks, bleeding and screaming like something mad. Stupid hound, Mitch thought. Though he knew it was unsportsmanlike, he decided to let Homer bleed to death on his own. "After all," he chuckled, his warm breath vaporizing in the cool air, "who needs a coon dog when you're out hunting crow?"

He considered Mary Crow and smiled. At last, she'd made her first mistake. Before he'd washed those messages scribbled on the rock away, he'd found out exactly what had happened to her and her friend and exactly what they were going to do about it. They'd even marked their trail, in case somebody came looking for them.

"You finally fucked up, Mary, girl," he said as he unwrapped one of the food bars in his pack. "And you fucked up big-time."

He finished eating and pushed on through the fog, finally breaking out of the thick woods into a narrow, level plain that seemed to have once been a kind of road. The feathery heads of pampas grass swayed from a field punctuated by small cedar trees that stuck up like exclamation points. A path of trampled weeds crossed the sward, then vanished into the forest above it. If he squinted, he could see a bright yellow dot on a tree about ten feet above the roadbed. Shifting the pack on his shoulders, he smiled. If the trail kept going as easily as this, he could probably have Mary Crow and company dead before breakfast.

"And what were you doing when Mary Crow was killed?" he mimicked aloud, parodying one of the last questions she'd hurled at him on the stand. "Hiking through the woods, your honor," he replied. "Experiencing firsthand how the fittest survive."

THIRTY-THREE

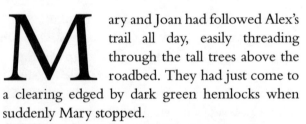

ary and Joan had followed Alex's
trail all day, easily threading
through the tall trees above the
roadbed. They had just come to
a clearing edged by dark green hemlocks when
suddenly Mary stopped.

"Something's happened," she said softly.

"What?" Joan was concentrating so hard on
trying to walk as silently as Mary that she almost
stumbled into her.

Mary pointed down to the roadbed. "Alex
has quit marking her trail."

Joan's old terror instantly reawakened. "But
why?"

Mary rubbed her eyes, as if that might make
Alex's bent thistles and stalks reappear. "I can't tell.
It looks like she walked to the edge of those hem-
locks, then stopped."

"What should we do?"

"I don't know." Drumming her fingers

softly against her paint box, Mary studied the clearing. Finally, she spoke.

"I'll go down and look around. Maybe the trail picks up past those trees."

"But what if it's a trap?" Joan plucked at the sleeve of Mary's sweatshirt. "What if Barefoot knows we're following him, and now he's down there, waiting?"

"We can't help that. Wait for me right here. I'll be back in fifteen minutes."

"But . . ."

Mary turned and glared at her. "Joan, I've got to go down there. We've got to find out what happened to Alex's trail."

Joan opened her mouth to protest, then closed it. She had learned, during the past three days, that arguing with Mary Crow was pointless. "Just please be careful," she said meekly as Mary slipped like a shadow through the trees.

When Mary had gone, Joan sat down beside a fallen pine and stretched out her legs. Once delicate and high-arched, her feet were now swollen and blistered. They protruded from Mary's jeans, looking as if they belonged to someone else. She wondered what Natalie, her favorite shoe clerk at Saks, would say if she could see them. *I'm so sorry, Ms. Marchetti. No more Ferragamos for you. You'll have to try the orthopedic store on thirty-ninth.* Joan's lips trembled as she bit back a sob. Alex had always laughed at her passion for shoes. What a kick she would get out of this. *Brooklyn's answer to Imelda Marcos,* she would hoot, *condemned to beige oxfords!*

Joan turned her gaze away from her feet and stared through the leaves. *Alex,* she thought, trying to sharpen the now hazy memory of her teasing friend. *Where are you? Has Barefoot done the same thing to you as he did to me, or has he done worse?* All at once his stink filled her nostrils as she recalled his rough fingers on her flesh. *Raped.*

Violare. Her parents would call down the worst of curses on a man who would do such a thing. Her Uncle Nick would gleefully hack off that man's balls. *And so would I.* The realization sizzled through her like a jolt of electricity. *I, too, could kill him.*

The shrill chirp of a wren jarred her back to reality. She frowned. Where was Mary? Wasn't she supposed to come back soon?

She stood up and nervously scanned the clearing. "Shit!" she cried, wringing her hands. Mary had been gone far too long. Had she gotten lost? Had she fallen and hurt herself? Had Barefoot sprung some sick trap? What was she supposed to do now? And what would happen to her if Mary never came back?

"Think," she told herself. "Think like Mary would think." She forced herself to stand still and try to come up with a plan. If Mary had walked into a trap, then Barefoot would either wait for her to fall into the same trap, or he might get impatient and come looking for her. Mary had taken the palette knife and the paint box; all she had was the nearly empty tube of yellow paint. Though the idea of creeping through the forest alone made her queasy, sitting here waiting to be violated again made her want to throw up.

"Move," she finally decided. "Mary would move."

Stashing the paint tube in the pocket of Mary's jeans, she crept down to the clearing. The trail led to a wider patch of trampled grass, then there was nothing. It looked like Alex and Barefoot had come to this spot and simply vanished.

Okay, Joan thought. *Where would Mary have gone from here?*

She turned in a slow circle, her heart thumping. No one direction seemed any more promising than any other, so she moved forward, hesitantly keeping close to the trees.

The afternoon sun cast long shadows on the ground while the forest lay eerily still. She'd felt the same anticipatory hush when she'd sung on stage, as the curtain rose and the audience waited, silent, for the notes to start soaring from her throat.

Mary, she thought, longing to sing out her name, longing even more to hear her friend's voice answering in return. But the only sound she heard was the hiss of golden maple leaves, shuddering on a breath of wind.

On the left the roadbed veered slightly uphill. On the right sprawled a massive thicket of twisting bushes. Laurel, Mary had called it. Appalachian kudzu. Suddenly, Joan stopped. Had she heard something in the dense foliage?

"Mary?" she called softly, peering into the tangled green darkness.

Nobody answered. Still, Joan knew Mary was in there, somewhere, searching for Alex. *Trust your instincts*, she thought as she ducked and stepped into the tangle of high bushes. *That's what Mary would do.*

She picked her way easily through the first spindly plants, then the leaves grew thicker, the branches more confining. Beneath them, the air smelled pungent, choked with rotting vegetation. She started having to shoulder her way between the reluctant bushes, then she had to turn sideways to penetrate them at all. The plants granted no admittance; the further in she pushed, the denser they grew. Suddenly she realized that this was crazy—Mary would never have traipsed through a tangle like this.

"I'd better get back," she said aloud. "Mary's probably waiting back at that log, pissed."

Shoving the scratchy branches away from her face, she turned. All at once her legs went limp. The coiling foliage had swallowed the path she'd just made: the laurel itself seemed to have closed behind her like a wall. Every plant loomed above her, blocking out all light and air.

"Mary?" she called, bewildered, a sudden cold sweat bathing her body.

There was no answer.

"Mary?" she called louder. Her voice edged toward panic. What an idiot she'd been. What had ever made her think she could navigate these woods like Mary Crow?

She turned quickly, then felt something slash against the top of her hair. She remembered the hawk, plummeting down from the sky, its talons like knives, and she started to whimper. Instinctively, she ran, tearing headlong through the unyielding bushes. Leaves clawed at her eyes, branches snatched at her legs as she fought her way through the malignant green maze.

"No!" she cried, thrashing through the twisted bushes that held her prisoner. She wanted to go back the way she'd come, but the leaves crowded around her, cutting her off from any place that looked familiar. Was she going forward? Or running in endless circles? Panic gripped her. She ran faster, growing dizzy, all the plants now tilting, thrusting maliciously toward the sky. Suddenly she stepped on something sharp. She cried out as a white-hot pain sizzled up her foot and into her thigh. She toppled forward. Lurching to her feet, she kept moving, charging recklessly through the thick plants. As she shoved between two towering bushes, her foot snagged on a root. This time, she fell sprawling, biting her tongue as her left cheek hit the earth. With the warm, metallic taste of blood filling her mouth, she crawled beneath a bush, seeking shelter like some stricken animal. Gasping, she sat up and examined her foot. A huge thorn lay imbedded just below her big toe. Already the fleshy part of her sole was hot and throbbing in time to the frantic rhythm of her heart.

"Shit!" she cried. "Shit! Shit! Shit!" Without thinking, she grabbed the thorn and yanked hard. The sharp point broke off, but most of the thorn remained buried deep in her flesh.

All at once she felt sweaty and nauseous, just as she had when she was five and her brother Frank had locked her in their hall closet. Then, hot woolen coats had pressed against her, robbing her of the air she needed to breathe. Now coiling bushes kept her captive, their branches trapping her in an emerald darkness where the air smelled like the moldy insides of an old refrigerator. How she would love to breathe fresh air again! How she would love to see the sky!

Suddenly she could bear it no longer. She grabbed the laurel leaves above her with both fists and tore them from their branches.

"Shit!" she cried, cackling like a madwoman. "Shit! Shit! Shit! I'm going to be strangled by a bunch of fucking bushes!"

All at once, the shredded leaves that flew around her turned into women. Every Mary she'd ever known floated to the ground smiling, radiant as pictures in a missal. Mary Crow. Sister Mary Ignatius. Sister Mary Magdalen. The Virgin Mary. "Help me," Joan pleaded, now sobbing uncontrollably. "I'm trying so hard. Please don't let me die here. Please tell me what to do. . . ."

"Joan?"

The sound startled her so that she was sitting up before she was even awake.

"Joan? Is that you?"

Joan struggled to focus in the dark, bracing herself to run. Hours must have passed since she'd collapsed beneath this bush. A figure crouched in front of her, someone dirty, hunkering down like an animal. The smell of fear hung rank in the air. Joan bit down a scream. Was this a dream, or had Barefoot found her? Would she die here without anyone ever knowing what had happened to her?

"Good God, Joan! Where in the hell have you been?" Mary grabbed her so hard Joan felt the breath leave her lungs. "I didn't know what had happened to you!"

Joan felt Mary's arms around her, felt her sweatshirt soaked with perspiration. She was trembling so hard she could barely speak. She was not dreaming! Mary had returned!

"Why on earth did you come in here?" Mary cried. "Why didn't you stay where I told you to?"

"I was looking for you," whimpered Joan. "Please don't yell at me . . ."

Mary let Joan go and stared into her eyes. In the dark her dirt-streaked face gave her the look of some aboriginal mud-woman. "You don't know what this is, do you?"

The warm comfort Joan had felt just seconds before evaporated. Trembling, she shook her head.

Mary looked at her fiercely. "This is a Hell, Joan. A dog-hobble. A huge sprawl of bushes that could go on for miles. Hillbillies write songs about people who wander into these things and never find their way out. I've been crawling through these bushes for hours. If I hadn't heard you snoring, I'd never have found you."

"Well, you don't need to be so nasty about it," Joan retorted, close to tears. "After all, I was the one who was lost—"

Mary gave a weary sigh. She released Joan and brushed a tangled snarl of hair from her eyes. "You're right," she said. "You didn't know, I should have warned you."

For a while neither of them spoke; then, with another sigh, Mary curled up beneath the laurel like a bone-tired child. She lay with her back toward Joan, and in the green darkness she looked no more animate than a lump of earth.

Joan watched her until the silence between them seemed to stretch for miles, and she felt as if the two of them suddenly inhabited separate islands in a distant archipelago. When she could bear it no longer, she whispered, "Are you mad at me?" Her voice cracked in the darkness like a child's.

"No," Mary answered flatly. "Just tired."

The thorn in Joan's foot was throbbing like a hot coal. "We're in trouble, aren't we?"

"Yes."

"Bad trouble?"

Mary turned over. Her expression was lost in the shadows. "I don't know, Joan. We're hurt. We're hungry. We lost Alex's trail, and now we've lost ourselves in this Hell. Does that sound like trouble to you?"

Again, Joan started to tremble. Mary made everything sound so hopeless. "Maybe when the sun comes up . . ." she began.

"The sun can't penetrate this laurel, Joan. It's never more than twilight in a Hell. There aren't any streams to drink from, and nothing edible to forage. It could take us days to crawl out of here."

Joan began to cry. How she had wanted to please Mary—to prove just one time that she wasn't the wuss Alex had called her. But she'd failed utterly. She'd gotten them both impossibly lost in this stupid tangle of bushes. She wished Barefoot had just killed her back at that spring. It would have made it easier for everybody. Then Mary might have had a chance.

"I'm sorry," she sobbed, her breath coming in gulps. "I'm so very sorry . . ."

She hunched over in a small knot as she wept, filthy, hungry, and more miserable than she'd ever dreamed possible. They were hopelessly lost and it was all her fault. And now Alex would surely die, if she wasn't dead already. Then suddenly she felt Mary's bracing arms around her, her breath whispering into her hair.

"Save your tears, honey. I learned years ago they never change a thing."

"But what are we going to do?"

Mary squeezed her. "We're going to rest a little while, then we're going to move on."

Joan blinked. "In the dark?"

"Dark, light, it doesn't make much difference in here."

"So we're not giving up? We're still going to look for Alex?"

Mary didn't answer at first, then she spoke, sounding as if she were a thousand years old. "No, Joan. Alex is gone. We lost her when we got tangled up in this Hell. From here on the only thing we'll be looking for is a way out of here. And we'll be very lucky if we find that."

Joan looked up through the branches that coiled high above their heads. Not a star or a glimmer of moonlight shone through the leaves, which seemed to press down upon them like a shroud. *What a rotten place to die*, she thought, and she crept closer to Mary, knowing nothing could save them now.

THIRTY-FOUR

I t's going to be daydown soon," Mitch
said, using the Real Life Cherokee's
quaint term for sunset as a line of pines
turned to somber silhouettes against a
wild tangerine horizon. "Time for tired little
trackers to make camp for the night."

But he walked for a few minutes more, watching as the golden light paled to mauve. Above him
an owl hooted hidden in the trees; on the ground,
the forest floor was spongy with moss and dead
leaves. He wondered what everyone was doing at
home. His mother was probably keeping company
with Jack Daniels and Oprah Winfrey while his
father barked orders from the library. Cal, he sus-
pected, was sitting in his cell, royally pissed that
their father hadn't been able to buy him out of this
mess. *Is my testimony still funny now, Cal? Does the
hour I spent for you being humiliated by Mary Crow still
crack you up like it did in court that day?*

"I hope so, bro," Mitch said aloud. "Hope
you still think it's just a scream."

When he tripped over the roots of a sprawling tree and nearly fell, he decided it was time to stop. No point in breaking an ankle, he thought. It's not like Mary Crow's going anywhere.

Beneath a white spruce he staked three tent poles in the ground, clipped his orange tent to them and crawled inside, pulling his rifle and gear after him. He dug in his pack for his lantern, which lay tucked beneath the duct tape and clothesline he'd bought at the convenience store. He switched on the light and a small radio, bathing the tent in a tropical glow and filling the air with the sounds of a scratchy R&B station out of Chattanooga. He knew he would be highly visible listening to music in a tent the color of a cantaloupe, but why should he care? He and the Beretta could deal with anything that appeared at his tent flap, and if Mary Crow and company came by, so much the better. It would save him a lot of shoe leather in the morning.

He heated some freeze-dried beef stew on his propane stove and topped off his dinner with a chocolate bar. Unrolling his sleeping bag, he remembered how the Real Life Cherokee had admired his gear, especially this bag. The Indian would have loved the Beretta, too, if he'd ever gotten a chance to see it. Oh, well, Mitch thought, as he climbed into the bag's featherweight warmth. Shit happens.

He turned up the radio. As Al Green's thumping "Let's Stay Together" filled the tent, he rolled over on his side and closed his eyes. He tried hard to revisit Rio Blanco, but his dreams took him in another direction.

Sandra is on top of him, her tongue working in lazy circles around his nipples and down the cordon of hair that bisects his belly. He's anticipated her ultimate destination; already his dick feels hot and swollen, rising to meet her touch. She's at his navel now; he feels the soft weight of her breasts sliding down his thighs.

Suddenly his cell phone chirps from his trousers by the bed. Sandra stops, looks up.

"You expecting a call?" she asks, her honey-colored eyes surprised.

"No," he tells her, trying not to sound annoyed. "Ignore it."

"I don't think you'd better," she says, rising off him as the phone chirps on. "It sounds important."

Irritated, he rolls over and grabs for the phone. Cal's voice, drunk, stoned, whatever else Cal is, comes on.

"No," he replies. "I can't come get you. Not now."

But Cal pleads, begs, even weeps. Christ, his twenty-one-year-old brother bawling like a baby! The cops will get me, Cal insists. If I get busted again Dad will kill me.

He sighs, knowing his brother will not give up; has never in his life allowed "no" to thwart him. "Okay, Cal," he sighs. "Stay right there."

He hangs up the phone and dresses, easing trousers tenderly over a dick that has not yet gotten the message.

"Where are you going?" Sandra asks.

"To get my asswipe brother," he answers, too angry to say more. "He's down at Five Points, stoned."

"Oh, bring him back here," she says. "I want to meet him."

"No you don't," he snaps, knowing what always happens when his handsome brother meets women. "He's a jerk."

"Oh, come on, Mitch. He can sober up here. Then he can go and you can stay." She looks up at him so sweetly, what can he say? No, I'm afraid my little brother will steal you away?

"Okay," he says, brushing her large, dark nipple with his fingertip. "But only till he's able to drive."

He picks Cal up. He's done a lot of coke and some other street drugs he's probably never heard of. Cal's head wobbles on his neck, but his eyes are bright, his cheeks red. Cal's knuckles are swollen; he complains that he's been in a fight.

Don't do this, a voice tells him, but he ignores it. He will not allow himself to fear his fucked-up little brother.

Later, she opens the door to both of them, smiling especially sweet when she sees Cal. "Hello," she says, like they were meeting at some damned cocktail party. "Mitch has told me so much about you!"

Which is a lie. He's told her nothing. He wishes he had no brother; wishes Cal would overdose on something and die.

They sit on her sofa; she in the middle between them. Cal pulls a bottle of whiskey from one pocket and a tin of white powder from the other. "Let's party!" he says.

Cal and Sandra do a few lines of coke and turn on the CD player too loud. The downstairs neighbor starts banging on the ceiling. The phone rings—another neighbor calling to complain about the racket, threatening the police. He turns down the CD, but Cal turns it back up again.

"You want to learn the fuck-me-blind polka?" Cal giggles, sweeping Sandra up off the sofa. He holds her tight, she seems to melt in his arms, giggling, almost swooning at Cal's handsome face. They gyrate around the room, then the loud music slows and their movements become a slow grind—her hips meeting his in a pantomime of sex, her gaze locking onto his as if she's wanted him forever. Cal smiles at her, holds her close, then over her shoulder he winks at Mitch.

Cal's grinning face ignites a poker in Mitch's gut. There's no point in sitting and watching this shit. He goes to the kitchen where he turns the cold water on full blast. He needs to take the heat, the hotness, away from his skin. He plunges his head beneath the faucet, letting the water douse his face and his hair and run dripping down the collar of his shirt. It feels good; cools him like the turquoise waters of Rio Blanco. He wishes he were there right now, and away from this stuffy apartment and Sandra Manning and his stupid asswipe brother.

He shakes the water from his face and looks back into the living room. He can hardly believe it. Sandra's panties are in a puddle around her ankles while her skirt is pushed to her waist. She and Cal are not doing the fuck-me-blind polka, they are simply fucking, hammer and tongs, like two dogs in an alley.

He turns away. Though he has no particular love for Sandra Manning beyond the roundness of her breasts and tightness of her twat, she was his first. That is his twat his brother is fucking.

Angry, accusatory voices crackle through the air.

"Stop!" Sandra cries, over Cal's "You fucking cunt!"

Mitch hears slaps, blows resounding against flesh. Leaving the water streaming from the faucet, he runs back into the living room. He knows what can happen to a woman when Cal gets mad.

They are standing by the fireplace now, no longer fucking. Cal's face is scratched and the front of Sandra's blouse is ripped away. They are struggling. Cal takes that mean right cross and smashes it into her jaw. A tooth goes flying, lands near Mitch's boot. Sandra leaps at Cal, yowling, nails scratching at his eyes.

"Are you two nuts?" Mitch yells. He rushes forward and tries to pry them apart, but both are too angry and stoned to be subdued. Cal's dick dangles like a limp, dark worm from his fly.

"Stop it, Cal!" Mitch cries, suddenly in the fight himself. His brother's fist glances off his jaw, while Sandra hisses at him like a cat. Finally he lowers *his head and shoves them apart. He pushes Cal backward on the couch, but Sandra is something else. Sandra he heaves as hard as he can. He wants her to know that he's the Whitman she needs to fear, not his stupid little brother. He laughs as she careens toward the fireplace, the panties around her ankles tripping her up. Suddenly, she's falling, waving her arms and screeching, but going down, down until her head shatters the glass fireplace screen and her skull smacks into the andiron behind it.*

He closes his eyes as the glass explodes around him. When he opens them again he expects to see blood. Instead, there is no blood, just Cal passed out on the sofa while Sandra lies there, her neck at an impossible angle inside the fireplace.

"Sandy?" he says. "Are you okay?"

But Sandy does not answer. Sandy is not okay. Sandy looks like a broken dummy in a department store, and when he bends and puts his hand between those big soft breasts, he feels no heartbeat at all.

For an instant, a panic bubbles inside him as the neighbor's broom bangs harder on the ceiling. Then, strangely, his terror congeals into an icy calm. He stands up with the realization that for the first time, he's found a way out of being Cal Whitman's brother.

Leave, he thinks. Just walk out the door and out of his life. There'll be no more cleaning up Cal's messes, covering Cal's tracks, camouflaging Cal's dirty little secret that two other girls met their deaths at his angry fists. Mitch smiles. As sorry as he is about Sandra, this was too perfect to pass up.

"You pack a mean punch, bro," Mitch says, lifting Cal's eyelids with his hand. His pupils are dilated, but moving. Cal will wake up with a head the size of Texas and a dead girl at his feet. And this time the shit's all yours, brother.

Then, as a distant siren wails closer, he moves quickly, wiping his fingerprints off everything he can remember touching, stripping Sandra's sheets from the bed and bundling them under his arm. The water is still running full blast in the kitchen sink, but there's no time to turn it off. He knows the back way out of this old apartment building: hell, his father owns it. He also knows that the old people who live here are too scared to open their doors and that the alley where he parked his car is unlit. If he hurries he can make it.

"Serves you right, Cal," he calls softly as he lets himself out the door, just as the police siren turns up Sandra's street. "From now on I'm gonna be reading about you in the papers."

.   .   .

Mitch sat up in the tent, gasping, his body drenched with sweat. The sirens were back. The police were here. But this time they'd come for the true killer of Sandra Manning.

He couldn't focus. His breath came hard. A bright red light bathed his body. Then the hard edges of his radio resolved against the soft bulge of his pack. The Colt lay on one side of his bedroll, the Beretta on the other. *It's okay*, he thought, *it was just a bad dream*. But it had been so real—the cops, the siren . . .

Suddenly, his muscles tightened. The siren hadn't been a dream. The siren was just outside his tent.

Eeeooowww. The sound pierced the thin orange nylon. No cop siren ever sounded like this. Nothing he'd ever tracked or hunted sounded like this. His heart raced as he tried to place the cry. It sounded like a woman, but no human female could approach that piercing volume. Gooseflesh prickled his arms. Maybe this was the Wendigo he'd once read about up in Maine—the forest monster that tore flesh from unlucky people's limbs.

Eeeooowww.

Leaves rustled on the ground. The thing was moving closer. He found the radio's switch and turned it off. Marvin Gaye died mid-verse as he reached for the lantern. Suddenly he sat in darkness.

Crouching in his sleeping bag, he listened. Nothing. Had the thing gone away? He reached for his rifle and flipped off the safety.

Eeeooowww!

He could hear snuffling now, and the crackle of leaves close to his tent. *Damn*, he thought. *What the hell is that?* Bears don't sound like that, and the little red wolves they've released up here aren't big enough to make a noise that loud. Boars? he wondered, desperate to pair something up with that noise.

Eeeooowww!

Suddenly, he knew. Though every game warden and ecologist in the country insisted it was not possible, Mitch Whitman knew. Outside his tent crept a mountain lion.

Eeeooowww!

The rustling grew louder. In the shadows he could make out a dark, low-slung shape slinking closer. It snuffled now against the base of his tent, knocking over the radio.

With sweat-slick fingers, Mitch strapped the rifle in a double loop around his arm and aimed at the tent flap. He didn't know where the first swipe would come, but he didn't care. Sometimes the not-knowing made it all the more fun.

"Come on, kitty-kitty," he murmured. He shook his head and chuckled. "I'm ready for you. This trip I'm ready for anything."

THIRTY-FIVE

T his story is so scary you can only tell it in
the daytime." Jonathan sits on the porch
outside Little Jump Off. He and Mary
had planned to go on a hike, but a cold
rain pelted down from a leaden sky.

"Ulagu was a giant wasp that swooped down
from the clouds and stole children away from their
homes. He had long yellow claws and a giant red
stinger on his tail. He flew so fast no one could catch
him, and he carried off so many kids the Cherokees
were in danger of dying out."

"What happened?" Mary squeaks like a mouse.

"The warriors tried to kill Ulagu with arrows
and spears, but they had no luck. Finally they prayed,
and the Great Spirit struck Ulagu's nest with
lightning . . ."

Craaawwww!

Mary jumped. She startled from her sleep,
her eyes grainy, her tongue thick in her mouth.
Ulagu, she thought, her heart hammering as she

struggled to her feet. Without thinking, she ran forward, ready to push against the Hell that she and Joan had fought through all night.

Crrraawww! Once more the sound split the still air.

Mary stopped, breathing hard. Perched in a pine tree just ahead of her was not Ulagu, the fearsome monster of her childhood, but a single black crow.

She blinked, never more grateful to see a bird in her life, suddenly realizing that the sharp laurel leaves that had so cruelly sliced her hands and face had been replaced by the scrub growth of the forest floor. "We're out!" she cried.

She turned around. Ten feet behind her Joan lay sleeping under a laurel bush, but Mary was standing upright among oak seedlings and scrub cedars. They had done it. All night they'd struggled through the sharp, cutting bushes, finally collapsing when they could crawl no further. Mary had been certain that this day would only bring more of the same torture, but for once they had chosen the right direction. They were free.

Her heart suddenly light, she looked up at the crow. Like her he was solitary; a singular member of a race that embraced pairs. Maybe he was a Spirit Guide sent from the Old Men, she thought suddenly. Maybe he would speak if asked the right question. "Can you tell me where Alex is, Koga?" she called, breathless with hope.

But the crow made no reply. Instead, he spread his tail and let loose a glob of green shit, then he lifted his wings and swooped up into the sky, a moving black rent in a field of white clouds.

"Well," Mary sighed. "So much for Spirit Guides." As the bird disappeared her joy faded. He probably knew exactly where Alex was, but he could not speak English, and she could not speak crow.

She looked around. Oaks, maples and mountain ash grew thick around the edge of the Hell. It was familiar vegetation, but unfamiliar terrain. Earlier, when they had followed Alex's trail from Atagahi, she had always had a sense of where they were. Crawling through the Hell had changed all that. Though she could still find east, she could no longer place it in relation to any part of the forest she was familiar with.

She sat down on the ground and gazed at the trees around her. That she and Joan had escaped the Hell was wonderful. But they were still miles from any part of the forest that she knew, and probably even further away from Alex's trail. Time, she knew, was running short, and every day sapped more of the little strength they had left. Yesterday they had lost Alex's trail; today they were badly lost themselves. She sighed. With a sick, sad ache in her heart, she realized then that she would never see Alex again.

She watched as an ant crawled around the toe of her boot and wondered if Alex was dead. If so, then had she become a ghost? Was she now chuckling from some cosmic plane, amused by Mary's anguish? "I hope so," Mary said softly, unable to bear the thought of her dearest friend waiting vainly for Mary to come to her rescue.

"Forgive me, Alex," she whispered. "I tried my best. Don't ever forget that I love you."

"Bella!" called Joan suddenly, twitching in the tangle of a dream.

Mary got up and hurried over to her.

"Bella?" she mumbled again.

"Joan, wake up," Mary said gently.

Joan sat up fast, scraping her forehead against a laurel branch. She blinked at Mary, her gaze still soft and unfocused. "Where are we?" she groaned.

"On the far side of hell." Mary smiled sadly at the irony of her words.

"Huh?"

"We crawled out of the Hell, Joan. I'm not sure where we are, but we're out of the jungle."

"We are?" Joan rubbed the sleep from her eyes. "What are we going to do now?"

Mary picked up a dead leaf and dragged it along the ground. "We're going to walk that way." She pointed east. "I think it's the way back to Little Jump Off."

Joan's jaw dropped. "But what about Alex?"

"We lost her trail yesterday, Joan. Crawling out of this Hell probably put us miles away from her." Mary shook her head. "You're injured, we're both starving and exhausted. It's time to call it quits."

Joan looked at her, unbelieving that those words had come out of Mary's mouth.

"If we get back to Little Jump Off, we can start the sheriff looking for Alex," Mary said. She made a little cross in the dirt. "Do you still have the oil paint?"

Joan fished it from her pocket. Mary took it to where the crow had perched in the tree. At shoulder level, she dotted out a small yellow X.

"I have no idea how far this Hell stretches, but if we walk east, and keep it on our right side, we should eventually come back to our old trail."

Joan frowned. "Why the X on that tree?"

"It's a marker. We'll always know where we started," Mary explained. "It'll keep us from circling this Hell forever."

Mary capped the paint, then shot a final, wistful glance over her shoulder at the distant mountains.

"We could look for Alex one more day," Joan offered.

Mary shook her head. "I'll join the official search whenever it starts. Right now we need to get you back to civilization."

Mary helped Joan ease the boots on her swollen feet and they started walking east. Joan had to walk on her right heel, giving her a hopping, peg-leg sort of gait. It made for slow going, and Mary knew it was just a matter of time before Joan's whole leg would be hot and swollen with infection.

They pushed through the trees, Mary helping Joan when she stumbled, wishing they could just slip through the forest like Jonathan did when he tracked wild turkeys. *Jonathan.* How she wished his arms were around her right now. Did he still remember what "Save me a seat" had meant to them, several lifetimes ago? If she ever got the chance, she would have to ask him.

"Hold on," Joan panted, as the sun began to heat the hazy air. "I need to find a bush. I've got diarrhea."

"Okay." Mary slumped down against a tree. "I'll wait here for you."

As Joan went to squat behind a patch of bushes, Mary pulled some hickory nuts from her paint box. She bit into one, wincing at its bitterness, but swallowed it anyway. A while later Joan eased down beside her.

Mary scooted over, sharing the spongy moss beneath the tree. Joan's slender body now gave off a hot, too-sweet smell. Though she'd made no complaint about her foot, she was limping badly. *She's got one more day*, Mary realized. Then the diarrhea will have purged her completely and the fever will bake what's left. Then the only thing she'll want to do will be to lie down under a tree and sleep. The infection in her foot will wither her, just like the laurel leaves. *Then the Old Men will have taken them both*, a voice echoed inside her head.

Mary handed the rest of the nuts to her. "Finish these. I've had plenty."

"They look like candy they used to sell at Dr. Bell's drugstore in Brooklyn. And they don't taste half-bad anymore." Joan cracked one nut between her teeth. "I guess you can get used to anything."

Mary gazed out at the trees below them, then, all at once, she sat up straight, her heart racing. She turned to her friend.

"Joan, do you sense anything odd?"

Joan frowned. "Do I *sense* anything odd?"

"Yes."

"You mean like ESP?"

"No. Just stand up and tell me if anything seems different."

"Okay." Joan struggled upright. She looked out over the russet colored valley below. A moment later she turned back to Mary, her eyes wide.

"I smell smoke."

Mary leapt to her feet. "That's exactly what I smelled. Some-body's here." A strange kind of anticipation sizzled through her. Close by, someone had lit a fire. It could be anyone from fishermen casting for trout to Barefoot. And Alex . . .

"Can you tell where it's coming from?" Joan asked.

The scent of the woodsmoke hung in all directions. Mary turned in a slow circle, trying to catch any sounds of people camping, but no noises drifted up on the breeze.

"What should we do?" Joan's voice was tight.

"Let's keep walking east. Maybe we'll run into whoever built the fire."

"And then what?" asked Joan.

"If they're campers or hunters, they'll have food and supplies. They can bandage your foot and help us get back to Little Jump Off."

"And if they're not?"

"Then we'll have to do something else," Mary replied evenly.

They hiked on resolutely, ignoring their discomfort, keeping now to the cover of the trees. Mary's eyes searched for smoke everywhere, but she saw none. Finally, they reached the top of a ridge. Here an ancient oak commanded a stunning view of the mountains below.

"Come on," Mary said. "Let's go get our bearings behind that tree."

They scrambled up to the tree, where they pressed themselves against the trunk and peered out into the valley. Hundreds of rusty autumn mountains rolled out before them. It was a magnificent vista. Both women stood silent, searching the hills for any sign of a fire.

"Look!" Mary cried suddenly, pointing.

Joan looked where Mary pointed, then gasped. A tiny sprig of smoke curled from the trees.

"There's the fire, Joan. That's where they are."

"How far away is it?"

"It's hard to tell," Mary said. "Maybe twenty minutes. Maybe an hour. Do you feel strong enough to go have a look?"

Joan stared at the curling smoke, then took a deep breath and nodded.

"Are you sure? It's okay if you want to stay here and wait for me."

Joan shook her head. "No. Bad things happen when we split up. I want to come with you."

"Okay, then. You keep the boots on, and we'll go slow."

"And we'll be careful, won't we?" Only the tremor in Joan's voice betrayed her anxiety.

"Very careful," Mary assured her.

"Good. Just remember if it's Barefoot and he sees us, then we're both dead."

THIRTY-SIX

Mary helped Joan down through the trees, in the direction of the smoke. Thimbleberries pulled at their scratched and bleeding legs, as if begging them to stay in the sanctuary of the ridge. They pushed their way down through the prickly branches to emerge in an old-growth forest.

"Jeez, these trees are tall," said Joan, gazing up at a hundred-foot hickory.

"The timbermen never got up here." Mary breathed easier as the air felt cooler, the earth springier beneath her feet. She squinted at the wilderness below, but saw nothing beyond the understory of the forest—young maples and hornbeams sprouting from a knee-deep evergreen carpet of galax and trillium.

With Joan following close behind, Mary crept on from one tree to the next. After a few minutes she gestured for Joan to stop behind a clump of locusts. Ahead, glimmering through the sun-dappled shadows, lay a broad expanse of tall yellow weeds. Could that be where the smoke was coming from? They crept on to a huge basswood that rose just in front of a weedy meadow lying like an island in the middle of the dense woods. Suddenly, Mary caught her breath. At the very back of the field stood a run-down cabin with a tendril of smoke wisping from the stone chimney.

Her muscles tightened. Was this just some hunter's remote cabin? Or had they stumbled upon the lair of Ulagu?

Mary slipped from behind the tree and was just about to pull Joan forward, when a flicker of a motion caught her eye. Quickly, she threw both of them back against the trunk and peeked out.

A figure emerged from the cabin. A man, wearing an old army camouflage suit and a Yankees baseball cap. A long hunting-knife scabbard hung from his belt. He raised his arms high above his head, as if stretching, then slung a bulging sack over his shoulder and stepped off the porch. Mary's heart froze. Though she and Joan crouched a hundred yards away, she could still see the dark beard and deep-set eyes.

"I see him!" she whispered, not believing their luck.

"Where?" Joan tried to peer around the broad tree trunk. "I don't see anybody."

"There!" She pressed Joan against the tree, barely daring to breathe herself, praying the bearded man would not walk toward them. He paused, lazily scanning the perimeter of the field, then strode away at an angle, into the woods that bordered the northeast side of the meadow.

"Come on," urged Mary. "Let's see if we can get closer."

For a moment Joan looked as if she might weep, then she closed her eyes and made the sign of the cross. "Okay," she said, sighing deeply. "I'm ready."

"Crawl from tree to tree now. Remember, he's out here some-where, so we need to be quiet."

"No kidding," muttered Joan as she dropped to her knees and began to follow Mary through the lush forest floor.

They reached a tulip tree, then crept on through some spicy-smelling sassafras. Once they thought they heard footsteps behind them. They froze, trying to press themselves into the damp earth. For an eternity they lay motionless, listening, scarcely breathing. What-ever it was came toward them, paused, then rustled slowly away.

Mary raised her head and looked toward the meadow. She saw a low pile of rotting logs just inside the edge of the forest—a perfect shelter if they could get there undetected.

"Over there." She mouthed the words and pointed her finger. Joan nodded. Her face was pale and her lips tight.

Inch by inch, the two women snaked through the underbrush. Thorns ripped at their skin; yellow jackets whined around their eyes and mouths. Crawling ten feet seemed to take ten years, and all the while Mary kept waiting for a shotgun to click and a male voice to bellow "Hold it!"

The woodpile logs were cedar, cut years ago and forgotten. Now silver with age, they afforded a knee-high shield behind which two people might possibly conceal themselves. Mary reached it first, then Joan crawled up beside her, breathing as if her lungs were clogged with sand.

"Thank God," she rasped. "I was sure I heard him fifty times."

Silently, Mary studied their situation. If they lay on their stomachs and craned their necks, they could peer through a gap between two logs that offered a narrow view of the cabin beyond. Cautiously, she raised up and peeked through the slit.

The cabin was barely standing. Both windows on the side were broken. The chink had crumbled long ago from between the logs; planks gaping in the front porch gave it the snaggletoothed look of a piano with missing keys. Smoke still rose from the chimney, but beyond that, nothing moved.

Then Mary saw a shadow melting through the woods on the far side of the cabin. She grabbed Joan, and they both turned back to the slit, trying to see everything and not be seen.

The dark shape shifted through the trees: Joan gasped as a green-clad man ambled into the clearing.

"That's him!" she cried, her voice a thin squeal. "That's the one who hurt me!"

"Shhh!" Mary pressed Joan down hard. *At last*, she thought with a strange satisfaction. *I'm going to gaze upon the face of Ulagu.*

He stood lankier than she'd imagined. The sun cast no highlights upon his snarled beard and his eyes glittered out from beneath the cap as a lizard might peer from under a log.

With a hitching gait he carried his sack to a rickety gambrel attached to the porch. Mary studied his walk. Could his odd, shuffling steps be the same curious tread she'd heard on the porch that afternoon, moments after finding her mother?

A brown bullet of tobacco juice flew from his mouth, then he knelt on the dirt and pulled a limp raccoon from his sack.

Mary knew what was coming as he hung the creature from the gambrel by its hind leg. "Turn away, Joan," she warned.

"Why?" Joan asked, still watching. "What's he going to do?"

With his knife flashing in the sun, he made one swift cut along the underside of the coon's legs, then began to peel the skin away from the flesh. Once something attracted his attention. He looked up and seemed to stare straight at them. *Not now*, Mary pleaded, unable to tear her gaze away from his face. *Please don't see us now.* He stared at the forest, unblinking. Then he spat again and turned back to his work.

"He must have a trapline somewhere," Mary muttered as he tugged the animal's pelt down from the fatty white carcass. When he began to make tiny cuts around the coon's eyes, Joan made a retching noise deep in her throat and rolled away to vomit.

"Close your eyes," Mary told her. "Sing Puccini in your head."

Joan obeyed, curling herself in mute misery against the logs. But Mary waited intently as the man untied the skinned carcass, then made quick work of another big coon and a small dun-colored rabbit. When he'd finished, he carried the skins and carcasses into the cabin. Mary waited, but he did not reappear.

Finally, she sagged back against the woodpile, feeling the small fire of hope she'd kindled for Alex die. She knew trappers loved leaving nasty little surprises everywhere they went. Leghold traps, deadfall traps, underwater traps. She studied the meadow that stretched between them and the cabin and felt her heart sink in despair. The field might as well be ringed with razor wire and land mines.

She looked down at Joan. Her friend's mouth was slack, her breathing shallow. She had taken herself far away, indeed. Maybe she was singing at La Scala, the notes soaring from her throat clear and beautiful, just as they had at Atagahi, so long ago. Mary gave a rueful smile. If she had somewhere else to go, she would be doing exactly the same thing.

She decided to keep watch on the cabin and let Joan sleep for a time. Then they could take turns watching until dark. The adrenaline rush that had carried her here had dissipated, leaving her shaking and exhausted. She settled back against the log, her eyelids gritty, her scratched arms and legs heavy as lead. *The Old Men have given me Ulagu*, she told herself as the warm sunlight made her drowsy as a shot of whiskey. *Now if only they'll give me Alex.*

THIRTY-SEVEN

Mary opened her eyes. A hard white circle of moonlight burned through the black lace-work of limbs above her. Joan snored softly beside her, curled against the logs that shielded them from the cabin. Panic shot through Mary. She had not awakened Joan to keep watch; instead, she had fallen asleep herself and both had carelessly dozed away the afternoon and most of the night. Her plan of watching the cabin in shifts had failed. She'd screwed up already. He could have sneaked up on them and slit their throats as they slept. How could she possibly expect to rescue Alex like this?

She rose and peered over the logs. The cabin sat silent in the silver meadow; not even a wisp of smoke seeped from the old chimney. Mary rubbed the sleep from her eyes and touched Joan's arm.

"Yeah!" Joan jumped awake.

"Have you been asleep the whole time?"

"I woke up about dusk. A big flock of bats or something came swarming out of the chimney." Joan shrugged. "I guess I fell back to sleep after that. Shit, my foot hurts like hell."

"Did you see anything besides bats?"

"No. Thank God."

"No sign of Alex?"

"Mary, if I'd seen Alex, I'd have woken you up," Joan said testily, rubbing her grotesquely swollen foot.

By the high angle of the moon Mary guessed it was close to midnight. She and Joan had been asleep for hours. What could Ulagu be doing to Alex in the cabin? If indeed Alex was still in the cabin and not buried somewhere in the mountains. She shook her head. Some thoughts were better turned away at the door.

Joan was shivering, although a feverish heat radiated from her body.

"What are we going to do now?" she whimpered.

"I'm not sure." Mary had hoped to sneak down to the cabin under the cover of night and peek in a window. But Ulagu's being a trapper had given her pause. She had seen what traps did to an animal's leg. The thought of those metal teeth snapping into her own flesh made her cold inside. She ignored the sudden queasiness in her stomach and said firmly to Joan, "First we need to see if Alex is really inside. If she is, then we'll go get her when he's out checking his traps."

"What do you mean *if* Alex is there?"

"Like you said before," Mary reminded her bluntly. "He could have killed her days ago."

"But sneaking up and peering inside?" Joan shuddered. "Jeez, Mary. What if you looked in and there he was, staring right back at you?"

Mary did not answer. The sky above them shone like a clear obsidian bowl. It was a hunter's moon, for sure. All prey would be illuminated tonight. She studied the terrain around the cabin. If she jumped over the logs and ran straight ahead, anyone who happened to be looking outside would see her the instant she left the cover of the trees. Circling around to the front offered no greater advantage, either. So that left the rear. She scowled at the weedy creek that ran across the back of the property. A trapper might have it studded with sets that could break her ankle as easily as snapping a twig. An injury like that would forever destroy whatever slim chance they had. But if she could make it unobserved to the water and then wade down the creek . . . then she might stay hidden until she could sprint across the back field to the cabin. The whole idea made her cold inside, but with Joan so crippled, it seemed like their only hope.

"How about this." Hastily, before her brain had a chance to reconsider, she blurted out her plan to Joan. "You have to stay up here and be my lookout. If anybody comes out, yell."

"Yell?" Joan stared at her as if she were insane. "Yell what? Fire? Police? Bloody murder?"

"Anything. Just something to warn me."

Joan's mouth curved down in disbelief. "And what will you do then, Mary, when I start yelling? That is, if I *could* yell. I'm dying of thirst."

Mary shrugged, her cheeks warming with embarrassment. Out loud, all her plans sounded ludicrous. "Have you got any better ideas?"

Joan scowled at her. Then her expression softened. "No, I don't guess I do."

"Okay, then. That's it." Mary braced herself. *More death might soon be upon your head,* she thought, but she couldn't help that now. As her mother had told her so long ago, sometimes there was no other direction to go but forward.

She tightened the laces on her boots and told Joan: "I'll take the paint box and bring us some water from the creek. And remember, if you see anyone, yell."

Joan studied her face, then reached over and touched her cheek. "Please, Mary, promise me one thing. Promise me you'll be careful."

With her paint box tucked under her arm, Mary Crow nodded, and slipped into the shadows.

She reached the creek with surprising speed. The brilliant moonlight allowed her to thread her way easily between the trees. Every few moments she glanced at the cabin to see if anyone was sighting down a gun barrel at her, but the yard remained vacant, the cabin eerily silent. As far as she could tell, she was the only creature moving upright on two feet.

In the moonlight the creek rolled like a ribbon of gurgling black ink. It edged the clearing as neatly as a fence, keeping the wild dark tangle of the forest back from the cabin. Mary knelt on its bank and looked for any submerged stumps that a trap might be attached to, but the surface of the water flowed smooth and unbroken. If this creek concealed a trapline, the sets were buried deep. She shoved her paint box beneath a thicket of bearberry as she sat down to remove her boots. Wet shoes might squeak. After she untied the laces, she felt Wynona safe in the pocket of her jeans.

She tucked her shoes beneath a bush and tentatively stuck one foot in the creek. Involuntarily, she gasped. The water pierced her skin like needles and a wet iciness began to numb her legs. If she was going to get there this way, she would have to move fast. She began to hurry forward, but her left foot slipped on a slick, algae-covered rock. For an instant she teetered over the chill water, then, miraculously, she regained her balance. More cautious now, she hunched over and began to creep down the center of the creek as if she were walking a tightwire, arms extended.

She moved carefully, testing the slimy bottom with her toes, waiting with every step for the snap of a trap to clamp down on her flesh. Twice, she felt something slither around her ankles, but she pressed her lips together and waded on through the black water. By the time she stood abreast of the cabin, both legs were numb from the knee down. Slowly, she edged to the bank, then stepped out of the water, lowering herself down among the weeds.

"*Wahdoe*, Wynona," she whispered as she peered over the razor-sharp rushes and studied the cabin, yards away. Though the back wall was windowless, the only cover between the creek and the house was a single maple tree. Anybody peering through a missing chink would clearly see her crossing the meadow. She looked up at the hunter's moon and had to smile at the irony: on one hand she was the hunter, on the other hand she was the prey.

Run! The warning rippled inside her head. *If he has a gun you'll be harder to shoot.* Without considering further, she took a last look around, then leapt out of the rushes and dashed across the meadow. Her feet hit the ground like frozen stumps, but she did not break her stride until she dived into the concealing shadows of the chimney, gulping air like someone drowning.

Lungs burning, her body pressed tight against the chimney, she waited. Then she realized she was safe. No one had awakened. No one had seen her. The meadow and the cabin were as silent as they'd ever been. Now she just had to find the right window to look into. Cautiously, she turned and moved toward the corner of the cabin.

Foot by precious foot she slunk along the back wall. A bat swooped low over her head; there was a sudden thick splash in the creek. *Dear God*, she thought, her heartbeat accelerating. *He's been out setting a trapline. Now he's coming home.* She dropped to the ground and pressed herself against the earth. With the blood rushing through her head she waited for him to lumber dripping from the creek, but the meadow remained empty. When her vision began to blur from staring at the muddy bank she realized that whatever had splashed in the water had nothing to do with her.

Still, she remained on her belly. It would be slower, but down low she would be harder to spot. She crawled along the ground, rising only to press her ear to the cabin to listen for any sounds inside. All she heard was the rattle of her own breath.

Finally she reached the corner. She tried to spot Joan across the meadow, but the woodpile was invisible in the shadows of the forest.

For a moment she lay still, thinking hard. The earth felt warm against her cheek; the sweet aroma of autumn grass filled her nose. *This is insane*, another voice taunted in her brain. *You are an assistant District Attorney for Deckard County, Georgia, not some Cherokee commando.*

"Oh, but tonight I am," she countered silently. "Tonight I am exactly that."

If she was going to do this, she must do it now. With a final flex of the cramped muscles of her legs, she crept toward the broken window.

THIRTY-EIGHT

Her toes dug for purchase in the stiff weeds, her fingertips sought the cold metal teeth of a trap. Inch by inch she crawled along the cabin wall. Finally, she looked up. In the moonlight, four grimy panes of glass glimmered above her head.

She studied them. Three were intact, but half of one bottom pane had been broken out. The jagged hole would reveal the interior of the cabin clearly. It would reveal her just as clearly, but she had no choice. With a swift, silent intake of air, she scrambled up, and pressed herself against the wall. The broken pane was just beneath her shoulder. She would have to crouch down to see inside.

Mentally cursing the glistening moon, she eased down and turned her face toward the gap in the window. The air inside the cabin smelled sour, its breath redolent of gun oil and roasted meat and another sharp scent she could not identify. She inched forward, peering inside.

The amber firelight revealed a kitchen of sorts. Embers glittered orange in a stone fireplace. Close to the window stood a small table; on it lay magazines and a bottle of vitamins. Suddenly, she caught her breath. Propped against the vitamins was the smiling photograph of Jonathan and a blonde woman. Jodie Foster. Ulagu had been at Little Jump Off! He must have been following them since Friday afternoon.

The banked fire illuminated the back part of the cabin, but it left the front shadowy and impenetrable. Her heart sank. She would have to look in the second window, too.

She withdrew her face from the fetid warmth and dropped back on her stomach. Again she squirmed forward through the dirt, still groping for traps. To her right a curious indentation dimpled the earth. Probably an old well, she decided. It seemed odd that anyone would put a well so close to the side of a cabin, but this was Ulagu. Ulagu could put his well any damn place he pleased.

She crawled for what felt like decades, the rustle of her body moving through the weeds thunderous in her ears. Ulagu must surely have heard her by now. Any second he would storm out of the door, shotgun in hand. But nothing happened. The cabin remained so still she wondered if he hadn't slipped away while she and Joan slept. Finally she neared the last window. She could make no mistakes now. Who knew what the snap of a twig might pull down upon her head?

Her whole body trembling, she rose to her feet. Except for a single top pane, all this glass had been shattered. If anyone was looking out this window now, she would soon be staring them straight in the face.

Resolutely, she steadied herself. *Just let Alex be in there*, she prayed silently. *And please at last let her still be alive.* Finally she turned to the empty mullions. Her eyes took a moment to accustom to the light, then the interior of the cabin materialized from the darkness.

A cot stretched beneath the window. Though the head lay cloaked in shadow, she could see two feet protruding from the end of a ragged blanket. Two feet with long toenails and a thick growth of hair. *Ulagu*, she realized with a calm which surprised her. *Now where's Alex?* She squinted into the darkness. A puddle of moonlight fell on a knotted rope looped around the man's ankle. The rope sloped to the floor, then led to a torn mat a short distance from his bed. Mary fought back a gasp. There, not six feet away, staring straight at her, sat Alex.

She huddled there nude, her eyes riveted to Mary's face. Her golden hair hung matted and limp. Her upper lip was bloody, both eyes were almost swollen shut. Her skin seemed pulled too tightly across her skull.

For an instant Mary could only stare helplessly at the beauty who had once reigned as Miss Chance Station, Texas. The features that two days ago she had known as well as her own now looked like a stranger's. How dare this man do that to Alex! How dare this man harm anyone. *Kill him now,* the voice thundered in her brain. *Roar through this window and tear out his eyes.*

Suddenly Alex blinked, then her mouth began to quiver in a feeble version of her old smile. She put one finger to her lips, then pointed at the sleeping man and shook her head. Mary nodded her acknowledgment, then smiled. Whatever else Alex was, at least she was still alive.

A row of raccoon pelts stood on stretchers across the room, while snake skins hung from the ceiling. In one corner stood a sagging table that looked like it might have been stolen from some flea market— trinkets and clothing and toys and sporting equipment jumbled together, dripping from the table to the floor. *Souvenirs,* Mary thought, the realization raising the hairs on the back of her neck. *Ulagu takes scalps.*

She pushed that out of her mind. Instead, she looked back at Alex and smiled. In the shadows, Mary could see hope rekindling in her friend's face. They would have to be beyond careful now. One sound from either of them would get them both killed. Cautiously, she reached through the shattered window and extended her index finger. Alex rose noiselessly, careful not to disturb the rope that bound her to Ulagu. In the moonlight they pressed their fingers together. Not much, but enough. The spark that had bound them together for the past twelve years passed between them again. Mary mouthed the word "later" and withdrew her arm. Alex raised her hand in farewell. With an extragavant wink, Mary grinned and nodded, then began to back away.

She had taken only a few steps when she saw Alex's mouth become a horrified gap in her face. Simultaneously she felt the ground beneath her right foot give way. With a deep *whump* she tumbled backwards. The base of her spine bounced once on something hard, then she began to slide. She scrambled to catch herself in the slick damp clay but the hole angled precipitously away; disastrously out of control, she slid lower and lower, until her left foot snagged something that felt like a small root. She trembled there suspended, her hands clutching the earth above.

Idiot, she scolded herself. *You've tracked Alex through hell and half of Georgia, only to fall in a stupid well!* She looked above her and saw only darkness and the stars, but then she heard voices. Alex's, then a second, deeper one. Angry, yelling.

"What the hell are you doing, Trude?" The deep voice boomed like a cannon.

"Charting my horoscope, you pinheaded asshole!" Alex's Texas twang sounded weak, but it still carried the sting of spurs. "Now just leave me alone! Go back to where you came from!"

The hoarser voice roared something back in a language Mary couldn't understand; Alex's shrill "Get out of here!" ended abruptly with a slap and a muffled cry.

As Mary struggled to cling to the ground above her she realized what was happening. Her fall had awakened Ulagu. Now Alex was creating a diversion to give her a chance to escape. By the sound of the voices overhead, she needed to move fast.

Quickly, she began to search for a foothold. Balancing on the one small root that held her, she nudged the earthen walls with her free foot. She had just found a small crack she could dig her toes into when she heard it. A soft, buttery sound. She cocked her head and listened. Surely she was imagining things. Surely this was just an old well this monster had forgotten to cover. But the sound continued. Suddenly it was joined by another; then a third.

"Oh, God!" she cried involuntarily, an icy sweat instantly bathing her skin. This was no well she had fallen into. This was Ulagu's lair, and she had fallen into Ulagu's snake pit.

Panicked, she dug her toes desperately into the earth. If she fell to the bottom she would die. You could survive one snake bite, maybe two. But a dozen? Two dozen?

"*Inadu*," she cried the Cherokee word for *snake* as she scrambled frantically upward. If she could just lift herself enough to get her elbows above ground maybe she could get the leverage to pull herself out . . .

She felt for another toehold in the earthen walls. A shower of crumbly dirt sifted into the darkness below; the snakes rattled louder as Alex and Ulagu bellowed through the darkness above. She searched the walls with her foot. Finally, one toe found another minuscule crack. She pressed her foot into it and pushed up. Her shoulders trembled with pain, but it felt like she moved a fraction of an inch upwards.

She clung with her fingers and now dug her toes into the earth, this time a little higher. She pushed up. More earth sifted down on the snakes, but her right elbow had almost reached the grassy surface above. She pushed and kicked once more, then suddenly she could bend her arm. Pressing it hard against the ground, she pushed with her left leg and abruptly her other arm and shoulders were free. Cool, sweet air caressed her face. She tugged herself upright, then turned to the cabin. She saw nothing, but she didn't need to. Alex's screams resounded through the moonlight like souls being ferried into hell.

For a moment she crouched frozen in place. What should she do? Her first instinct was to run back and rip out Ulagu's heart with her bare hands. But Alex had screamed "Go away" and "Get out of here" too many times for her to ignore. Was she just yelling at her captor, or was it some kind of message for Mary?

She cringed as their shouts still echoed in the air. Ulagu was big and strong. His blood would be hot now, his muscles limber and warm. She would have little chance hand-to-hand with someone like that. *Better to leave now*, the voice whispered inside her head. *Better to sneak up and surprise him later. That was what Alex was trying to tell you.*

She turned and wriggled through the grass as quickly as she could, certain she would be discovered; waiting for Alex's screams to stop and a bullet to snap her spine. Her breath sounded like a windstorm in her ears. When she reached the back side of the cabin she gathered her strength for the final sprint to the creek, then, with only thirty more yards to go, she took off. Her lungs were on fire but her legs, her heart, kept pumping. Finally, the shadows of the bushes reached out for her as she plunged into their forgiving darkness. For an eternity she lay flat on her belly, the cool, damp rushes soft against her cheek.

When she caught her breath she sat up and looked back at the cabin. Once again it was silent and ominously still. Alex had either been beaten to unconsciousness, or to death. Suddenly Mary felt a heat begin to bubble inside her. A rage. A hunger. A desire for revenge. All at once she remembered the six stones piled upon her mother's grave, and she realized that the one act that would redeem her lay ahead.

"Tonight you have six, Mama," she said quietly, thinking of the mystical Cherokee number that would grant her absolution. She stared up at the high, white moon. "But tomorrow you shall have seven."

THIRTY-NINE

From that moment on, a high whine keened inside her like the hum of angry wasps. It warmed her as she waded through the icy creek to her boots and paint box, the only weapons she possessed, and it did not stop when she filled the box with water and threaded her way back to Joan. She moved supple as a panther in the jungle and she wondered, as she neared their woodpile, if she wasn't glowing in some spectral shade of blue.

"Mary?" Joan crouched low to the ground, peering nervously into the woods. "Is that you?"

"It's me."

"Jeez, Mary! What happened over there? All I heard was screaming!"

Mary slid to the ground beside Joan and told her that the barefoot man kept snakes and traps and a curious collection of souvenirs; that Alex had been tied up but that she was alive; that

Mary had fallen into a snake pit kept by Ulagu. She did not, however, reveal to Joan that the barefoot man may well have beaten Alex to death just minutes ago.

"It sounded horrible." Joan shuddered. "I didn't know what to do. . . ."

"You did okay," Mary assured her, offering Joan some water from the paint box. Her own throat felt as papery as the snake skins that decorated Ulagu's rafters. "You did just fine."

"What are we going to do next?" Joan eagerly slurped some of the water.

"I'm going to go back and kill him." The words came out of Mary's mouth so fast and blunt that they surprised her. She'd just announced her intention to kill a man as casually as if she were going to debone a chicken.

Joan's eye gleamed like a pearl in the moonlight. "You're going to what?"

"Go back and kill him." Mary stared at her, unsmiling.

"But couldn't we just kidnap Alex back, when he's gone?"

"He'd be after us in a heartbeat," replied Mary, the wasp-hum inside her rising. "Even if we got a full day's head start, he'd catch us."

"How?"

"Joan, we marked our way with yellow paint," Mary reminded her. "A myopic cripple could follow our trail. This monster would be eating our livers before dark."

Joan drew herself up into a small, ragged ball. For a long time she stared mutely at the cabin, fear and misery both twisting across the planes of her face.

Suddenly Mary was stung by a poisonous guilt. If it hadn't been for her, Joan would be back in Atlanta, safe in a sunny hospital room banked with flowers, talking her trauma out with some kind-eyed therapist. Instead she sat here—sick, feverish, huddled behind a rotting pile of logs, playing hide-and-seek with a madman. The hum notched higher inside her. Joan had been a brave woman to come on this trek. She deserved to survive. Mary knew she alone had the best chance of making that happen. She leaned over and said:

"If I kill him, we can rest. He's got a fireplace where we can get warm. He's got food we can eat. He's even got a damn bottle of vita-mins." She squeezed Joan's arm. "With him dead we can all walk out of here alive."

For an instant Joan gaped at her as if she didn't recognize her—as if the Mary Crow who'd crept into the darkness an hour ago had returned as someone else. Then her face contorted, as if she were remembering that afternoon at Atagahi, when a man had appeared from nowhere and ripped her world apart. "Okay," she replied qui-etly. "How do we do it?"

Mary smiled. "Do you remember how tall he is?"

Joan shrugged. "I don't know. Taller than Alex, probably."

"Okay, let's say over six feet. I'll have to aim pretty high."

"Aim what?"

"I'm going to take one of these logs and sneak back down to the porch. When he comes out in the morning, I'll be right beside the front door, waiting."

"And?"

Mary felt the hum again. "And then I'm going to smash his fuck-ing head in."

Joan pressed herself tighter against the logs. "Do you honestly think you could do that?" There was a quaver in her voice.

Mary looked into Joan's mutilated face and remembered Alex's bruises, then thought of her mother, lying still and broken, so many years ago. "There's not a doubt in my mind," she replied.

They talked on in the dark, working out the details of the plan. This time neither of them slept. A breeze rattled the trees. Shadows danced on the ground, and leaves tumbled across the meadow as if swept by an invisible broom. A front was blustering through from the north. This day would dawn frosty, rimmed in ice. Hog-killing weather, Mary thought with an odd little jolt of anticipation.

Joan finally wore out. She splashed some cool water on her infected foot and slumped down behind the logs, fitfully sleeping. Mary knew that she, too, should get some rest, but she did not feel tired. From the moment she had decided to kill Ulagu, a hot, expansive energy had infused her. She felt as if she could stay up all night, kill Ulagu, and party all day tomorrow. Maybe this was what made them kill, she thought, remembering Cal Whitman and the five other men she'd nailed in court. Maybe delivering death was the headiest thrill life had to offer.

She shook her head. She couldn't allow herself to dwell there.

The old logs glowed like dull silver in the moonlight. She crawled over and pawed quietly through the pile, searching for just the right one. Most were too big and heavy for her to hold comfortably, but underneath some leaves she found a smaller one that had tumbled from the stack. It was almost a yard long and tapered at one end, like a thick baseball bat. She wrapped both hands around the splintery bark and swung it tentatively. The heft felt sweet and firm, and she knew without a doubt that it would cleave a man's skull like a melon.

When the dark began to soften into dawn, she touched Joan's shoulder.

"Joan," she whispered. "I'm going now. I'll need my jeans to crawl through those weeds."

Joan blinked, sleepily. "Did we just plan to kill Barefoot?" she asked. "Or did I dream that?"

"No." Mary untied the laces on her boots. "You didn't dream that at all."

Joan tugged off the pants and handed them to Mary.

"Is there anything else I can do to help?" Joan asked as Mary pulled on her jeans and relaced her boots.

Mary shook her head. "Just do like before. Keep watch and yell if you see him sneaking up on me. And you might say a prayer to whatever saint's in charge of putting mad dogs out of their misery."

"I can do that," Joan promised, smiling crookedly. She wrapped her arms around Mary's neck and held her close, as if trying to fill her with whatever small strength she had left. Mary felt the fever burning within her. "Thank you," Joan whispered.

"Thank you?"

"For keeping me alive."

Mary hugged her, then kissed the swollen cheek of the tiny

soprano from Flatbush. "Your courage humbles me, Joan. Whatever happens now, I want you to know that you're a true War Woman. And I've never called anybody that before in my life."

Joan smiled up at her. Her eyes were wet with tears. "And I want you to know that you did the right thing by coming up here. What is it you guys say? It's a good day to die?"

Mary chuckled. "I heard that once in the movies."

"Then it must be true." Joan wiped her eyes.

"See you later."

"*Addio, amica del cuore*. Here. Take this. At least it's some kind of weapon." Joan held out the palette knife.

Shouldering her log, Mary dropped the knife in the pocket of her jeans and slipped back through the trees. This time, however, she stopped at the back of the cabin. The weeds, she noted, grew taller here. She could creep through them and still remain hidden from anyone looking out.

"Okay, Wynona," she murmured as she cradled the log in her arms and dived belly-down into the tall grass. "Stay with me one more time."

The dew had made the weeds slippery and wet. She crawled with her elbows forward, always seeking the rim of another snake pit or the sharp metal edge of a trap. For every three feet she pushed herself through the cold, slick tangle, she felt as if she slid a foot back. She didn't want to raise up from the grass and expose her position, so she picked one pale star from the Pleiades overhead and crawled directly towards it. Already it seemed to glow less brightly than when she'd started. If she was going to reach the porch before the sun rose, she needed to hurry.

She crawled on. Husks of ragweed tickled her nose. To her left she heard a rustling in the grass. She froze. Ulagu? Could he have seen the tall grass moving in the dark? She held her breath, then the *who-who-who-whoooo?* of an owl came from the creek. Her heart sank. *Uguug*. To the old Cherokees, owls foretold death. "So be it." She shrugged as she crept on. "Let's just hope Uguug's calling for him."

The hum pulled her forward. Her senses were sharp as razors; the dawning world blazed fiery green; she felt as if she could hear spiders spinning their webs in the forest of grass. Had Cal Whitman felt such power when he committed murder? *This is what it's like*, a seductive voice whispered inside her brain. *This is why they kill.*

She crawled on. When she thought she had crept far enough to be hidden behind the cabin, she rose up.

"Twenty more feet," she whispered, burrowing back into the weeds. Now the goldenrod was intermingled with some kind of plant whose tiny thorns tore at her cheeks and forehead as she pushed through. Wincing in pain, she narrowed her eyes and crawled on

Surely she must be there by now. Again, she lifted her head. This time her position was perfect. She had a straight shot down the windowless side of the cabin and onto the porch. Betting her life that no more traps or snake pits awaited her, she stood up.

With the log clutched against her chest, she sprinted to the shadows of the cabin wall. When she reached them, she stopped, half-expecting a man in green camouflage to pop out from the porch and greet her. "Why, hello," he would say. "How nice of you to drop in! I've been waiting for you for hours."

But no such thing happened. The cabin remained as quiet as when she'd first visited. She crept along the wall, listening for the sound of someone stirring, a human body awake, but by the time she reached the porch she'd heard nothing except the frantic thunder of her own heart.

The slate-colored light revealed the porch and the door, but little else. From here on, however, she could make no mistakes.

She grasped the log and eased her right foot on the porch, testing the strength of the board. Tentatively, she shifted her weight. The wood did not give or wobble. She held her breath and straightened her knee, moving her left foot up beside her right. Triumph flooded her. She'd reached the porch without making a sound.

The door stood ten feet away, the latch on the near side. She would have to cross to the other side to get the needed leverage to shatter Ulagu's skull. She inched her right foot three boards toward the door, then shifted her weight. Amazingly, the ancient boards again held firm.

She crept along for what seemed like a century. She had to crawl below the single front window, and she froze once when a board squeaked loudly beneath her. She pressed herself up against the cabin, waiting for Ulagu's bellow, but nothing happened. *Heavy sleeper*, she noted with a quickening in her veins. *Smug in the protection of his damn snakes.*

Finally, she reached the door. With a single swift motion she crept across the doorway and positioned herself on the other side. She was here. She was ready. She'd gone over what to do a million times in her head, but it wouldn't hurt to rehearse it again. First wait, when the door opens, to make sure whoever is coming out isn't Alex. Then, if Ulagu comes out fast, swing like hell for the back of his skull. If he comes out slow, smash his face first, then his head if he goes down. If he doesn't go down, smash his balls, then the back of his skull. *And if none of that kills him,* she thought as an early-morning robin began to chirp, *then the death song that Uguug was singing must have been meant for me.*

FORTY

Morning, sugar." The words startled her so, she almost dropped the log. "I was wondering when you'd drop back by."

A coldness seized her body. How could this be? How could he have slipped out of the cabin without her seeing him? Reluctantly, she turned. With a long intake of breath, she lifted her eyes. For the first time, she was going to stand toe-to-toe with Ulagu.

He glared down at her, yellow eyes burning beneath woolly brows. Three fresh red scratches scarred the left side of his forehead and continued down his cheek. In his right hand glittered a hunting knife, the point of which now trembled an inch from her throat.

He grinned, his frank gaze a circular assessment of her face, then her breasts, then her face again. "You're Cherokee, aren't you?"

She gave the slightest nod.

Ulagu frowned. "You made an awful racket

in my snake pit last night. You weren't much quieter when you were scampering back to that log pile, either."

"Sorry," she managed to croak, her last wisp of hope evaporating like dew in the rays of the sun. She hadn't fooled him for an instant. He had known all along. Joan! He must have slit her throat the moment Mary had taken off for the cabin.

Ulagu grinned. "You know what I do to people who trespass on my property?"

Mary stood there, unflinching. "Kill them, I imagine."

"Mostly." Ulagu's amber eyes glittered. "But not right off the bat. First, you tell me why you're here."

"You kidnapped one of my friends and killed another. And I think you killed my mother."

"Killed your mother?" Ulagu pressed the knife blade against her throat as if making a pin hole in a piece of paper. "What gives you that notion?"

"The way you walk," Mary replied evenly.

"Well, I might have helped a few pilgrims on to Glory, but I don't know that any of them were your mother." His upper lip snarled away from teeth brown with decay. "And here you are, fixin' to kill me with that stick."

Mary looked at him without speaking.

He traced the tip of the knife down her throat and between her breasts, bringing it back to rest just under her jaw. "Why don't you drop that log on the ground and come inside with me? I think Trudy and I need to have us a little family conference."

For an instant she considered trying to bash his head right then and there, but she remembered the swiftness with which he'd skinned that coon. *Wait*, she decided as she let the log thud to the porch boards. *Your time still might come.*

The cabin was not much lighter than it had been the night before. The dripping snake skins gave the place a feeling of macabre festivity, like decorations left over from a witches' ball. Animal hides adorned the walls like posters—a fox, a skunk, a dingy piebald thing that had once been a Jersey calf.

As her eyes adjusted to the shadows, Mary saw what she'd come for. Alex. She lay curled on the floor by the cot, her back to the door, one hand scratching limply at her scalp. Relief swept over Mary—whatever else Ulagu might have done, at least he had not yet killed Alex.

"Get up, Trudy! We got company!" Ulagu slammed the door behind him. Alex jumped. Slowly, she twisted toward them. This morning both her hands and legs were bound tight together, and a shorter leather cord tethered her to the cot.

"Mary!" Even beaten and tied, she still managed her old smile. Mary wanted to cry, then she felt a hard shove between her shoulder blades.

"Go sit on that bed. I need to think about this."

Mary stumbled over to the cot and sat next to Alex. She smelled of old smoky fires, and an ugly grid of switch marks crisscrossed her breasts. Her face was swollen and bruised. Still, she looked at Mary and smiled.

"I was wondering when you were going to show up," Alex said, giving a wheezing chuckle. "Then I remembered you've never been on time for anything since I've known you."

"You shut up, Trudy!" Ulagu barked. "My business is with *her* today." He waggled his knife at Mary. "This is amazing. I didn't even know you existed, and here you are, the girl tracker of the century, coming to avenge her mama." He squinted, then grinned as if a marvelous idea had just occurred to him. "Why don't you stand up there and take off those clothes? I'm ashamed to say I've never seen any Native American pussy."

Mary stared at the blade of Ulagu's knife. A thousand scenarios flickered through her head. She could wrestle it away from him and cut his throat. Or she and Alex could knock him down and stab him to death with the palette knife. Even if he was armed, it was two against one. But Alex's hands and feet were bound, and what good was a flimsy painting knife against a Bowie? Still, there must be something she could do. She sat motionless, feverishly thinking.

"Hey! *Sacajawea!* Look up here! Now's not the time to be shy!" Ulagu swished the knife. "All your girlfriends have done it. Now it's your turn. I need to make sure you've got all your parts."

"*Shogwa.*" Mary began to count in Cherokee, stalling for time. "*Talee, zoee . . .*"

"Don't give me that Indian shit!" Ulagu screamed, the veins standing out in his neck. "Get up and get your clothes off! The three of us are gonna have some fun today!"

"Do what he says, Mary," Alex advised wearily. "Little Henry here can throw a real tantrum when he doesn't get his way."

Mary stopped counting. With Ulagu's eyes upon her, she stood up and walked toward him. Only the creaking of the floorboards and the rasp of his breath broke the silence of the old cabin.

Brank made a soft moan of anticipation as Mary stood before him, her fingers fluttering at the button of her jeans.

"Any particular way you want this done?" she asked, drawing out the moments between them.

"The knife don't matter," Brank chuckled. "As long as the fruit gets peeled."

Slowly, she grasped the hem of her sweatshirt as if to pull it over her head, then she stopped. She pulled her sweatshirt back down and began to unzip her jeans. She had just eased them over her hips when suddenly she plunged her hand in her sweatshirt pocket and pulled out Wynona. Faster than she'd ever moved before, she aimed, hurling the little statue at Ulagu's head. It struck him just below his left eye. Not a heavy blow, but it was enough. For an instant, she had surprised him.

Mary lowered her head then, and threw herself into him like a tackle on a football team. As the top of her skull plowed into his chest, she felt the breath whoosh out of him. With one startled "*Uhmpf!*" he fell backwards, his knife clattering. Together they tumbled to the floor.

"Try to get loose, Alex!" she screamed as she tried to pin him down. He twisted and bucked beneath her. With her knee pressing hard on his throat, she groped for the palette knife. It should be here, somewhere in the pocket of her jeans, but she couldn't find it. She pressed herself desperately onto his chest, hoping the sheer weight of her body would keep him down until she could get the knife, but he was writhing like a wild animal. With a sinking feeling in her gut she realized that he was too strong for her; in just moments she'd be on the floor with a madman on top of her.

"Try to get out of here, Alex!" she screamed. "Try to get out of here *now!*" She was losing this fight, fast. She gave up on finding the palette knife and wrapped her hands around his throat, trying to bang his head against the floor. His neck was thin, but tightly corded with muscles. She tried to squeeze his windpipe shut, but his eyes only seemed to brighten. He connected with hard, sharp blows to her breasts and ribs, then, with an insane grin, he winked and brought his fist smashing into her left ear. A flash of bright pain jolted through her head and all she could do was try to hold on to him, blind, and hope that Alex could break her ropes and get away. She struggled with all her strength, but she knew she had lost; already she could feel him squirming away. Soon he would be free.

Frantically she tried to knee him. A blow to his scrotum might slow him down. He was too quick, though. He twisted on top of her and with one move, pinned her shoulders to the floor. "You're a regular wild Indian!" he snorted as he sat down on her stomach, his stench filling her face.

With the bulk of his weight over her hips, he grabbed her sweatshirt and pulled it up over her face. She could see only blackness now, as she felt his rough fingers pawing her breasts. Alex began to yell as he lifted himself off and yanked Mary's jeans and panties down around her knees.

"Look, Trudy," she heard him cry. "Just look at what your little brother's gonna do to your friend."

Alex thrashed to get loose from the cot. Mary squirmed, struggling to pull the cloth away from her face. She needed to look him in the eye while he did this.

He perched on top of her grinning, feasting on her nakedness. He pried her legs apart with one knee while he fumbled with his fly. "Didn't your poor dead mama teach you that it's not nice to hit people with logs? Didn't she tell you it's not *höflich?*"

He pulled his penis out. Huge and hard, it was violet with anger and desire. *Don't look away,* Mary commanded herself. *Die with your eyes open. Honor your mother's memory.*

She was trying to stare into his face when a small movement caught her eye. She glanced toward the door and gasped. Joan stood just inside the cabin, her eyes blazing.

She's not dead, Mary realized, her hopes catching fire. *We still have a chance. Keep him busy and we still have a chance. . . .*

Mary turned her gaze back to Ulagu, and stared at his penis. "You call that a dick?" She guffawed.

"It's big enough for you, Pocahontas," he growled, prying her legs farther apart.

"Looks like a funny little frankfurter to me, Ulagu. Doesn't it, Alex?" Looking over at Alex, Mary shook her head and gave an extravagant laugh.

"Don't you talk to her!" He slapped Mary hard. "And don't you laugh at me!" He smiled. "You know, that little Native American mouth is a lot prettier than your pussy. How about we put it to good use?"

Reaching backward, he pulled something from his boot. At first Mary thought it was a pencil, but he flicked his wrist once and a slender, sharp blade whisked out.

Mary caught her breath. An old-fashioned straight razor, the weapon of choice for her third conviction, a skinny carpenter who had a penchant for carving his initials in female flesh. The pictures in his evidence file still made her queasy.

"Ha!" Brank laughed at her expression. "This little beauty gets your attention, don't it?"

She did not answer.

"Okay, Sacajawea." Brank scooted toward her head, his penis thrusting forward like the prow of a ship. With one hand he held the tip of the razor at the inside corner of her left eye. "You know what to do. But I warn you—if I feel one tooth nibbling at my frankfurter, you're gonna kiss your face good-bye. *Verstehen?*"

Mary nodded, her heart thudding. *Where was Joan? Had she lost her nerve?*

"Here we go, Cherokee gal." Brank's foul breath blew hot in her face. "Open wide and suck hard."

"Suck hard yourself, you fucking asshole!" screeched a voice from above them.

Brank's eyes grew wide, then he made a sound as if a rat were crawling up his throat. The razor clattered to the floor as he released Mary and clutched at his neck with both hands. Joan stood just behind his left shoulder, her black hair wiry and disheveled, her one good eye gleaming crazily. She leaned over and spoke into Brank's ear.

"*Stupratoré!*" she screamed. "You filthy, cock-sucking *stupratoré!*"

Brank blinked at her in astonishment, then his body arched backward as blood began to pour from his mouth and nose. With his head bobbing woozily, he looked over at Alex, his glazed eyes pleading in a curiously tender look of betrayal. He moved his lips and tried to speak, but only grunts came out, and soon even they were drowned in a cascade of foaming red bubbles. Mary felt the wet warmth of his blood as he slumped forward on top of her, then Mary Crow felt nothing at all.

FORTY-ONE

The cabin lay wrapped in a hollow silence. Nothing moved, except an errant fly that buzzed over Ulagu's head and landed on his shoulder. Mary looked up. Joan and Alex stood above her, Joan holding the straight razor, Alex's bindings dangling from her wrists. Angels, Mary decided. One short and dark, the other tall and fair. They're both angels now.

"We're dead, aren't we?" Mary's voice echoed through the cabin like an actor addressing an empty house.

Joan shook her head. "He is. We aren't."

Mary blinked at the bloody bulk collapsed on her chest, then she looked back at her friends. "Then help me move him."

Alex and Joan kneeled and grasped Ulagu's leg. Mary pushed against his shoulders. With his body heavy as stone, the three women shoved together. He flopped over on his back, which pushed the Bowie knife all the way through his chest. Blood spattered Mary's face and neck. The stink of feces permeated the air.

Alex stared down at the oozing body. "Good-bye, Henry," she said, her voice a low rasp. "Give my love to Papa."

Mary sat up. Whatever fire had burned within her had consumed itself; she now felt charred to cinder and crumbling ash. Had all this really happened? Had Joan Marchetti really stabbed Ulagu to death just moments before? She looked over at him. Though the knife had completely pierced his chest, his mouth hung open as if he were about to speak, and his yellow eyes still stared at her with a curious combination of menace and astonishment. Mary thought of her mother. *Was this the last face she saw before she died?*

"I hope not," Mary whispered.

"What did you say?" Joan frowned.

"Nothing," Mary replied. "Let's get out of here."

Mary pulled up her bloodied jeans as bright gold sunlight streamed inside the broken windows. Joan grabbed her Yankees cap from the cot while Alex helped Mary to her feet. Together, the three women started for the door.

Suddenly Mary stopped. "Wait," she told her friends. "I think something here might belong to me."

"I've got Wynona." Alex held up the little figurine.

"No." Mary shook her head. "Something else."

She turned and moved toward the rickety junk table, sifting through Brank's grim collection of memorabilia.

"Jewelry," she muttered, rattling through a stack of old eight-track tapes and dog-eared paperbacks. "Where's the jewelry?"

She lifted some moth-eaten scarves and uncovered an old tackle box. Her fingers fumbled with its lid. A dazzling array of cheap, gaudy jewelry had been dumped inside. Glass bead necklaces tangled with dime-store brooches and fly-fishing lures. She rifled through a handful of the stuff; one glittery rhinestone bounced to the floor. *Damn,* she thought. This is going to take forever.

"It's not there, Mary." Alex's voice floated across the cabin.

Mary turned and stared at her.

"You're looking for your mother's medal, aren't you?" Alex sagged against the doorway. "A knight fighting a dragon. It's not there. I've looked."

"But . . ." Mary began.

"In the daytime he tied me up with a rope that reached across this cabin. I've spent hours staying sane by looking for Saint Andrew when he was out checking his traps. It's not here. He didn't kill your mother."

"But maybe he hid . . ."

Alex's eyes flashed with pain. "Mary, every night we played show-and-tell. Of course I had to show first, but then he would tell. I got to hear exactly what happened to all the people who owned that stuff." Alex hobbled over and rummaged in the tackle box, pulling up a high-school ring with a bright green stone.

"Remember the girl whose picture was on the bulletin board at the store? This was hers. You don't want to know what happened to her. And this," she pawed through some ragged clothing and pulled out a child's baseball cap. "This belonged to the little boy whose picture was beside hers."

"Jimmy Reynolds," Mary murmured, tracing the worn Milwaukee Braves emblem with her finger.

Alex put her arm around Mary's shoulders. "I'm sorry," she said, her voice thick with regret. "I got to hear about every one in great detail. Your mother was not among his victims."

Mary retrieved the photo of Jonathan and Jodie Foster, then the three women closed the door of the cabin and limped into the sunshine. Walking as if of one accord, they made their way to the creek. At the water's edge, they pulled off their clothes. Something far beyond Ulagu had stained them all today. Maybe the water could wash it away.

Mary stretched her arms to the bright sky for a moment, then she stepped into the stream. The sunlight danced like fire on the water, and she gasped as the frigid current sent shock waves up her legs.

Breathing deeply, she dropped first to her knees, then lay on her stomach, letting the stream roil around her. Though the freezing water nearly paralyzed her, the gummy bloodstains that covered her began to float away in clumps, revealing the clean skin beneath. She sighed as the water caressed her body like icy silk. Maybe this little stream was the true Atagahi. Maybe when she rose dripping from this creek, she would be clean. Maybe she would even be healed.

Alex sat down next to her with a splash, then Joan joined them, easing herself down onto a soft bed of underwater moss. Mary turned to Joan.

"How did you do it?"

"Do what?"

"Everything. Avoid getting your throat cut. And then coming after me."

"I couldn't stand just to stay and watch anymore. I crawled through the bushes to the front of the cabin. It was the only place I could see everything."

Mary frowned. "Did he come looking for us at the woodpile?"

"I never saw him until he was behind you, when you were hiding by the door. I didn't know what to do, so I waited. When nothing happened, I figured things had gone sour. Then I knew it was time for me to do something. I've been such a wuss . . ."

Alex frowned at her. "What was that word you called him when you killed him?"

For a moment Joan only stared into the rippling water. Then she raised her head and looked at Alex, her face calm and unashamed. "*Stupratoré*," she replied. "Rapist. I was raped, you know."

Alex nodded, her eyes full of pain. "I know."

Joan turned to Mary. "Do you think I'll go to jail?" she asked evenly. "I mean, I did kill a man."

"They ought to give you a medal for killing him," Alex growled as she stroked the raw, blistered skin where her wrists had been bound together. "Maybe mint a few million new quarters with your face on them."

But Joan kept her eyes on Mary. "Barring that, will they indict me for murder?"

"I doubt it, considering the circumstances. You could claim about ten legitimate defenses. *Lex talionis*, for one." Mary scrubbed fiercely at the blood on her arms and fingers.

"Eye for an eye?" Joan frowned. "But he didn't kill any of us."

"Yes, he did." Alex said it flatly. "Just because he didn't stop our hearts doesn't mean he didn't kill us."

For a while, no one spoke. Only the monotonous gurgle of the creek rose around them as they each counted the cost the barefoot stranger had exacted of them. Finally, Mary broke the silence.

"Alex, did you ever find out his last name?"

"Brank," Alex replied. "Henry Brank. His father was a butcher. His mother made chocolate cake called *Kuchen*. He was absolutely convinced that I was his dead sister, Trudy."

"His dead sister?" Joan frowned. "Why would he want to kidnap a person who's already dead?"

"He was way gone, Joan. He'd spent thirty years hiding in these woods," said Alex.

"But I don't understand . . ."

"Years ago, he couldn't bring himself to kill a deer, so his big sister Trudy made fun of him." Alex's laugh was bitter. "He got mad and killed her, then he got scared and ran into the mountains. Somewhere along the line, the edges began to blur. He believed Trudy was hunting him. To him, everything became Trudy. And every Trudy, he killed."

"But he didn't kill my mother!" Suddenly Mary's voice broke with rage and pain. "Somebody else did! I can't catch the one who killed her!"

Alex leaned over and gathered her in her arms. "Honey, it's okay—"

"No, it's not," cried Mary in a fury. "You don't understand!"

Alex held her tight. "No, Mary, you don't understand." She looked into Mary's eyes, now sparkling with angry tears. "The whole time I was in that cabin the only thing that kept me going was that I knew if you weren't already dead, you'd come after me." She smiled. "You saved my life at least fifty times a day."

"That's right, Mary," added Joan. "You might not have been able to save your mom, but you certainly saved the both of us. That must count for something!"

For a long moment Mary stared at them, as if measuring their words, then she nodded. "I'm freezing. Let's go lie in the sun. We'll catch pneumonia sitting here."

The three women climbed to the bank and let the warm sun dry them, then they put on what clothes they had; Mary lacing her boots, Alex buttoning up her old shirt, Joan pulling on her underpants and ceding Mary's jeans to Alex. After that they walked over to the bright meadow behind the cabin and stretched out beneath the maple tree.

Joan fell asleep immediately, but Alex could not be still. She walked around the cabin several times, once returning with a small shard of glass from one of the broken windows, another time carrying the cedar log with which Mary had meant to kill Brank. Finally she settled in between Mary and Joan. She sat down with her arms folded, and stared intently at the cabin, as if Henry Brank might reappear and pursue her once more.

"He's not coming back, Alex," Mary said, looking at her friend's odd collection of weapons.

Alex shrugged. "You know, when I was a kid I wasn't afraid of anything. Not Dracula or Freddy Krueger or any of the gross stuff my brothers tried to scare me with." She pried a weed up from the dusty earth and shredded it. "Now I can hardly stand to blink my eyes."

"Lie down," Mary said. "I'll stay here beside you."

"I don't think that will—"

"Alex, remember our freshman year in college? All those nights you listened to me until I fell asleep?"

Alex nodded.

"Well, now's payback time. Close your eyes and sleep. And this time I'll keep watch."

Alex frowned, but then she curled up obediently while Mary leaned back against the tree and watched two squirrels play on the roof of the cabin. For a while Alex twitched and cried out in her sleep, but gradually her arms and legs relaxed and her breathing became soft and rhythmic. Mary pulled the photograph of Jonathan from her sweatshirt pocket and studied it. How sweet he looked, standing there beside the beautiful actress, his arm lightly on her shoulder, his smile genuine, but also amused at the unlikeliness of his picture being taken with a movie star. Mary traced around his image with her finger. He would not have given this up without a fight. Was this the souvenir of Jonathan that Henry Brank had stolen for his collection? She stared at the picture for a long while, then she put it back in her pocket. Waves of a new dark ocean of pain lapped against her, but she would not plunge into them now. She would do that later, if she ever made it back to any place where tears could be shed safely and in private.

All at once she felt as if her whole body had been leeched of all the strength it had ever possessed. With a deep yawn, she lay down and turned her face up to the afternoon sun. They would have a long, hard hike back to Little Jump Off. They would need to be rested. She took one final look at the cabin, then she laid her head down. With a single sigh, she closed her eyes and allowed herself to relax into a soft heavy nothingness that was very like what she imagined death to be.

FORTY-TWO

From a distance he knew they were dead. He'd swung wide around Godfrey's Hell and approached the old Babcock logging camp from the ridge above it. The battered dogtrot cabin looked like a hundred others, remnants from the last century. No smoke wisped from the chimney, and no dogs dozed beneath the porch. Even when he drew closer it seemed harmless, save for the broken floorboards and jagged windowpanes. Not until he scouted the area from the close perimeter of the trees did he see them. There, in the back, sprawled in the weeds, he found Mary and her friends, semi-clothed and motionless, like dolls abandoned by some careless child. His throat closed as Homer whimpered. Whitman had beaten him here.

First Billy, now Mary. Jonathan felt as if an Atagahi boulder had been suddenly heaved against his heart.

He tied Homer to a tree and clicked off the

safety of his shotgun. With his hands sweating, he walked toward the three women.

They lay in the grass beneath the single tree that grew behind the cabin. The tall one wore a plaid shirt and ridiculously short jeans, and her face looked like a prizefighter's the morning after the night before. The curly-haired one still wore her sweatshirt and Yankees cap, but her left foot was red and swollen with infection. Jonathan stared at her nose, unbelieving. When she'd been at the store she'd been a beauty. Now she was something else entirely.

Reluctantly, he looked at Mary. A filthy sweatshirt covered the upper part of her body, but her legs were bare. He could see no apparent wounds or injuries, although blood dotted the tops of her hiking boots like spatters of dark red paint and her legs were torn and scratched.

He frowned. It didn't add up. Why would a man gut-shoot another man, batter two innocent women into hamburger, and then leave his intended victim virtually untouched? Why not line them up with their faces to a wall and simply execute them? And why did he see no bullet holes? If these women had been shot with the same gun as Billy, the wind should be whistling Dixie through the holes in their chests.

He glanced back at the cabin. It sat there still and sad, as if Babcock's loggers had just picked up their axes and moved on. Even as he watched, a tiny brown wren began hopping through one of the broken windows. The cabin was empty, he realized. Whitman had gone. But where? Was he scurrying through the distant trees, trying to put as many mountains as possible between him and his victims? Or was he hiding just beyond the creek, waiting to see who might wander by?

Jonathan's eyes narrowed. He scanned the forest that surrounded the cabin. He would be the proverbial sitting duck if Whitman was out there, watching. But he had to take care of Mary. He would just have to take his chances.

Keeping his gun pointed at the ground, he crept through the grass without a sound. When he reached Mary he extended two fingers, seeking a pulse in her throat.

Her eyes flew open the instant he touched her. He flinched at the look in them. She saw him, and yet she didn't see him. She pressed herself against the earth, silent and wary.

"Mary, it's me!" He spoke softly, not wanting to frighten her any further. "Jonathan. Jonathan Walkingstick."

"What?" She blinked at the war paint smeared grotesquely across his face.

He rubbed Billy's dried blood from his skin and touched her cheek. "It's me," he repeated. "I've been looking for you."

For a moment she stared at him as if she'd never seen him before, then she said, "Jonathan?"

He nodded, and only then did she fling herself around his neck and cling to him, as if he might carry her out of some building that was burning inside her.

"I thought you were dead," he said as he locked his arms around her. She trembled in his grasp. He held her tight and buried his face in her hair, once again losing himself in the softness of her skin.

"We were in so much trouble!" She pushed back and looked at him hard, as if to make certain he was not a dream. "I thought he killed you, too."

"Why would anybody kill me?"

"He had this." She held up the photo of Jodie Foster.

Jonathan stared at the picture. It made no sense. Mary had been tracked by a killer from Atlanta. A brain-fried mountain trapper had snitched his snapshot. He shook his head, baffled. "I'm sorry. I don't understand."

"Come with me." She grabbed his hands. "I'll show you."

"What about your friends? Don't they need help?"

She glanced at Joan and Alex. "They're sleeping, thank God. Don't wake them yet."

He helped her up and pulled off his army jacket for her to wrap around her waist. She pressed herself tight against him, as if she were afraid he might disappear.

"Did you know this is Babcock's old Wolfpen camp?" he asked. "The place they used to warn us about when we were kids."

"I figured it might be when we started tracking along the railroad bed. They were right to keep us away from here. Just look at that." She pointed as they passed a gaping black hole in the ground.

He peered into it, then he looked up at her in astonishment. "That thing's ten feet deep. There must be a dozen rattlers at the bottom."

"Come on." She grabbed his arm and tugged him toward the cabin. "There's more."

They hurried on to the porch, their footsteps breaking the sunlit silence of the clearing. At the cabin door, Mary stopped.

"There's a man in there. He attacked Joan and Alex at Atagahi. He raped Joan, stole all our clothes and supplies, then kidnapped Alex. Joan and I tracked them here."

Jonathan said, "Yellow dots on the south side of the trees."

Mary nodded. "That was us."

"But what about Billy?" he asked.

"Billy?" Mary frowned. "You mean Billy Swimmer?"

"Yeah. Our old friend Billy. You tracked the guy who stole my picture and kidnapped your friend. Didn't you ever see Billy?"

Mary shook her head. "I haven't seen Billy since the day we drove up to Little Jump Off." She pushed open the cabin door. "Just look. There's a whole table of trophies from the people he's murdered."

He knew someone was dead long before his eyes adjusted to the dark. The smell of blood and shit poured from the cabin like a malevolent cloud. In the shadows he could hear the hum of busy flies. Mary took his hand and pulled him across the room.

She stopped well before they neared the corpse, watching motionless as Jonathan knelt beside it. With the tip of a Bowie knife still protruding from his chest, lay the man he'd last seen at Little Jump Off.

"Jesus Christ, Mary! When you ladies kill somebody, you don't mess around."

The man's skin was mottled with death and blackened blood. A fly was dining on one open, unseeing eye. Mary knew nothing about Billy or Whitman, Jonathan realized. She had killed the man who'd attacked her friends. She was totally unaware that someone else was tracking her. He looked up at her.

"Mary," he began, choosing his words carefully. "You may not have killed the right man."

"But that's exactly what Mary Crow does best." A deep voice rang out behind them. "Or haven't you figured that out yet?"

FORTY-THREE

N ow turn around, both of you. No sudden moves, okay?"

Mary and Jonathan turned. A tall young man stood in the doorway, long legs spread wide in a shooter's stance, muscular arms pointing a pistol directly at them. Mud and beggar-lice covered his camouflage suit, while soot had been smeared over his cheeks and forehead.

Mary gasped. "Mitchell Whitman!"

The sunlight trapped Mitch's eyes like two pale prisms as he pointed his Beretta at Jonathan. "Put that shotgun down on the floor. Do it slowly, and I may let you live long enough to kiss Pocahontas here good-bye."

Jonathan knelt with infinite care, setting the shotgun on the floor as if it were an offering to some god. As he bent over, Mary saw that he pulled his shirttail surreptitiously from his belt, letting it fall loosely around his waist. *Ribtickler*, she thought.

"Haven't seen you since last Thursday in court." Mitch grinned at Mary's filthy appearance. "I gotta say, you don't look like the same girl."

Mary met his gaze steadily, her eyes the color of steel. "Oh, I'm the same girl, Whitman. Believe me."

"Oh, yeah? Still just as bad a bitch?"

"Maybe even a worse one. It might be better not to fuck with me today."

"Awww, sugar." Mitch threw back his head and laughed. "I haven't even *begun* to fuck with you!"

"Just like you didn't fuck with poor Sandra Manning?"

"Sandra Manning? Didn't we exhaust that subject on the stand last week?"

"Pretty much. Except I think you killed her, Mitch. Your brother was involved, but I think you were the one who really killed her."

"How so?"

Mary regarded him with a bitter smile. "Because if you didn't kill Sandra Manning, then why else would you be up here pointing that pistol at me?"

"Maybe I wanted to teach you some manners. Maybe I wanted to show you that you can't torch people on the witness stand and not expect to pay the consequences."

Mary shook her head. "I didn't call you to the stand, Mitch. Defense did."

"But once you got going, you just couldn't stop, could you? You really got off on having a rich man's son up there, sweating like some petty thief. You knew you'd never get a shot at Cal, so you took it all out on me."

"I just tried to make my case, Mitch."

"But you didn't, did you?"

"Not then. I bet I could now."

"Tell me how you figure that, Miss DA."

Mary glanced at Jonathan. Though he had no bow, he was staring at Whitman with the same look he wore just before he let an arrow fly.

"I figure Sandra belonged to you, until your handsome brother came along. Then Sandra switched brothers and that made you mad.

Both you and Cal were at her place the night she died, but you were the only one who was sober. Cal's blood showed traces of every drug cooked in the past fifty years, and Sandra's wasn't much cleaner. Something, probably something sexual, pissed you off to the point that it felt good to knock one of Sandra's teeth out. And it felt even better when you pushed her into that fireplace and broke her neck."

"Don't stop now, Ms. Crow."

"Then, I imagine Cal passed out—all those free-range pharmaceuticals in his system could have killed an elephant—and you had your big chance."

"My big chance?"

Mary nodded. "To get rid of your pesky little brother who was handsomer than you, infinitely more charming than you, but who was, and always would be, a weak fuck whose messes you'd had to clean up all your life. Murder investigations can dig pretty deep, Mitch. We learned all about your and Cal's history."

"So how did I get away with this frame-up?"

"You hadn't had sex with Sandra that night, so you knew you were safe from DNA tests. You stole the sheets and wiped your prints off everything you'd touched. Why you left the water running in the kitchen I have no idea."

"Chamomile tea," Mitch chuckled.

"Anyway, you sneaked out the back of Sandra's apartment while the cops came in the front. They found her dead and your brother so stoned he couldn't even zip his pants up when they arrested him."

"Even if he was stoned, don't you think he'd remember if he'd beaten a woman to death?"

"Cal's not nearly as bright as you, Mitch. And your little mind games had confused him." Mary shrugged. "Or maybe he remembered everything, and your father decided to let his loser, drug-addicted son take the fall. Big Cal's no fool. Why lose two of his boys when one would do?"

"How'd you come up with this fairy tale?" Mitch taunted.

"Because I'm good. I know how expensive defense attorneys work. And I've read enough evidence files to put all the little loose ends and jagged edges together. What I can't figure out is how you found us. Nobody but Cherokees and mountain men know the way up here."

"I can tell you that," Jonathan interposed. "He drove up from Atlanta looking for you. When he couldn't find the Little Jump Off Trail by himself, he offered Billy Swimmer a thousand dollars if he'd lead him to you. Claimed he worked in your office. And Billy believed him. He took him as far as Atagahi, then I'm not sure what happened, but Billy wound up with two slugs in his belly, floating facedown in the spring."

"Billy's dead?" Mary murmured, stunned.

"This man killed Billy Swimmer." Jonathan's eyes locked with Mitch's. "Billy figured it out, didn't he?"

"He pulled a knife on me." Mitch shrugged. "I had no choice."

"You've got a choice now," Mary told him. "Even if you've killed Billy Swimmer and Sandra Manning, put that gun down, and you'll live. I promise you."

Mitch grinned. "And what are you gonna do? Make sure I rot in the same cell as my idiot brother?" He gave a sharp bark of laughter. "No thanks, Ms. Crow. I've got a happier life plan in mind." He cocked his head toward the door. "Both of you put your hands behind your head and walk outside, slow. It's time for you to join your friends."

With a swift glance at Jonathan, who nodded at her, Mary did as she was told. Jonathan lifted his hands and followed behind her.

When they walked around the cabin, Mary gave a sharp cry. Joan and Alex sat under the leafy yellow maple, bound and gagged with duct tape, in a hunched-over posture like prisoners of war. Above the silver tape, their eyes looked wild and wide with fear.

"Subduing those two was like shooting fish in a barrel," Mitch chuckled, behind her. "I practically had to wake them up to tie them up."

Turning, Mary searched his face for any hint of mercy or remorse. "Let them go, Mitch," she said, desperate to strike a deal. "Take me wherever you want, but let them go. They've done nothing to you."

"Come on, Miss Deckard County DA. You know it doesn't work

like that." Mitch poked his gun in her back. "You two Indians sit down beside your buddies. I need to decide who I'm going to kill first."

Jonathan sat down beside Alex, Mary beside Joan. All watched as Mitch towered in front of them, a thin, raw smile creasing his soot-streaked face.

"Let's see." He aimed the Beretta at each of them in turn. "Eeny, meeny, miny, moe. I say Crow is last to go."

"Mitch, it doesn't have to be like this," Mary tried again.

"Sure it does," Mitch snarled, angered by her calm. "If I let you get back to Atlanta, you'd have me in jail before dinner. Anyway, there's a little question you raised on the witness stand that I want to address."

"What's that?"

"Remember how you asked me if I knew what sexual intercourse was?" Mitch's dark eyes blazed. "Remember how that question just cracked up everybody in the courtroom? And how they showed it about sixty times on the news that night?"

Mary gave a sad nod, sickened.

"Well, after I get rid of your pals, here, I'm gonna show you exactly how much I know about sexual intercourse." Mitch laughed. "You might be surprised."

He grinned at Mary for a moment, then his gaze fell on Joan. "I think my mother told me to choose *you*."

Whitman aimed the pistol at Joan's head. Joan shrank against Mary, squirming frantically, screaming something unintelligible behind the duct tape. Mary leaned over, trying in vain to shield her with her own body. She knew this was the end of their hike. They'd all be dead soon.

But Jonathan was watching Whitman like a tiger about to pounce. Suddenly, with his hand moving so fast she thought she'd imagined it, he grabbed Ribtickler from his belt and hurled the knife forward, end-over-end in a single, fluid motion. It hurtled through the air, silvery as a trout, finally landing deep in the flesh an inch below Whitman's collarbone. Whitman yelped, then Mary heard the deafening *pop* of his gun. A wave of agony gripped her left shoulder as Whitman's bullet tore into it. In a haze of shock and pain she saw Jonathan spring forward and leap at Whitman's throat.

Jonathan hit Whitman hard, knocking him on his back. The two men rolled on the ground, Jonathan trying to pry the gun away from Whitman's huge hand. Whitman struck out with a roundhouse left that smacked into Jonathan's jaw. Punching furiously, he shook the blow off. In a tangle of legs and fists they fought, thrashing like infuriated boys on a playground, moving ever closer to Ulagu's snake pit.

"Jonathan!" Mary called, trying to struggle to her feet. "*Inadu!* Don't forget the *Inadu!*"

She couldn't tell if he'd heard her as they rolled in the dirt. The whole side of her body was on fire. Blood spurted down her arm as she watched, helpless.

She knew she had to do something. Heedless of the pain, she forced herself upright. The whole world spun as she drew her left hand up into a fist, her fingers slick with blood.

A weapon. I need a weapon. She'd stashed Wynona and the palette knife in the pocket of her sweatshirt, but both would be useless at this range. She needed something else. Something heavy. She looked around desperately. Both men struggled for the gun, rolling closer to the pit, Whitman pummeling Jonathan relentlessly with brutal jabs to the throat and ribs. *Do something*, Mary told herself. *Do something* now.

Suddenly, Alex fell over on her side and began squirming to the other side of the tree. She flopped like a fish on dry land, and for a moment Mary was distracted. Then Mary saw what she was moving toward. On the grass beneath the tree lay the log she'd intended to use on Brank.

That was it! Alex had figured it out. Mary scrambled over behind the tree.

She grabbed the log Alex had carried from the porch with her right hand. Fierce tendrils of pain shot up her arm when she tried to swing it. Could she do any real damage with a shattered and bleeding shoulder? As she saw Whitman's fist again crashing down into Jonathan's face, she knew she would have to try. Jonathan needed her now more than he had ever needed her before.

Jonathan turned his head. One eye was already swollen shut and his upper lip was gashed and bleeding. Both men were within a yard of Ulagu's pit.

Jonathan called out something she didn't understand, then she watched in horror as Whitman wrenched the gun away, and suddenly Jonathan was grasping nothing but air. Whitman smacked the butt of the pistol down viciously on Jonathan's forehead, then scrambled to his feet.

"Told you you were fucked, Squanto." Mitch laughed down at Jonathan, aiming the gun between his eyes.

"Not quite, he's not," Mary said.

Whitman jumped, distracted. As he started to turn, she lifted the log above her right shoulder, like a baseball batter at the plate. Ignoring the pain that blazed along the left side of her body, she tried to focus on her target. *Help me, Wynona. Guide my arm.* Gulping air, she concentrated all her strength and swung. Hard and high, the log slammed into Whitman's skull. His legs crumpled like pipe-straws, dumping him on the edge of the snake pit. He teetered for a moment, struggling to regain his balance. Without another thought, she ran forward and rammed the log deep into his chest. A groan escaped from his lungs, and he plunged backward. One muffled cry of surprise grew into a scream as Mitchell Whitman's long fall ended, head-first in the writhing nest of Ulagu's rattlesnakes.

FORTY-FOUR

Whitman's screams had stopped by the time Jonathan wrapped Mary's shoulder in a bandage.

"Do you think he's dead now?" Mary asked as they huddled together in the sudden, strange silence.

"I hope so, for his sake. Can you imagine getting hit by a dozen snakes?" Jonathan grimaced. "Too bad the fall didn't break his neck."

"At least that awful screaming has stopped," Joan said.

Jonathan unfolded himself from the ground. "I'm going to check out what Whitman brought with him. He might have something we can use."

The three women watched as Jonathan walked over toward the cabin, then suddenly, Alex began to cry.

"I can't stand this anymore," she sobbed, tears rolling down both cheeks. "This was supposed to be a fun weekend. Now every time I open my eyes there's some man in fatigues with a gun!"

Joan put one arm around Alex's shoulders, while Mary crawled over and sat on the other side of her. They held her while her huge wet sobs gave voice to all the rage and terror that she'd kept hidden from Henry Brank. As her tears finally subsided into a low, inarticulate weeping, Jonathan reappeared.

"Hey," he called. "Guess what I found? Whitman had a VHF radio in his backpack. I called the Santoah Ranger station. Most of the law enforcement officers in western North Carolina and east Tennessee will be landing here in about an hour."

"Will they take us home?" Joan's voice rose with hope like a child's.

Jonathan nodded. "They'll take you to Robbinsville or Tellico Plains, anyway. Until then, you might enjoy some of these." From his own backpack he dug out a red plaid blanket, a handful of candy bars and a carton of Virginia Slims.

Snuffling, Alex took the blanket and candy while Jonathan offered Joan the smokes. She looked at them a long time, then shook her head.

"No thanks," she said, touching the swollen mass of her nose. "It sounds crazy, but after all that's happened, just breathing plain air is good enough, you know what I mean?"

Jonathan smiled. "Actually, I do."

Suddenly Alex spoke. "Are there telephones in Robbinsville?"

"Yes."

Tears welled again in her eyes. "Then I'd like to call Texas. I'd like to ask my mother if she's put up any Mayhaw preserves."

Mary started to laugh. "I don't think that will be a problem, Alex."

Jonathan helped Mary stand and the four of them hobbled over to the cabin. They sat on the porch and stretched their legs out in the late-day sun, letting the warm light bathe their cuts and bruises and soothe their exhausted muscles. Jonathan brought Homer out from the woods, and soon the dog lay sprawled at their feet, his tail thumping the ground. Alex held him close, burying her face in his soft coat and feeding him peanuts from her candy bar.

They sat like that until the distant hum of a rotor floated in on the breeze. As they watched, a North Carolina police helicopter came into view and lowered to the meadow, flattening the weeds as it landed. Two men with a gurney jumped out, followed by the sheriff and half a dozen patrolmen. Alex and Joan scrambled to their feet as a second chopper full of Tennessee state troopers landed nearby.

"Come on, Mary," Alex urged, wrapping the blanket around her. "Let's go home."

Mary smiled. "You two go on ahead. I'll catch up in a minute."

She watched as Alex and Joan limped eagerly toward the waiting officers, Homer bounding after them. In that moment, she had never loved any two people so much in her life. Joan, who had managed to kill Ulagu when she could barely walk, and Alex, who'd taken on Henry Brank so that Mary could crawl out of a snake pit. What terrific friends they were. War Women, both of them.

"Mary?"

She turned away from Joan and Alex, now safely in the care of the troopers. Jonathan sat beside her, grinning despite his split lip and blackening eye. "I'm just fine," she told him, reading his mind as she always had. "How are you?"

He rubbed his bruised jaw and chuckled. "Hoping the next guy I fight is some old, ninety-eight-pound geezer who's terrified of guns."

Mary smiled. "You did okay, Jonathan. In fact, you did better than okay." She gazed into the sunny meadow, watching as a Monarch butterfly bobbed on a bloom of Queen Anne's lace. "I'm awfully sorry about Billy," she added softly. "He was a good friend."

Jonathan shook his head. "I still can't believe he's dead. I'll have to go back up to Atagahi and bring him home."

"I'll call Tam as soon as I can. I'm sure there's something I can do to help," Mary said.

Jonathan smiled at her, then they sat in silence, watching as the police jabbed at a topo map and argued over whose jurisdiction this was. After a while the Tennessee cops got back in their helicopter and flew off, leaving the North Carolina troopers to take statements from Alex and Joan and to haul Mitchell Whitman's body from the snake pit. Only then did Jonathan speak.

"Here," he said, tossing a small rock in Mary's lap. "I found this over by the snakes. Isn't your birthday January fifteenth?"

Mary nodded. "*Dunolutani*. The middle of the Month of the Cold Moon."

"Then those red flecks are your birthstones."

Mary looked at the rock. It was a piece of quartz the size of a buckeye, sparkling with chips of blood red garnets. "I'm amazed you remembered," she murmured, smiling.

"I remember a lot." He leaned closer. "What do you remember?"

"Everything," she said. "And I always wish things had turned out differently."

"Me, too." He took the quartz from her palm and looked down at the garnets, glittering in the sun. "Do you think things ever could be different? I mean, do you think we could change them now?"

She sensed his gaze on her face, searching, probing. Suddenly she wanted to touch him. A fountain of words and colors exploded inside her head, but when she tried to answer, her voice came out hesitant, as if she were trying to speak a language she was no longer fluent in.

"We can't change the past." She searched for the right word, but all her soft ones were rusty from disuse. "But the future, maybe."

He moved closer. She could smell his skin, feel his warmth radiating toward her.

"Mary, I . . ."

"Walkingstick!" A voice boomed through the air like a cannon.

They both jumped. Sheriff Stump Logan stood at the far end of the meadow, motioning to Jonathan.

"Oh, shit." Jonathan handed the quartz back to her. "It's that asshole Logan. Don't move. I'll be right back."

Jonathan strode down the porch toward the tall figure in a cowboy hat. They conferred with troopers and the paramedics, then Jonathan helped them maneuver the heavy gurney through the narrow cabin door. As the sheriff came to take her statement, a sudden chill slithered down Mary's spine. For an instant she was eighteen again, back at Little Jump Off the afternoon her mother died.

Stump leaned over and put one hand on her unbandaged shoulder. "Hello, Mary," he said. "I hear you've got a swing like Mark McGwire."

Mary smiled as she looked up into Stump Logan's familiar face. Time had grayed his hair and flabbed his belly, but to her he looked the same—handsome, rough-hewn features shaded by a white Stetson hat; a pack of chewing tobacco stuffed in the pocket of his khaki shirt. Though his wide mouth stretched in a smile, his gray eyes bored into her, as intense as they had been twelve years ago, when he questioned her about her mother.

"You want to tell me what happened?" he asked now, just as he had then.

He sat beside her and took notes on a little spiral pad while she told of tracking Alex and finding this cabin. The sheriff shook his head when she described what happened when Ulagu threatened her with his razor. When she finished up with Mitchell Whitman and the snake pit, he took off his hat and wiped his forehead with a big white handkerchief.

"Mercy," he drawled, spitting a dollop of brown juice on the ground. "You gals have had quite a time."

He put his pad back in his hip pocket and looked at her, studying her face so long it made her uncomfortable. She looked down and smoothed the jacket that was tied around her waist. Could Stump Logan possibly think she was making all this up?

Finally, he spoke, his voice tolling like a bell on the still air. "Why'd you come back up here, Mary?"

"For fun." Mary flinched at the ludicrousness of her reply. "For a long weekend of camping."

"Are you sure you weren't doing a little investigating of your own?" His eyes measured her face.

Mary met his gaze evenly. Like all good cops, the sheriff was adept at hearing the unspoken; but like all good attorneys, she was skilled at cloaking the true meaning of her words. "I was taking my friends to Slickrock Springs," she replied, using the English name for Atagahi.

"I see." He nodded at her. "That's good. I'd hate to think a pretty girl like you was up here nosing around a dusty old unsolved murder."

"Actually, I had my hands full with other things." Mary glanced at the troopers who were hauling Brank's body out of the cabin.

"Well, I don't think you gals need to worry about anything here. This all seems pretty much like self-defense, although the DA in Robbinsville will want to talk to you."

"That's not a problem," said Mary.

Logan stood and looked down at her, his eyes now kind. "Mary, can I give you a little advice? Go on back to Atlanta. Forget about us up here. There's a whole bunch of criminals down in the city for you to hang. Up here, you've got nothing but a million acres of bad memories."

"A million acres of *memories*, Sheriff," Mary corrected him. "Not all of them are bad."

With a brief smile he said good-bye, then left her. This was the second time she'd had an official conversation with Stump Logan. Time and a legal degree of her own had not made the process any easier.

Two troopers zipped Mitch Whitman into a body bag, while two others stood jimmying long sticks, wrangling the rattlers out of the pit at Jonathan's direction. *Inadu* were honored by the Cherokee. She knew Jonathan would never have left any to starve in the bottom of a pit.

Two more helicopters landed—one a medevac air rescue, the other bearing the bright logo of the Asheville TV station. The second disgorged two men carrying video cameras and one snappily dressed reporter. Mary watched as he shoved a microphone in Stump Logan's broad face, then stood in front of the cabin himself, regurgitating what he had been told for the viewers of the evening news.

A beefy-armed state trooper appeared, holding up a blanket for her.

"It's time to go, ma'am," he said, eyeing the blood-soaked bandage wrapped around her shoulder. "Medevac's waiting."

"But I need to return this man's jacket." Mary looked over at the snake pit, but Jonathan was no longer standing there.

"Sorry, ma'am. I'll see that he gets it. The DA's waiting for you at the hospital in Robbinsville." He offered his arm; apparently his duty was to help her to the helicopter.

"But it's vital that I speak with him," she protested.

The trooper just looked at her, his face unmoved.

Sighing, she scooped up the rock Jonathan had given her and accepted the officer's arm. Stump Logan ordered the TV crew to stop filming as the cop escorted her to the helicopter. She searched for Jonathan, but she saw only a sea of gray uniforms topped with Smokey the Bear hats.

"Could you wait just a moment?" Mary lagged behind the officer, her shoulder throbbing with a vicious heat.

"No, ma'am. We gotta go. Sorry."

Stump Logan yelled something as she felt the trooper's arm gently but firmly propelling her toward the chopper. Alex and Joan were already on board—Joan was having the wound on her foot treated while Alex sat clutching Homer on her lap. The trooper directed Mary to a seat over which a paramedic hovered, anxious to take a look at her shoulder. Panic rose in her as she was nudged up the steps to the passenger bay.

Two troopers strapped her into the seat. Scanning the crowd, Mary saw policemen, the cabin, even the two body bags laid out on the front porch, but no Jonathan. Where could he be, she wondered, craning her neck to peer around the paramedic who was inflating a blood-pressure cuff on her right arm.

"One fifty-two over ninety-six," the young man reported. "That's pretty high."

"Yeah, well, getting shot raises your numbers," Mary snapped as she continued to search the crowd. Had Jonathan gone without saying good-bye?

Suddenly a tall figure pushed through the knot of troopers watching the chopper. One officer's hat went flying; he turned and grabbed at the man who was trying to get past. Mary leaned over the paramedic and yelled out the still-open door.

"Jonathan!" she called.

"Hey!" He shook the big trooper off easily and ran up to the chopper just as the rotors started to turn with a heavy *whump*.

"Aren't you coming too?" Mary called.

He backed away from the turning blades and held his hands out. *He can't hear me*, she realized in despair.

"Aren't we taking everybody with us?" Mary glared at the paramedic.

"This medevac's full. Your boyfriend will have to ride with the troopers."

Mary turned back toward the open door. Jonathan watched her helplessly for a moment, then he cupped his hands around his mouth. "Hey, Mary—Would you ever think about saving my seat again?"

His words resounded inside her head. He had remembered! For an instant she tried not to cry, but it was hopeless. As the big rotors turned, tears began to spill from her eyes for the first time in twelve years.

"Yes!" she cried.

He frowned and shook his head, unable to hear her above the din.

Nodding extravagantly, she lifted her arm as the paramedic began to close the door, and gave him a thumbs-up sign.

Jonathan grinned and turned his own thumb up.

The hatch closed, the helicopter tilted to the right, and they rose into the sky. Laughing and crying, she waved out the tiny window as his face became smaller and smaller until finally it was just a bright dot on the golden meadow; then she could see him no longer. She looked down at the red-flecked stone he'd given her. Suddenly, she knew. This was the stone she'd sought for so long—the seventh stone! It lay in her palm. Finally, she was free!

The paramedic held out a disposable thermometer. "You want to do this now or later?" he called above the engine's roar.

"Later," she answered, the tears still flowing down her face.

She leaned her head back against the seat and looked down at the Old Men. Although they were brilliant with autumn now, by this evening the thick white mist would float up from the forest and conceal them once again. *Disgagistiyi, Dakwai, Ahaluna.* Though they had not given her back her past, they had offered her a future rich with promise.

"Keep your secrets for now, Old Men," she told them softly. "I'll be back. Crows always know the straightest way home."

ABOUT THE AUTHOR

SALLIE BISSELL is a native of Nashville, Tennessee. She currently divides her time between her hometown and Asheville, North Carolina, where she still makes occasional forays into the Nantahala National Forest. She is at work on her second novel, which will feature prosecutor Mary Crow and will be published by Bantam in 2002.